*For Lauren, whom I love with all my heart
and who always encourages my crazy ideas.*

*And for Star Wars, which I love differently, but just as deeply.*

# THE KNIGHTS OF NINE

## THE LIGHTNING KNIGHT

SEAN P VALIENTE

Copyright © 2020 Sean P Valiente

Cover design by Rebecca Haley
Cover illustration by Anthony Yoingco
Cover copyright © 2020 Valiente Publishing
Maps by Soraya Corcoran

First Edition: December 2020

ISBN 978-0-9600381-1-4 (hardback)
ISBN 978-0-9600381-0-7 (paperback)
ISBN 978-0-9600381-2-1 (ebook)

Printed in the United States of America

*"Every magical action has an equal and opposite reaction."*

– *The First Law of Magic*

# CONTENTS

MAGIC WASN'T REAL / 2

A LAST FIRST DAY / 15

WHISKEY DANGER / 26

QUESTS / 33

CARPENTERS / 43

THE BOOK / 52

ONE SMALL THING / 63

THE KNIGHT ANGEL / 68

THE BLUE FISH TAVERN / 81

MISTAKES / 95

A DAMSEL NOT IN DISTRESS / 101

THE SPIDER'S WEB / 107

THE FORGE / 114

HARALABOS / 121

THE BLACK PRINCE / 131

LOVESICK / 144

THE STARFALL CITY JOUSTING TOURNAMENT / 151

HOMECOMING / 162

THE LILYTHORN / 169

THE PRINCE OF ROMIR / 174

THE ERRANT KNIGHT / 185

THE FOOL / 190

THE TEMPLE OF ROMIR / 196

THE WORLD CHAMPIONSHIP / 203

A QUEST ENDS / 213

# CONTENTS CONTINUED

THUNDERCLAP / 221

THE DARK MIND TEMPLE / 225

AZEL'S STORY / 230

THE MERITS OF MAGIC / 240

THE EASY PART / 248

THE STAFF OF THE SEAS / 262

THE IN-BEWTEEN / 271

A GRAND ENTRANCE / 280

THE FIFTH BEST FIGHTER / 292

THE STRANGER / 297

AN UNEXPECTED GUEST / 314

THE ELIXIR / 322

THE SON OF THE CHIEF AND THE DRAGON PRINCESS / 332

THE DANCE OF THE WATER DRAGONS / 340

THE PERFECT STONE / 352

THE DRAGON CHAMPIONSHIP / 358

ENTER THE DRAGON BENDER / 370

THE HIGH QUEEN OF SORAYA / 380

AROUND THE WORLD IN ONE NIGHT / 387

QUEST: IMPOSSIBLE / 403

THE KEY / 422

THE LIGHTNING MAGIC / 430

THE PRICE OF MAGIC / 442

CONSEQUENSES / 450

MAGIC WAS REAL / 461

EPILOGUE: THE STRANGER AGAIN / 470

THE DRAGONLANDS

The Northern Tribes

Kandahart

Gate
of Kandahart

Land
End

Romir

Mercyhold

The
Floating
Isle

Starfire Bay

Soledad

Starfall

THE SOUTH

Dragon's Gift

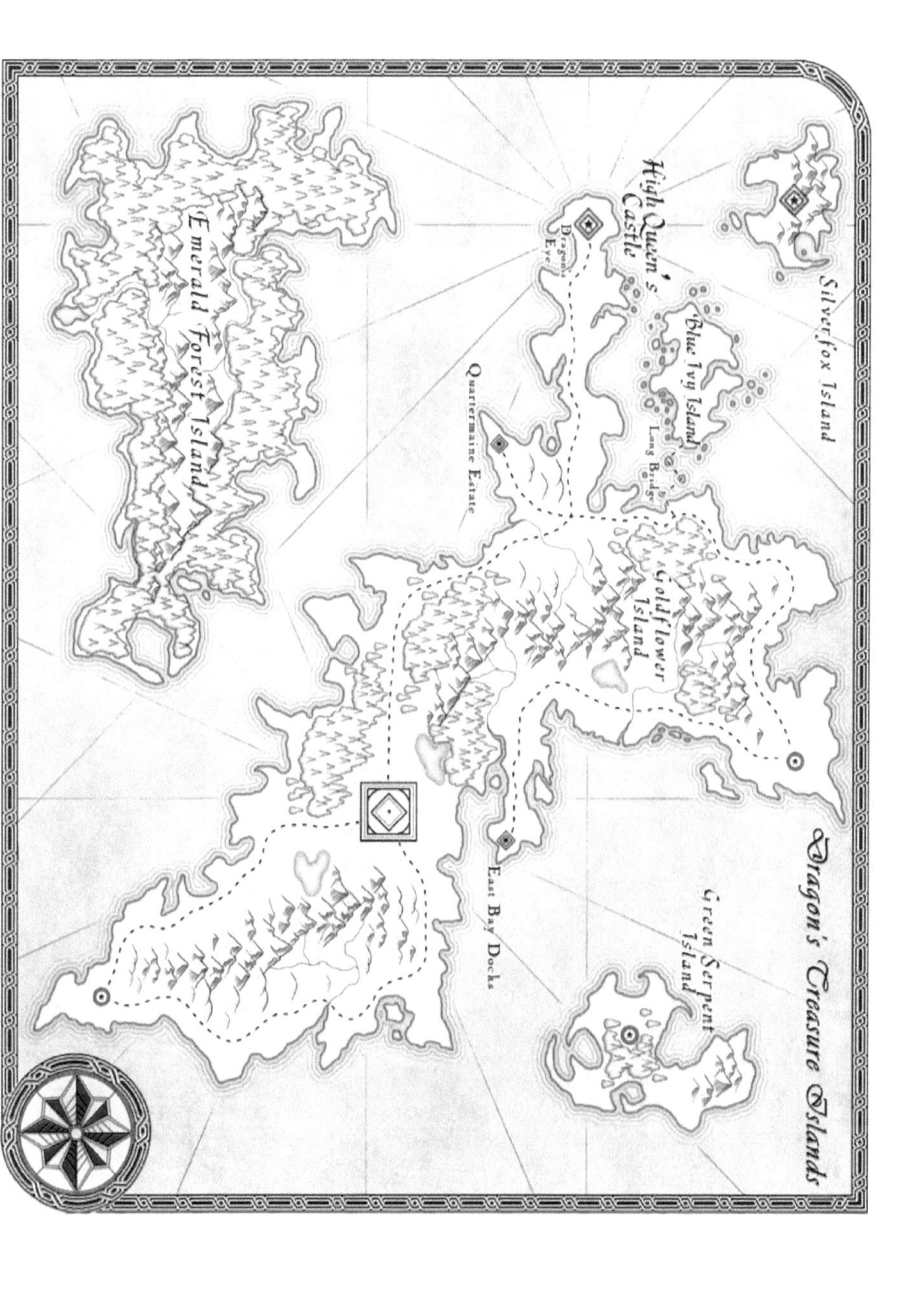

# PART ONE
## OLIVER QUARTERMAINE

# MAGIC WASN'T REAL

**M**agic wasn't real, not anymore. Not like it used to be, or like it was in the fairy tales. Even the mention of magic was forbidden. Or at least, it was supposed to be.

"Magic isn't real," I repeated to myself even as doubt crept in. It was only the stuff of myths and old books, and yet, it was the only explanation I could think of for my current predicament. I didn't know where I was or even how I had arrived at this dark place. Maybe this was a dream, but an intangible voice inside me contradicted that idea.

Something moved through the air, shimmering with faint light and vibrating, playing tricks with each of my senses. I smelled the charred aroma of a fire and heard the echo of soft taps of rainfall on stone. My mouth watered with something both sweet and savory, and a warm embrace coiled around my entire body. It was utterly intoxicating. I wanted it to never end.

My final sense was the one that betrayed the mirage. In one of his many attempts at imparting his wisdom, my brother once said, "Never trust what you see." Of course, I was blindfolded in the middle of the Forest of Kel and I was nine years old, but the lesson stuck. I hated to admit it, but in this moment, he was correct. An image of a face appeared before me; a face I saw every time I closed my eyes at night. She appeared radiant and wonderful and... impossible. She was back home in Starfall City, where I'd left her, hundreds of miles away.

That's how I knew none of this was real.

The illusion collapsed and the tastes, smells, sounds, and sights disappeared. I found myself returned to the dark room, my feet bare against a cold stone surface. I searched in all directions, peering into the darkness, seeing nothing but the emptiness that surrounded me. I wasn't one to panic, though now would have been an exceptionally fine time to do so.

"Hello!" I yelled, curious if the absence of light meant an absence of sound. My voice echoed along the stone floor, and maybe even against the walls, if this place had any.

"Can anyone hear me?" I hoped someone or something would answer my call, but none did. I took one step forward, and suddenly the ground lit up around my foot in a blaze of white light. It faded as quickly as it had burned, and by the time my eyes had adjusted, I was once again in darkness. I took one more step, lighter this time, and just as I had guessed, the illumination along the floor was not as pronounced, lasting much longer and not dazzling my eyes.

As fleet footed as I could, I ran forward, swiveling my head from side to side in search of anything. I stopped suddenly as a freestanding door with no wall nearly laid claim to my face. Before the light completely faded, I pushed open the door and entered, stumbling onto the floor of what appeared to be a library. Books and scrolls adorned the walls, and a large fire flickered and danced, lighting up the entire room.

"He's not ready," a soft voice echoed. The voice sounded almost familiar, although I was sure I hadn't heard it before. I stood up quickly, looking for its source, only to find empty furniture and more books.

"He will have to be," a second voice replied. This voice seemed weary, as if it had lost hope long ago. Or maybe I had lost hope? My chest heaved with emotions. Despair and rage pounded against my heart, but they felt foreign. Not my despair and rage, then, but someone else's.

"Your Knights were destroyed. He was to be the first, but it's too soon! Who will guide him?" The anger in the soft voice was rising even as my foreign feelings increased to match.

"You will," the somber voice said as a hand pulled on my shoulder. I turned and the library shifted too, turning like a kaleidoscope until all that remained were two chairs and two people to match the two voices. I had many questions, so I remained standing, unable to move for fear that even the slightest breath would shatter this fragile reality.

"That was not the future we saw," the figure with the soft voice argued. It was a tall woman, dressed in an outfit I had seen only in paintings of the long-extinct Elven people. The man standing next to her took one of the seats, crossing his legs and directing a fierce look at the woman.

"We have no time left—"

"And who's fault is that?" the woman interrupted. Her soft voice had lost its warmth and was now rather stern and annoyed.

"Um, hello? Hi, I'm Oliver. Nice to meet you both. Love what you've done with the place. The whole books and not books anymore thing, it's all a real mind-bender. Quick question if you will, can someone explain what's going on here?" I had never been shy of using my tongue even in the most precarious of situations, be it in a fight or with group of strangers or… whatever this was.

The man turned back to me, quickly measuring. "Quartermaines," he spat, shaking his head. He stood quickly. "Listen to me carefully," he said. The floor beneath him turned into a river of stars and heavens, flowing from left to right in constant motion. The man bent down and touched the floor, creating a bright point within the stream. "There is a boy, a boy from Starfall City. He is the key."

The woman joined in, though her demeanor softened when addressing me. "But first you will win your match. We have seen it."

"My match?"

"Against Sir Declan. You will win, and the future will solidify as we have foreseen." Her eyes darted back to the man still kneeling in the river of stars. He looked away, shame flitting across his face. The woman continued. "You will only remember pieces of this moment. Like a dream, this will fade, my child. You must remember to find the boy."

I shook my head, a haze settling in that made me feel like I was about to fall over. "Find who?"

The man stood and shook me by my shoulders, staring into my eyes. "Po. You must find Po. Protect him. He is the key."

"The key to what?" I asked as I felt the pull of the ground below me.

"The key to…" But the woman faded from view. The chairs and two figures swirled as I fell for what seemed forever, until suddenly my eyes opened to a familiar sight.

I lay on the dirt ground, my body annoyed at the clumsiness of my fall, and a faded memory flirted at the fringes of my mind. I tried desperately to hold on to it, but the more I tried to grasp the vision, the more easily it slipped through. Only two solitary words survived: magic and Po.

But magic wasn't real, and I had no idea who or what Po was.

"Di-did you fall asleep again?" Yokel grabbed my arm to lift me back up.

"Only for a moment," I replied teasingly. I squeezed my hand and felt my uncle's necklace, which was once hot, grow cold until it turned to dust altogether. "Let me ask you a question."

My friend was shuffling his notes furiously within our dimly lit tent. The notes leapt from his hands. "Ye-yes, Oliver?" He dove toward the ground, grasping at the pages while a single word forced itself through to my throat and I clumsily relayed my question.

"Magic. What do you know about magic?"

Yokel looked at me wide-eyed, pausing in his frantic attempt to collect his meticulous notes. "I spend all this time preparing a-and you…" He began arguing with himself for a time before giving in to an answer. "Magic isn't real, you know that." His answer had an air of finality, but his gaze remained on the ground.

"But what if it was?" I prodded. He knew more than he was letting on; he always did. Yokel was the most well read and knowledgeable person I had ever known, and I had known quite a few people.

"Children's stories," he replied almost too quickly.

"What if they weren't?" I agreed with him, and yet I wanted to be wrong.

Yokel sighed. "We shouldn't even be speaking of this. What if someone overheard us?"

"The Black Sun aren't going to take us away for talking privately in a tent, Yok."

"No, bu-but what if someone else hears you talking about… it?" That someone else, of course, was Roc. Magic was a sensitive topic around him, being that it was the reason his parents were gone. For years, High Queen Amukamora had obsessively hunted any and every hint of magic in all of Soraya. It would have been easier to collect every grain of sand from the seas, but still she persisted, and for hundreds of years she had success.

The High Queen was known to hate magic more than anyone, and she had been sent to Soraya from a distant land by the Nine Gods themselves to rid our world of it. They'd blessed her with eternal life, and she used that life to further her quest. Her Black Sun Battalion was charged with destroying all rumors of magic and all the people related to it.

Before the High Queen, all the kingdoms and queendoms of Soraya were splintered and separate. Magic was used by those who could summon it for all manner of tasks, including waging war. The legendary Knights of Nine were said to help quell those wars and protect those who used magic, but the Knights had been defeated by the High Queen and were never seen again.

Or so the children's stories went. How much of that was true and how much was embellished was up for debate. What wasn't, was the High Queen's ongoing war against all things magic, even if it all seemed a fool's errand. Magic was nothing more than lies and rumors, meant to trick those desperate enough to believe in it. But rumors, true or not, have consequences.

One of those rumors brought the Black Sun Battalion to Starfall. Everyone joked about it, children and adults alike. We all knew there was probably no such thing, but people still pretended their sword or shoe or stick was the famed magical object. The Black Sun didn't like the joke and destroyed any thought of a magical object in Starfall. In the process, a riot broke out, a building burned down in the Narrows, and Roc's parents were collateral damage. All in the name of preserving the safety of the kingdoms. Magic wasn't real because the High Queen said it wasn't. Commanded it wasn't. There were no magicians, no spellcasters, no witches or warlocks, wizards or mages. No one could do magic, and she made sure no one would ever try.

I let the dust from the necklace fall to the ground, contemplating what I knew to be true in my mind and what I felt to be true in my heart. I stared at Yokel, knowing he knew more, because of course he would. But we weren't in Mercyhold to talk about things we weren't supposed to. We were here to finish off a summer of tournaments with an undefeated season. The discombobulation of Yokel's notes and my taboo questions were wreaking havoc on his analytical mind. He would break sooner rather than later if I pressed. Smiling slightly, I bent down to help gather his notes, handing them to him and forfeiting the argument to allow my oldest friend this small victory.

Yok fumbled for control, and the entire portfolio fell once more from his desperate grip, showering the cold dirt floor with its contents. Utter defeat visibly washed over his body.

"Yok, I'm sorry," I said, giving his shoulder a friendly squeeze.

"N-no, it's n-not you," he stammered, fighting to control his frustration.

His skinny body seemed to shrink even more. "It's all here, I just can't keep it straight." He sighed heavily.

"Yok," I whispered, letting my voice carry along the stale air. "Just breathe."

"But I can't just, with, with, and..." He waved frantically at the scattered information at our feet. I grasped his other shoulder firmly, pulling him around so I could peer directly into his eyes. Cutting through the wall built against the mockery he'd grown accustomed to, I saw the young boy I met over nine years ago at a party among the high nobles, a place where neither of us felt we quite belonged, though our family names would suggest otherwise.

A small, skinny, bespectacled boy stood nervously next to his mother's hip as she mingled with the other noble families. His white-knuckled hands clung to her dress, and his eyes darted from towering adult to towering adult.

"Hi, I'm Oliver," I declared. As nervous and shy as this little boy appeared, I was the complete opposite. I stood there, curiously waiting for his reply, but the boy was frozen, as unreachable as one of the monstrous stone figures mounted atop the Shearson Library.

Undeterred, I continued to talk without waiting for an answer. Blatantly invading his personal space, I pushed his spectacles back up his small nose. "I like your eyeglasses! Do you wear them all the time? My uncle has a pair, but he only needs them when he reads, which is pretty often since he works at the library in Kandaheart. I usually see him every summer, but this summer we couldn't because Mother was busy—"

I continued to somersault my way through my entire life story, when the small boy interrupted my babbling. "M-my eyeglasses?" He seemed confused at the mention of the nearly invisible eye shields. "Y-you... like my eyeglasses?"

"Yeah, they're neat. Though the frames make your head look funny." I giggled. The frames perched awkwardly on his small nose, not unlike how they would look on his slightly older, more proportional teenage face. The young boy retreated again, his smile dissolving.

"I'm sorry," I apologized, eager to settle any tension between me and my new friend. "I wasn't trying to tease, I was only letting you know. My brother says I talk too much for someone my age, but then again, he once fell off a boat looking for water-dragons, so, like, what does he know?"

"You have a b-brother?" The boy's face lit up.

"Yep! He's at the Forge with my dad tonight, so it's just me and my baby sister, but she's already asleep."

"I d-don't have any brothers or sisters." The boy glanced toward the ground, fidgeting with his mother's dress as she brushed him aside like a pestering fly. I studied him, this skinny, sad little boy, and wondered what was wrong. Why wasn't he happy like me? I was always happy and, knowing no other existence for a seven-year-old boy, I was convinced he should be too. Maybe it was because I had a brother and sister and he didn't. I would be sad too if I didn't have them, I thought.

"Well... I'll be your brother!" I said. He needed a brother, and I had nothing else to do that night.

"W-what?"

"You're sad because you don't have a brother, so we can be brothers!" Happy with my solution, my thoughts wandered to how I could smuggle to my room some of the tasty lemon cakes being served.

"That's not how it works, I d-don't think," the little boy replied, scuffing his shoe into the floor.

"Who cares?" I said, starting to formulate my plan of attack. First, I could make my way around the back of the table, possibly knock something over to create a distraction, but that would mean I still needed the servant looking after the desserts to leave. It was risky but possible if I had help...

"W-well, if you d-don't mind hanging out with me." He let go of his mother's dress and nervously shifted around. "I can be a little..."

"Yeah, yeah, I don't mind," I said absentmindedly. My focus was now on "The Great Lemon Cakes Quest," but it would take two to pull it off. "You hungry?" I asked slyly.

"W-well, I'm allergic to—"

"Perfect! I need your help. What did you say your name was again?" I asked while I pulled him over to the wall behind a suit of armor. A loud clang sounded against the stone floor where a servant slipped on a cloth I had laid, dropping his silver platter.

After the ringing subsided, I could hear the end of the boy's muffled response. "-mir Yokel."

"Okay, Yok, here's what we're going to do..."

My mind cleared as I pulled myself away from memory and back to the young man who stood in front of me, spectacles sliding down the bridge of his nose once again. Pushing them back up with my index finger, I smiled.

"Okay, Yok, here's what we're going to do. You're the best tactician I know, and I wouldn't be here without you. You have everything you need already, right here." I pointed to his forehead. I walked over to the stool and began to armor up. "So, give me the rundown."

"Promise you won't fall asleep this time?" Yokel teased as he straightened his shoulders. "Your final match is against Sir Declan, one of the Old Guards for the King of Mercyhold." The name sounded oddly familiar, but I brushed off the feeling just as quickly as it had come.

"A real knight?" I asked. My giddy tone couldn't be held back, but neither could Yokel's.

"A true knight," he responded in kind. Knights were rare in Soraya, and it was even rarer to be fighting one in a tournament like this. A win against a true knight would make me famous, even beyond Mercyhold.

Yokel continued with his rundown as he helped me lace my armor. "He won this same tournament when he was our age, some forty years ago, but hasn't competed since. According to my sources, he's quite the hero in this kingdom, some say legendary, even at his age. He prefers Form Twelve for offense and Form Seven for defense, but I've witnessed him merge Forms Ten and Fourteen, and quite uniquely if I do say so. He's got strength and skill, but he's never approached longer than five minutes in any of his matches so far."

Yokel's assessment was, as it always was, thorough and concise. The best fighters in the world, whether in a tournament like this or on the battlefield, always fought using the Elven Forms of Fighting. There were twenty-four forms in all, twelve offensive and twelve defensive, and although each weapon had its own variation, they all used the same forms as their base.

Based on what Yokel was saying, the knight would use a mildly aggressive offensive attack form with a very conservative defensive attack form, which told me everything I needed to know about the man. He was cautious when attacking but would take calculated risks. The same could not be said about his defensive technique, which would take no risks at all. It made all the sense in the world how Sir Declan had defied the short life of a knight.

"So, I wait him out and then take him on the back fifteen points?" I asked, shoving my arm through the uncomfortable chest plate.

"That would be the strategic thing to do, yes, but a knight doesn't get to be his age by being predictable," Yokel acknowledged, tying my laces to an almost unbearable tightness.

Bursting into the tent like a tornado, Roc began yelling. "What are you two doing?! Oliver was due in the ring minutes ago!"

"But we haven't finished going over my notes and—"

"No time for that, nerd! Any longer and we'll be disqualified." Roc snatched my helmet with his enormous hands and shoved me out of the tent into the blinding light of the afternoon. Yokel trailed close behind, his portfolio of unneeded notes still out of order.

Bouncing off spectators as we rushed toward the ring, I heard Yokel spewing more tactics as I fidgeted inside my armor. The heavy steel never allowed for the full range of motion I so desperately desired. I guess belonging to the most famous smithing family in the South hadn't afforded me any unique advantages. Having the most famous inventor in history as a father hadn't afforded me any advantages either.

Roc pulled my shoulders around and craned down. "You ready? You win this and you're undefeated this summer. Can't think of a better way to start off your career. And I bet Iris would love to be courting a..."

Iris. I suddenly pictured her in my head, and fragments of a vision flashed before me. Iris. Magic. Po. A door.

But there wasn't time to think about these things. I ignored his last comment and ended the conversation.

"You mean we won't have to spend the ride home listening to Yokel complain about not preparing enough."

Roc slapped the top of my helmet with gusto, pushing down my visor and spinning me around once again. "Exactly!"

Twirling my sword, I let my body relax within the metal shell. This was the last match I would have as the Summer Tournament Series concluded. Victorious in the five previous tournaments within Sunset Mountains Circuit, truth be told, I was a bit spent. My mind wandered briefly, back to magic and the mysterious Po—

BONGGGGG!

I snapped back to reality and to an immediate clash of sword on sword. Sir Declan saw my mind wander and took the opportunity to introduce himself forcefully, to shouts of delight from the crowd.

We circled each other, weighing one another's movements. Sir Declan appeared much nimbler than a man his age ought to, and he held his sword with a balance that confirmed his practiced knowledge. He wore the same light steel armor I did, but whereas mine was smooth and blank, his was adorned with designs and details marking his battles. In the middle of the chest plate sat an ornate blue sapphire that caught rays from the setting sun. My admiration became critique as he began his attack with Form Twelve, just as Yokel predicted.

We danced, the ting of our weapons keeping the count as the motions came naturally to us both. With a quick shift in tempo, Sir Declan began to embrace the unexpected, improvising deftly into Form Two, a basic attack every swordsman mastered early in their training. However, he took the form and stretched it, sprinkling hints of more advanced techniques to throw me off my guard. Perplexed, I struggled to counter each small manipulation of the assault.

A quick glance at the scoring wall showed twenty red flags to my lowly eight blue flags, a strategic eight-point sacrifice on Sir Declan's part that allowed him to amass such a lead so quickly. For every defensive parry and block I managed, he responded with a slight variation of the perfect counter, all within the construct of Form Two.

The simple elegance of his strategy made it hard for me to focus and not applaud the knight's brilliant tactics. Sixteen years and I had convinced myself I had learned and mastered all there was to know about the Fighting Forms. My arrogance had cost me valuable points in the match, and Sir Declan's technique had restoked a fire within me; the joy of indeterminate combat flooded through my heart. The rush of facing an opponent of such high skill and ambiguous strategy brought a broad grin to my face. His strategy was bold and tested successfully against every opponent before bringing him to this final match today. It was perfect. Simply perfect.

I almost felt sorry for him.

Almost.

Sir Declan finished his sequence with a flourish, hesitating for a moment to gather his breath and composure. His five minutes were up. The nimbleness and energy he had started the match with had quickly faded, matching the faded sapphire in his armor. The moment he took to collect himself was one moment too long. I pounced. He had relied on the wide point margin to afford a break from our dance, but my quick succession of slashes and forward thrusts broke through, turning his strategy into a handicap. His simplified offensive tactic never translated into a defensive scheme, and appropriating his gambit, I began an intricate reworking of a highly modified attack myself.

The result was a blitz of strikes he was unable to defend, and within minutes, the scoring wall read twenty-nine red flags to twenty-nine blue flags. As we entered into a final contest of blows, we both knew what would transpire. As it had so many times before, the world seemed to slow down, if not stop altogether. Various paths illuminated before me, showing me the result of each different action I could take. A thrust on one path might lead to my defeat, whereas a parry and slash would lead to victory. I saw it all clearly before me, as well as the path to victory. But I had seen beyond that too, beyond the final flag on the wall and past the ceremony to the world that followed after. It was a world I'd seen in a river of stars. One full of outcomes I felt no control over. It was as if I had no choice in the matter, and something about that felt wrong.

So, I forged a path I had not seen.

The final sound of the gong rang loudly, and the audience was silent as they vied for a look at the scoring wall. A red flag posted, and an exuberant crowd burst into cheers. Exhausted, Sir Declan knelt to the ground, his armor rising and falling viciously with each breath he tried to collect. It had looked like a clean match, with Sir Declan scoring the last point on my final missed thrust, but we both knew what had truly happened. It was in fact a draw, with my unseen strike scoring at the same time as his. I stood there, victorious this summer no more, and smiling all the same.

Roc and Yokel jumped into the ring, rushing toward me.

"What happened?"

"We thought you had him!"

I didn't answer but rather watched Sir Declan across the ring, still on one knee. He looked up at me and I shook my head, conceding the match to him. He was holding himself up by his sword, and with every breath he took, years of fighting released from his body like a vapor of worries and troubles. He was savoring this moment, this final match of the tournament.

The crowd began to clap slowly, and Sir Declan rose, leaving his sword and helmet standing in the hard-packed ground as he began to unlace his boots methodically and deliberately. Walking to the center of the ring, the old knight placed his boots down somberly. Allowing one final pause, he gazed out into the crowd, tears streaming down his cheeks as he received the admiration of his screaming fans. They adored their old hero, and he loved them back.

He eyed the three of us, a smile creeping along his wrinkled face. He nodded slowly and the full weight of the moment overtook me. He would never fight in this, or any tournament, ever again, and the finality of his retirement sent shivers down my spine. It was rare to meet a knight old enough to see his hair turn the pale gray that Sir Declan sported. He had chosen to leave on his own terms and in his own way, not face down on the ground but on his own two feet.

I raised my fist over my chest, beating it softly, and Sir Declan responded in kind. He knew the match should have gone to me, but I had chosen the path I wanted instead of the one everyone expected. I had chosen, and that was all that mattered to me.

We departed, leaving Sir Declan to revel in his final moments in the arena. Instead of remaining for the closing ceremony, we gathered our gear and headed straight to the station, waiting for a steam locomotive, an invention of my grandfather's, to arrive against a setting purple sky.

"Where are we off to next? We never did make it to the Northern Tribes," Yokel asked, picking up his bags while Roc leaned against the post in giddy amazement at the rumbling machine.

Peering out along the tracks, I thought back on the summer, the tournaments I had competed in, the parties at my uncle's house in Kandaheart, and all the mischief the three of us managed to accomplish. I thought of my mother for the briefest of moments before shutting that door in my mind once more. After her death I had left my life in Starfall to travel the country under the presumption of competing in tournaments. I thought the time away would help, but the thought of her stung all the same.

So instead I thought of my sister and wondered what adventures she must have had without me. I thought of my father, undoubtedly spending his days at the Forge, as he always did.

And I thought of Iris, who was the singular obsession of my heart. I thought of the girls I had rejected, much to Roc's chagrin. I thought of how I missed Iris's smile and her laugh, and the way we would spend all night talking about nothing and yet seemingly everything. Finally, I thought of the kiss she gave me as I boarded a train to leave her. The same train that was now blasting a cloud of steam as it rolled slowly to a stop in front of us.

I looked at Yokel, his figure silhouetted against a setting sun and stationary planet above, and I smiled. "We're going home."

Yet even as my voice charted our course, my mind lingered on a different topic.

Magic wasn't real.

Or was it?

# A LAST FIRST DAY

The sun had not yet risen, but the faint dusk light from the planet above provided just enough light to guide a path. This path would take me from the edge of the Narrows and the outer wall, through the alleyways and compact streets that lined the shantytown, and even past Roc's home. At this hour he would most surely be asleep.

Sweat dripped off the small hairs on my chin as I raced around corners, over obstacles, and past the inner wall of Starfall City. Ever since our return home, I had been unable to sleep. Restless nights gave way to running as a means to physically exhaust myself. Some nights it worked, but others not so much. It was as if some energy I had never felt before was coursing through my body, depriving me of normal weariness.

Or maybe I was running away from something. I didn't quite know. Ever since Mercyhold, I couldn't quiet the thoughts in my head, of magic or of this mysterious Po. I hadn't even been able to muster the courage to see Iris, though I'd had plenty of opportunities. Instead I hid in the shadows, away from her and away from the world. However, today I could no longer hide. The Institute beckoned me.

I finished my run and arrived back home at the top of Nobleman's Hill. The easternmost edge of the city sat upon a hill and cliff overlooking Starfire Bay. The most powerful and affluent families lived there, and my home was at the very top, both literally and metaphorically. Being one of the oldest and wealthiest families in all of the South meant that in a kingdom with no king, as was the South, we were the only family with an actual castle.

As I began to ready myself for the day, I could hear the city below come to life. The sun broke the horizon and faint sounds of birds and sailors danced along the sea breeze. I enthusiastically put on my uniform, a Southern-style outfit, and stared at my reflection in the mirror. The ease I felt in the sword ring translated to other fields of battle. A formal dinner or a meeting with the City Council or even the Institute. Each of these was a different arena, each with a different purpose, and each with a different suit of armor. If they could see only a Quartermaine, they might not see who I really was underneath: a kid with no idea what he was supposed to be. If I could just survive this final year at the Institute, maybe I would find a purpose.

The Institute at Starfall was attended by high and low noble families from not only the South but also the rest of the country. Noble families from kingdoms as far as the Northern Tribes or as far west as Kandaheart would send their children every year for instruction and education. Well, all kingdoms except for Romir, because that kingdom was the worst. The Institute was the premiere educational organization in all the world, and no private tutor, maester, or other teacher would ever compare. Some royals through the years had even attended, though for the most part they stayed in their own kingdoms, with their own instructors.

The Institute worked simply enough. If you were wealthy or lucky enough to be sponsored, you would attend five years of curricular instruction on a variety of subjects. After five years, you were expected to do something with that knowledge and the connections you made along the way. For many, it meant continuing their family's fortune well into the future, instead of squandering it. For others, it meant making a mark on the world in their own way. For quite a few, it was just another box to check off on their list. Uneducated nobles weren't noble for very long. But for me, it meant I finally had to decide what it was I wanted to do with my life.

Theoretically, I could do nothing and be one of those "checklist" nobles. My family's wealth would last a hundred generations, as it had a hundred before. I could live my life competing in tournaments, attending parties, being a royal in all but name and responsibility. But even as I contemplated a life of decadence and debauchery, I shook my head. I was a Quartermaine, and that meant certain expectations were set for me. I was expected to do something great, be someone great, just as everyone else in my family had been.

My father, the famed inventor, as his father was before him. My uncles and aunts, all of whom either held attendance in royal courts or were famous for any other variety of reasons.

But I didn't know if I could be great. I just wanted to be Oliver.

I made my way downstairs, walking fast. The paintings passed and I stared at a slightly askew portrait in the hall. It was an answer to a question I had posed during the night. My father may have been known for his metalwork and his inventions, but few knew of his more obsessive eccentricities. A slightly crooked painting was my trap for him, knowing he could never let it remain so. I sighed. He had not come home once again.

Dejected, I picked up a weekly news periodical that was funded by my family and entered the kitchens. The chef was hard at work, his culinary artistry unnoticed by my sister, Reagan, who perched on his prep table. Legs swinging playfully, she swiped a biscuit and tossed it with a smile.

I caught the soft bread. "He's still at the Forge?" I knew the answer, but I asked anyway. Maybe one of these times I would be wrong.

But I was never wrong.

She beamed. "Still working on a project, I believe. You know how he gets. One moment he's here, the next he's not around for weeks. Then comes some life-altering invention that changes the world." I never quite understood how Reagan could be so understanding of his absenteeism, but then again, I never quite understood Reagan. I could go with one fewer invention if it meant more time with my father.

I looked like my father, whereas Reagan looked like a fifteen-year-old version of our mother, and the sight of her would sometimes remind me of what I had lost. It wasn't Reagan's fault. She was beautiful, with sharp features and a sharper tongue. She wasn't quite a woman, but neither was she a child, and the thought of all the boys I'd have to beat up who came calling for her hand lifted my spirits. It's what brothers were for, after all.

"We received a letter last night with the Imperial Seal. It was about—"

"I don't want to hear about it," I snapped, a quick simmer of unbridled anger and resentment bursting out. Seeing her expression, I apologized immediately. "I'm sorry, I just don't want to talk about him."

Reagan hopped off the table and picked up her pack, gesturing toward the door. "It's been over four years, Ollie. He's still our brother." She was right, of course, but my emotions never allowed for rational thinking when it came to him. The coming spring would mark five years since my brother left Starfall. Five years since he split up our family. Five years since I said his name aloud.

Reagan and I left the house, letting the morning sounds of our city guide us toward her heart. A cascade of feelings rose alongside the sun, clouding my thoughts with bitter emotion. For a shred of a moment, I imagined myself in a different life, a different family. My father would be here, on my last first day at the Institute. He would have visited me this summer, bearing witness to my victories or at least feigned interest at a bland recount of my adventures. My mother would still be alive, wishing me the very best while also making sure I pushed myself as hard as I could. My brother would be working at the Forge instead of fighting whatever war the High Queen was waging currently.

I tried to take my mind off my family, instead focusing on a story I had read in the *Starfall City Journal*. "So what's this about a 'Knight Angel'?"

Dang, that was a great name.

"A vigilante of some sort," Reagan answered gleefully. "The City Watch is none too happy about it."

"I wonder who he is?" My eyes darted to the side, trying to discern Reagan's body language. She always had her pulse on the mysteries about our city, but how she did it, I had no idea.

"Who said it was a he?" she replied, before changing the subject. "So," she said, skipping backward beside me, "have you seen her yet?"

"Seen who?"

"Oh, I don't know, maybe..." She imitated an exaggerated and passionate kiss, taking many liberties in the pantomime.

"I haven't the foggiest idea what you're talking about," I lied, choking back laughter while conceding a small smile.

"I thought that might cheer you up," she retorted, but her voice abruptly dropped. "Ollie..."

"Yes?" I replied as we approached Merchant's Square. Reagan became uncharacteristically quiet.

She hesitated, looking out at the buildings surrounding us. "It's been a long summer."

I raised an eyebrow. "I'm pretty sure it's been as long as all the other ones."

Reagan scowled. "No, you don't understand, just listen. I mean, you've been gone for months and... and we aren't kids anymore and I don't think you've noticed how different everything is. How different everyone is.

People change."

"People like you?" I shot back. She did seem different. More mature, and less of the kid I had left behind. She may have only been a year younger than me, but it wasn't until this moment that I really noticed those changes and how she carried herself differently.

"People like people," she snapped. "People like Iris." I stopped walking. What was she trying to say? I had thought of Iris every day this summer, and surely she had done the same. I could feel it in my bones and in my heart. We were connected, and more than that, we were meant for each other.

"What do you know about it?" I snapped. "I think I know her a little better than you do, and it's not even like that yet. And... it wasn't even that long a time."

Reagan stopped abruptly, hands planted firmly on her hips, lips pursing into an all-too-familiar expression. She had somehow acquired a gift for knowing exactly how and when to exploit any weakness in your argument, a gift she had grown to use judiciously in our family. I had to put an end to this and fast.

"Just shut your... all the holes... in your face," I eventually fumbled. For all the books I had read and all the years of education at the Institute, my inner thoughts were complex and often eloquent, but when it came to turning those thoughts into real words for real people to hear, I always seemed to revert to speaking like the teenage boy I was.

Reagan's expression softened and she leaned in for a hug underneath my tensed arms while my defenses crumbled.

"I just don't want you to get hurt. I realize how close you two were..."

"Are."

"... and you're not kids anymore."

"We're only sixteen! When did life suddenly become so serious?"

"Why are you being so hostile?"

"Why are you being so, so... so YOU!" I retaliated, forcing us both to burst into violent laughter.

"Maybe you take this year to work on your insults, huh, big brother?"

"Maybe," I quipped. "You know, I'm the one who should be looking out for you, right?" I planted a kiss on her forehead. Hoping she'd infer the apology and move on, I questioned her upcoming school term. "Who's your

Head Professor this year?"

"Professor Harwich," she replied absentmindedly.

I gave her a wry smile. "Bring him a candied pear and you'll be set for the year. He loves those."

"Where did you learn that trick?"

Without responding, I turned and left in the opposite direction toward the Narrows, the memory of candied pears lifting my spirits.

The city was buzzing as I reached the Narrows, dawn finally breaking over the horizon and filling the streets and alleyways with a faint blue-green glow. Roc lived in a communal living space above a variety of shops in an enormous three-story building. I always imagined the fun of living in such a frenetic space, but Roc often described it as "a crap place full of crap people who'll steal your shoes, but for some reason, not your socks." Thinking of it, that's probably why Roc's feet always smelled so bloody awful; presumably, he never removed his shoes, not even to sleep.

Though his uncle was a knight, he wasn't afforded a custom of wealth and station. Rather, Sir Roclan's lord had died on his watch many years ago, and a knight without a lord to serve was lost to bid his talents to anyone willing to pay. It was a sad affair, especially for someone as great as Sir Roclan. The old knight never made any excuses for it, though, and neither did Roc.

"How was your morning?" Roc asked, initiating our handshake ritual.

"More of the same." I sighed. "Yours?"

"More of the same."

We continued on our way, his long strides outpacing mine. He was by far the largest student at the Institute in both height and breadth, a measurement wholly unique among his family, or so he told me.

Walking through the Narrows and back toward Merchant's Square, a small smile crept across my face. Roc and I had made this same walk to the Institute every day for the last four years; the idea of this fifth and final year was already proving to be bittersweet. We'd become nigh inseparable since we met eight years ago.

By happenstance, my mother had run into the lowly hedge knight Sir Roclan and invited him to one of her famous Black Sunday dinners. Yokel and I were right in the middle of one of our more complicated pranks, desperately trying to rig up a system to drench my brother with a bucket of water as he passed through a narrow doorway and into our gardens. True to fashion, I was entangled in an elaborate net of ropes when in walked a towering eight-year-old, his quizzical gaze meeting mine as I dangled in the air.

"Hey, kid, you wanna do me a favor?" I asked as I spun around uncontrollably. The kid glanced up, following the rope and tracing its path into Yokel's less capable hands. The rope started to slip and burn against Yokel's skin. Without warning, Yokel yelped and let go, sending me and my bucket hurtling toward the unforgiving ground below. With mere inches separating my head from the cold stone, I miraculously jolted to a stop. I turned my focus from my certain death to the benevolent giant holding my tether. He lowered me down gently and turned toward Yokel, who looked equal parts embarrassed and amazed.

"You're strong," I said, picking myself up and looking at the bucket as it sloshed water over the brim.

"Thanks," the kid said. He cocked his head like the dogs would when we asked them a question. "What are you two doing anyway?"

"Well, it's a long story—" Yokel started.

"No, it's not. I have a bucket of water and I want to dump it on my brother. We're just running into some—"

"Logistical problems," Yokel added.

"Lo-gis-ti-cal?" the kid asked.

"He means we haven't figured out how to get this bucket up there in a way that will fall on my brother when he walks through."

"Oh," the kid answered cautiously. "Why are you trying to do that?"

"Because he's my brother."

"Oh, right," the kid settled, looking to Yokel for help.

"What are you three doing?" my brother demanded in all of his thirteen-year-old righteousness.

"Uh..." I started, surprised at his sudden entrance. I glanced at Yokel, the bucket of water still sloshing in my very guilty hands.

"This!" the new kid yelled, deftly snatching the bucket and drenching my brother through his finest dinner wear.

"Was that him?" he whispered, checking in a bit too late on the intended target's identity.

"Sure was," I gasped, wide eyed.

"You little... my hair... I'm going to kill you!" my brother howled, coming to the realization that it was only water and he was the largest person currently in our quartet.

"Time to go," I said, grabbing the new kid by the back of the shirt and sprinting for an escape. "What's your name?" I asked him as we huddled behind a carriage, watching for any sign of my furious sibling.

"Riley Roclan," he answered, shifting uncomfortably.

"I'm Oliver, he's Yokel." I squinted at Riley Roclan. "What's your favorite food?"

"Uh, I don't know." His eyes lit up, "Ox tail?"

"Favorite knight?"

"Summer Solstice Night, I suppose."

I shook my head. "No, like your uncle."

"You know my uncle?" His face lit up.

"Of course, he's Sir Roclan!" Yokel said. "I have his Knight Card at home!" Yokel was speaking of a card game featuring both real and fairytale knights. Given the scarcity of knights in Soraya, even a hedge knight such as Sir Roclan would be known to collectors.

Riley Roclan's back straightened at the mention of his uncle's name. "Oh, uh, then I guess probably Sir Dewie of the Mountain," he answered.

"The legendary jouster?" I was puzzled. It was a curiously obscure choice. Rare was it to hear a Southerner mention a Northern Tribe jouster as his favorite knight.

"Yep, that's what I want to do when I grow up." The boy puffed up his even-then enormous barrel chest.

"Cool, cool, cool." I pondered. Ox tail, Sir Dewie, and the fact that he threw water on my brother confirmed what I had suspected from the moment we met.

"We can help with that, right, Yok?"

"Y-yes, my grandfather was teaching me some fun things w-with a lance the other day and—"

"Wonderful, Yok. So, what do you say, Riley Roclan? You want to become the greatest jouster this world has ever seen?"

"Wait, you want to help me? Why?"

"Because," I said with a wry smile, "you're one of us."

Riley Roclan stared at me, then at Yokel with a broad smile. "You can call me Roc."

"Like a rock? Rock? Roc... whatever. Alright, Roc, but we can't help you if we don't survive the night."

"Which knight?" Roc asked, looking around.

"No, I meant... never mind. You know, if there's more than two of us we're going to need a name for ourselves."

"Why?" chimed Roc and Yokel in concert.

"Because all the best teams have names. There's Ghost Company in the Imperial Army, or even the City Watch here in Starfall. My brother and his friends call themselves the Stonemen, but that's super dumb. We need something better."

"Something more dangerous," Roc added.

"Exactly, something more, more... Yokel, what are you holding?"

"Uh, I don't know, I just f-f-found it in this carriage." I crawled over to Yokel and snatched the object from his hands—a bottle of whiskey from Romir.

"Whiskey... danger," I muttered to myself.

"What?" Roc asked, sliding over to us.

"Whiskey Danger. That's what we call ourselves," I said, confident in my thought, the greatest in the history of eight-year-old thoughts.

"I love it!" Yokel proclaimed.

"I hate it," a voice from the front of the carriage boomed.

"RUN!" I yelled as we sprinted away from my brother and his Stonemen.

"What are you smiling about?" Roc asked as we walked past a bakery.

I slowly returned to the present. "Nothing," I replied as he grabbed a pastry from the shop. He left a coin and continued on his way while I added three more coins to complete the transaction.

"You didn't bring any supplies for school."

"Nah, with a mind like this, who needs to take notes?" He pointed to his forehead. I grimaced at his compliment and he laughed. "Oh right, me. But, come on, what are the chances they make a mistake for the fifth straight year?" Roc was speaking about the clerical mistake they had been making since we first started going to the Institute. Each year his tuition was paid in full, though he never knew how.

"I'd say pretty good. What odds are you giving?" I asked, amused.

"Ten to one," he joked back.

"I'll take that bet, but if I win, I'm not your herald this year, Yokel is!"

"Yokel!? That dinkus is literally the most annoying herald in the entire city. He'll go on and on, making up grandiose stories—"

"Grandiose?"

"I read it in a book."

"Who taught you how to read?"

"Your sister!"

I shook my head and we continued on. We approached the Square and made our way past the western side where the merchants set up their shops. Directly across we spied the hundreds of daily workers, or "Rabbits," that lined up for any number of odd jobs they might secure. We would have seen Sir Roclan, but the hedge knight was usually one of the first to arrive each morning and would be long gone by the time we walked through the now-busy square. It was how he received his sigil of a rooster.

Roc punched my shoulder. "So, you seen her yet?"

I shot him a look from the side of my eye, and he responded with an exaggerated expression. "I thought that'd be the first thing you did when we got back. The way you yammered on about your girl all summer, I thought—"

"She's not my girl," I corrected quietly.

"Oliver," he began, taking a deep breath before plunging in, "you've been pining after her for years and you haven't made a move. How many times did we have to listen about her this summer?"

"Not that oft—"

"Every. Single. Day. Listen, bro, you're the top student at the Institute, you come from one of the most powerful families in the city, hells, the entire country. You're Oliver Quartermaine! You get to be whatever you want, have whatever you want, and whoever you want. So, you can be with Iris, and I can be with all the girls you turn down."

"Obviously," I replied. Roc had more than enough confidence for the both of us.

Roc smirked. "So... MAKE A DAMN MOVE! Or I will."

"Okay."

"Okay, what?"

"Okay, I'll make a move this year."

"This week."

"Today." I squinted into the morning light. The moment had taken full hold of me, and as usual, I was in over my head. I knew I wasn't ready to test those waters yet, but for all of my supposed intelligence, Roc had outsmarted me.

Fantastic.

Roc let out a held breath. "Finally! This is going to be great. I'll be apprenticing with your father at the Forge, win the Homecoming tourney, you'll be with Iris, and I'll be with all the rest." His eyes glazed over in a daydream as we arrived at the gates to the Institute.

"Hey, guys! Guess what, Roc? I'm in all your lectures! We can talk strategy for the lists all day! I've been reading up on tourneys since we got back and I think if you—" Yokel squawked, running up to us.

"Yokel, get out of here! We were having an important conversation," Roc bellowed, clearly not happy about his dreams being interrupted.

"Geeze, Roc, you d-don't have to yell, I was only—"

"Yokel!" Roc and I hollered in unison. Yokel skipped ahead of us, trying to avoid the reach of Roc's fists.

"Nine Gods, I hate you, Yokel," Roc muttered, shaking his head. I knew he could never hate Yokel, which was a very good thing because Yokel would definitely be his herald this year; Roc simply didn't realize it yet. I was going to win our bet; I had already made sure of that, just as I had these past four years.

"You're smiling again, dweeb," Roc pointed out. Uncomfortable with expressing anything more than masculine affection for one another and in the typical fashion of our friendship, he punched me in the crotch.

I doubled over and replied with a groan, "Yeah, I know."

# WHISKEY DANGER

"So, what's the verdict?" I asked, leaning against a window in full view of the Forest of Kel. The haunting forest sat on the southeast section of Starfall City, just beyond the boundaries of the Institute's grounds. Rumors abounded that the forest was unending, the few adventurers courageous enough to explore her deep, dark mysteries rarely returning. At least, that's what our professors threatened as an embellished punishment underneath the forest's branches.

"Looks like I'm stuck in this place for at least one more year," Roc answered as he emerged from the damp basement where the ledger-nerds kept the Institute's financial records.

"Paid in full?"

"For the entire year." He shook his head, clearly flabbergasted. "I don't know how I get away with it sometimes."

"You're just lucky, I guess, and I'm lucky too. Because that means—"

"Don't even say it," Roc interrupted, threatening a punch.

The Institute was as old as Starfall, maybe even older, but I had never delved into its history. Yokel would know though. He loved this city more than anything and would undoubtedly have read up on the Institute years ago. But the Institute was mainly for the noble and wealthy, and a boy like Roc would never have been able to attend, if not for his luck.

We leaned against the wall, our attention drifting to the multitude of students filing in through the doors. Roc was a veritable celebrity. He may not have had the station of most of the other students, but he was by far the most popular. His jovial attitude along with his sheer size made him stand out. People just gravitated toward him, like a planet. It was something I admired, if not was outright envious of. It also probably helped that he was the reigning Homecoming Jousting Champion, which meant he was the most popular athlete in all the South. Just being associated with Roc as not only his best friend but also part of his jousting team meant I was afforded a modest amount of popularity as well. That, and being a Quartermaine helped, of course.

But after a series of hugs, hand slaps, and intricate handshakes with fellow students, I felt a jolt of pain along my ribcage that knocked me out of my internal roll call. I exaggeratedly recoiled as Roc began pointing toward a line of First Years.

He clapped his hands together and rubbed them back and forth proclaiming, "Ahhh, fresh meat." Their faces displayed a range of emotions: some looked excited, some nervous, and some were attempting a false sense of bravery. One of them, a smaller-than-average freshie in the front of the line, looked up at Roc with his mouth agape.

I glanced at Roc, repaid the jab to the side, and motioned with my head toward the freshie, my eyebrows raised. Most if not every jousting team always had their own would-be squire— a bright-eyed and eager child who could do the tasks no one else wanted. Typically, we reserved that for Yokel, because he was Yokel. But after winning a bet against Roc in Kandaheart, we had agreed to find a freshie to join our team. The only question was, would this kid be up for it?

"Better close that hole in your face, freshie, before you catch flies," Roc joked, walking over to crane his neck down.

"You're... you're... you're Riley Roclan!" the freshie yelped. His excitement caused his whole body to vacillate back and forth, and I was confident his limbs had stopped listening to his head.

"That's right, freshie, I am the great and mighty Riley Roclan. You may address me as 'mister,' or 'sir,'" Roc trumpeted, puffing out his chest in a familiar fashion.

He was such an ass.

"You're not a 'sir,'" I corrected.

Roc murmured angrily, "I am to them."

Returning his attention to the first-year, he continued, "And what's your name, freshie?"

"Freshie? My name? Name? Who? Uh... Freshie?" This kid needed to calm down before he hurt himself, but I could tell right away he would be a perfect addition to our group.

"The freshie seems to have forgotten how to speak. See, you're 'fresh meat,' but the professors don't like that, so we call you 'freshies,'" Roc explained.

I attempted to throw the kid a lifeline. "Your name, buddy. Like me, I'm Oliver, this here is Roc, and you are?" I motioned kindly, trying to save him from himself. He had an air of awestruck innocence, exactly the kind of squire we were looking for.

"His name is Hugo Pondarion," a voice declared, and my heart threatened to leap from my chest. "He's one of my summer students, so treat him well or you'll be answering to me," Iris commanded, slight amusement in her tone. Our eyes met, and I thought I caught a look of distress before it was quickly masked with a quiet smirk.

Hugo shifted from a shade of red I thought only occurred in tomatoes to ghostly white. The kid was going to have a stroke before he even made it to his first class. Meanwhile, Roc looked around at all the other students whose attention hadn't wavered from their newly met hero.

"Hugo, is it?" Roc bent down to Hugo's level. "That's a good strong name. No doubt named for someone important?"

"My grandfather, sir," Hugo replied with a timid grin that threatened to envelop his entire face. "But you can—"

"People are going to remember that name, and do you know why? Because you're going to be my squire and join my team. What do you say?" Roc raised an eyebrow to wink at Iris while gesturing toward me and the fast-approaching Yokel.

"Hey guys, I just spoke to the clerk an—"

"Shut up, Yokel! Ahem, well, babe, how's that for treating the freshie well?" Roc said to Iris, pointing his thumb at Hugo as Iris's leg swung back unnoticed.

"I told you not to call me that," Iris said, deftly making contact with Roc's shin. He jumped back, yelped, and all the freshies giggled.

"And that, kids, is how you deal with a Roc."

"I was joking!" Roc insisted, standing like an awkward flamingo.

"So how about it, Hugo, think you have what it takes to help Roc win the Tournament this year?" I asked deliberately so every one of the freshies clearly heard. If this kid didn't faint from excitement, he would make a decent squire yet.

But my reasons weren't entirely altruistic. I figured maybe this could win me some points with Iris. By the Nine she looked fantastic. A memory instantly shot to the front of my mind, clear as day. Iris was in the library, arranging books and scrolls back into their stacks. She hadn't noticed me approach the end of an aisle. I lingered there, watching as she reached on tiptoe, stubbornly refusing a nearby ladder, her dark hair cascading well past her shoulders.

Nine Hells, I'm creepy.

"New hairstyle?" I asked her, snapping back out of my memory, still waiting for Hugo to start breathing again.

"Yes!" she exclaimed, smiling her wide smile that threatened to devour my entire being. "Do you like it? I'm trying something new for fifth year." She swung her head back and forth as her hair danced lightly on her shoulders.

Damn, that's cute.

"I love it," I said immediately. Maybe too immediately. "Uh, uh, Hugo! So, what'll it be, bud?"

After a moment's thought, Hugo yelled out as loud as he could, "HELLS YES!"

The entire hall fell silent, and Roc smacked Hugo's back, his hand encompassing almost a third of it. "Well then, Hugo, welcome to Whiskey Danger. We start training this afternoon. Don't wear anything you like." After eyeing Hugo up and down, he added jovially, "I suppose you can keep wearing that then!"

An onomatopoeic clicking announced an uninvited guest. "Tck-tck-tck, ah look, boys, the would-be hedgie is recruiting children because no one else will tie his boots. How utterly pathetic."

Iris's eyes closed slowly and her lips pursed together as Ridhan Shipwight and his Sharks pushed their way through the crowd.

My heart detached itself from my chest, entered my stomach, and shattered into a million tiny shards of disgust and revulsion when Ridhan pulled Iris in for a kiss on her cheek, all the while glaring at me.

Iris was courting Ridhan? Ridhan Shipwight?! This couldn't be.... It had to be some sort of mistake. Yes, it was definitely a mistake. A ruse. A glib attempt at comedy and nothing else, because that was the only way to describe this tragedy.

Glib? Tragedy? I'd been hanging out with Yokel too much.

I couldn't comprehend what I was witnessing. If I hadn't seen it myself, I would never have believed it. A shared kiss months ago, the imagined future I had daydreamed, the fullness in my heart at the thought of her... it all began to crumble in an instant.

Iris tried to pull away, but Ridhan's long arms ensnared his trophy.

"Oh, you didn't know, Q? Lady Kentaro here is all mine. Isn't that just, tck-tck-tck, wonderful?" A sinister look and a thin smile betrayed his true self, but Iris's expression remained a puzzle to me. He pulled her in close for another vomit-inducing demonstration of affection; however, this time Iris resisted, driving Ridhan to instant fury.

"I thought I told you—" Ridhan began, raising his hand.

"Hey!" Roc exclaimed, lunging toward Ridhan without hesitation. This is what made Roc a legend. Beyond the bravado, the size, or any trophy he may have won on the field, he was fearless when it came to those in need. He was my hero, and in this instance, he needed to be Iris's too. Caught by surprise, Ridhan let go of his prize and prepared to defend himself, but Iris intervened, keeping Roc at bay.

In my own mind, I moved swiftly, pinning Ridhan up against the wall by his throat, his feet barely scratching the floor below. I would threaten him with all the pain and anguish I could imagine, and he would vow to never look Iris's way ever again. She would thank me and fall into my arms and everyone in the hall would clap at my heroism as we kissed.

But I merely stood there, paralyzed. The surprise of Ridhan and Iris, the anxiety about this last year at the Institute, and all the other troubles in my life weighed me down. I was supposed to be brave, but in this moment that mattered, I wasn't.

Come on, Oliver. Move!

"How dare you try to touch me, you worthless sandeater!" Ridhan yelled as he spat on Roc. Ridhan was a high noble, and if there was one thing he hated in this world more than anything, it was people he deemed beneath himself. People from the Narrows who could barely afford a roof above their head. People like Roc.

A voice of some kind stirred deep within my mind, within the recesses of my very soul. It urged me to take action with a surge of energy. I had felt this fantastic feeling before, but I couldn't quite place the memory.

A warm embrace. The tapping of water on stone.

As I contemplated the familiar sensation taking over my body, Roc's courage won through as he escaped Iris's grasp and landed a punch on Ridhan's forehead. Our antagonist fell flat on his back and a chorus of groans sounded from the onlooking students gathered around the commotion. Iris shoved past me and down to her suitor, but an outraged Ridhan rebuffed her.

He hollered, "Get off me, you—" but before he could finish, my body took control of itself, pushing Roc aside. I tripped as I tried to defuse the situation and accidentally shoved Ridhan back to the ground.

"Oliver!" Iris wailed as she pushed me away.

"I didn't mean to..." I apologized reactively. I don't know what had come over me, but a more pressing question stuck in my head.

Why was she defending him?

"Just leave!" she cried, tears in her eyes as she reached toward Ridhan for forgiveness.

"Young lords!" The low voice boomed from the bottom of the stairs. The High Steward of the Institute approached in his gray suit, a vision of rules and order.

Fearful of his reputation, the crowd of students instantly dispersed at the first sound of the High Steward's voice. Ridhan lay on the ground, a wild expression in his eyes as he looked at a ring he wore on his right hand. He withheld his Sharks from engaging further and I looked at Roc and Yokel, motioning that we should leave while we still could.

Turning my head back around, I caught Reagan and her friend Jocelyn carrying candied pears in a basket, walking in through the main doors. Reagan looked at Ridhan, still on the ground, now with his back to the wall and a trickle of blood tracing his head. A scowl of disappointment appeared on her face as she looked back to me. I shrugged.

I left, walking along the torch-lit and windowless hallway toward the fifth-year spire named after my family. Next to the sign that proclaimed my family's status, a deep bellowing voice from under a bushy mustache bounced off every wall of the stairwell. It was my stout, diminutive, and intimidating instructor, Professor Lortho.

"Mr. Quartermaine, follow me."

My shoulders dropped at the thought of a detention on my last first day.

As I approached the first step, I felt a tap on my back. Turning around, I found Hugo waiting patiently for me to speak.

"Hey, Hugo, sorry about all… well, all of that. It usually isn't like that on the first day."

His eyes lit up and his mouth opened wide. "Are you kidding me? That was epic! That guy is a jerk. I can't wait to be on your team. I mean, that is if you still want me?"

All the heartache I had felt earlier at the loss of Iris was subdued and my heart was full once more. Hugo's earnest sincerity is what would set him apart.

This kid, this kid was special.

"Hugo, of course we want you on the team."

Hugo smiled wide and skipped along toward his first-year tower. Just before he was out of sight, he turned and yelled back to me.

"Oh, and Oliver, you can call me Po!"

# QUESTS

**M**agic. Po. I was stunned.

These words had stuck in my head and I knew there was more to it; however, I was due to follow Professor Lortho. The mystery of my new young friend would have to wait.

The professor stared at me from behind his desk. "Arithmetic, highest marks. Sorayian Language, highest marks. Apothecary, highest marks. Law, highest marks. Highest marks, highest marks... highest marks," Professor Lortho repeated as he slapped a report from each of my classes down onto his oak desk. "Even the dead language, Elvish, highest marks." He peered over the rim of his eyeglasses, his judgment all but palpable. "Tell me, Mr. Quartermaine. Why are you here?"

"You told me to follow you, Professor."

"No, no. I meant, why are you at the Institute? You clearly not only have an aptitude for these studies but are far beyond anything you'll learn in your fifth year. So, I ask you once more"—he paused, leaning over his desk, hands folded over the scattered reports—"why are you here?"

I inhaled slowly, taking the time to study the rotund professor, searching for a glimpse at his agenda. This was the first time I'd received grief for high marks in anything. I decided to hold close to my truth, lacking inventiveness at the moment, and gave him the answer that came easiest.

"I suppose, Professor, that I'm here because this is what is expected of me."

He raised an eyebrow. "You always follow expectations, do you?"

"As well as I can," I replied, the small burdens of my life falling into line within the Institute's prescribed structure.

The professor let out a small sigh, sitting back into his large study chair. "Disappointing, Mr. Quartermaine. Disappointing indeed." He stared at me for longer than I was comfortable with, until finally, our conversation took a turn I never would have expected.

"Mr. Quartermaine, what do you know of magic?"

Was this a trap? Did he work for the High Queen? Could he read my thoughts?

"Magic isn't real, Professor," I answered. Suddenly my defenses were up, and this was no longer a professor who lorded over me with the power of this Institution. He was now an opponent in a ring, and I had to treat him as such. Any slipup of thought or my tongue would surely be disastrous for me.

Professor Lortho looked at me once again with disappointment. "What if it were?"

"Children's stories, Professor." I'd had this conversation before, be it in a tent a world away with Yokel, except in reverse.

Magic. Po. A dark room. A door.

Images flashed through my mind as if a locked door in my mind temple had briefly cracked open. My expression gave away my cards, and the professor noticed.

"Are you sure about that, Oliver?"

In four years at the Institute, Professor Lortho had never once called me by my first name. I felt the energies flow through me once more, and the smell of fire tickled my nose.

I had but two choices. Trust the professor, who had given me countless detentions in the past, or lie to him and lose the chance to learn more.

What would my brother tell me in a time like this?

"Honestly, Professor, I'm not sure."

A large smile appeared underneath his bushy mustache and the professor clapped his hands together before moving to the front of his desk. He took a small black obelisk out of his pocket and placed it on the desk, spinning it. A dullness emanated around us both, and all sound from beyond the room evaporated.

"I was hoping you would say that. Listen carefully, Oliver. Magic is real," the professor said. "It is lost, locked away, hidden from us. But we've come to the moment where it must be found. Your talents are wasted here at the Institute, and I very much doubt you will learn anything of importance that you do not already know. Therefore, I have a special assignment for you, the only one you will have all year. Complete it, and you may graduate. Don't, and I fear there will be worse things to consider."

If I had thought my shock from this morning's kerfuffle was intense, the professor's words promptly took the breath out of my lungs. I was lucky to even form words in response.

"What is the assignment, Professor?"

Professor Lortho checked his obelisk once more. "To find and save magic."

"Save it? Save it from who?"

"Whom," he deftly corrected. "The High Queen. She intends to destroy magic for good."

"Magic is already gone, I thought."

"Yes and no. But it lingers just so in magical objects throughout our world. Once those are all destroyed, I'm afraid we may never see magic again. But if you can find real magic, apart from relics and the like, then I believe we may have hope yet."

This was well beyond anything I had expected, but it intrigued me.

"Hope for what?"

"Hope that we may save this world from what is to come."

I had hundreds of questions running through my mind. "What of my other professors? They'll want me to—"

"I have taken care of that. This is your assignment, so take great care, and trust no one. There is more to this world than you realize, Mr. Quartermaine." The obelisk disintegrated into dust, sounds from outside the room resumed, and a loud bell rang. The professor pinched the dust between his fingers, sighed, and quickly left.

I sat alone in an empty room with my thoughts. Magic was real? Or wasn't anymore? I was utterly confused and also excited. The professor was correct in that I was floating by at the Institute. Everything being taught I had already learned. This new assignment had not only a complicated quality to it but also an air of danger.

Danger. Whiskey Danger.

The professor had said to trust no one, but surely I could trust Whiskey Danger. Yokel and Roc were my best friends, and if I was going on a quest, I would need their help.

Nine Gods, I had a quest!

This was like every fairytale and children's book I had ever read. The hero was given a quest, and the adventure began. I had spent the entire summer and even this entire morning begrudgingly contemplating my future, and here I was with it spelled out for me. I was to be a hero and go on a quest to save magic.

Nine Hells, where should I begin?

The image of two chairs and two figures flashed in my mind.

Magic. Po.

Protect Po.

Did the kid have something to do with this? Why was I to protect him? Was I on two quests? If I had to protect Po and save magic, I thought, I was going to need help. Sorry, Professor, but where there's danger, there's Whiskey Danger.

The rest of the morning's sessions came and went without much fanfare, and my mind occupied itself with my two new quests. A third thought kept impeding my progress, however. Suddenly Iris was all I could think about. Ridhan simply could not be courting her. Could it be for political reasons? Could her family have pushed her to do so? Why would a family as high as the Shipwights court a family as low as the Kentaros? As progressive as Starfall may have been within the South or even Soraya, there was still a good amount of joining of families through marriage. But that wasn't the Iris I knew.

Maybe I didn't know her as well as I thought.

The rest of the day passed without notice, the only thing on my mind being Iris. Even with the allure of my magical quest, she was all I could think about. As I sat in our study session, a beam of light shone through the colored glass in the study hall. The light softened to a color reminiscent of this morning's walk through Starfall. That seemed so long ago, and yet only hours had passed. Everything was different now. Iris was different.

Or was she? Maybe I could save her.

"So, the Second Elven War is what ultimately led to..." Roc fished while I stared absentmindedly at the wall.

"The Uprising," I stated, uninterested.

"Well, yeah of course," Roc retorted. "Then the Battle of the Blood-Red Moon was..."

"Between the vampires and the werewolves."

"I knew that," Roc replied, scribbling furiously onto his parchment.

"Don't forget about the Giant Riot, you'll get higher marks," I added as Roc continued to scribble away.

"How do you remember all this?" I smiled and he rolled his eyes. "Never mind. Why is it again you're not doing this?" Roc sighed, admiring his shoddy but complete coursework.

"I was given a special assignment by Lortho. I'll tell you about it later," I replied. A large bell from the center of the Institute rang once more, signaling the end of the day.

Roc hurriedly shoved his parchment into my pack. "See you at practice? I need to pick something up from the armory."

I grabbed my belongings, joining the sea of students as I navigated the hallways, dreaming of a world where Iris and I could be together... and the Nine once again heard my thoughts.

"Oliver! Oliver! Wait up!" a voice yelled at me, snapping me out of my daydream. I turned to see Iris approaching quickly, books in hand, words flooding from her mouth as if they must leave or forever be held captive. "Oliver, hi, I'm sorry about this morning and everything. I'd been meaning to tell you about Ridhan but you were away and I was here and... I'm sorry." She dropped her gaze to the floor when I tried to answer her, but my words caught as my throat seized, my breath frozen tight.

She continued softly. "I was wondering if you could stop by the Shears on your way home today. I have a book I think you'd like. Honestly, I know I shouldn't bother you with it, but you're the only person who I think can help..."

I blinked rapidly, trying to make sense of the conversation. She was asking me for help. She needed help. I could help her. By the Nine, I wasn't crazy. I could save her! This would be my third quest! Protect Po, save magic, rescue Iris. If they didn't write books about me in the future, it would be a shame. I felt blood rushing to my cheeks.

She continued, almost apologetically. "It's been a long time. It's just... Well, anyway. I know how much you like to read. Well, insomuch that the rumor is that you've read almost half the books and scrolls in the Shears. Which I find hard to believe, by the way, given the amount of time that would take." She giggled, music to my hopeful ears, but stopped suddenly. The pause was enough for my mind to react, and I wasn't quick enough to hide my sadness.

"But I'm rambling. Am I rambling? Oh Nine, I feel like this used to be easier. This used to be easier, didn't it?"

With my throat still seized, I stood in awestruck silence, absolutely no help to the conversation. She gently touched my shoulder and then pulled away. The entire exchange was more awkward than anything I had ever experienced.

What was wrong with me?!

"Is this weird? Sorry. Ah. Okay. Well... anyway. If you're free, do you think you could stop by?"

My mouth opened but the only words I could muster were, "To help you..."

"Right, to help me, with a book."

"Oh, right, the book," I replied sheepishly, all the while running through every possible scenario leading to her dumping Ridhan and running off with me. Iris looked around, embarrassment washing over her beautiful face.

"If you're busy, I suppose I could—"

"No!" I yelled, forgetting normal human speech at that moment. An orc would have addressed her like that, and in all my swirling emotion that's what I was, an orc: loud, dumb, and obnoxious, just as Steward Balon described them in his histories. Iris was giving me the opportunity I had dreamt of; all I needed was to take hold.

"I'm sorry, Iris, I meant no, you're not rambling. You're fine, in fact, you're great! I mean... Okay, stop." I fought to control my breath and catch my tongue. "I have practice now, with Whiskey Danger." I struggled with my conflicting thoughts, desperate to communicate. "I can absolutely stop by after... around dusk? I missed you..."

She stared blankly at me. "Sounds... good, it's a date!" she said apprehensively, awkwardly patting my shoulder. Her brow furrowed, and I felt her hand leave my shoulder as she turned to walk away.

A date?!

She quickly escaped from sight as I stood, hopeful for the future. I was gazing longingly down the hall after her when my thoughts were rudely interrupted by a hand on my shoulder and a swift fist to my stomach. I groaned, folding over in pain, not too surprised to hear Ridhan's voice address me coldly.

"Tck-tck-tck, hello, Q."

I quickly ran through my options, the urge to run out of the building prevailing. But I didn't run. Instead, the internal voice from that morning stopped me. It was as if every courageous fiber in my soul was forcing me to confront this challenge head-on.

Ridhan stood not an inch from my face. He was handsome enough, but his true disposition had grown into his expression, souring his overall appearance. We had known each other all our lives, and I had seen him grow from a kind and caring child to the bully he was today. At one point, I would have even counted us as friends, but those days were long ago. Maybe my friend was still inside, deep within the mask he now wore. A mask of terror and power and privilege. I would have been lying if I didn't say I missed him.

Was this another quest? Redeem Ridhan? How many quests could I take on in one day?

He paced around me, measuring my defiance with his eyes as I gained my composure. Few people ever stood up to Ridhan, his family name and innumerable lackeys affording him his boorish, self-serving attitude. The bully sauntered back around to face me, his cackling laugh echoed by his encircling Sharks.

With the characteristic clicking of his tongue, Ridhan continued his heavy-handed torment. "Tck-tck-tck. It's funny, you know, my Q? You and I, we are so much the same. The prospects of our names, stations, our futures, all wrapped up in tiny little boxes, sitting in wait under our childhood beds as we fly high above those who do not understand."

Apparently when Reagan had said people had changed, she must have meant Ridhan as well. He had developed his "ticking" sound a few years back, but this nonsense he was rambling on about was a new development. I leave for a few months and all of a sudden everything has turned upside down. But what game was he trying to play, and how could I gain the upper hand? I let him continue, trying to anticipate where the conversation was going.

"Tck-tck-tck... but alas, my earthbound friend, you once again disappoint me. I should string you up and let you bake in the sun for how you touched me this morning!" His voice curdled in rage but just as quickly settled into a hint of glee. "Such a curious thing I saw."

"You spat on my friend."

"Ah yes, the gutter rabbit. He deserved it, no? Imagine retaining that pitiful existence when you could actually be useful as... fish food."

At his final hiss, three of the Sharks moved swiftly, pushing me onto my knees and pinning me motionless. Ridhan bent slightly, looking me directly in the eyes.

"I could kill you now, you know. As easy as an accident..."

This was new. I had never known Ridhan to talk like this, let alone act like this. His eyes were wide and soulless, a dark husk of the boy he used to be. Yet maybe, just maybe there was a hint of light still inside him. If I could appeal to that, maybe I could get out of this situation unscathed. Ridhan may have been lost, but that didn't have to mean forever. He snapped his fingers and I was released.

He laughed heartily and his Sharks followed suit. "I jest, my love, I jest. Or do I? Who is to say? Minds are so easily changed these days."

Was he rhyming now?

The situation was getting away from me. He was winning his game, and if I kept playing, I was afraid of what the outcome might be. I needed to change the rules of engagement.

My eyes closed briefly; something in my chest burned hot and bright as if to counter the cold abyss that had taken hold of Ridhan's soul. Without warning, my world stood still and my mind entered the familiar patterns of my Carpenter fighter training as I took a survey of my environment.

Four Sharks, Ridhan, three students passing by... Target Makolio first, sweep the leg and throw him into Baskin, neutralizing them both. Dodge under Lemond's haymaker punch, his forward stumble revealing Porbea, and throw him into the passersby. Head kick to Lemond, use Baskin's momentum to snap his wrist out of a grapple, relieve Makolio of the knife on his back, target Ridhan.

In one swift blur of motion, I was holding the tip of Makolio's knife to the point of Ridhan's nose as a sinister grin of amusement grew over his face.

"You might want to rethink who you threaten, Shipwight," I hissed, watching as Ridhan brought a single finger to the blade, drawing it across the well-honed edge until he drew blood. He pulled his left heel backward, stepping away slightly as he licked the blood from his finger.

"Oh, how I've missed you, my Q. I promised my Iris I wouldn't hurt you, my sweet. However, that promise does not extend to any of your little friends."

"Ridhan, if you lay a finger on—"

"You'll what? Accidents happen all the time. This city is a dangerous place, after all. The Narrows are full of all sorts of unsavory types."

My heart fell from my ribs and, ceding my pride, I strove to safeguard Whiskey Danger's future. "What do you want?"

"Your Shield of Kandaheart," he said coolly and quickly, sending my mind into scrambles. The shield was a simple family heirloom, generations old. It was as much a part of my family as the Forge or Anvil, treasured by my family as little more than an ornament; it didn't even technically work as a shield. Yet, what cost was too great to assure the safety of my friends, my brothers?

I sighed in defeat. "You'll leave them alone?"

"Well," Ridhan replied, a sickening smile overtaking his pale features, "I will not go out of my way to hurt them, which you know I so badly want to do. I cannot, however, guarantee that upon meeting your destitute friend in the joust, he will leave the field of his own accord." Every word Ridhan spat struck me as if laced with poison, but his arrogance had left me the opening I was waiting for.

Maybe I could win this game.

"I hadn't realized you were competing at Homecoming this year, Ridhan. Let's raise the stakes." Never one to falter in the face of a challenge, Ridhan seemed enticed, but I needed to assure his contemptible cooperation. "If you win, I'll hand over my family's shield and your family's Staff of the Seas. You know, the one that currently resides in my father's armory. If Roc wins, you leave them alone. And Iris. Unless you don't think you can beat him. He is the reigning champion, after all."

"Goading me, Q? Tck-tck-tck. I expected more than that from you, but I have to admit, I am intrigued. That staff hasn't seen my house since..." He looked me over, clearly questioning my motives. Curiously, he seemed not to care about the second part of the wager, the one concerning Iris. Maybe their relationship wasn't that strong, and I could figure out a way to her.

"You have yourself a deal. I will not touch your little friends until the Homecoming Tournament. When I win—and I will win, my dear, sweet

Q—I expect the Shield of Kandaheart and my family's staff." As if an afterthought, he added with a hiss, "Oh, and when I win, I think I'll be killing all your friends as well, including the little one my Iris is so fond of. And I will finally have you all to myself."

The terror in my stomach was palpable, but I saw no solution. Was he joking as before, or was this threat serious? Should I trust this madman? At this point, I had no choice. I had to trust him.

"And what of Iris?" I demanded.

He looked at me, calculating. "She is mine." He was clearly relishing the moment. "But if I lose, she is yours." He walked closer, looking me up and down before resting his hand on my shoulder. "Sweet, simple Q. I doubt you'll want her though..." His last words were punctuated by a sharp pinch of my cheek. He smiled, drawing his tongue across his lips. Immediate nausea took me over. Nine Hells, what did I just agree to?

As Ridhan and his faithful peons walked out of sight, I struggled to understand all that had transpired, thinking about what would happen to all of us if Roc didn't win this autumn. Then I heard his telltale shuffling footsteps behind me.

"What are you still doing here?" Roc asked, oblivious to the stakes we were now playing for. My newest quest wasn't that of redeeming Ridhan but rather saving my friends. Not wanting to read him into the current circumstances, I deflected.

"Nice helmet!" He had donned his newly feathered jousting helmet, and inspired by his focus, I spared him the turmoil eating away at my mind.

Protect Po. Save Magic. Rescue Iris. Save my friends.

"Let's get to practice, Roc. You're going to need it."

# CARPENTERS

"Hugo! I mean, Po! What are you doing after practice?" I asked, picking up my pack. My first quest was to protect Po, but from what or who, I had no idea. I didn't even know if it was a quest or just my own mind playing tricks on me.

The kid had immediately fit into our group, like a missing puzzle piece we never knew we needed. We'd never had a squire before, and it felt great to not have to do all the grunt work ourselves. He was eager to do anything and everything we asked and had once pointed out a flaw in Roc's technique that even Yokel had missed. He was a perfect addition to Whiskey Danger.

I figured there were only two ways to protect him, if that really was what I was supposed to do. First, I'd have to get to know him and keep him close, training with Whiskey Danger. The second would come now.

Po responded in a matter-of fact tone. "Just heading home, I suppose. If I don't get there before dark, all the best beds will be taken." There was no hint of embarrassment in his voice, but I was struck by the answer.

"You live in the Narrows?"

"Yep. My gran works for Miss Iris's family, so she lives in the Gardens at the Kentaros with my sister, but she's just a baby. There wasn't room for me, so I stay in the Trees."

I cocked my head. "Roc lives in the Trees also. Maple Three."

"No way!" Po yelped. "I live in Birch Two." I smiled at his enthusiasm, and we exited the Institute's training grounds.

"What about your mother and father?" I asked.

Po grew silent before finally answering. "They're both gone. Died a little while ago."

"I'm so sorry, Po," I said. This kid was a smaller version of Roc, and my heart felt for him.

"It's okay, Oliver. I have Gran and my sister."

"Does your sister have a name?"

"Not yet. Gran said I get to choose a name for her on her name day, which will be in a few months. Until then, I just call her Stinky." Po giggled to himself and I resorted to a small smile. A person's name day typically occurred on the solstice following their birth, which meant the baby Pondarion couldn't have been more than a few months old. That also meant the loss of his parents wasn't so long ago either. When I lost my own mother, I fled from everything I knew, but this kid charged into making a better life for himself at the Institute, instead. I had to admit to myself, I was envious of this boy.

"Well, if you don't mind not getting the good bed, how about you tag along with me for a while, eh? I could use the company."

"Sure, where we going?"

I smiled ominously. "You'll see."

We made our way through town to the city center, the deep blue sky dotted with bright white puffy clouds sweeping across the horizon of the planet above like something from a painter's brush. The rustle of the roadside trees was quickly drowned out by Market Square, easily the busiest place in all the South. As we walked past the merchant's stalls, I reflected on my quests.

Obsessing, really.

I'd spent my whole life never committed to one thing. Even my studies at the Institute had been a collection of every subject I could weasel my way into. I had never wanted to just be one thing in life, and I could never decide which path to choose. Now, it seemed, life was choosing for me. If I was to be a hero on this adventure, I needed focus.

I stopped briefly at a stall, handing off a few coins and picking up a couple of kabobs. I turned to Po, who was out of breath from keeping pace with my longer and much stronger legs. I walked at a brisk pace, conditioned from years of keeping up with Roc's long strides. Handing Po a kabob, I turned my attention to the boy, looking for a glimpse of information.

"So, Po, tell me about yourself, little buddy," I asked, slowing my pace considerably. "What I mean is, what's your story?"

"Um, well I don't really have a story."

"Everyone has a story, bud, and everyone's story is important."

"I don't, Oliver. I'm no one special. Just a kid from the Narrows. My parents weren't special either. My pa was a quarryman and my mum worked for the Kentaros with my gran. We're not special like you or Roc or Yokel." His expression soured until his face lit up. "My grandpa was special! He was a soldier in the Imperial Army. He was on the front lines at the Sunset Mountains when goblins attacked. See, here's his ring he sent me before he died."

I looked at the heirloom on his hand but was more surprised by the pride with which Po talked about his grandfather. With all the death the kid had suffered, one more loss I was sure would have destroyed him. Instead, it seemed as though he held no ill will toward the world. No, to him, his grandfather was a hero. A hero he bore the name of. And an heirloom that I was pretty sure wouldn't fetch a silver coin at the market but was priceless, nonetheless.

We continued walking and I decided to investigate more into who Po was as a person, beyond his family. His family was not important in the traditional way, and his grandfather was a simple soldier in a border war half a world away. So why did this nobody from the Narrows need protection?

"So, what is it you're looking to get out of life, Po?"

"Um, well, probably more kabobs," Po said between bites. "This is amazing. WAY better... than... chompfchommm... mmm..."

"Slow down there, kid. I mean, what is it that you're looking to become in life? A soldier like your grandfather?"

A determined conviction flashed across his small face. "I want to become a knight, a real, true knight. For a high lord, and buy my gran and sister a cottage outside the city and move out of the Narrows. I'll build a great big porch to overlook our land and, and, and I'll be famous and lords will invite me to their parties and we'll dance and sing and there'll be..."

I looked at him in awe. This was so simple, so easy in his mind, however long a shot it was in reality. Becoming a knight was one of the hardest titles to attain in the kingdom. He wanted to try, regardless of the odds, to help his family... not just himself. He wanted so badly to help people, most importantly the people he loved.

"Po..." I hesitated, wondering if I really could destroy this dream so soon after its inception. It wasn't as though the kid didn't deserve to be a knight, but the odds were against him. "Po, that's a great dream. I want you to make me a promise. You think you can do that?" I asked, lowering my voice.

"I promise, Oliver," Po said without a second thought.

"I haven't told you what to promise yet, bud." Nine, this kid was outright special.

He slumped his shoulders. "Oh, right, sorry."

"Promise me this. Promise me that you will try as hard as you can in everything you do. That you will not let anything stop you, and that you will become a knight."

"I promise."

My eyes glazed over as I stared off across the bay. We continued toward the northeast side of the city, the crowds dwindling to an occasional passerby. There was only one way in or out of the inner city, and that was through the Narrow Gate.

Starfall had been founded and built around the docks, Shears, Market Square, and the Institute, but over time it had needed to expand. Those with less means and money were forced out of the inner city and expanded into narrow buildings outside the city walls. A single gate—the Narrow Gate as it was called since it could only fit a single wagon through at a time—separated the two parts of the city. The Narrows, as the part of town east of the wall was called, acted as an informal barrier against would-be invaders from the land, and the city wall and Narrow Gate acted as another defense.

In the years since its founding, Starfall City had never been sacked. We didn't have a large army, given the only soldiers were the City Watch, who mostly policed the city on behalf of the Council. The Starfall Reef and our Merchant Navy led by the Shipwights saw that no invaders would ever attack by sea. It was the only kingdom in the world without a king or queen, and thus it was always referred to as the City.

My City. And I loved her more than anything. It was a place that accepted anyone and everyone. Northern Tribes, Floaters, Romirians, Kandaharim, and strangers from even farther distant lands. Starfall welcomed everyone, as long as they were willing to accept all of its peoples. It didn't matter what you looked like, where you were from, what your family name was; the South, and more importantly Starfall City, was the place for you.

My plan was progressing as we moved through the Narrows. If I was to protect Po, and if he was to become a knight, I knew of only one place that could accomplish both.

"Well then," I said, "since you want to be a knight, I may be of some help to you." I turned, leading the boy through an inconspicuous door and into the Workshop.

As we entered, the Carpenters halted their practice, the dull thud of their wooden practice gear echoing through the otherwise silent room. I watched as Po took in the room, the most elite training center in the entire world. All of Starfall's best warriors, four of the eight current Black Hawks, and seven of the last eleven Dragon Champions had trained here: If you wanted to become the best, you trained at the Workshop.

"This... is... AMAZING!" Po was practically levitating with excitement.

"Continue," I said, motioning to the students by tapping my left shoulder. Po looked on in awe, gazing up at me as I led him through the ranks. I had been coming to the Workshop since I was old enough to walk, and my family had been highly involved in the training program for generations. I probably spent more time here than in my own home, and I had the scars to prove it. In truth, all Carpenters were of equal rank in the Workshop, even those who had been training for years and those who had started only weeks ago. Looking down, I could see that Po was already hooked.

"These are Carpenters, Po. We are all Carpenters, and that is the only title in the Workshop." I motioned around the busy room, explaining the structure as best I could to the eager boy. "We're called Carpenters because of how we handle problems. You see, we take a challenge and pull it apart, turning it into something new, something with purpose. Just like a trade carpenter takes wood and makes a chair, we take a situation and make a solution. We take what others can't handle or see, and we fix it. If you really want to be a knight... well, here is a good place to start."

Po was clearly overwhelmed, his chest heaving erratically. I tried to redirect his energy. "Bud, this isn't even the hardest part. Take a breath."

He stared up at me, his brow furrowed. "What's the hard part?"

"First, you have to meet Azel."

And that's when he fainted. I shook my head, amused.

Kids.

I stood over Po's small form in a small room holding a flagon of water.

"Po, Po! Wake up. I'd like you to meet someone."

I splashed his face with the water and gave him a healthy slap on the cheek. He blinked rapidly, then warily eyed a woman in the corner of the room who was methodically sliding a whetstone down the length of a handsome blade, my second-favorite sound in this world.

"Po, I'd like you to meet Azel. Carpenter, this is Po."

Azel stood up from her stool, modest dark leather clothes adorning her slender frame and long hair pulled back into a ponytail. This small room served as her personal quarters; there were no windows and no adornments other than the two lanterns that hung useless to her from the ceiling.

"Po, is it?" she said in a steely tone I had been used to hearing since my birth. At times I would hear her voice narrating my thoughts as I read to myself late at night.

"Let us take a look." Bending down onto one knee, Azel's milky grey eyes stared sightlessly into Po's wide gaze. "Who are you, Po? What is your story?"

Po stood like a statue, his stiff form threatening to shatter at a hair's touch. Meeting Azel was something that hit hard, her blank stare sticking with a person long after they left. Po gasped, his eyes never falling from Azel's, but he remained silent.

I handed the Carpenter her quarterstaff, with its round colorless stone on the top, and she twisted the shaft, pressing it into the kid's chest over his heart.

"I see your story, Po Pondarion. You are a strong young man, a good brother, a good grandson. Your story is important; you will help to shape this world. I see this—" Suddenly, Azel's face drew itself into a curious contour. "But... I also see fear..."

The words cut into me like cold steel. I remembered that stare when she had looked into my eyes. She had pressed the very same staff to my heart, saying, "You have a power within you, more power than anyone I have seen in a long time... so familiar, but so distant. Strange that I cannot see it all."

Po's answer brought me back from my memory.

"I'm not afraid," he stammered, resolving his posture and straightening his spine.

"Oh, but you are. I see it all.... The fear of letting your mother down, fear that your gran will never leave the service of others, fear that your sister will never know a good life, fear that you will fail them as you did your grandfather... fear of failing in your duties to this Carpenter here." Azel waved her hand toward me, knowing without seeing exactly where I stood. I inhaled sharply; Po was afraid to let me down?

Oh, kid. You're going to be okay.

"Ma'am—"

Azel stopped him, motioning her hand to her own chest. "Please, Mr. Pondarion. Call me Carpenter."

"Carpenter..." Po continued hesitantly, "I lied. I am afraid. How can I be brave all the time?"

Good job, bud. You passed.

I sighed in relief. To become a Carpenter, there was only one test. It didn't matter who you were, the family you came from, the money you could offer, or even your skill. The one and only test was based on honesty. If you couldn't be honest with Azel, you could never be honest with yourself. You could never be honest in a fight, or when it mattered most.

Azel's shoulders lowered ever so slightly, accepting the young boy's answer.

"Fear is not something to hide from, and together, we will learn how to control that fear, and how to use it to help others. You may leave now, Carpenter Po."

Po's eyes lit up, his mouth opening to speak to little avail, not an uncommon thing to happen to a new Carpenter. Azel continued, a kindly smile on her weathered features.

"Carpenter Oliver here will assist you. You will learn from other Carpenters, including me, and you WILL learn to harness that fear into something greater." With this last promise, Azel stood and made her way back to her stool, took up her sword, and began honing the edge in the same slow motion as before.

Po still hadn't moved. In fact, I hadn't seen him take a breath in what seemed like minutes.

Nine Hells, I've got to teach the kid how to breathe!

I grabbed him from behind by both his shoulders, spinning him around and moving him out the door. Po staggered and looked up at me.

"I can't, I can't believe what just happened. I... wait, what just happened?! I think I blacked out."

"We all black out, bud," I said, laughing. "You're a Carpenter now. That about sums it up."

"But I can't afford this! I have no money..." Po began, sadness creeping in his voice.

"Carpenters don't pay at the Workshop."

"What? How?... What?!"

"Well, my family has known Azel's family... well, forever. I mean, I'm not entirely sure we're not related, come to think about it. Ancient family lines and all. Anyway, a long time ago, my family agreed to fund the Workshop, which meant that lords weren't the only ones who could become Carpenters."

Po's wide eyes threatened to overtake his whole face, and his jaw went slack.

"I don't know what to say. I..." Tears were streaming down his cheeks, but his resolve won through and he continued. "No, I can't. Even if it's free, I can't not give you anything."

I had seen this before and knew no matter what I might say, I would be unable to convince Po differently. He was like Roc, like most in the Narrows. They never wanted handouts, charity, or even help. I'd spent my entire life disguising the help I gave Roc. People without means were still people, with pride and dignity. They wanted to earn what they got, unlike most nobles I knew. It's why I loved Roc so much. He'd never known an easy life, but he never asked for an easy way out. He worked hard for everything he got, and any way I could help, I would, albeit disguised.

But I was trapped in this moment, without an escape. I quickly tried to think of a multitude of ways Po could "repay" me or even the Workshop, but each scenario seemed too obvious. I didn't have to think long though, because Po interrupted with his own solution.

Sliding the loose ring off his thumb, he held it up toward me. "I know I don't have much, but this means a lot to me. I want you to have it."

I took a step back, as if I'd been pierced in the heart with an arrow. "I can't take this. It was your grandfather's. You really don't have to—"

"Take it, Oliver. I want to pay my own way. It doesn't look like much, but I know it's special. Training here is the opportunity of a lifetime, and I don't want to always think back on how I didn't pay my way. Please, take it." His eyes were drowning in more tears ready to stream down his young face. I knew it was useless to argue with him, so I took the ring.

It was a curious weight, almost perfect in a way. Too small for my own thumb, it slid quite nicely onto my right third finger and I held it up to the torchlight. It was a simple design; a thick silver band encircled the outer edges while the middle of the band contained a false sapphire. Inside the blue were intricate yellow weaves of knots, all concluding with a curious nine-pointed star I had never seen before. It wasn't flat enough to create a seal of any type, but the detail of the metalwork and filament signaled something important.

Or maybe it was just a trinket Po's grandfather sent him. I spun the ring around on my finger, letting the feel of it settle against my knuckles.

I looked at Po and smiled. "Thank you, Carpenter." He wiped the tears from his face and started to laugh away the emotions that had built up.

"So, Car-pen-ter," Po started, exaggerating each syllable in excitement, "when do we start?"

"We start now!" I replied. "Let me show you to the barracks. I wouldn't want to lose this ring of ours. Did your grandfather tell you anything about it?"

"Nothing too much. Only that it was a key," Po answered as we made our way down a hall, but I stopped dead in my tracks.

Did he just say a key?

"A key to what?" Could this be it? Could this be a clue to my quest for magic? Is this why I was supposed to protect Po? Was I going to solve two quests in one day? Was I the greatest hero in the entire history of the world?

Po turned. "I don't know. It came with an old journal we had lying around, but it was blank. I guess he never got around to writing in it."

My excitement sank as my dreams of fulfilling my quests early were summarily dashed. We reached the barracks, where Po would now be living, and his breath stopped once more. The room was pristine and immaculate, filled with furniture and clothing and equipment one might expect only to see in a royal castle. There was probably more wealth in this one room than in all the Narrows.

"Oliver?" Po asked after regaining his breath.

"Yeah, Carpenter?"

"How rich are you?"

I patted him heavily on the back, grinning ear to ear. "You wouldn't believe me if I told you."

# THE BOOK

Dusk came quickly, and I was not entirely ready to begin my third quest. I stood on the steps of the Shears with a bouquet of flowers, a riot of colors against the white granite shell of the building. I craned my neck at the massive structure in front of me, often referred to as The White Jewel of the South.

If the Institute was one of the oldest buildings in the city, then the Shearson Library was its grandest. Larger than even the Institute, it housed more knowledge in the form of scrolls and books than any other single place in the known world. Stewards from every kingdom and country pilgrimaged to the Shears to study, scribe, and learn. The height of the building was only superseded by its depth—an underground labyrinth of rooms and halls that may never have been fully explored. Forgotten texts, secret genealogies, and other wonders awaited anyone who ventured through the door.

The Shears was a veritable playground for my appetite for knowledge. As a child of the woman who had run the entire operation as High Steward, I'd spent countless hours in these halls, voraciously reading anything I could get my hands on. Given the way my mind worked, I needed only read a scroll or book once, and it was with me forever. If not for the Workshop, this would have been my true home and safe haven. Yet the life of a pure scholar would never be for me. As much as I loved the old texts and stories, it would never be my only passion. Maybe in the next life, if the Northern Tribes were right about death.

I stood on the threshold, trying to summon the courage to walk in. Iris wasn't the only reason for my apprehension. I hadn't stepped foot inside the Shears since my mother died. The massive oak panels creaked with a submissive groan, tired from centuries of safeguarding the knowledge within, and even though my stomach dropped, I entered the old building.

Dusk was turned to night as torch-lit shadows danced along the corridors and I entered the maze. My feet sprinted me down and down until I had reached the level where I knew Iris would be.

Bursting through a door on the third basement level, I paused to catch my breath, rolling my shoulders back as I casually entered the room with a feigned nonchalance.

Don't seem too eager, don't look like a fool.

I turned a corner to find Iris placing books neatly on shelves.

Nine Hells, she looked great.

Inhaling deeply, I thought of how to address her.

"Hey, pretty lady, those books sure look..."

No, that's dumb.

"Heya baby, do you come here often, because..."

Ugh, STUPID. She works here, idiot! Come on, Oliver. Do better.

Lost in this conversation with myself, a tap on my shoulder spun me around so suddenly I nearly knocked a startled Iris off her feet with the namesake I held clutched tightly in my left hand.

"Whoa there, killer, last thing I want is to be known as the girl who died from being smashed in the head with flowers!" She was grinning and holding on to my arm as if I might fly across the room had I not been restrained.

"Oh! Uh, sorry. I was just... Uh, yeah. Sorry. This is for you. Welcome back." I motioned to the now-battered flowers, disarmed completely by her smile and her hand still squeezing my forearm.

"Thanks, Oliver, but you're the one who's back, remember?" She took the flowers hesitantly.

"Oh, right. Of course. I mean, it's nice to see you again. Those don't mean anything," I said apologetically. Seeing her hurt expression, I added quickly, "Well, they do, but nothing like... Never mind." This girl was driving me crazy! Here I was, once again fumbling for words.

"Thank you, Oliver, it means a lot." Her tone was intoxicating, her sincerity undeniable, but the vague sadness in her voice distracted me. She took the flowers, placing them on a nearby table, and grabbed hold of my hand. "Come with me!" she said with a flirtatious smile. She pulled me through the stacks, a maze of books and shelves and hidden corners. Following closely, I escaped into a memory, the whirl of stacks blurring into a dark room in my first year at the Institute.

I was seated, bent over a desk with my forehead drumming the wood, keeping an unheard tempo in utter boredom. I was frustrated and hurt that my older brother had left, and my first assignment seemed worthless. My mind and my emotions were undisciplined, and my equally undisciplined tongue had made sure my time would be spent as it was now, in a tedious detention in the Institute's dungeon.

"Oi, I see you didn't complete Professor Harwich's assignment either," a voice said from the doorway. This girl was in my class. She had an unusual accent. She was pretty, with long hair and an unkempt appearance. Her clothes and accent were more a style from Land's End than they were of the South.

"Nah, I'm not really into this stuff," I said, trying to sound more audacious than I was.

"Is that right? And what 'stuff' might that be?" she asked, taking a seat next to me. Her wide eyes were framed by her long hair as she threw her boots up onto the table, letting her long coat fall away to reveal pants. She was more unusual than any girl I'd ever seen in Starfall, and I was instantly hooked.

"Oh, you know. These dumb assignments they give us," I said dismissively.

"So, you're not long for this place, love?"

Love? We just met; did she love me already? Was I ready for love? I had never even courted someone before!

I looked at her curiously, trying to recall my knowledge of the people from the Imperial Capital. I remembered their peculiar accents and dialect and realized she was goading me into looking like a jerk. She was right; I was being a petulant jerk.

"Honestly, that's not me. I actually like it here! It's just... things at home have been kind of..."

"Bonkers?"

"Um, sure," I responded, not quite sure what bonkers meant. "Between my brother and my parents, and now this assignment, which I totally meant to do, but I just got..."

"A little sidetracked?"

"Yes!"

"Me too." A smile punctuated her rosy cheeks. "My family can be tossers too."

I instantly relaxed, the weight of my situation dissolving at this lovely girl's commiserative and confusing words. I smiled back.

"You're new here, right?"

"Aye, my family just moved down from Land's End," she said, clearly apprehensive about the move. She fidgeted with her clothing. "Da's establishing his new shipping business here with the Shipwights."

She was so obviously out of her comfort zone, I turned back to our embarrassing surroundings.

"So, do you have detention too?"

She stood up, smiling slyly. "Nope!" Reaching into her pocket, she pulled out a candied pear. "Come with me, little lord."

"Oliver, you're doing that thing again."

I snapped out of my memory, blinking quickly, my mind racing to review what she had just said to me, my subconscious playing scribe for my escapist daydreaming. I turned to Iris and smiled briefly, my attention solely on her.

"Anyway... as I was saying, I have this book. But there's something strange about it that I don't quite understand." Her accent was no longer noticeable, unless she was extra tired or a little drunk. She reached above her head, drawing down a small brown book. In any other place this book would have been ordinary, but here in the stacks—huge rooms dedicated to housing the giant, overstuffed volumes and scrolls scribed over centuries—the informality of the small book stood out like a freshie at a joust.

The book had a clasped binding on it, as if it could be locked. But the clasp was unhinged and the book easily allowed its contents to be read.

"You found a book..." I teased. "A book. Here, in the largest library in the world."

"Well, no. Just shut up and listen, will you! This book is different. I've been researching on this level all summer, and there's no mention of something like this."

I looked around. This level contained a collection of personal histories of noble families throughout the continent. They would often have not just genealogies but also stories of their deeds, holdings, and even details about nonfamily members. If you were clever enough, you could ascertain information about a family that wouldn't easily be known.

"Everything here is histories of noble families. I don't understand how that connects to your book."

"You've read all of these?" she asked, clearly amused if not convinced. "I'm going to test you on that another day. This book didn't come from a noble family, but I was trying to find any mention of the sigil in these histories. I found nothing." She handed the book over to me and I began my own inspection. It came with a locking mechanism that had clearly been tampered with, and the cover felt odd in my hands. I was having trouble pinpointing its age. The leather spoke to an older finish, but the detail on the front cover looked as clear as if it had been burnished yesterday.

"Did you just smell it?"

I glanced up at her. Iris had her nose scrunched up and brows furrowed downward. I was incapable of holding back the smile that overtook over my face; she was so overwhelmingly cute, I thought I might explode. I felt much like I had my first year at the Institute, and a sudden sympathy for the overwhelmed freshies that morning grew in my heart. I grinned mischievously, and without warning shoved the book into her face.

"Yep, here, take a whiff!"

She immediately recoiled. "Ohhh, I'm going to get you back for that, little lord!" she cried playfully, shoving my arm clear and conceding a small laugh.

This was the kind of weirdness in Iris I knew and loved.

Liked, not loved. Get a hold of yourself, Oliver.

"I look forward to it!" I smiled nervously and an awkward silence stretched between us as we stood looking into each other's eyes.

"So... this book..." I finally broke the strange spell.

Iris took a heavy breath, snatching the book from my hand and holding it up to a lantern. "Yes, this confounding book. Here's the odd part."

She opened the cover, deftly flicking through page after page, each leaf devoid of any inscription or illustration. She handed the book back to me, clearly at a loss. I turned back to the sigil on the front, a nine-pointed star. I looked at the ring on my hand, the one Po had given me, and wondered.

"You said this book didn't come from a noble family, and yet you spend all summer on this level researching noble histories." The puzzle was starting to piece together. "One of your summer students, right?" I asked. "His grandmother works in the kitchens of a noble family."

Iris smiled back, happy that I was finally catching up. She grabbed the book, running her hand through the pages once more. "Po gave me this book, told me it belonged to his grandfather. I saw the sigil but couldn't find any mention of it. Five-pointed stars, eight-pointed stars, every star in the sky except this one. A blank book with an unknown sigil. It could mean nothing, just an old book. But Po was adamant it was important, at least to his grandfather."

"Only noble families have sigils. Why does he believe it's so special?"

"Because he says his grandfather told him so in the last letter before he died."

I turned away, pacing about the aisle of the books we were in, readying myself.

Time stood still, and I retreated into my mind. Before me stood a vast temple, and before it stacks of books in rows. As a young boy, I would panic and freeze when my mind was overloaded with too much information. It was as if a scribe constantly recorded everything I experienced. Every sound, every sight, every feeling was all catalogued in my head. Even things I didn't want to know, like the number of bricks in a building or the weather on this same day three years ago. The information would become too much and I would collapse, falling asleep to escape reality.

Then my brother taught me how to build a temple, my mind temple, with thousands of rooms where I could store my knowledge. I could close the doors, opening them only when needed, and live my life without the constant rush of all that I experienced. Over time, I'd created sort of a "garden of books." It contained the knowledge I wanted more readily to hand and allowed me to process thoughts quicker than delving deep into my mind temple. But this was not a time for quick knowledge. I entered the temple, and before me was an empty white room. I spoke aloud my search.

"Information on sigils, symbols, and other markings." The room rushed around me, filling shelves with countless tomes and scrolls. I needed to narrow my search.

"Noble families throughout all history," I modified. The shelves shifted around me in a circular pattern like the mechanisms of a clock. But it was still too much.

"Let me try something different," I spoke, and the shelves melted into dust.

"Children's stories and fairytales." The familiar rush of stacks once again rustled my hair.

"Stories about magic." The stacks disappeared and reappeared rapidly.

"A nine-pointed star sigil." The stacks melted into dust once more.

"How about just nine points?" A pedestal rose in front of me, holding a single book that I had seen once when I was a small boy at my uncle's library in Kandaheart. A mythos about nine legendary heroes called The Knights of the Nine. Everyone knew of the story, their legends entirely fictional. Every child dreamed of being a Knight and fighting monsters and saving princesses. Why would I pull this book up now? Made-up children's stories weren't what I was looking for.

I approached the large book and noticed it was bound similarly to Po's. On the front was a locking mechanism, with three triangles set within the binding's strap. I touched the book and was pulled to a memory.

"Uncle Bruce, can you read me this one?"

"Come now, Oliver, I'm sure you've heard those stories before."

"But, but, what if there are NEW stories in this one?"

"That may be the case, but, well, do you want to know a secret?"

For a six-year-old, a secret was the most exciting thing in the world. I hunched down low and sidled over to my uncle.

"I can keep a secret."

"You have to promise not to tell anyone. Not your brother. Not even your parents."

"Can I tell Reagan? She's just a baby and won't tell anyone either." Reagan may have only been a year younger than me, but she would always be a baby.

He patted me on my head softly. "Not even Reagan."

"Okay," I said, hoping beyond all hope that this secret would be amazing and not a trick. My uncle liked to play tricks on me.

"This book is a special book. You see how it's locked? Only a special key can open it."

"What if you don't have the key? Can you use a knife?"

"No! Only the key can unlock its stories. If forced open, you'll only find blank pages, and we wouldn't want that, would we?"

"Maybe it doesn't want to tell me its stories," I said, dropping the book to my lap in defeat.

Uncle Bruce took a ring off his finger and placed it into the mechanism of the book, unlocking the binding as my eyes lit up in wonder. "All stories are meant to be told," he whispered.

I rushed back to my mind temple and then back to Iris. She had stood there this entire time while I was off in my own world.

"I'm sorry, how long was I away for?"

She tilted her head at me and frowned. "What do you mean? You haven't been anywhere." I had never entered my mind temple for so long in front of someone before, but my curiosity about how it appeared to others would have to wait for another time.

"Never mind," I replied. "I know why you haven't been able to find this sigil."

"You do? What do you mean?" She stepped closer. For a moment I thought to step closer as well, but would that be too much? So many thoughts were rushing through my head, it was as if my mind temple was broken.

"You can't find it because it doesn't exist." Iris's frown deepened. "It doesn't exist because it's from a children's tale. You recall The Knights of the Nine, right?"

"Everyone knows those stories. They're cute when you're a child but they purport all the wrong stereotypes of women, if you ask me. Damsels in distress! More like men who don't know how to handle a situation until a woman shows up to—"

"Thank you for that, but do you recall any symbols from those stories?"

She put her hand to her chin and mouth, tapping her finger against her mouth as she thought. "I think there was something about a triangle?"

I took the book and showed her the front cover, tracing the star I counted. "One triangle. Two triangles. Three…"

"Triangles," we finished together.

"But what does this mean? Why did Po's family have a children's book, or rather, why is it blank?"

I took the mechanism and the broken clasp on the cover and clicked it back into place, locking the book once more.

Iris looked annoyed. "Why did you do that?"

"Shhhh, just wait." I took Po's ring and placed it on its side into the mechanism, turning both left and right until I felt the tension break. The clasp snapped back open, and the book was once again free.

Iris took the book and started searching its pages. "It's blank," she said, searching my face for an explanation. She threw the book back at me and I opened it up.

"Well... except for the name."

"What name?!"

"There's a name on the first page. See?"

"What!? No there isn't." She snatched the book from my hands, gasping at the simple scrawl on the first page. "Oliver, you did it! You really did it!" she yelled as she jumped into my arms. We both hugged tightly until we realized what we were doing and immediately pulled apart.

I scratched my head awkwardly. "So, who or what is Haralabos?"

"I have no idea!" she exclaimed, her eyes beginning to twinkle. "Come on, wonder boy, I thought you'd read every book in this place! Not ringing any bells?" She smiled, goading me on.

I moved away, circling my gaze around the entire room. "I've never heard that name before. It could be a place, or a person. An object or even just a made-up word."

"All words are made up," she joked. "Do you remember anything about The Knights of Nine and that name?"

"No. None of the Knights had names. Other than their awesome Knight names!" I said, reverting to the six-year-old who was fascinated with these heroes. Iris began to pace and I found myself watching her, the brilliance of her emotion shining through her expressive face. I wanted to stretch this moment, to hold on to it forever. No family, no jousting, only us standing here in this room, together.

No Ridhan.

This last thought hit me like a punch to the gut. Ridhan was courting Iris; that fact hadn't changed. His earlier threats began to ring through my mind and a sour taste rose to my tongue.

"What's wrong?" Iris asked.

"It's just..." I wanted so badly to fly into a tirade of emotion, to tell her everything I was feeling, denouncing her courtship with that jerk as what I knew it to be, a disgusting lie. I hesitated and looked down at the book in her hands.

"I know what you're going to say, Oliver. I'm sorry. I just can't get into it now."

Seeing her sincerity, I yielded, realizing that a confrontation would prove fruitless. I was supposed to be helping her with this book, even though my own quest was to rescue her.

Iris looked back up and, reading my forlorn expression, bent to meet my fallen gaze. She smiled softly.

"Hi."

"Hi," I replied, predictability easier to muster than any sense from the whirlwind of my thoughts.

"Well, it looks like we have a mystery on our hands, little lord. We may just have to spend a bit more time together," she said, smiling. She moved one shoe closer to me but immediately drew it back and planted it back next to its mate. My mind imploded. The energy from this morning took hold through the mayhem of my emotions and I took a full step closer to her.

Her smile nervously returned. "So, what do you say? Do you think we can handle it?" She stepped closer again with a soft motion, her reluctance visibly melting as she touched my arm and her dark brown eyes gazed deep into mine. I searched her face, taking in every detail, each dimple, every small crease around her smile.

Somehow, without my direction or control, my body closed the remaining gap between us. I could feel every fall and rise of her breath, her delicate form pressed lightly against my own. I took the book from her and placed it in my pack while my other hand moved gently toward her face. She turned her head slightly toward my palm, not noticing my sleight of hand.

"I say... let's solve a mystery." I moved my fingers through her hair, tucking a stray strand behind her ear. A slight breeze moved through the room, catching the lamps and throwing shadows into a celebratory dance on the walls. Iris stood up on her toes. I leaned in. Our lips a hair's breadth apart.

But my lips would go no further, and I pulled back slightly in what had to be the dumbest move made by any boy in all of history. Her eyes went wide and her lips quivered when I spoke.

"You're with Ridhan..."

Pulling away slowly to look into my face, she answered in a voice softer than the hair still trailing through my fingers.

"Not here... Not now."

I raised both hands to cup her face and pulled her back in, searching her eyes desperately. Suddenly, a familiar twang hit me in the stomach, and as I moved away, I prayed to the Nine that I would do the right thing.

"I'm sorry," I confessed, turning to leave her in the library basement, once again alone. As I climbed the stairs, I muttered the only thought screaming through my mind.

"I hate you, Oliver. I really, really do."

# ONE SMALL THING

There were stories about people like me. People who had everything they ever wanted handed to them on a silver platter, only to mess it all up. I had a quest to rescue Iris, and I could have completed it! It was right there! She wanted me to kiss her, and I wanted to kiss her. Yet I messed it up, just like all those stories my sister read. Guy gets girl. Guy loses girl. Girl wants guy. Guy is too stupid to realize everything he did wrong.

Classic.

Did I return that night to profess my undying love? Did I find her the next day and tell her I'd made a mistake and I did in fact want to be with her?

No, no I did not.

Did I avoid her every chance I could for the next week, and when I did finally see her in the hallway, trip over at least half a dozen freshies as I dove into the nearest stairwell?

Yes, yes I did.

You're so stupid, Oliver.

It was all I could think about, even while Po trained against the other Carpenters. We'd come to the Workshop after jousting practice every day, and every day, he'd grown more and more frustrated. Po had been a decent enough scraper for his age. But he lacked any sort of formal training, which in turn caused him to lose every sparring session.

"Again!" I yelled from my chair as I balanced it on its back legs. I would admit, I wasn't the best teacher at that moment. My mind was preoccupied with Iris and our almost kiss. I'd given up even thinking about my other quests. Magic? Meh, it'll turn up. Ridhan's threat? Roc can handle practice just fine with Yokel. Protecting Po? That's what I was supposed to be doing right now.

As I heard the loud thump of Po being flipped onto his back once more, I motioned toward the Carpenters.

"Again."

Suddenly, my balance was thrown off and I was flat on my back. My chair had been kicked out from under me. The upside-down image of my sister's scowl resembled that of a deranged smile, and immediately my mind was off Iris and on Po's training.

"I understand," I groaned as I got to my feet, not wanting to hear the berating from Reagan. Po sat on the floor, disgusted with himself and his progress. I'd seen this before, with other Carpenters and even me. You start training and you see all the others around you, how graceful and amazing they are, and you wonder if you've got what it takes. Maybe you were a decent fighter outside of these walls, but inside, everyone started at One.

"Carpenters, circle up!" All the other trainees created a circle around Po and me. Even Reagan joined in, being a Carpenter herself. "What's wrong?" I asked Po.

"I can't do this. I'm not good enough." Po was trying to hold back tears. He was at rock bottom, broken from a week of learning that in fact he did not know anything about fighting. Growing up in the Narrows, no matter the age, fighting was a way of life. People fought for food, fought for personal possessions, even fought just trying to walk down the street. Bullies were abundant, especially if you were seen as special. Po attending the Institute was the definition of special for a Narrows kid. If you didn't join a gang when you were young, you rarely made it to your seventeenth name day.

Po had avoided joining such a gang, although he was at risk without one. Once anyone else found out that he was now a Carpenter, he would need to defend himself. Narrows gangs loved nothing more than to test Carpenters and knock them down a peg. Po had assumed his rudimentary street-fighting skills set him apart as a student here, but he soon learned that he was actually much further behind than he would have guessed.

On his first day, we'd evaluated his skills, or lack thereof. They mostly consisted of grappling and wildly swinging his limbs. He overcompensated for his lack of technique with sheer energy, which would be consumed and leave him fatigued in a matter of moments. So, we spent every day trying to break his habits, like breaking a horse. Each day he would come to the Workshop, and each day he'd leave defeated. It was painful to watch, almost cruel. But there were two lessons to be learned, and now he was ready for them.

I bent down to one knee as all the Carpenters stood around us. Placing my hand on Po's shoulder, I began. "You're correct, you can't do this."

Po's face rotated through a myriad of expressions. First surprise. Then disappointment, followed by anger. Then crushing doubt that what I spoke was true. Lastly, and most importantly, came resolve. Before he could respond, though, I continued. "No one can do this. Not in the way you're trying. Tell me, what have you learned this week?"

Po thought for a moment. "Well, I've learned how to get my butt kicked." I smiled slightly, letting the joke defuse an otherwise tense interaction. He continued. "And I learned that I'm not that good at anything and that I'll probably never become a knight." His eyes were watering once again, but in the Workshop, it was okay to embrace emotion.

"No, that's not what you learned at all."

Po sniffled. "It's not?"

"No. This week, you learned how to fall. Everyone falls, and they think it's the end of the world. That they've lost. That they can't get back up. But each day you came back, and you fell again. Do you know how many times you've fallen this week?"

Rubbing his lower back, he tried to count. "At least a few dozen..."

"Sixty-eight times," I answered. His eyes widened. It didn't seem like that many, but I was never wrong when it came to minute trivia. "And on this sixty-ninth time, will you stay down? Or will you get back up?"

Po was exhausted mentally, physically, and emotionally. Anyone else would have stayed on the ground. Anyone else would have given up. Every single Carpenter in the room had all chosen to stay seated, myself included.

"I want to get back up," Po said, "but I don't know how."

"I do." I reached out my hand. The Carpenters in the room started to slap their legs with their hands, creating a rhythmic chant with the sound.

"Together," I said.

Po took my hand and I pulled him up and the room cheered. Carpenters were the best in the world because we knew one simple truth: We can't do it alone.

"Basic Stance," I commanded, and Po moved into position, one foot slightly in front of the other, his wooden sword held with both hands in front of him. "There are twenty-four fighting forms, and you will learn them all. But first, you start at One. What is Form One, Carpenter Po?"

"Form One is the first defensive form. It is the most basic and the foundation for other forms."

"Correct, and why has it failed you this week?"

"Because... because... I don't really know. I kept falling to the ground. I think I kept losing my balance?"

"Correct again. Form One teaches us not only how to defend, but also how to move. How to keep our balance. Balance is the key to everything you will learn in the Workshop." I smacked his thigh with my wooden sword. "Balance here." I pointed next at his temple. "Balance here." Lastly, I touched his chest with my hand. "And most importantly, balance here."

"How can I master all these forms, Oli— I mean, Carpenter Oliver?"

"Easy," I said with a smile. "First you learn one small thing. And then another. And then another after that. One small thing is all you need to make a big impact."

I was suddenly thrown into the thought of Iris, of how to rescue her. Of how to win her back after I'd left her. I would follow my own advice and do one small thing. But first I would finish my lesson with Po.

"Balance comes from your entire being," I explained. "Balance your body, like this."

I moved into a Basic Stance, and all the other Carpenters followed suit. Unlike Po's narrow stance, our feet were slightly wider than our shoulder width. He saw the difference and adjusted. I bent my knees slightly, and he unlocked his, like a mime in a mirror.

"Balance also comes from your mind. Close your eyes and breathe slowly. In through your nose, hold for the slightest of moments, then release out through your mouth. Clear your mind of all thoughts except the present. Not the past, not the future. But right now."

After a few moments, his shoulders relaxed, his breathing steadied, and he naturally opened his eyes.

"Lastly, and this is the most important part. Your heart must be balanced. Do not hold anger, or fear, or pride, or hubris. Instead, have respect for your opponent. Respect for the fighter they are, the person they may be, and respect for yourself. In a fight, you are responsible for them, and they you."

"But," Po began, "what if they are a bad person?"

It was the moral question we all raised each time we fought. Inside the confines of these walls, it was easy to treat an opponent with respect. Outside, in the real world, it was more complicated.

"If you fight with a bad person, does that in turn make you bad now? How do you determine the moral stance of an opponent? Does stealing make them bad? What if they stole so their children wouldn't starve?"

"But, if they attack me, I can defend myself, right?"

"Of course, but remember, you're a Carpenter now. That carries with it a responsibility. You are responsible for everyone in your life. Strangers in the street or opponents in the ring. How you treat them, whether you fight them or not, is a reflection of you. Balance in your heart, and you'll do the right thing. I promise."

Po looked at his sword, a plain piece of wood. His expression spoke for him. He would understand now that he not only held a weapon, but he was a weapon. How he chose to wield it was as important as anything else he would learn.

"I understand, Carpenter Oliver. Regardless of who I meet in a fight, regardless of the reason, it's my duty to do the right thing. Just like a knight would."

"Couldn't have said it better myself."

Po's sly smile crept upon his face. "I'm ready for number seventy."

"And if we fall?"

Po beamed at me. "Then we get back up, together."

# THE KNIGHT ANGEL

Standing in front of the Shears once more, I held Haralabos's book in my hand. The one small thing I had decided would get me back into Iris's good graces was to give her the book back. Or at least tell her why I took it. The mechanism on the giant door seemed infinitely louder when I pulled on it tonight, the ancient oak somehow mindful of my wish to remain discreet.

I descended to her level, but to my surprise she wasn't there.

Her schedule says she was supposed to be, you weird stalker.

"Okay, stop," I snapped at myself. I needed to backtrack. I moved back to the entrance hall, looking toward the main doors and the marble double staircase leading around the foyer and up to the main levels. Walking to level seven, I noticed no one seemed to be working tonight. Strange, given that there were any number of people roaming the stacks at all hours of the day. Muted and unfamiliar voices broke the now-oppressive silence.

Most strange.

I slowly made my way through the stacks.

Click.

I faltered at the unexpected noise, looking along the row of volumes for a hint as to its origin. The voices were echoing off the walls, but I couldn't place their source. Coughing, I started to feel disoriented, a strange heaviness weighing on each breath.

Focus, Oliver.

Why was it so difficult to focus? A strange odor filled the hall. Something wasn't right, something was off. My palms were sweaty, knees weak, arms heavy.

Why was the wall... sideways?

I tumbled, my head glancing off a stack to my right, and a loud thud accompanied my limp weight falling full-force onto the floor. The cold marble reminded me of my bedroom on early mornings and I idly wondered if they had problems with their fireplaces as well.

I should ask.

... Who would I ask? No one works here.

The cold pressure of the floor was oddly comforting on the contours of my face.

This is my life now. I think I'll stay here.

No, focus, Oliver.

Who's Oliver?

Need... to... focus.

I closed my eyes, fighting for clarity, and was met with an image of Iris, hair floating around her face in front of a dark night sky. She looked at me, gentle eyes beckoning me to come closer. I moved to meet her, only to find that my limbs had been restrained, bound tight. She called out to me, her voice echoing through my mind as I struggled.

"Wake up!"

My eyes snapped open, my muscles tight in rebellion against my very real restraints. I struggled briefly, my eyes darting around the room. I was surrounded. Six cloaked figures were circled around me, peering out from under their hoods, their faces shrouded from the torchlight.

"What in the Nine Hells... Who are you?" I said groggily.

"Who we are is of little consequence," a metallic voice bellowed from the far side. The voice was unfamiliar and had been altered past even a human identity.

"Okay..." I responded, still struggling with what I was seeing. "Right. But even so, aren't the robes like, a bit much?" My voice was muffled by the half-mask that had been pulled over my lower face. Confidence coursed through me, knowing my identity was protected even if only by the thinnest of barriers.

"Silence!" cried the same voice, raising one hand and motioning to an unseen person in the shadows. A robed girl not much taller than Reagan stepped into view and walked toward me, her identity hidden within her own mask and hood. She seemed different than the others, younger, and not draped in the same robes but instead in a fighter's outfit. Even in the torchlight, the inside of her cape shone with a multitude of colors, like a rainbow after a late evening rain. More alarming than her colorful cape was the fact that she had Haralabos's book in her hands.

She set it down on my lap, and the cloaked man's voice from behind her barked at me. "Where did you find this book!"

I looked around desperately. "Um, well we are in a library…"

"Enough of your insolence! Lady Nightshade, please unmask the intruder you caught so we may ascertain his identity. We'll make him talk one way or another."

"Your binds… a false knot…" she whispered in her own metallically cloaked voice as she whipped around to address the room. "I'm sorry, my lord, but I must inform you of something first. It's quite important."

The circle of insane robed people turned about, looking at one another, seemingly unsure what to make of her claim.

She continued. "Do you know what a Knight Angel is?"

Audible gasps escaped the mouths of the various members of the group.

"You have disrupted us for the last time. Kill them both," the robed leader said coldly.

Three armored guards carrying long swords stepped out from the shadows, ready to engage.

Lady Nightshade, or the Knight Angel, or whoever she was, looked quickly at me as I sat there dumbfounded. "I hope you're ready," she said.

I looked at her in panic, for instead of getting out of my bonds, I had been caught up in her revelation. She sighed.

"Fine, I'll do it myself."

She held out her hands in a defensive posture, feigning forfeit. "You wouldn't hurt a girl, would you, boys?" she flirted slyly as the guards continued their steady advance.

"Oh, we'll treat you nice and right, girl," the lead guard spat. I frantically began trying to untie the ropes around my wrists, hoping to help even the odds. Three trained and armored guards against a girl? She didn't stand a chance. I needed to save her, and myself, but first I needed out of this chair.

The Knight Angel was unfazed, however, bantering back to the guards. "Now, I'm going to give you blokes one last chance to surrender, and I'll let you go free and clear." I couldn't see her smirk under her mask, but I was sure they could hear it in her voice.

"Shut up, girlie. Tonight, he dies, and we have our fun with you."

"Tonight, he dies?" She scoffed. "You couldn't think of anything better than that? Blimey, you're going to be boring, aren't you?" She turned and eased her pack from her shoulder, putting the book inside. She winked at me. "Just a moment, love."

The guard on her right advanced with his sword out, lunging with a thrust. She dove forward, passing his longsword by less than an inch, parrying his arm across his body and smashing his helmet against the wall with a loud metallic thud. Grabbing his falling sword, she spun it vertically toward the ceiling and parried away the second guard's downward slash. He tumbled forward unexpectedly and directly into the path of their leader who immediately tripped off course. Her tunic swayed behind her, casting odd shadows along the wall.

I think I'm in love.

Sword in hand, she smashed the second guard's face into the marble floor with the pommel. Showing unbelievable control, she spun her sword and in one swift motion planted the tip under the throat of the leader. His eyes widened in astonishment. She addressed him curtly, accentuating each word, cockiness ringing clearly through.

"Oi, I'm going to ask you a question and your life depends on whether you answer me truthfully or not. Understand?"

The guard stared at her, his brow tightening into a familiar expression.

"Yes," he muttered.

"Are you just here for the gold or are you here because you believe in… this."

"Gold," he spat, attempting to keep his throat clear of the sword tip.

"Good. Then I suggest you don't take this job again," she stated in a demeaning tone.

His face twisted, souring with each word. "Why you little…" he began, his last word inaudible as she spun the sword and raked it against his helmet, knocking him unconscious.

Finally freeing myself, I searched for the hooded figures who had retreated from sight. The room was empty, save the three fallen guards and the Knight Angel. She walked over to me, her face still hidden beneath her mask and hood.

"Took you long enough."

"Well, if you'd tied a better knot—"

I was cut off by a sound echoing into the room.

She turned quickly and grabbed my hand, pulling me toward the exit. "We need to leave before they come back."

We escaped the Shears through one of the many hidden exits I had found over the years, and made our way through the Inner City. My mind was reeling, and I fought to remain tuned in to my senses as the night's events pulled at my attention. We didn't slow until we reached the Narrows and the maze of buildings and streets it afforded.

"So... who were those people?" I asked, leaning against the wall of an alleyway.

"None of your concern," she replied bluntly.

"Well, actually, it seems they were after my book, so it does concern me. And also, they probably know who I am—"

"No, they don't. I put the mask on you, you idiot. Because of you, I had to blow my cover. Do you know how long it took me to infiltrate them?"

"No, because I don't even know who 'they' are!" I yelled back, waking a pair of birds perched on the roof above.

"It doesn't matter. They don't have your book, and they don't know who you are. So, you can forget about them, and me."

The Knight Angel began to turn, but I grabbed her quickly by the shoulder and before I knew it, I was face first on the ground.

"Oi! You know better than to touch a girl like that, little lord," she said with a chuckle. As I struggled, she released me and I sat up, rubbing my aching shoulder.

"Look, I just want to help," I said, trying to win over this amazing, strong, and presumably beautiful girl.

"It's..." She hesitated, looking out into the darkness of the alleyway. "It's complicated. I'm complicated. Go home, Oliver Quartermaine. And forget about mysterious books and secret societies."

At that, a rope descended from the roof, and she scaled the wall deftly, disappearing from sight.

I stood up, pulling the book from my shirt that I had pocketed while the Knight Angel threw me to the ground. All this fuss over this silly little book? Who were you, Haralabos? And who were you, Knight Angel?

I made my way back home to the Anvil and looked back across the city and the roofs where my heroine had disappeared. I tossed the book into the air playfully and whispered, "Now we're both complicated."

I spent the next week contemplating everything that happened with the Knight Angel and the secret society. Jousting practice once again went by without much thought. I avoided Iris entirely. The only bright spot was Po's training, which had improved beyond my wildest dreams. The kid was a natural, and he was starting to grasp the tiniest of details in everything he learned.

Black Sunday was upon us, the fortnightly day when the sun didn't rise above the horizon so we stayed in perpetual darkness during the day, and the dusk light from the planet above would be at its dimmest during the night. Our customs dictated we celebrate and feast with our neighbors, to show the Nine we believed they would once again raise the sun and our planet above would return to us. Obviously, without these celebrations, our land would fall into a darkness and we would never see the light of day ever again.

Or maybe it was just a way for parents to appease their frightened children.

I exited the private bathing area connected to my room. Tonight's celebration at the Shipwight's estate was an obligation I couldn't skip, as much as I wanted to. After my meeting with the crazies and being introduced to the Knight Angel, I was actually happy to enter an arena I was familiar with: high society. I smiled, looking over my finery in the mirror perched over my dresser.

Damn, could I wear a suit.

"You two need a room?" Roc grinned as he entered my quarters. He shifted uncomfortably within his burgundy suit, a gift from my mother. He wasn't as keen on formal wear as I was, nor accepting of any hint of charity. Although it was far outside his comfort zone, Roc had worn this suit as a sign of gratitude to my mother every Black Sunday since she'd given it to him. She was as much a mother to him as she was to me, which is probably why he was more than happy to leave with me on my sabbatical from life.

"It's okay to be jealous, I'll allow it," I replied as I donned some finishing accessories. Roc looked away and I realized that my joke had hit too close to the mark of our social stations.

As we walked down the hall toward the balcony stairs, Reagan's voice sounded from a half step behind us.

"Hi fellas, don't you two look dapper tonight." She adjusted Roc's ascot flirtatiously while his eyes widened at her smart hairstyle and much too revealing gown. My baby sister was growing into a beautiful young woman, even though I prayed against it.

"Who are you trying to impress?" I asked sharply.

"Oh, you never know who you'll meet at these parties. Maybe a cute little Shipwight lord..." She stared off dreamily for a second before winking at the still dumbstruck Roc, then turning to walk briskly down the stairs.

Oh, Nine no, not one of Ridhan's cousins.

I wanted someone to just kill me now, in the face, with a spiked axe. I looked sharply at Roc, his stupid expression inflaming my hatred further.

"What the hells are you grinning at?"

His jaw closed slowly as he turned to respond. "Your sister is hot."

That got him a sharp punch to his shoulder. "I hate you, so much."

At the Shipwight estate we exchanged pleasantries with other lords and ladies. The Yokels arrived shortly after us, and Whiskey Danger found a corner, trying to avoid any contact with Ridhan. We stood somewhat sullenly, music from the chamber orchestra in the front hall filtering through the room. I nodded absently while the always-strategizing Yokel walked Roc through his latest jousting plans, but my eyes were constantly searching the room for any sign of Iris. Our peaceful nonexistence, however, proved short lived.

"Tck-tck-tck, Q, you've brought the help, how sweet."

My eyes narrowed as I turned on my heel at the sound of the saccharine voice behind me.

"Ridhan. I'd say it was nice to see you but, well, it's not."

"I'm surprised the guards let the ogre in, but I suppose Father allows anyone into his company these days."

"Hey!" Roc exclaimed, "I'm right here, you—"

"Tck-tck-tck. Silence, you buffoon. Can't you see your betters are talking?"

It took every ounce of speed and strength I had to intercept Roc as he lunged. I couldn't let Roc jeopardize an already fragile armistice with this bully.

"What are you doing? Lemme after him!" Roc implored.

Ridhan walked up close behind my back, sneering into my ear as I held Roc tightly.

"You should have more control over your dog, Q, before he gets put down for disobeying his master." His voice curdled with disdain, and for a fleeting moment I thought about letting Roc have at him.

"Hello, gentleman," Reagan said, moving to pull Ridhan away from us. "Ridhan Shipwight, I don't believe you've ever had the pleasure of showing me around your wonderful home. Would you be so kind? For me?" She was smiling flirtatiously and Ridhan eyed her up and down, measuring her beauty with all his lust. In a sudden shift, I found I was the one being pinned back by Yokel and Roc, struggling to get free as I watched my sister walk off arm-in-arm with Ridhan.

When they were no longer in sight, I felt Yokel's grip on me loosen. He shook his head.

"Nine, I hate that guy."

I looked around the room once more and caught sight of the Kentaro family who had just arrived. For a moment, Iris's gaze met mine. My heart soared but was immediately dashed as I watched Ridhan approach her, looking at me with a sinister smile as he groped her. Iris squirmed, causing Ridhan to grip her tighter and only let up when his father walked in to greet his newly arrived guests. Lord and Lady Kentaro had turned a blind eye to Ridhan's assault, their inclusion among the high nobles an obvious priority over their daughter's distress. My mind raced, running Ridhan through all manner of torturous retribution and how the grateful Iris would thank me for saving her.

My anger took over and I left to seek refuge in the gardens behind the Shipwight mansion, using all my Carpenter training to calm myself. I could teach it, but I sure had a hard time practicing it. Iris disrupted the balance I needed in my life, confounding my thoughts, my emotions, even the beating of my heart. My thoughts, as obsessed as they were, quickly pivoted to the Knight Angel. Our brief interaction had left me enamored. She was a most graceful fighter and her confidence was impressive. The mystery of who she could be added even more to her allure.

But what if she was hideous under her mask? Would I still be thinking of her in the same way? My immediate reaction was no, but I couldn't quite help but think she might be hiding a disfigurement or some other blemish.

Nine Gods you're shallow, Oliver.

I quickly tossed away that notion. Anyone who could fight like that, handle herself in that way, was beautiful no matter how she looked. But who was she? I reverted into my mind temple, examining every aspect of that night. Her accent was from the capital, so she was definitely not from Starfall. She must have arrived just after I left for Kandaheart this summer. Her other physical features were mostly hidden beneath her outfit, and she seemed a bit taller than Reagan, with maybe wider shoulders.

So, all I had to go on was that she was as skilled a fighter as anyone I knew of in the city, she was from Land's End, and most importantly, she knew who I was.

That wasn't too much of a surprise. I was a Quartermaine, after all.

I plucked a purple flower from its stem and gazed longingly at it. My mind was back to my flower's namesake, and I smiled. A stranger in the night held no comparison to my crush, even if I couldn't be with her.

"Do you two need a moment?" Iris smirked as she entered the garden.

"Well, if I can't be with one Iris, I guess I'll settle for another," I replied, once again brave beneath the armor of my fine clothing.

"Oh, I see. You've found another. I won't get in the way of you two, then," she flirted back. I laughed and tossed the flower into the fountain. Iris sat down on its edge, tracing an intricate design on the surface of the water.

I wanted to tell her everything in my mind. How I was sorry for leaving her. How I went back. How I had taken the book from her, and how I had come upon an unsavory group within the Shears. I wanted to tell her of my quests, and how I was going to be a hero.

I would maybe leave out the part about the Knight Angel. I didn't quite want to share that part with anyone else.

"Oliver," she started. "I know you took my book."

"Actually, it's Po's book."

"A book he gave to me. I would like it back please," she asked, holding out her hand as if I had it on me this very instant.

I did, of course, but I wasn't about to tell her that.

"I don't have it here."

"You know I can tell when you're lying, right?" She looked up from her tracing. The lines of the nine-pointed star disappeared as quickly as she had drawn them.

"Why would I bring it here? This isn't exactly a book club," I lied, trying to figure out a way out of this. Iris slid closer to me, peering deep into my eyes, getting ever closer to my lips. Would she really be so bold as to kiss me here and now, at Ridhan's own home? Would I really be so bold? I adjusted my legs and pants awkwardly as her hand slid behind my back, pulling me closer to her.

"Ha! I knew it!" she proclaimed as she pulled away, Po's book in hand. I was dumbstruck, very uncomfortable in my clothes, and furious all at once.

"Hey! You can't have that!" I quickly snatched the book back. She may have been sly, but I was quick.

Together we'd make an excellent fox.

I held the book high above her head where she couldn't reach, and she shoved me backward out of annoyance. "That's mine, Oliver. Or maybe you don't remember, I'm the one who even showed it to you."

"Yes, but that was before…"

"Before what?"

I was mere seconds from telling her the truth, but I knew I couldn't.

"Nothing. It's dangerous."

"So dangerous that only you get to have it?"

"So dangerous that I'm not going to let anything happen to you." She turned to pace, scowling. Her frustration reminded me of when she'd come to my terrace at night after a fight with her parents. I missed those nights. I missed my friend. Now we were just people who maybe liked each other but the timing was wrong.

"We were supposed to solve this mystery together," she finally argued, but my thoughts were no longer on the book. They were on us and our lost friendship. Our missed opportunity at love.

"Just tell me something. Why him, of all people?"

She looked away, fidgeting with her gown. "You don't understand."

At least we could agree on that.

"He's everything you vowed you hated. He's everything you swore you would never be. So why? For the love of the Nine, why, Iris? Do you love him?"

"…no…"

Oh, thank the Nine!

"Is it your family? Is it something else? Because I can't think of any reason in this world you should be with him instead of—"

"Instead of who? Instead of you!? I'm not some damsel who—" Iris's expression grew tense and cold and angry. "Who I'm with or not with is not for you to decide. I have my reasons. Now give me the book. Please."

"You didn't answer my question."

"I'm with him because I am. Okay? Besides, who are you to talk? You're the one who ran out on me. Where have you been recently, huh? Avoiding me because you have my book! We were supposed to do this together. We were supposed to be friends. Give it to me, please."

She was right. I had run out, I had avoided her, and I had been a bad friend. But there was more to this book now than just a simple mystery. Bad people, really bad people were after it. I couldn't put her in danger. She was safer away from the book.

"I can't do that right now. You don't know what I know about the book."

"What do you know? What do you mean?"

"It's dangerous. People are willing to kill for it."

"I can take care of myself."

I fidgeted back and forth. She wasn't a fighter; she was a lady. Her house was that of merchants, not warriors.

"I can't, just trust me. I'm doing this to protect you."

Her cheeks flushed and anger dripped from her voice. "We were supposed to do this together."

"No," I replied simply.

"No? What do you mean no? It's MY book!"

"Now it's mine. Three things. First off, a book that's blank and suddenly has words. You and I both know what that means. Second, and I say this with the utmost respect for you, there is literally no way in the Nine Hells I'm giving you that book back. It's dangerous, and I will not stand by and have you put in harm's way."

"You have no right to—"

"Third, I'm in love with you."

She stopped talking, maybe even stopped breathing. I hadn't meant to say that or say it in exactly that way. But now it was out there and there was no taking it back.

"Oliver, I... I can't."

I was feeling more confident by the second that I did in fact love her and that she loved me back. "Yes, you can. Just tell me how you feel. How you really feel. Stop trying to pretend and just be honest."

"Oliver..." Tears were falling down her cheeks and her makeup was smearing. "Oliver, I can't. I told you I can't. It's too complicated right now."

Complicated. Why was everyone suddenly so complicated? I hadn't the energy nor strength to fight her any longer. This quest to rescue her might very well be my hardest one, and I vowed to myself I would succeed, but maybe not tonight. Tonight, I needed her to stay away from me and the book, so I could keep her safe.

I pulled her in close for a hug and her face fell into my chest, just under my neck. My arms wrapped around her tightly. "I can't do this anymore," I said.

She looked up at me through her blurry eyes. "Can't do what?"

"This. I can't do this anymore. Or at least, not right now. The world has changed, Iris. There are people out there that... well, I need to keep you safe. I'm sorry."

I kissed her on the forehead and left with the book. I left her again, just as I had in the stacks, like the fool I was. I couldn't be with her for now. She was with Ridhan, and as much as I hated that idea, she would be safe. If I wanted to rescue her, I needed to solve the mystery of the book and stop the people who were trying to kill for it.

Instead of attending the Black Sunday dinner, I headed back to the Anvil, which was only a short hike up the hill. I walked up the stairs, noted that the portrait was still crooked on the wall, and went into my room. I stared into the eyes of the boy in my dressing mirror, finding no answers to the hundreds of questions milling around in my mind.

My gaze fell to the floor, where Po's book lay on a pile of clothes. This book had done nothing but cause me trouble. The secret society didn't know who I was, so maybe if I just got rid of the book, they would never bother me. But something told me I couldn't. This book was important. For starters, the same day I was given a quest to find magic I was also given a ring that made a blank book suddenly show words.

I sat on the floor, holding the locked book, fidgeting with my ring.

Laughing, I placed the ring into the mechanism, absentmindedly asking a question.

"Haralabos, what do you think I should do?"

The lock snapped open and I turned to the first page, finding the name in its center just as before. I sighed, turning to the next page, but instead of the expected dead blankness, I was met with four new words in scrawling script across the middle of the page.

Find the Knight Angel.

# THE BLUEFISH TAVERN

"Ahem." Johanous coughed from the doorway as I sat on the floor in disbelief.

"Yes, Jo?"

I looked at our butler. Of all the house workers, Jo was by far my favorite. It may have been because he was solely dedicated to the Quartermaine children, or it could have been because he was as much my family as my parents were. One thing was for certain, Johanous could keep a secret.

"Good evening, Master Oliver. I assumed the usual was needed tonight. They are in your wardrobe."

I jumped up in glee, knowing this master tailor would have something extra special for us. "Thanks, Johanous, as always. That will be all for tonight."

"Be safe, Master Oliver. If you require anything more, I shall be in my quarters."

I ran to the wardrobe and pulled out three new outfits tailored, as always, with precision. When we returned from our trip, I tasked Johanous to start on new outfits for Whiskey Danger's Black Sunday adventures. Johanous knew all our measurements and I expected the outfits would fit perfectly, allowing us to move freely in comfort. Knowing Johanous, we'd also be moving around with a bit of style as well.

Grabbing my new suit, I marveled at its texture. What was this made of? It was so light and flexible, yet sturdy. Would it stop a knife or a sword pierce?

We'd have to practice on Yokel.

I donned my suit and stretched in as many positions as I could think of, occasionally jumping and throwing my knees to my chest and feeling the freedom this strange fabric allowed me. Johanous had truly surpassed himself this time. Well done, indeed.

The crown jewel of the suit was still lying on the bed: a black hooded cloak. Inside the hood was a circular leather… belt?

Interesting.

I put the cloak on my shoulders, clasping it into the predetermined inlets of the suit. It draped down to just above my ankles, and it seemed as though the bottom of the cape was weighted somehow? I threw the hood on and the leather circlet settled on my head, a perfect fit.

Of course it was.

I stood in front of the mirror, inspecting the shape the hood took around my face, the rigid circlet of leather keeping its form true. The top of the hood came to a point while the sides rested just behind my peripheral sight lines. When I turned my head to the right or left, the hood followed, contouring to the movement, which meant I could wear the hood and never have to sacrifice my sight lines.

"Johanous, you, my friend, are a cut above the rest," I said aloud to the empty room.

I pulled the neck of the outfit up onto my face, just over my nose and ears, allowing only my eyes to remain exposed. The fabric was light and breathable. It too came with a clasp that attached to the leather circlet. I turned in front of the mirror, enjoying the master craftsmanship. There was some detailing on the chest, and I slowly moved my hand over the embroidery. The shining symbol looked like a bird with wings outstretched, as if flying straight in the sky.

I loved it.

I packed the book and Roc's and Yokel's outfits in a pack and headed out across the terrace, making my run through the city, into the catacombs of underground tunnels before I reached the Narrow Gate, and popping back up in the Narrows.

Starfall City was built upon a preexisting ancient city of the peoples who lived in Soraya thousands of years ago. They had built sewers and wells underneath the city before mysteriously abandoning the lands. Most of the major kingdoms in Soraya were similarly built upon abandoned settlements, and over the years the infrastructure had been improved, leaving the original catacombs for the use of any number of reasons. Gangs and guilds used them for their hideouts, whereas some people and animals used them for their homes. Whiskey Danger used it for quick and unseen access between the Inner City and the Narrows.

I met Roc and Yokel on the roof of Roc's building. After some coaxing, they put on their new suits and, as I expected, they both loved them. Yokel put up a bit of a fight over the new emblem on the chest, but Roc quickly punched him out of that idea. The suits also came with perfect holsters for our individual weapon scabbards. I sported a classic knight's sword, allowing for maneuverability and speed. Roc enjoyed the longsword, double-handed hilt, perfect for his brute strength method of attack, and Yokel carried a slender rapier, complete with an intricately designed guard.

"Okay, boys, what's on the agenda for tonight?" Yokel asked gleefully.

We had met atop Roc's home in an effort to help patrol the Narrows. Although the City Watch patrolled Starfall within the Inner City, they rarely if ever ventured beyond to the people who needed it most. People who couldn't necessarily pay for protection. My brother's Stonemen had once patrolled these same roofs, and after they graduated from the Institute, they passed that vigil to us. For five years, we had roamed rooftops, alleyways, and the back of taverns, always on the lookout for someone who needed us.

More often than not, our skills were used to escort someone home or break up a drunken fight. Nothing was ever really important or truly dangerous, but nevertheless, we felt like heroes.

"Nothing from me other than the normal patrol route," Roc replied, sounding distant.

"How's your uncle?" I asked. The old knight had been unwell these last few weeks.

"Some days are better than others. Tonight, was an 'other.' Let's get on with it. I need something to take my mind off of life."

I smiled at my friend. "I have just the thing you need. It's time we had an actual mission."

"Are we getting paid?" Roc asked.

"Nope."

"Well, it's not like we were ever paid before, so let's hear it!" Roc exclaimed enthusiastically.

I paused, contemplating how much to reveal. In the end, I decided that

I needed to trust my two friends entirely, especially if what I had guessed was true.

"You're going to want to sit for this," I started, but neither of them sat. "I've been given a quest. Actually, two quests. Then I gave myself two more. So, four quests total."

Roc looked incredulous. "Quests? Did you hit your head?"

"No, it's obviously some kind of joke," Yokel proclaimed, waiting for a punchline that would never come.

"I'm serious! Professor Lortho gave me—"

Roc interrupted. "You mean to tell me a professor at the Institute, the same Institute we all have been going to for the last four years. That Institute. With the most hard-ass professor in the place. That professor. He's the one who—"

"Yes! He said I had no assignments other than this one."

Yokel nodded. "Ah, so he just gave you an assignment."

"No, it's a quest. Just listen, you jerks." It was going to be hard to explain the quest without upsetting Roc. I knew that going in. It had to be done, but my mind started racing through all the pent-up thoughts I'd been saddled with on my own.

"There's also Po, and a book, and the Knight Angel, and Ridhan and —"

Roc picked me up by my shoulders.

Nine, I hated him.

"Put. Me. Down."

"Not until you start making sense."

He finally relented only after I kicked him.

Being the voice of calm and reason, Yokel spoke up. "Oliver, start from the beginning. That always seems like the best place to begin."

So I began with my conversation with Yokel in Mercyhold, and the two words that had buried into my mind like a mole in the winter. I glanced at Roc from time to time as I spoke, trying to ascertain his mood. His expression remained the same, and I took that as a sign that he wasn't too angry with me. After coming to the conclusion that my first quest was to protect Po, I relayed my conversation with Lortho, and my second quest to find magic.

"Magic isn't real," Roc muttered.

"Yes, it is."

I looked at Yokel in shock and with a small sense of betrayal. I had asked him point blank about it.

"I'm sorry, Oliver, but I may not have been as truthful in Mercyhold as I wanted to be. Magic is real, just not in the ways you both think."

Roc shook his head. "We shouldn't be talking about this."

"We have to! It's our quest!" I countered.

"*Our* quest?"

"You know I can't do this without you two."

Roc looked at both of us, sighing and letting his shoulders drop. He nodded and Yokel continued.

"According to some of the legends—"

"You mean children's stories," Roc corrected.

"The legends speak of many types of magic. The magic in those 'children's stories' were one type. Spells and potions were another. Those kinds of magic were said to have faded from the world, or at least that's what they'd have you believe. My family holds many texts that not even the Shears have. Texts of the Purge, hundreds of years ago. We were told it was to save our world from invaders from the Sunset Mountains, but really it was to rid the world of magic."

Roc scuffed his boot along the roof. "Seems like they succeeded."

"Yes, that is what it would seem. But in reality, there are more kinds of magic in the world than powers and spells and potions. There are magical items, left behind from long ago. Although people can't perform magic, the old magical objects still exist."

I thought about my uncle's necklace that had disintegrated in Mercyhold. And of the obelisk on Lortho's desk. Maybe there were more of these magical objects than rumored. But if we were to find and save magic, it had to be more than magical objects, and Yokel's family may have been one of the very few in the world to have any information on these other types of magic.

Yokel took a breath and continued. "Roc, your parents, when the Black Sun Battalion came…" He paused, unsure of his next words. "They, they came because there was a magical item in the Narrows. A magical key of sorts. I know because my grandfather was captain of the City Watch. The Black Sun Battalion never found the item, thinking that it was probably destroyed in the fire. But it wasn't."

Roc stood up quickly, his body trembling. "You, you knew. This entire time you knew and you said nothing. I always thought… I always thought it was for nothing. That it was a rumor about magic and that's why… How could you not tell me?"

"I wanted to, I promise. I just didn't know how. I'm s-s-sorry," Yokel stuttered. I couldn't judge Yokel. I don't know if I would have had the courage to tell Roc the truth about his parents.

Roc walked over to Yokel, and I didn't know if he was about to throw Yokel over the edge of the roof or beat him senseless right there. Instead, he pulled his friend into a big hug. "It's okay, Yok. It's okay." He pulled away quickly.

"Okay, so quest number two is to find magic, and destroy it," Roc proclaimed. Yokel and I looked at each other and begrudgingly agreed. We needed to find magic, but I wasn't ready to go as far as destroy it. Roc continued. "You said there were four quests?"

"Oh right! Yes, so the third quest is to rescue Iris from Ridhan."

Roc cocked his head. "Rescue her? Is she being held captive?"

"Not in so many words."

"And I suppose that after you 'rescue' her, she'll be courting you?" Yokel asked.

"That would be the plan, yes."

"Interesting," Roc started, "but does she even know you like her like —"

"I told her I loved her tonight," I blurted.

"No turning back now, I suppose," Roc said.

"Nope! But that quest has to be put on pause, because there's something that connects all three quests." I pulled out the book. I told my story of getting my ring from Po, of the book's origin, of Iris in the stacks, of the secret society, and finally the Knight Angel. Yokel examined the book enthusiastically. Roc refused to touch it.

"This is a most peculiar thing," Yokel said. "And you say the ring unlocked it?"

"Yes, Po said it was a key…"

And right there and then we put the puzzle pieces together. The magical key in the Narrows that had caused the death of Roc's parents was the same key I held in my hand at that very moment. The key was to unlock a book, and from everything I could tell, a magical book.

Yokel looked at me. "Who is Haralabos?"

"I have no idea."

"What does this mean on the second page, 'Find the Knight Angel'?"

Roc walked to the edge of the roof, peering out along the buildings. "I think it means exactly what it says. We find the Knight Angel, and maybe we find a way to destroy magic, and this key. No one else gets hurt because of it."

"But where would we start?" Yokel asked.

"Oliver, where did you say the Knight Angel took you after you escaped the Shears?" Roc responded.

"Over near the Bluefish Tavern."

"I say we start there. Grab your weapons, boys, we have a Knight Angel to find!"


We arrived atop the roofs along the alleyway near the tavern, waiting patiently for any clue as to the Knight Angel's whereabouts. What sounded like a quick adventure slowly turned into a tedious one. No sign of the Knight Angel, or anything out of the ordinary for that matter.

We sat, kicking rocks back and forth to pass the time. Occasionally we would arm wrestle or play a guessing game with our hands.

"Wait!" Roc exclaimed. "Wasn't there one more quest?"

"Oh right! Yeah, so this one heavily involves you."

"Only the best quests do." Roc said.

"You need to win the Homecoming Tournament."

"I was going to do that anyway."

"Yes, but if you don't, I lose my family's Shield of Kandaheart to Ridhan."

"That thing doesn't even work as a shield, anyway," Roc said.

Yokel glanced our way but then returned to his stakeout.

"Yes, I know, but Ridhan said he would kill you and Yokel if he won. And Po."

I let the threat sink in.

Roc nodded slowly. "So, I guess it's really more a part of the first quest, to protect Po?"

"Oh, yes, I suppose that's technically accurate." I felt a little deflated. There was something nice about having more quests than fewer, but in the end, it really didn't matter all that much. The only thing that mattered was I had my friends to help.

"Well we can check that one as done and done because with Yokel here as my herald, there's no way I'll lose." Roc said.

Yokel pointed down at the alleyway. "Guys, something weird is happening down there."

All three of us peered over the edge of the roof like birds on a tree branch.

A hooded figure made her way behind the tavern to a back alleyway that led to a dead end. She was about the Knight Angel's height, but the inside of her cape was black instead of the rainbow of colors I remembered from the other night. Were there two of them? My confusion was interrupted by another thought: her position. It was an interesting place she had walked to, a horrible position if ambushed.

What was she thinking?

The Knight Angel turned around and was met by two men with large brimmed Romirian hats. As they talked, both parties seemed to become more and more agitated, leading to the Knight Angel pulling out her sword. This wasn't going to be a pleasant exchange, and the three of us unsheathed our weapons.

"Okay, boys, you know the drill. Protect the Knight Angel, take out the hat guys, get answers," Roc said as we all raised our masks over our faces.

Rappelling down on a rope, I bounced gracefully off the walls as though it were second nature.

Thanks, Carpenter obstacle course.

We landed in formation, albeit with Yokel's foot tangled in his rope. Roc led with his towering stance that would intimidate just about anyone. A half step behind, I flanked his right and Yokel his left. I might have been the money, and Yokel might have been the brains, but Roc was our leader, and that's how I preferred it. He could have all the glory, all the fame, all the women.

"Hello there. A little late at night to be meeting behind a tavern, isn't it, my lords?"

Roc got his sarcastic tone from me, and it kind of worked for him, though I personally thought he was missing some flair. The men turned quickly, but their faces were hidden from the torchlights on the building, and they didn't seem nervous.

How peculiar.

"What are you three doing here?" the Knight Angel whispered in her metallic voice, clearly annoyed at our intrusion.

"Saving you?" I replied.

"You're going to get yourselves killed," she said loud enough to be heard by the two men.

"Best to listen to the lady. The Narrows can be a dangerous place, you know. Lady Nightshade, Knight Angel, whomever you are it makes no difference. Return the book and we'll let your friends here go." The men's voices were also metallic and obscured.

"I told you I don't have it," the Knight Angel replied angrily.

"We thought you'd say that, but it matters not. We will get it from you one way or another. Preferably another."

As if born from the darkness, five more guards in very light armor appeared. Of the five, three looked familiar... from that night in the Shears!

So much for being in it for the gold.

"Sirs, I don't believe you want to do this. Turn around and leave and we won't hurt you," Roc offered again, knowing they wouldn't accept, but it was the thought that counted.

"Are you stupid? We have the numbers, and you have no escape," the leader stated. It was the same voice from the other night. I chuckled to myself, remembering the loud smash when the Knight Angel's hilt crushed his helmet. I could see the dent.

Yet, the guard's words had struck true. With our backs to the dead-end wall, our only escape was a slow ascent on the ropes that had brought us down.

Roc scowled. "Outnumbered, yes, but make no mistake, we will defeat you. I'll give you one last chance. Leave."

Pointing his sword in the Knight Angel's direction, the leader yelled, "Get them! Kill those men but leave that one for me!"

The guards pulled their weapons from their hilts, throwing their torches to the ground and advancing at a pace.

Roc turned his head toward me. "Your turn," he said.

He was born for leadership, but now was my time to do what I did better than anyone. Courage that flowed through me in the fighting ring flowed through me now. I was in my element, and I reveled in it. The energy enveloped my body, and I was balanced once more.

"I've got the two on the right. Think you three can handle one apiece?" the Knight Angel yelled as she charged two of the guards, seemingly taking my job. I was the Carpenter of the group; I should be the one to take on more than anyone else.

"See you on the other side," Roc yelled as he parried and tackled the guard in front of him.

"Welcome to class," Yokel said, trying his hardest to sound like Roc and me.

We needed to work on his fighting banter.

I rushed and skidded to a stop in front of the leader while the Knight Angel attacked her two opponents. She was precocious and swift and did not lack discipline. Her moves were good, admirably so, but she left herself open too often when she didn't need to. Her form was aggressive, maybe too aggressive. I had to hand it to her, though, she was an amazing fighter who would be able to keep up with most anyone in the Workshop.

I should find out where she trained.

"I'm going to kick your ass," the leader said to me, "and then I'm going to kill her, nice and slowly."

See the paths, Oliver.

I played out the various paths in front of me. I chose the one that led to the guard being knocked unconscious and injured enough to not make this mistake a third time.

Excellent.

"Not tonight, dirtbag!" I yelled. I somersaulted to the left, joining the Knight Angel in her fight. My chosen path was quite clever. I'd taken the few moments to size up her fighting style and determine how we could work together. I only hoped she would understand my idea in time for us not to make a mistake.

"Fancy meeting you here," the Knight Angel said, holding out the point of her sword. The ting of my own point sounded the beginning of the duel. I feinted to the guard on my left and thrust my sword at the one to my right. She quickly turned and parried the leader's slash, spinning around to grab the first guard and throw him in front of the leader, causing both to tumble. She knew the first rule of fighting multiple enemies: divide and conquer.

We flanked the remaining guard, who was much better than he was the other night, given the ample space and familiarity with his opponent. But he would be no match for our combined skills. We needed to remove him from the board quickly before the other two got up. I parried and ducked under his attack, raking him behind his knees as the Knight Angel landed a blow across his chest. On the way down, I swung my sword in a circular motion with the broad side directly against his helmet, knocking him unconscious.

One down, two to go.

"Not bad, for a man," the Knight Angel jested.

"I do my best with what I've got."

The other two guards managed to untangle themselves from each other and popped up quickly. I grabbed the downed knight's sword, adding a level of spontaneity I was sure they weren't ready for. They approached and attacked in unison, though not as coordinated as they should have been. The Knight Angel was able to disarm her guard, leaving him flat on his back as I moved in for the assault on the leader.

One left.

I moved in a blur of steel and shadow as I parried and followed up with small attacks and feints, using both swords to fullest advantage. I saw Roc struggling with his guard and motioned to the Knight Angel.

"I got this, help him!" I yelled as I waited for the leader to make a mistake. As if on cue, the leader overreached in his slash, and I parried him into a spin that caused him to trip over his downed compatriot. It was a move I'd learned long ago in the Workshop.

Rolling to his feet as quickly as he could in his exhausted state, he looked up at me with a deranged smile. "You fight like your brother—recklessly." He turned and ran toward the Knight Angel, whose back was to us as she helped Roc with his opponent who'd found himself in a reverse headlock, slowly choking. Yokel didn't notice as he was putting the finishing touches on his man, small cuts to various parts of the guard's body.

"I'm going to kill you!" the leader yelled as he staggeringly approached the Knight Angel. This was not a path I had seen, and it was evident by the paralysis I was feeling.

Energy rushed through me and a voice yelled from within.

Move, Oliver, move!

My body was back in control and I moved faster than I could have imagined, closing the gap between me and the Knight Angel and placing myself directly in front of the guard's haymaker. I parried instantly and the guard started to fall forward, his momentum taking him toward the ground. I followed my parry with an upward thrust, piercing straight through a weak point in his armor and into his chest.

The bones in his breast separated as my sword sliced through, the ease and quickness of the thrust taking me by surprise. As if in slow motion, I saw the man's face change from surprise to blank. His eyes looked at me as he dropped his sword and clutched at the sword in his body. Blood dribbled from the corner of his mouth and a rattling noise erupted from his throat and he fell to the ground. I pulled my sword out quickly and stared at the blood on my blade.

"What happened!" Roc yelled as his enemy lost consciousness. Yokel ran over, his guard out as well. The Knight Angel quickly checked the fallen guard, looking up to reveal the answer we already knew.

"I... I... he... you..." What had I done? What just happened? I hadn't seen this at all. We were supposed to render these knights immobile and unconscious.

What had I done?

A warm feeling started to make its way up my throat, and my mouth was suddenly filled with saliva. I turned toward Roc and Yokel and vomited onto the ground.

"We need to leave, now!" Roc yelled, but his voice was muffled by a ringing in my ears.

What was going on? Where was I? Oh no, I needed to puke again.

"Ollie, we have to leave!" The Knight Angel shook me, to no avail. I could see everything that was happening, as if I were floating outside of my body. But try as I might, I couldn't get myself to respond normally.

"There's no time for this! Let's get to the roof, now!" Roc commanded as the Knight Angel and Yokel rushed me toward the wall. Somehow my hands took the rope and I pulled myself to the roof. We raced along the rooftops through the darkness. If we hadn't run these same roofs thousands of times before, we may have misstepped, but even in my panicked state, I was as surefooted as ever.

We arrived at Roc's building and took a moment to breathe.

"I'm sorry," the Knight Angel said as she disappeared over the edge of the roof and back into the Narrows. I felt a haze cover my eyes. I saw the face of the knight, dead eyes staring into my soul.

"What have I done!" I yelled.

"Shhh," Yokel implored, "we'll figure it out tomorrow. Tonight, we need to get you home."

Roc put my pack on my back and we headed into the tunnels, making our way to the Anvil. Johanous was waiting by the gate, and after talking with Roc and Yokel, ushered me into the safety of my home.

I sat on the edge of my bed, staring at my reflection in the mirror. There was some blood speckled on my face and I walked over to the desk, taking a rag to desperately try to rub the blood off.

Why wouldn't it come off? Nine Hells, get off!

I was rubbing as quickly and as hard as I could when Reagan burst into my room and snatched my hand.

"It's okay, big brother, it's okay. Let me see." Her expression was determined, and she pulled my hand away from my face.

"I'm trying to wipe it off. It won't come off. Why won't it come off?"

She dabbed the rag with her tongue and wiped at my face. "There, it's gone, see?"

I looked in the mirror but couldn't stand the sight of myself. "I'm sorry. I'm so sorry." I wept, convulsing as I tried to breathe.

"It's okay, Ollie, it's okay. It's not your fault." She pulled me in tight for a hug and my head fell onto her shoulder.

"You don't understand, Rea, the light just went out of his eyes." It felt so good to confess, but also so horrible.

What had I done?

"You did what you had to do. You saved your friends."

"But maybe I could have done something different. A way where he lived... I just couldn't find that path..."

"You can't think like that. You're a hero, Ollie. A hero. If it weren't for you, there would have been a different death tonight. Maybe more than one."

She was right. She was always right. I did the right thing; I saved the

Knight Angel's life. Why did I feel so horrible?

"I'm so sorry, big brother. You've never had to do this before, choose between two lives. You train and pretend, but it was never for real, was it? But you did the right thing. Try to calm down and get some sleep. You'll feel better in the morning."

I didn't know if I could love my sister any more than I did at that moment. How did she do that? Know exactly the right thing to say, at the right time.

"Can you stay for a bit?" I didn't want to be alone.

"Sure thing, Ollie."

I lay in bed, still in my full vigilante garb, and she sat next to me, her back to the wall. My body trembled and my mind raced and my chest burned with heartache.

"How do I stop feeling like this, Rea?"

"I'll show you, big brother," she responded confidently.

"How do you know what to do?"

She paused, staring into the dimly lit room. "Because I've seen it before, and I know the way out."

"What's the way out?"

She held out her hand, as I had to Po. "Together."

# MISTAKES

The Workshop had always been a sanctuary for me, in my happiest or my darkest times. My family was never overly religious, but nor were most of the nobles in the South. We held on to the customs and holidays of the Nine, but they were more ceremonial than spiritual. No, my true faith was in my Carpenter training. My temple was a catacomb of rooms and buildings hidden within the belly of the Narrows. My gods were swords and staffs and bows and tonfas. My religious texts consisted of the twenty-four fighting forms, and my confessions happened in the ring.

It had been two weeks since that night by the tavern, and try as I might, I couldn't stop seeing the guard. The blood on my sword, the sound of his body collapsing around my weapon, and the blank stare as his life escaped. If I had been a true believer of the Nine, I would have gone to the temple, confessed my sins to the Eighth God, and begged forgiveness. Instead, I came to the Workshop and never left.

I'd avoided the Institute, avoided jousting practice, and even avoided another Black Sunday on Roc's roof. I had gone through the obstacle course four hundred and seventy-two times and failed each run. I had practiced against the wooden and metal sparring dummies and against other Carpenters. Yet, whenever Po arrived in the afternoon, I would disappear to a different area.

I couldn't bear to have him see me for who I was.

A killer.

A murderer.

I wasn't the person he'd put his trust in. I wasn't the one who could train him. Or even protect him.

I couldn't protect anyone.

As I walked through the halls beneath the Narrows in my daily sojourn to avoid Po, a glint of steel stopped me from moving further.

"Not today, big brother," a voice from the darkness spoke.

"Out of my way, Rea," I said, trying to push past her.

"No. When I said together, I meant it."

I wanted to argue with her. I wanted to scream at her. She didn't know what I was feeling. She had no idea what I was going through. I couldn't face what waited for me above.

I turned around in a ruse and quickly spun to catch her off-guard. I was able to grab her sword, but in the tight hallway, she slipped under my disarmament and flipped me to my back. I may have had the sword now, but she still had the upper hand. As I held the sword defensively, she pushed dangerously upon the blade with her chest.

"What are you doing!" I yelled in a panic.

"You won't hurt me."

"I might," I said with gritted teeth. Her weight was pushing both edges of the blade against our bodies. The slightest miscalculation of angle or force and one, if not both of us, would be spilling blood.

She pushed herself up. "Prove it, then."

She grabbed the sword and we raced up through the catacombs and back to the main training room. It was empty, but that wouldn't last long. Reagan tossed me her sword, which I recognized as a blunted practice weapon that wouldn't have cut a loaf of bread. I had been fooled once, but I was determined to best her in this match, just as I had in every match we'd ever fought against each other.

"I know what you're doing," I said as I readied myself.

Before any match, be it sparring at the Workshop or in the ring at some tournament, I made sure to find my balance. Taking a large breath, I closed my eyes and readied myself.

"Ollie, you have no idea what I'm doing," Reagan replied with a wry smile. She took up a staff and began to exercise it around her body in tight circular spins. Moving into Form One, she got low into a stance that would give her an advantage against my longer legs.

There was no offensive form that would give me an advantage or disadvantage against her form, so I settled into Form Two. If she wanted to start at the beginning, then I would too. But before our match began, a rush of novice Carpenters and their more experienced teachers entered the training room and sat on their knees around the perimeter of the room. It wasn't often that two Carpenters of our stature put on a session like this in front of them.

I looked over at Po, eagerly watching me. How could I tell him I wasn't a hero? How could I stand here and look him in the eye?

Before I could finish another thought, I was met with an opening stab from Reagan. My mind couldn't focus except on what was in front of me: my sister trying her hardest to win. We shifted stance and circled each other, and a rush of excitement and fire flowed through me.

"Carpenters, today's lesson is about adaptability," I began while Reagan took the opportunity to move into an aggressive Form Twelve. I settled into assertive Form Fifteen, deflecting and parrying her attacks in a way that allowed me the chance to continue the lesson.

"Notice how Carpenter Reagan moves between different forms, letting her position dictate her actions. What is she trying to accomplish?"

I pushed against her in an attack of my own.

Carpenter Petr from the east coast of the South answered. "She's testing your defenses, trying to understand how you will react to each form."

"Correct, but you're still missing it," I said as Reagan again pushed into multiple different forms in a single combination. I reverted back into Form Seventeen, the most complex of the basic defensive forms. She wasn't able to penetrate my defenses, but that wasn't the point of her exercise.

Although Po had been quiet up until now, I knew he was working through the solution. He was the quickest study of any Carpenter I'd ever seen. Quicker than Reagan, maybe even me. I somersaulted into a dive and jumped up right in front of him, giving the young boy a wink.

He finally burst out. "She's learning to anticipate you. You always drop your heel back when you're a move and a half away from switching into a different Form. She's trying to understand the pattern."

Reagan spun her staff in a dazzling fashion. "Not trying, I already know it!"

That's when the room stopped. Time stopped. Once again, I found myself playing out each scenario in my head. Her combinations weren't random but strategic. But they were combinations, nonetheless. They took time and practice, which meant she followed a pattern of her own.

Patterns were everything in battle. Understanding how a weapon moved and the lines it followed could help you anticipate and react accordingly. Very few people, if anyone, had the reaction time to properly counter an attack by any weapon, be it a sword or a brick. Knowing the motion of the arm, the placement of the feet, the slight variations in body weight as an opponent shifted would allow one to anticipate, even if for a split second, and execute accordingly. It always came down to patterns.

I saw it all, in that timeless moment. If I did anything to counter her, she would defeat me. All the forms I knew would result in the same outcome. What I needed was something unexpected. Something no one would ever do in a battle.

This is the way.

Time resumed and Reagan yelled, beginning her assault and moving into the combinations I knew she would. I did exactly as she would have anticipated, and when the time came for my final shift onto my heel, moving into a form she would instantly have countered for the victory, I instead did something no one in the room expected.

I fell.

Dropping to the flat of my back, I exposed my body to an easy and open strike. In any other moment, I would have been obliterated with a hit, and lost. But the strike opportunity just wasn't one Reagan was prepared for. In her attempt to follow my pattern and exploit the flaw in my defenses, she had gone for the knockout hit with all her power, causing her to miss widely and stumble forward to where my feet were waiting to trip her. She landed on her back, her staff sprawled along the floor and my sword along her neck.

Match over.

The only sounds that could be heard were our heavy breathing as my sister and I lay on the floor, exhausted.

"What was her mistake?" I asked the Carpenters still surrounding us.

Carpenter Katarina answered first. "She didn't make a mistake. It was perfect. She set you up."

"The score would indicate otherwise," Reagan said as she sat up.

"But you did everything right! Carpenter Oliver made the mistake," Carpenter Katerina argued.

Regan held her hand up. "No, Carpenter Oliver never does anything by mistake. Isn't that right, Carpenter Po?" She looked at Po, who was quickly putting the pieces of the match together.

"No, he didn't, but rather I think he set you up. You were testing his defenses, but he was also testing you. He made sure you would notice that heel shift and when you finally went to use it against him, he…" But Po couldn't quite finish the tactic.

"I did what no other person would think to do. I left myself defenseless to allow her to overcommit and miss. Carpenter Reagan had chosen a plan of attack that required her to win on the final strike. Once I took away that option, there was nothing left. Her strategy is aggressive, but hard to complete if your opponent is willing to sacrifice everything."

"So, you didn't make a mistake. You meant to fall, to allow yourself to be open like that. You knew it was the only way," Carpenter Katarina replied, wide eyed.

I stood and walked around as I finished the lesson. "You must be able to adapt. You must be able to sacrifice. Every circumstance, every fight, every interaction is a battle between you and those around you. We teach you to practice and to look for patterns. Doing so will make you a good fighter. If you want to be a great fighter, you have to be willing to risk your strategy and adapt to your opponent. I've fought Carpenter Reagan for years. She knows all my moves, all my combinations. The only way for me to survive was to break free of the expected. I needed to adapt, and I needed to be willing to do whatever it took."

Reagan rose beside me, capping off the lecture. "Everything we do here in this Workshop is to prepare you for what's out there in the real world. When a Carpenter fights, they don't make mistakes. They do exactly what they are supposed to do. *Every time.*" She emphasized the last two words while looking directly at me. "Carpenter Oliver is one of the greatest this Workshop has ever seen. Pay close attention to him and you might be great too. He doesn't make mistakes, and neither will you."

After a round of applause, the rest of the Carpenters began sparring with each other, trying to imitate the intricate combinations Reagan had strung together. I walked over to a basin of water to wipe the sweat from my face and was joined by my sister.

"So, how'd you like my lesson?" she asked.

"I thought it was a little on the nose," I replied through my wet towel.

"Ollie, you know it wasn't your—"

"I know, Rea. That doesn't mean it doesn't hurt."

"If it didn't hurt, if it didn't pain you to think about, then you wouldn't be you," she replied. She was right, about everything, as usual. I don't make mistakes, not when I'm fighting, at least. I may not have wanted to kill that guard, but I did the only thing I could do at that moment. I still grieved, but it had been the right thing to do.

I stood, watching the other Carpenters practice. Their enthusiasm was infectious and for the first time since that night at the Bluefish Tavern, I smiled. Happiness brought back life within me. But there was sadness too. I wondered if both could live inside me at the same time or if it would split me apart. It was a feeling I'd known all too well since returning to Starfall. It was the feeling I had when I thought of Iris.

If I had made a mistake, it was with her. I might have made many mistakes, I realized as I thought more about it. I missed the life I had planned with her in my head, but more importantly, I missed my friend. I had hidden for too long, and it was time I fixed things.

Reagan threw her towel at my head and I snapped out of my daze. "So, where'd you learn that move anyway?" she asked.

I receded into my memory of a match against my older brother, whom I was sure I would defeat. I'd studied him for months, learning every pattern and combination he practiced. When the time had finally come, I'd ended up in the same position as Reagan did.

I hadn't smiled at the thought of my brother since he left over four years ago, but the thought of my family keeping a tradition couldn't dissuade me from a grin.

"It's a family thing."

# A DAMSEL NOT IN DISTRESS

"Don't even think about it," I threatened at the large oak door as I stood on the rain-soaked steps of the Shears. I'd come to make amends for the mistakes I'd made with Iris. The mistake of leaving her more than once. For betraying her trust with Po's book. For forgetting what we were and always would be: friends.

Could I hide my feelings from her? No, I didn't think I could. But I had decided that it didn't matter. Even if she was courting Ridhan, I could still be in her life. I was being foolish and I knew it. I knew it and I still did it. Why?

Because boys are dumb.

I didn't have a plan as I walked into the foyer. If I was honest with myself, I didn't want one. I wanted to speak from my heart, to tell her everything that had been going on in my life.

Maybe not everything.

After searching through a few levels, I followed two familiar voices until I was neatly hidden behind the stacks. Iris and Ridhan stood near a window, seemingly arguing.

If I could be so lucky.

I snuck closer and closer, tempting fate that I would be caught. But it was worth it.

"Why do you even care?" Iris asked.

"You have no idea what's happening right under your nose, Lady K," Ridhan replied as if shooing away a fly.

"I know enough. Now why do you care about him? Are you jealous?" Iris moved to face Ridhan.

"Of you? Always. What he sees in"—Ridhan gestured up and down along Iris's body—"you, I will never understand. But I have plans for him.

Plans you can't even fathom."

"Let me take a guess, they involve something dangerous?"

"Of course."

She picked up a stray book and flipped through it absentmindedly. "Deadly, even."

Ridhan hissed excitedly. "Maybe."

Iris threw the book onto a chair. "Magical?"

My breath was, well, it wasn't working. I had stopped breathing. Did she just say magical? What did she know about magic? How did Ridhan fit into this?

"You're smarter than you let on. It's a shame I have no use for you any longer," Ridhan replied. My heart was beating so loudly I thought they could hear it, but I didn't care. Did this mean what I thought it meant? Were my prayers finally answered?

"I could be useful," Iris replied. My heart sank once again. I couldn't handle the ups and downs of the emotions. One moment I was on top of the Shears and the next I was a puddle of goop.

"Just tell me what you want him for."

"Tck-tck-tck, you show your motives too swiftly, Lady K. Always ready to throw in your cards if you don't have the winning hand. You should learn patience. You'll find out soon enough about my plans. Until then, I believe our business is concluded."

Ridhan left the stacks, passing dangerously close to my hiding place.

Iris spun around and landed on a chair near a window. She stared listlessly into the bay. I could barely make out her face in the reflection of the dancing lantern light. Was she sad? Angry? Happy? I was about to explode like the volcano at the Forge and couldn't wait for a second longer.

"Beautiful night," I said as I sat opposite her, and though I had memorized her face long ago, I stared into her brown eyes and was surprised at their depth despite her torpid stare into the distance.

"Oliver, what are you doing here?" she finally replied, still not turning to face me. Her strange melancholy disturbed me, and I reached for her hand, gripping it tightly. She exhaled slowly, tears welling in her eyes as her hand began to shake. I concluded that she and Ridhan must have ended their courtship and that was the reason for her sadness. She gripped my hand to steady her own as I squeezed slightly.

Don't worry, Iris, I'm here to rescue you.

"It's over, Oliver, I failed." She finally turned to look at me, her eyes watering with tears.

"It's okay, Iris. I never thought you two were right for each other anyway." I was looking for any opening I could find. This was my moment; I just knew it!

She chuckled to herself. "Oh, is that right? I never would have guessed you felt that way."

"Was it that obvious?"

"No, no, it was cute. You're right in a way, but you don't know the whole story."

I scooched to the edge of my seat, never letting go of her hand, "So why don't you tell me?"

She took a deep breath, then looked out into the bay once more, staring for what seemed an eternity. "I was never with Ridhan because I liked him, and I'm sure he felt the same. Our courtship meant more than a couple of kids' feelings, and that's what hurts the most."

My heart twisted into a knot that dropped into the pit of my stomach. On the one hand, she was admitting her courtship had no romantic element, and on the other, seemingly she felt distraught at the loss.

"I'm not quite following, Iris. Are you two finished now?"

I wanted clarity. I wanted an answer. The mess of emotions I was feeling was jumbling in my mind and I latched on to rules and order. Was this just a fight, or was she actually free from him?

"Let me start at the beginning. Oh my, the beginning seems so long ago. I guess I'll start months ago when you left Starfall. We'd kissed—"

"So, you do remember!" I blurted out like an ogre.

"Of course I remember. I liked you for so long and we finally were... well, I don't know what we were, but I'd finally stopped waiting for you and made a move." She smiled mischievously and my body got incredibly warm and my skin danced.

I shifted in my seat to adjust my suddenly uncomfortable clothing, and she continued without a second thought to my plight.

"I thought about writing to you, or even coming to visit, but those hopes were dashed as soon as I returned home. My parents met me before I even made it through the door and told me how they needed me to court Ridhan

Shipwight. It was part of a scheme they had come up with to join their business with the Shipwights and, apparently, to commemorate the deal in full, Lord Shipwight wanted his son to finally be seen courting a lady."

She was avoiding looking at me, but I was entranced by the story. Although my mind would usually handle multiple topics at a time, I was fixated by Iris. If only she had made it out to Kandaheart, none of this would matter.

"I refused at first, and at second, but finally they wore me down. So, I trudged up the hill to their mansion, to talk with Ridhan about the arrangement. That's when I overheard him and his father talking. I could only make out a few words, but they mentioned magic, Starfall, the High Queen, and something called the Spider's Web. I knew immediately it was something nefarious and dark, but what could I do? I'm just a nothing noble from a small house in the Gardens and they were the Shipwights. Before I left, I heard them mention your name, though, and that's when I knew I had to do something. So I began to court Ridhan, to learn everything I could about what they were up to, and more importantly, what they wanted with you."

My hand fell from Iris's and I sat back. For one of the few times in my life, I was speechless. I had been wrong about everything.

She was with Ridhan for me. To protect me.

I'd spent the entire time since my return thinking I was to rescue Iris, and in reality, she was rescuing me, and I hadn't even known I was in danger.

"I played up the part, pretending to grow closer and closer to Ridhan and his father. My parents were thrilled. I suspected Ridhan was using me for his own purposes, and we came to an unwritten agreement. Neither of us would let on what we were really doing, but both of us would keep pursuing our own goals."

"I have so many questions right now," I said.

"I know, and I'll try to answer them all. I promise." Nine Gods, I was smitten with her. She was powerful and strong, stronger than I ever was, that much I was sure of. There was so much more to her than I had known.

"Okay, my first question is, are you two done?"

"Yes," she said definitively. "We're through. He's done with his use for me, though I still don't know everything I wanted to find out." My heart soared, and I could swear there was music playing a tune of jubilation. I started shaking at the thought that I might finally be with the girl of my dreams.

You need to play this cool, Oliver.

I took a breath to calm myself, letting other questions fill the space before I finally asked for her hand. "So, what did you find out?"

"Well, to start, the Spider's Web is a secret society of people throughout all the kingdoms who are bent on bringing magic back into the world. They hate the High Queen, and beyond that really any sort of government or royalty. They want to sow anarchy in this world, and magic is their means to do so."

"How do you know all this?"

"Because the Shipwights are Spiders. I don't know how high they are, but given their status in the South, I'd have to imagine fairly high. They plan to use magic and take over Starfall, and then the entirety of the South. It would be the first step in rebellion against the other kingdoms and against the High Queen. It would mean war, Oliver." She stood up and began to shake off the tension. She seemed as though it felt good to finally talk about this. Keeping it all to herself must have been torture, and even quite lonely.

"I talked to Professor Lortho. He was the only person I could think of who would believe me and understand me, given he was the most senior professor of histories. Luckily for me, he did, and during the summer we began to work out the Spider's Web's plots."

Wrong again, Oliver.

"Beyond that, I've been trying to track everything I know about them. I've researched the noble families here at the Shears for any clues. I've tried to attend their meetings, glean any papers at the Shipwights, but they cover their tracks well."

"What about me?"

Iris put her face in her hands and rubbed them down in frustration. "I still don't know what they want from you. Or what Ridhan wants, really. All I know is he's obsessed with you, and that makes it very dangerous for you."

It was a complete reversal of positions. Weeks ago, I had left Iris alone, thinking Po's book was putting her in danger, and the entire time she was in the frenzy of the sharks, trying to keep Ridhan distracted from me.

Iris grabbed both my hands, tears spilling down her cheeks. "I'm sorry, Oliver. I really am. I tried to find out, I tried to protect you. I failed." She buried her head into my chest, and I held her tight.

This whole experience had torn her up inside, I could see that now. She had tried to do everything she could to protect me, and she was broken from the experience. But it was okay, because now it was my turn. I knew a damsel in distress when I saw one, and my quest to rescue Iris would be fulfilled.

"Don't worry." I kissed her lightly on each cheek, scrunching my face at the saltiness of her tears. "I'm going to fix you."

I smiled at her, but suddenly her expression hardened into pure rage. The hands from her hug turned into talons as they pinched me fiercely. For a second I saw each of the Nine Hells in her eyes as she inhaled sharply.

"FIX ME? You think I need fixing? Who do you think... by the Nine... In what world do you think I'm in need of fixing?! FIX ME!? You sound just like... FIX ME? What makes you think you need to FIX me? Am I not good enough for you now? Am I broken? I should punch you square in the face, Oliver Quartermaine!" Practically choking in her anger, she turned abruptly, all but igniting the building around us with her eyes. "You think you're some hero and I've been waiting all this time for you to RESCUE me? Are you out of your mind? Did you even hear what I told you? It amazes me that... FIX ME?! Who in the hells do you think you are?"

I flailed. "M-maybe fix you wasn't the right word. What I meant was... help you? Save you! Yes, save you!"

"SAVE ME!? Oh, Mister Big Hero wants to save me. Save me from what? Myself? I'll have you know I've been doing quite alright by myself over here trying to make sure that... I swear to the Nine... Ahhh!" She threw up her arms in exasperation.

Slap!

Ow.

"For someone so smart, who claims to love me, you sure are stupid."

With that, she turned and walked out, leaving me stunned. I rubbed at my stinging cheek and looked around at the lifeless stacks of books.

"Well, that went better than expected."

A voice from behind me answered.

"Tck-tck-tck. Oh, Q, I think that went splendidly."

# THE SPIDER'S WEB

I couldn't remember the first time I met Ridhan Shipwight. It wasn't because I didn't have my mind temple or because of any lack of memory. It was because we met when we were babies. I had known Ridhan my entire life, and even from an early age, I knew something was off about him.

It may have been that he was an only child. Or maybe it was because his mother died giving birth to him. Or maybe people are just born a certain way and that's who they are. Maybe it's how they are raised.

Regardless, what should have been a lifelong friendship between the children of the two most powerful families in the South, never happened. Instead, there was a budding rivalry that gave way to a quiet ostracization. He'd kept to his interests and friends, and I'd kept to mine. We crossed paths from time to time, and each time we did, Ridhan seemed a little worse and a little less the boy I'd known.

He always had a slight fascination with me that I couldn't quite put my finger on. Even when we were really small, Ridhan would talk to me like I was a favorite pet or even a trophy he coveted. I was understandably put off and did my best to avoid him. During our time at the Institute, we'd kept our distance from each other, or at least I'd kept my distance from him. I'd avoided trying to measure myself against Ridhan my entire life, for fear that I would be looking at some poor reflection if I stared too long.

All of that had now changed. He'd courted the girl I loved, threatened my friends, and apparently was part of some plot to destroy the city I loved. I could no longer avoid a confrontation with him. At the very least, I needed to know that I wasn't like him.

"What are you doing here, Rid?"

"Tck-tck-tck, I should be asking you the same question, Q, but we both know the answer to yours. I knew my dalliance with Kentaro would bear fruit, and here you are, just as I hoped."

"So this was all just some plan?"

"Oh, Q, I have so many plans for you. Now that you know a fraction of what's going on, you can finally start to be useful." He sat in a chair, crossing his legs and waiting for me to mirror him. This wasn't a battle with swords or steel but of mind and words. I needed to tread carefully if I wanted to defeat him.

I needed to exploit his patterns, just as I had with Reagan.

I sat down, crossed my legs just as he had, and we continued like lords would.

"Okay, Rid, I'm game. I know you, maybe I'm the only one in this world who does. The real you, that is. I know there is good in you and that this… facade, is just that."

Sure, Ridhan was a bully, a jerk, and sometimes downright sinister. But I had seen him be good, or at least a facsimile of good. I wanted to speak to that Ridhan, if only he would show himself.

Ridhan sat quietly for a while. Maybe he was wondering if he could finally let his guard down. Maybe he was trying to think of a way to get the better of me. His face was an indecipherable puzzle.

"No one knows me, Q," he finally said. "Not you, not my father, not my Sharks, not even your little Kentaro."

It was a moment of honesty I'd rarely seen from him. Did he really feel so alone in the world? Is that where his hatred came from?

"I do, Rid. You're someone with the potential to change the world, with the means to affect everyone around you, and with the opportunity to help those in need. You act tough, and if I'm being honest, a little crazy. But I've seen you do good, be good."

Ridhan laughed a hearty and not wholly disingenuous laugh. "When was that, Q? In a dream?"

"No, on my tenth name-day party."

A small smile crept at the corners of Ridhan's mouth and he played with a ring on his right hand. He held the hand out. "Tck-tck-tck, show me."

I could feel my forehead crinkle as I stared at his outstretched hand. A pattern was emerging, but I didn't know exactly what it was. My only option was to continue with this line of thought. But what was he doing? Why did he want my hand? The energy in my body, the same energy that would encourage me silently toward action, was now controlling my body. I reached out and grabbed Ridhan's hand and suddenly I was pulled into my mind temple.

No, we were pulled.

"Interesting place you have here, Q, although you could do something about the decor."

"How are you doing this?" I asked, panicked. My mind temple was the only place in the world I thought impenetrable.

"In good time, my sweet. Now, off to your memory," he answered, and we floated through the temple. Most of the doors we passed were simple and had only a doorknob, but we stopped in front of one that contained five different locks.

Ridhan examined the door and sighed. "Yes, I have one of these as well."

The door began to shake and my anxiety about what was behind it caused me to step back and away. Ridhan looked at me sympathetically, and we moved on and finally came upon the door of the memory Ridhan was searching for. The memory of my tenth name day.

In the tradition of my siblings, my name-day party had consisted of small tournaments with tiny contestants. The children competed in standing joust, sword on foot, and even an obstacle course race while the adults watched and cheered. Thinking back on it now, it seemed crazy the adults would even allow such a thing, but despite the danger, we survived.

Children from all around the South and some beyond had been invited to my party. High and low nobles along with random Narrows kids and more had come for the promise of a good time and a generous parting gift from my parents. Roc had won the standing joust, which was not wholly unremarkable. After weeks of nonstop studying, Yokel had miraculously won the obstacle course, and the final sword on foot match pitted Ridhan against me.

"Let us pause for one moment," Ridhan said as my memory stood still, and we walked around the entirety of the scene. "I remember this now. Quite the party. It's a wonder any of us survived this cockfight our parents put us through."

"It's funny, I was thinking the same thing, Rid," I responded, trying to gain common ground with my rival. "I'm surprised you've forgotten this moment."

"Oh, really? Why is that?" He seemed genuinely curious. He may have been able to hide who he was from the world, but within the confines of my mind, his true self was the only version allowed.

"You don't remember? I beat you. I shouldn't have, but you misstepped at the very end and I scored the point."

I resumed my memory and the fight bore out just as I had described. Except, upon closer examination, I noticed something new. Ridhan hadn't misstepped but had thrown the match.

"Ah yes, I remember. My father was quite upset that I would lose to a Quartermaine." He smiled mischievously.

"We had so much fun back then, but after that, you changed. You became…"

"I became what I am now. You can say it. Call a shark for what it is, but you are right. My transformation catalyst, however, came later, that much I remember perfectly."

Ridhan walked about the memory as it continued, adults talking with each other as children ran around playing with all manner of wooden swords and shields.

"So many strays, I thought you'd open up an orphanage," Ridhan spat as the images of children ran through him.

"Why do you do that?"

"You should know better than anyone that there are those who are us and those who are not. We're better than they are, and they need to know that."

"I don't think we're better than anyone else."

Ridhan strode quickly toward me, stopping mere centimeters from my face. "That is what I love about you, Q. That naivety, it's so refreshing."

"Everyone deserves a chance to become who they were meant to be."

Ridhan didn't break his gaze from mine. "Everyone deserves whatever we allow them."

I shook my head. "What happened that night?"

"I think that is enough for now," Ridhan said and took his ring off.

Suddenly I was ripped away from the memory, from my mind temple, and physically thrown to the ground. Ridhan was sitting comfortably in the chair, juggling the ring between the fingers of his right hand. I tried to pull myself up when suddenly Ridhan took hold of my arm.

"I see you have one, too," he said, examining my own ring.

I sat up, trying to overcome the strange exhaustion I was feeling. "How did you do that?"

"Tck-tck-tck, not tonight, my Q." He let go of my hand and I rolled to a seated position on the floor. Ridhan moved to the front of his seat and looked down at me, still fidgeting with his ring. "I saw something in you that day at the Institute. It was just a flash of a moment, the quickest of visions, but I know what I saw."

My head was pounding but curiosity still got the better of me. "And what is it that you saw?"

Ridhan bent down off the chair and kneeled in front of me. "That we are the same." My expression betrayed my disagreement and he stood up quickly. "There's more going on in this world than you know, Q. Tck-tck-tck, the question is, will you be someone who is in my way or someone who helps me achieve what I want?"

The pattern clicked into place within my mind. My recent interactions, as well as our visit to my mind temple, helped confirm my theory. When Ridhan thought he was in control, he made that ticking noise. When he wasn't, it was absent. I filed the detail away.

"What is it that you want, Ridhan?"

"What do you know of magic, my love?"

How much could I lie to him? How much could I say without giving too much away? Do I tell him of my quest from Professor Lortho? Do I tell him of the book? I wasn't a good enough liar to admit ignorance, but perhaps I was skilled enough to get by with a lack of education on the matter.

"Magic isn't real, everyone knows that," I answered with a wry smile, trying to bait him.

"Tck-tck-tck, I think we both know better than that," he said while flaunting his ring. The insignia showed against the lamplight. A spider web.

Do they all have the same ring? I'm a little jealous now.

I stood up and looked around, pretending to look for eavesdroppers. "Well, now that you mention it, I've heard rumors that there may be some items that are magical."

A thin smile enveloped his mouth and his teeth began to bare. "Yes, that is correct. Some may even possess such items without their knowledge.

Family heirlooms thought to be useless and suchlike. An item one may have lost on a bet at a child's name-day party."

It struck me instantly. The Shipwight's Staff of the Seas that I had so carelessly bargained with Ridhan. The one that sat now in my home. His father must have wagered it against my own, the victor getting the prize. That must have been what Ridhan was referring to when he said everything changed that night. He'd not only lost an heirloom but a magical item, most likely one of the only ones his family owned.

"No matter." Ridhan waved a hand. "I'll soon be in possession of it, along with your own family's magical item." He was talking about our Shield of Kandaheart, although I had never known it to be magical.

Then again, I hadn't thought anything was magical until recently.

"So, what do you want with me?" I asked, trying to put the pieces of our conversation together. "What makes me so special?"

"Tck-tck-tck, oh, my sweet Q, you are very special. You're going to lead me to magic. Real magic, not these trinkets we vie for. Of course, you know of the prophecy, don't you?"

"No, I can't say that I do," I said, utterly confused.

Ridhan tore out a page from a book, and on the blank backside of it, took a quill and ink and started to scribe.

"Out of the shadows and into the light,
Find the lost, stand and fight,
A Champion will reunite,
Beware the power of The Lightning Knight."

He threw the paper to me and I read it, and read it again, trying to quickly ascertain the meaning. It was familiar to me, but it wasn't something I'd read in a long time.

"This isn't a prophecy, it's from a children's book."

"Yes, it is. But then again, so is magic. You said it yourself, Q, magic isn't real. So, maybe neither is this prophecy."

He was goading me. As much as I'd not wanted to admit it, he was right. If magic was real, maybe so too was this poem. But I still didn't know what that had to do with me.

"I don't see how I fit into all this."

"If I am to become the Lightning Knight, to have real magic, I will need my champion to find magic for me. You shall be my champion, Q. Go! Find magic and bring it to me."

Ridhan turned and began to leave, but I was overcome with defiance.

"And what if I don't choose to be your champion?"

Ridhan stopped but didn't bother to turn back around.

"Tck-tck-tck, oh my sweet Q, you have no choice. You're caught in the Spider's Web now."

# THE FORGE

"He's not ready," a voice echoed in the dark room. I stepped forward and the sound of liquid underneath my foot echoed along the wall-less room. It wasn't water. I bent down to investigate. It was dark and congealing, its texture almost rich. Sounds of a scream and of sword cutting through bone filtered through the room, and suddenly I knew what the substance was.

"He'll have to be, we're running out of time. He will not fail us, I have faith," another voice answered.

Who were they talking about? Fail at what? I wanted so desperately to yell out into the darkness but found my throat closed up. As if to answer my apprehension, the second voice addressed me.

"Soon, my child. We will need all of you."

My legs were sucked into the blood-soaked floor. I scrambled around, searching for escape before finally submitting to the dark liquid, only to find myself standing at the edge of a pier.

I touched myself all over, checking if I was still covered with the fallen guard's blood. Even as I felt relief from the knowledge that it had been a vision, I couldn't shake the feeling of being watched. I looked at the ring on my hand, which looked as though it was dimming until its natural dullness resided.

The world had grown a little bigger and a lot more complicated. For years I had trained as a Carpenter, roamed the rooftops at night as a would-be vigilante, and even spent the summer competing in tournaments. But it was all a façade. I was playing at being a hero, pretending at the consequences of real life, and it had finally caught up to me. The world was different now. I was different now. I had taken a life, and it ripped away at my soul.

Reagan had done her best to help me, but the grief lingered. Intellectually, I knew I had done the right thing. But in my heart, I still hurt so much. I was in a maelstrom of emotion, and I thought I would drown. I'd lost Iris, again, and whatever Ridhan's plans were, they couldn't be anything positive.

I needed my friends again. For weeks I had abandoned them, exiling myself.

Why did I do that?

I suppose I felt shame. Maybe a sense of dishonor. Or maybe I just couldn't bear it if they didn't forgive me. When my life became the hardest, I had retreated. It was the worst possible thing I could have done to myself. Being alone... being alone and isolated felt like I was slowly dying.

I stood at the edge of the pier watching the sun rise over the water of the eastern edge of the bay; waves of blue and green ocean were breaking violently over the rocks and pilings underneath and throwing a cool salty mist into the air. My concentration broke when Yokel approached, yelling out as he made his way down the long wooden steps to the pier.

"Oh, hey, Oliver! I ju-just had the b-best breakfast of m-my life!"

"Yokel... shut... up!"

He smiled at the friendly tease and we exchanged our Whiskey Danger hand signal, a closed fist with outstretched pinky and thumb with a slight oscillation back and forth. We used this signal in nonverbal solidarity, serving as anything from a greeting to emphasis, a moment of joy or frustration, quiet agreement or shared excitement. Sometimes Roc got a little too excited and went at it with both hands, flailing around like a drunkard on the Summer Solstice. At the very least, we were pretending things were back to normal.

A moment later Roc arrived with Po in tow. Reagan had said that in my recent absence, Roc and Po had been spending a lot of time together, with Roc thoroughly enjoying his little fan's adoration.

"Hey, guys!" Po said in his youthful excitement, flashing our hand signal. With our permission, he had appropriated it very quickly, using it as often as he could. "So, what are we doing here? Are we going for a swim, because I have to be honest, I don't know how." His face flushed in embarrassment, but Roc gave him a hearty back pat in reassurance.

"It's okay, kid, we're not going swimming today, but remind me to teach you how. No, today we have a special surprise for you. If you're going to be in Whisky Danger, if you're going to be one of us, then you're going to have to pass the… the test!"

Roc was improvising. I looked at Po, at his all-too-familiar expression of being overwhelmed.

Just tell the kid already, you know he's bound to pass out with too much excitement.

Po's words wavered slightly. "Test? What test? I hope it's not swimming because like I said before, I don't really know how—"

"It's not a swimming test, bud, just relax," I said, pointing out to the ocean. "We're heading out there." He followed my finger with his eyes, squinting to make out whatever was behind the morning's breaking fog. As if on cue, sunbeams burned through the remaining mist, revealing a huge mountain standing in solitary vigil in the middle of the bay. The volcano hadn't erupted for generations, but its molten bowels were the lifeblood of the Forge's many furnaces, without which none of my father's many high-volume production lines would have fallen dead long ago.

"We're going to the Forge!?" Po squeaked, jumping up and down and punching Yokel in the kidney. We all laughed at his exuberance and hopped on a skimmer to make our way across the bay. Normal ferries ventured to the island on a schedule, but my family had a collection of yachts, skimmers, and other boats for private travel across the bay. While Roc and Yokel manned the oars, I taught Po how to run the sheets and rudder. A slight breeze made for a smooth sail to the island, and a pod of good-mannered dolphins followed us part of the way, playfully popping above the water line to breathe before they resumed their underwater journey.

The island had many interesting quirks, such as the impenetrable ring of coral formations surrounding the island. This funneled all traffic through one channel that was maintained and moderated by the Forge's Guards of the Coast. Their floating stations along the channel served to direct ship traffic through this marine causeway, and rumors had run rampant in the city for generations of certain sinister surprises lying submerged in wait for malicious vessels.

We docked quietly, then moved quickly through the small market at the foot of the mountain to reach the entrance of the obsidian castle. It was less of a fortress and more of an homage to the master masons involved in its construction. Large panels of black glass teased captured sunlight into brilliance, forming an incredible piece of architecture embedded directly in the walls of the volcano. The glass was demonstrably resilient against pounding waves and coastal weather, but any weak point in the construct would leave the whole structure fragile, negating it as a defensible stronghold. Luckily for my family, our enemies were few and a military siege was not in our foreseeable future.

"So, kid, I hear you want to be a knight?" Roc quizzed Po as we entered the Forge through the main doors. Moving down the hall to the main workshop, the smell of brimstone grew until its acidity burned my nostrils. I watched each of my friends as the smell hit, Yokel covering his face and scoffing audibly as Po gagged into his sleeve. Roc, however, looked more at home here in this hot, sulphuric tunnel than anywhere else, sniffing the air like he had caught a whiff of a fine perfume. With his chest puffed up, he led us confidently, continuing to impress his knowledge on the clearly nauseated Po.

"You know, a knight has a very important job, some say one of the most important. I've met knights from all over the country, and let me tell you, they are something else." Roc was really laying it on thick, but Po appeared to eat up every second of it. Po stalled briefly before responding very deliberately.

"Yes, I want to be a knight. I know it's impossible, but I know I can do it! I want to help people... just like your uncle!"

Roc stopped dead in his tracks, caught off-guard by Po's high regard of a lowly hedge knight. He looked at Po and found nothing but genuine respect, so he continued in his 'older brother' tone.

"Impossible is right. You know why knights are so rare? Only the High Queen can dub you a knight and service you to a lord. But in order to even become a knight, you must first complete the Three Knightly Acts. Do you know what they are?"

"An act of honor, an act of valor, and... an act of service," Po answered, counting on his fingers.

"That's why there aren't many knights, and why becoming one is so important. It's not so easy to accomplish all three acts in a manner satisfactory to the High Queen. Many a man and woman have gone their whole life trying and failing to do so."

Po's expression turned grave. "My grandfather died before he could become a knight." It was the first time we had heard Po openly talking about his grandfather. Other than the book and the ring, I didn't know anything else about patriarchal Pondarion.

"He dreamed of becoming a knight and did everything he ever could to complete his three Acts, but he only ever did an Act of Valor, saving the High Queen. That's when she gave him the ring I gave you, Oliver."

I looked down at the ring on my hand and lost my breath. This ring wasn't just an heirloom or magical item but a token of a Knightly Act.

"He was a general, you know, in the Imperial Army," Po went on. "He and my father had gotten into a fight and I never saw my grandpa again. Then one day my gran and I got a package in the mail and a note saying he had died in battle, and he wanted me to have his ring."

"Po, we had no idea." Roc sounded a bit choked up.

"It's okay, Roc. Grandpa couldn't become a knight, but I still can. I won't fail you."

Roc smiled. "I know." Never comfortable with emotions, Roc turned quickly to his workstation and grabbed a slender wooden box from the table. Roc was an accomplished smith, and heir apparent to my father in terms of talent.

He stood in front of Po, holding the box behind him. "First, you have to answer a question for me."

"I'm ready," Po said proudly.

"It's really the only question that matters."

What was he getting at? I thought I knew what was about to happen, but Roc hadn't let me in on his full plan. I glanced at Yokel, who seemed like he knew something I didn't.

Oh, Nine Hells, Yokel knows something I don't. Kill me now.

"The question is this: Will you swear to protect all those in need, no matter the costs? Will you protect your friends, even if it means taking the life of an enemy, an enemy that gives you no other choice..." Roc's gaze rose past Po's and met my own as he continued speaking to us both. "Will you sacrifice your life, maybe your soul, so that others may live free? Being a knight is no small matter, no lighthearted feat. You will be forced to choose between a bad option and a worse option. The real question I have is, when the time comes and you are expected to make that choice, can you forgive yourself, knowing you did the right thing?"

I furled my forehead tightly, and Yokel put his hand on my shoulder as I blinked rapidly and smiled at Roc, thanking him with a nod.

"Um, I think so. Sorry, Roc, I kind of lost you in the middle there," Po said, scrambling in all his innocence to say the right thing. Roc smiled, lowering his huge frame onto one knee as he placed a hand on Po's shoulder. "I know, kid, my fault. Let me try this again. Will you follow your heart and do the right thing at all times?"

"Yes, sir."

"Good." A smirk accompanied an eyebrow rise. "Every knight in the realm requires one thing, and one thing only." He swung the box in front of him and unclasped the locks, revealing a squire's blade housed in a velvet casing. It was thin and lightweight, like Yokel's rapier blade, but a hand smaller to account for Po's small stature.

Yokel and I walked around and stood behind Roc, noticing Po's expressionless face. He was definitely dead now.

Great, we killed the kid. Guess I'll be the one to have to tell his gran. "Sorry, GranGran, his heart gave out from excitement."

Without warning, Po lunged at Roc, wrapping his arms around his neck, sobbing and muttering into Roc's chest. "Thank you, thank you, thank you!"

Roc embraced him back with a smile and then peeled Po off and picked up the box and sword that had fallen. "Take good care of this. I made it myself. It will serve you well if you serve it well."

Po freed the sword from its box and began to test its weight, slashing at imaginary enemies.

"Let's see what you've got, kid!" Yokel yelled, grabbing a practice sword off the wall. He grinned. "Just try to take it easy on me, I'm not much of a fighter."

Roc and I followed silently as the two moved into the courtyard to find room for their contest. Never before had I felt this kind of gratitude for Roc's undying friendship. I looked at him and smiled, flashing a subdued, grateful version of our hand signal. He responded in kind, and realizing that emotions were threatening to well up in us both, I leaned over and punched him square in the crotch.

He doubled over, gasping for air. "So, you think it's time we bring him to Black Sunday night?" Roc asked as he leaned against the wall for support.

"If I know Johanous, he's already made him a suit," I answered as we watched Po and Yokel trade strikes, Po's Carpenter training already outpacing Yokel's technique. "Five to one the kid beats Yok," I said, stopping to lean against a banister.

Roc chuckled, pride beaming from his eyes. "I'd put all my money on that kid."

# HARALABOS

"A slap to the face?" Roc asked as he walked over to me. "Yeah, I don't know if there's any coming back from that."

"You're a lot of help." I was stretched out on the roof in defeat. It was Black Sunday night, and while we waited for Po, I had recounted stories from my absence since the Bluefish Tavern.

"It's not as though she cou-could hate you forever, right?" Yokel laid his head directly next to mine. Roc joined us and we stared up into the night sky that was blanketed by stars.

I began to think aloud. "I mean, she was courting Ridhan to protect me, so you'd have to assume she won't hate me forever, I guess."

"I don't know about that. Knowing Iris, I bet she could hold a grudge for a while," Roc replied.

"What makes you say that?" Yokel asked.

"Because she's a girl, and girls are like that. Don't you know anything about the opposite sex, Yok?"

"You know, in some interpretations of Elven history, there's thought that they recognize upward of three different—"

"Shut up, Yokel!" Roc and I said in unison.

Damn, we're getting good at that.

We all laughed, and Po hopped over the edge of the roof in his new attire. As predicted, Johanous had crafted Po his own suit, just like ours. He was officially Whiskey Danger now. Without hesitation he lay down with us, creating the fourth point in our makeshift human star.

"Why are we lying down like this?"

"Because Oliver is a jerk."

"Hey!" I yelled, trying to aim a punch at Roc's head, only to hit Yokel.

"Is it because of Lady Iris?"

"Yes, yes it is, Po," I answered, utterly defeated.

"Wait, Po, ho-how do you know about Iris?" Yokel asked.

Po took his sword and playfully started counting stars with it. "Oh, that's easy. I saw her the other day when she was talking with her friends."

I eagerly sat up. "Did you happen to hear what they were talking about?"

Roc and Yokel sat up too, looking a little too eager to hear more of the drama that was my life.

"Yep," Po replied absentmindedly as he traced constellations.

I waited for more, and after what seemed like an eternity, burst out, "And? What was she talking about? Was it me? Did she say anything about me?"

"Sure did."

"Well? Out with it! What did she say?" If she was talking about me, maybe she had calmed down and forgiven me. Maybe she was ready for us to finally be together!

Po sat up and cleared his throat. "She said for me to tell you that you are an ass and that you're full of yourself and that if you think she's not still mad at you than you are as oblivious as you don't think you are." There was a certain delight in his tone, probably from the pride of remembering the tongue twister word for word.

The excitement that had lifted my lungs and coursed through my heart moments ago fell flat to the earth, and suddenly I felt even worse than before.

"That's... Well, that's not very good now, is it?" Roc eloquently summarized.

I put my head in my hands, stretching the skin under my eyes in aggravation. "Did she say anything else?" I asked, hoping against hope for a glimmer of forgiveness.

"Well..." Po started.

"Just say it."

"She basically hates you."

"Hates me?"

"With the fiery passion of one hundred exploding volcanoes, if I remember correctly."

I fell back to the ground with a groan.

"Well, at least sh-she's thinking about you," Yokel said.

"She's not thinking of anything good..." Roc countered.

"Yes, however..." Yokel began to protest, and they argued back and forth on the merits of whether a girl thinking about someone in various situations was good or bad. I tried to block out their voices and recede into my mind temple, a fortress where I could be alone with my thoughts.

"He's the most popular kid in school, of course she should want to be with him!" Roc yelled as their argument started to heat up.

"You don't get it. She doesn't want to be with the popular kid, she wants to be with Oliver," Yokel countered.

"How is that any different than what I said?"

"Because being popular isn't as special as being..." Yokel searched for the word he wanted but I snapped out of my trance and answered for him.

"It doesn't matter, I messed up." They both stopped arguing and Po stopped stabbing imaginary foes with his blade. "Sometimes you have to admit when you're wrong. I spent this whole summer thinking she 'would' be with me, and then I spent the autumn thinking of how she 'should' be with me. I never stopped to think about Iris independent of me. It was always us together. I was trying to be a hero when, in fact, I was the one in need of saving."

"Sounds like she's quite the girl," a metallic voice from behind us said. All four of us whipped around to find the Knight Angel standing on the roof's edge, her colorful cape playfully dancing from the slight updraft between the buildings.

"Maybe we should be meeting with her tonight instead?" A second metallic voice responded from the opposite side of the roof. We all twisted around once more as a second Knight Angel, this one with a black cape, crouched like a frog on the roof's edge.

"There's two of you?" I asked.

Roc nudged me and whispered, "Oh, by the way, Oliver, we found the Knight Angel while you were gone and invited her—I mean them, to our meeting tonight."

I stood up, pointing at both of them back and forth in false anger. "I knew there were two of you!" I yelled excitedly. The Knight Angels dropped down from the roof edge and introduced themselves.

The slightly taller one who had saved me at the Shears began first.

"'ello everybody, pleasure to meet you all. You may call me Pathfinder."

The second, slightly shorter one, who we saved at the Bluefish Tavern, spoke next. "And you may call me Windrunner."

They were naming themselves after legendary Elven folk heroes. Bold, but I liked it.

Any thought of Iris or the plight that was our nonexistent relationship disappeared. I was transfixed by our new comrades and something instinctive drew me to Pathfinder. Maybe it was the unique way she spoke with that Land's End accent, or maybe it was the fact that she had saved me. Either way, I was enamored.

"I'm Roc, and this here is Yokel, Po, and Oli—"

"Shouldn't we have our own special names?" Yokel interrupted.

"Oh, honey, we already know who you all are," Windrunner said as she rubbed Yokel's cheek with the back of her hand.

"How did you find them?" I asked Roc.

"Well, they uh, actually found us. They wanted the book, and I explained to them we should be working together, not separately."

"And it's always better to work together than apart, especially when dealing with what we're dealing with," Yokel added gleefully.

Po looked from face to face. "What are we dealing with?"

"One moment, please," I asked the Knight Angels, then pulled Yokel and Roc into a quick huddle. "Okay, so we're only doing this because we think they're hot, right?"

"Yes, completely," Roc answered.

"One thousand percent," Yokel echoed.

"Good, glad we're all in agreement." I clapped. We broke our huddle as Po tried and failed to interject himself into the conversation.

"Okay, so now that we've agreed to let you in on our quest—" I began.

"Oi, excuse me. Your quest? No, no, no. We're the ones letting you in," Pathfinder interrupted.

"We're the ones with the book and the ring!"

"But we're the ones who actually know what's going on," Windrunner proclaimed. Pathfinder and I had moved so close to each other, I could almost make out the contours of her face under her mask. It was a standoff, and I wasn't about to lose against her. But there was palpable energy between us, and I was for sure in love and pretty confident she felt the same.

Our babies would be amazing fighters AND beautiful.

Yokel, ironically, was the one to calm the situation down. "How about we agree that we are all partners i-in this situation."

I nodded and Pathfinder did the same. We all sat in a circle, and I put the book and the ring in the middle.

"Hey, those are my grandpa's!" Po said.

Windrunner looked at him. "They're much more than that, Po. These are actually magical items. The ring unlocks the book, and the book belonged to a man named Haralabos."

"You mean the Lightning Knight?"

No one said a word in response. The stories of The Knights of Nine never divulged the secret identity of the Knights, only their Knight names. The Lightning Knight was their leader, along with Skyjumper, Peacemaker, Starfire, and others with just as fantastical names.

Po continued in our silence. "My grandpa used to tell me stories of The Knights of Nine. He said that only very few people knew their identities, to keep their friends and families safe. But he knew a secret no one else did, and that was the name of the Lightning Knight. He said he'd always remember it because it was so unusual. But yeah, his name was Haralabos."

Yokel perked up. "Why would your grandpa know the name of a character no one else knew in a made-up story?"

"Because the stories are true," I answered.

Pathfinder spoke next. "What better way to erase history than to make it into myth. That must be what happened. In the story, the Knights were defeated by their most powerful foe from over the Sunset Mountains, the Destroyer. If that enemy wanted everyone to forget about the Knights, the best way would have been to turn them into fiction. They'd be remembered, but not how they were. It's quite brilliant."

Roc tapped the pommel of his sword. "So you're saying that a children's book is actually real?"

Windrunner nodded. "Precisely. The question is, what happened to them? And what does that have to do with this?" She picked up the book and held it in the air, inspecting it.

"Why don't we ask it?" I asked jokingly.

"Great idea!" she said and tossed me the ring.

I put the ring to the mechanism on the front of the book and turned. It unclasped and we all turned the pages in anticipation. The first page said the name. We quickly turned to the second page, which said, "Find the Knight Angel."

Yokel flipped through all the pages and put the book down in defeat. "They're all blank," he said sadly.

"Anyone have any ideas?" I asked. We all sat quietly thinking. I racked my mind temple for answers but couldn't focus as much as I typically could. Pathfinder penetrated all my thoughts, and my infatuation was causing an uncomfortable situation with my outfit.

"How did the name get there in the first place? And this other part?" Po asked. I explained how I used the ring to open the book and the name suddenly appeared, and how the advice from Haralabos had appeared the second time I had opened it as well.

"Did you say anything when you did that?"

"Well, I asked whose book this was… and then I asked Haralabos for advice with—" I looked around, suddenly embarrassed. "… Uh, never mind. I just talked to it, I guess."

We all looked at each other as the thought struck us simultaneously. Pathfinder clasped the mechanism again. I touched the ring to the book.

"Haralabos, what do you want?"

I paused and looked at Pathfinder, our eyes meeting for this momentous moment. I knew something was going to happen, and I was happy to share this moment of magic with the people here. My very best friends, and my two newest. I smiled awkwardly at Pathfinder, and I think she may have smiled back, but I would never be able to tell.

"Open the damn thing!" Roc complained loudly as he punched me in the shoulder. I apologized and Pathfinder and I opened the book. On the first page was the name, Haralabos. We turned the page once more and saw the sentence about the Knight Angel. But underneath that, instead of a blank sheet, three new words appeared.

It's about time.

The five of us exchanged glances. Yokel began to pace, trying to connect what he had seen with his own eyes to everything he knew, mumbling through his thoughts. Pathfinder and Windrunner were staring blankly at each other. Roc stared at the book strangely. I couldn't tell if he was utterly disgusted or slightly intrigued. It was always going to be a risk one way or another with him. Po never took his eyes off the book. He yearned for more, and so did I.

I was hooked. I had now used magic thrice.

THRICE!

Each time I had felt something special, entirely seductive, and my entire being craved more. I had never been addicted to anything, but I assumed this is what it felt like to be on the spice. Curiosity overtook me.

"Who are you?"

My comrades jumped at the sudden noise. None of us had ever been privy to any type of magic before. What we were doing was tantamount to treason and punishable by death; however, at that moment we all silently agreed we couldn't stop. I pressed the ring to the page of the book this time, hoping to circumvent the normal order of operations.

Words formed as if being written in front of us.

Who I am does not matter.
I have limited time.

I pressed the ring against the book once more. "Are you the Lightning Knight?"

Not anymore.

Two simple words and yet we could feel the sadness in his voice. If he had a voice.

"What do you want?" I whispered.

For a moment, he didn't reply. I couldn't blame him. If any of the stories were true, then losing out on being the Lightning Knight would have devastated me too. But an answer did appear.

I've been waiting for my progeny.
To become the new Lightning Knight.
It is the only way to save magic.

"Wait, is he saying someone related to him is alive?" Po asked.

Yokel looked up from the book. "I think h-he's s-saying that one of us m-might be r-related to him."

We all stiffened our backs and shifted in our seats. Could Yokel be right? Was the descendent of THE Lightning Knight one of us? I thought about the idea quickly, running through the scenario in my head where I was the one to carry the mantle. It was exhilarating and beyond anything I could have imagined. I spied Roc drifting off into what I had to assume was a similar dream, and Yokel was counting his fingers in an obvious attempt to understand his own lineage.

Before I could ask another question, Haralabos answered.

Hugo.
He will be the one to save us all.

Stunned wasn't the right word. Po, to his credit, wasn't breathing at all, so this must have been as much of a surprise to him as it was to us.

"Po, did you know that you were related to the Lightning Knight?" Pathfinder finally asked.

Po gasped for air as if he had just broken the surface of the ocean after a visit to its depths. "I had no idea. It can't be true. I'm not that special. I'm just... just—"

Haralabos spoke once more and the initial dive of the five of our heads collided in spectacular fashion.

You must find the Th'aumaturgy Codex.
Go to Romir and find the Fool.
He will be your guide.

"What's a Th'aumaturgy Codex?" Yokel wondered. I wondered who the Fool was supposed to be and why he was in Romir. Haralabos continued at a frenetic pace.

The Spiders are searching.
They must not get it.
She must not get it.

I panicked. "Who is she? Who's the fool? Why are the Spiders looking for it? Where are you?" I could feel the power waning, but I didn't want Haralabos to leave us.

I am out of time.

Find the Codex.

Train the Lightning Knight.

Save m

And like that, Haralabos was silent once more. We stood staring at the book, each of us willing ourselves to understand. Yokel was the first to speak.

"Where did he go?"

"What did that last part mean?" Windrunner sounded almost annoyed.

I knew the answer to her question because I could feel it.

"I think he ran out of, um, magic? Or power? Whatever he was using to talk to us, I don't think he'll be doing it anymore."

Pathfinder stood up and started pacing, repeating all the aspects of our conversation with Haralabos. "Why did he have to be so mysterious about it all?"

"So, if anyone found this, they'd have just as hard a time deciphering it as we would," Roc explained. "I don't like this."

"Don't like what?" I asked defensively. I knew this was going to be a fight, but it was one I felt we needed to have.

"You know what. Magic, Po, all of it. It's dangerous!"

He wasn't wrong, but he wasn't right either. This was bigger than his fears, bigger than all of us. It was my quest to protect Po. It was my quest to find magic. I couldn't let all that go.

I wouldn't.

I searched for a persuasive argument. "Look, we have to do this. If we don't—"

"If we don't, then what? Someone else will? Good, let them. I say we throw this book into the ocean and forget about it. We don't need this."

"Yes, we do!" I yelled back.

"Boys, settle down!" Windrunner said as she pointed to Po, who wore an expressionless face. He must have been nervous beyond belief, and here Roc and I were arguing around him.

"Po, what do you think about all this?" Pathfinder asked. Po didn't speak for a full two minutes, but I could tell his little mind was processing everything.

Finally, he spoke. "Magic is real, and I know who I am now. I'm Hugo Pondarion, named for my grandfather, descendent of Haralabos, and I am supposed to be the Lightning Knight."

Roc fell to his knees in front of his small friend. His voice trembled when he spoke. "Po, it's too dangerous."

"I know, Roc, but I need to follow my heart and do the right thing, and the right thing is to save magic."

Po was truly a knight in everything but title.

I walked over and took a knee next to Roc. Yokel did the same, and Pathfinder and Windrunner followed. I took out my sword and held it in front of me.

"I pledge myself to you, to go where you go and fight what you fight. I will follow you to the ends of the world and beyond if need be. You have my sword."

Before everyone else could pledge similarly, Po held up his hand to stop them.

"No, please stand up." We did as he commanded, albeit looking at each other in confusion. "My grandpa used to tell me something, that people weren't meant to be masters, they were meant to be in service to one another." Po was now the one kneeling, his small sword pointed toward the roofs below.

Roc was the first to speak. "What do we do next?" All the reservations he had about magic, about Haralabos, and about the danger it posed must have been overshadowed by his love for Po.

Po stood and put his hand out in front of him, inviting us all to join in as he replied, "I don't know, but I do know, we do it together."

# THE BLACK PRINCE

Wat had once been my solitary quest to protect Po was now ours. Po was going to be the new Lightning Knight, so he would need all the help we could give him. Yokel would tutor him with his studies at the Institute, and Windrunner would mentor him even further with special access I gave her to the Shears's restricted books. Of course, no section in the giant library was off limits to my family, given our history. I would continue with his Carpenter training, and Roc and Pathfinder would act as his personal bodyguards day and night. We weren't taking any chances with the Spider's Web out there.

And there was Ridhan, who also wanted to become the Lightning Knight. I just didn't know how he planned to do it. I knew it had to do with me, and probably that Elven-sounding codex, but beyond that it was a mystery.

There was only one small problem with our plan. We were supposed to be training Po to become the Lightning Knight, which meant he needed to learn to use magic, which none of us knew anything about. Yokel's knowledge stopped at the years of rumors and the incident that killed Roc's parents. Pathfinder and Windrunner only knew scraps of information they gleaned from their infiltration of the Spider's Web. Roc either didn't know or didn't care to know anything even remotely related to magic. All my knowledge came from children's stories, of which I couldn't be sure what was exaggeration and what was truth. The only thing we had to go on was half a world away in Romir, a kingdom notoriously unwelcoming to foreign travelers.

And so, the task of learning anything we could about magic in Starfall fell to Pathfinder and me.

It was wonderful.

We'd spent the better part of every night for the last two weeks scouring rooftops, eavesdropping on conversations, and searching for any clues that might aid us. Any rumor, theory, or drunken bard's tale we listened to, all the while growing closer and closer to each other.

I was smitten.

There was something familiar about her, like the smell of my room after a long trip. She was smart—no, she was intelligent. Athletic and nimble. And she had that cute little accent. And she was beautiful, she had to be, although I didn't know for sure because she hid behind her mask at all times.

"Oi, you're off in the clouds again, mate," she said with her metallic voice, bumping me with her shoulder. I'd met her atop the roof of the Shears, surveying my city below. Starfall was pulsing with life and music and people. Homecoming would begin tomorrow, and the annual weeklong festival would pack Starfall with more people than the city could handle. Taverns, brothels, and inns would burst at the seams with travelers coming in from the seas before the winter storms began. The piers would be lined with every type of boat, spending the months at dock being serviced. Even traveling out to the Forge would be rare as the billowing waves would toss even the sturdiest of ships.

The festival was named Homecoming because that's exactly what it was, a homecoming for all the sailors at sea, merchants who had traveled to other kingdoms, farmers, and everyone else from all over the South, from Starfall to the Neck. The festival was bookended by the Starfall City Jousting Tournament. It was a tournament unlike any other, a true spectacle, and only dwarfed by the World Championship in Romir.

Everything was going according to plan.

If Roc could win the Starfall Tournament for the second year in a row, we would have the perfect cover for traveling to Romir to find the codex. If we left the South without a valid enough reason at this time of year, when everyone was supposedly coming home for the winter months, we feared it might put the Spider's Web on our trail and signal to them our true identities. We needed the Web to stay in the South.

We also needed a way to leave the Institute for a month without being expelled for the year. But we would deal with that problem when we came to it.

I nudged Pathfinder back. "It's really something, isn't it?"

"How do you mean?"

"You're not from here, but Homecoming is a big deal in these parts. The biggest deal really. It's the one time when everyone comes together to celebrate. It's my favorite time of the year."

"How you know I'm not from here?" Pathfinder swung her legs over the edge, dangling them dangerously out from the safety of the rooftop.

"The accent. Land's End, right? Imperial Capital? I know a girl who came from there, but she lost her accent a while ago." I sat next to Pathfinder, my stomach dropping as I looked down.

Pathfinder leaned on her arm, placing it excruciatingly close to my own. "Oh, tell me about this girl. Maybe I know her."

I laughed awkwardly. "I highly doubt that. She moved here maybe five years ago, and I don't think you run in the same circles."

"And you think I run in squares or something?"

Nine Gods she's cute.

"No, no, I meant she's a lady, a noble. And you, well, you are..." I couldn't find the right words, and I was fumbling everything. I would have thought that after two straight weeks with Pathfinder it'd be easier, but it never was.

"A vigilante? A ne'er-do-well? A villainous huntress?"

I smiled widely. "A badass."

She laughed and I thought about how I didn't know her real name, nor had I ever seen her face. But my heart beat so loudly when I was with her, I thought I might die.

"So, this noble, this laaaaaady. I take it you fancy her?"

The thought of Iris overcame my infatuation for Pathfinder, as if I had dusted it off after taking it from an old shelf. The feelings came back so easily, and I began to rattle off my thoughts. "Well, yes I do. She's, wow, she's something else. She's strong and fierce and independent and... did I tell you she actually was courting my mortal enemy? Yeah, courting Ridhan himself, but not really. It was all to protect me. She's smart and funny, oh gods so funny. And when she laughs her nose crinkles up like this and—"

"Sounds like she's the one," Pathfinder interrupted as I mimed Iris's laugh. "So why aren't you with her tonight?"

"Because I messed up, royally. Like messed up in a way that will be retold for all time."

"I doubt it was that bad."

"I treated her like she was helpless and then she slapped me," I said with an air of finality.

"That'll do it, mate," Pathfinder replied. "But… and speaking as a member of the sisterhood, I very much doubt she hates you."

"No, she hates me alright. Did I mention the slap?"

"You did, but how 'bout I let you in on a little secret we women have. Now don't go telling the others, or else I'll be kicked out of aforementioned hood, but she slapped you because she still likes you. You were just an arse, and now you've got to win her back."

For weeks, maybe months, I had given up on a life with Iris. I had tried to bury my thoughts and feelings for her deep down where I couldn't find them, and now there was hope! Hope from the person to whom my affections had shifted. Was Pathfinder moving me into the friendzone? Did she even like me like that? Did she like women instead? She did mention something about a sisterhood.

"You really think so?"

"I'm certain of it. All you need to do is show her she's worth fighting for. Show her you're not afraid to embarrass yourself like you embarrassed her."

"But what if there was someone else?"

"Oh, I didn't know she was courting someone new."

"No, I didn't mean Iris," I said, leaning closer to my masked friend. I could just about see her eyes, but even as I tried to ascertain her features more closely, my focus blurred and her ornate choker shimmered. Whatever she was using to mask her voice apparently also helped mask her eyes. She moved closer to me, and instinctively I reached for her mask.

She popped up from her seat and drew her sword playfully. "Come here," she commanded, and I obeyed. I drew my sword and stood in front of her as the setting sun threw brilliant colors into the sky above us.

"A quick match to one point," she said as her sword danced.

"What do I get if I win?" I asked, spinning the sword in my hand. We'd sparred each night but always in a controlled environment. Never to see which of us was truly the better.

It was me, of course.

She put her hand to her chin. "If you win, I tell you a secret."

I was thoroughly intrigued. "And if I lose?"

"You'll see!"

She lunged. I parried her attack easily, following her step into a right-sided feint, her double grip affording her the fulcrum to complete a swift leftward sweep. Suddenly, she pulled into the space on her right, slapping her pommel sharply with her left hand, jarring into my own sword and knocking it from my hands so it went skidding across the roof. Continuing her momentum, she hip-checked me, throwing me over her shoulder and flipping me to the floor. She mounted my torso, her knees pinning my arms down, her face and her blade inches from my throat.

As far as losses went, it could have been worse.

We both stayed there as the light escaped the horizon and the darkness of night enveloped us both. I struggled my left arm away from her knee and she relented. I reached for her mask once more.

"No." She stopped my hand gently and placed it over my eyes, blinding me. My body quivered and a breeze danced along my cool lips. Suddenly they were met by warmth and softness and all thoughts ceased. It could have lasted a moment or a thousand years and I wouldn't have known. Pathfinder pulled away and I put my own hand over my eyes, praying for another kiss.

Instead, I felt pressure along my cheek and a voice whisper into my ear, "Go get your Iris, little lord. She's waiting for you."

The pressure on my chest lifted, but I stayed still for another minute, unsure what to do next. Letting go of my face, I looked around and found myself alone. Did that just really happen? What just happened? I was so confused I thought my heart would explode. Was I supposed to go after her? Was I supposed to go after Iris? A million and one questions ran through my head, and as the sky darkened, I let my thoughts dance along the wind. But eventually, the dinner scheduled by Reagan awaited me at the Anvil, so I headed home, utterly confused.

I joined Roc on the third-level interior balcony of my home, peering over the banister to an orchestra below, and relayed my conversation with Pathfinder, leaving out some of the more intimate details.

"What do you think that means?" Roc asked as he fidgeted in his formal suit. Reagan hadn't given us any clue as to what was happening tonight except to dress for the occasion.

I shook my head. "I don't know."

"Discussing anything interesting?" Reagan asked as she sauntered up to us.

"Oliver's love life," Roc said quickly.

"What love life, am I right?" Reagan joked and they both laughed too loud and too hard and I hated them. I walked away and down the stairs, exasperated with them both, but they followed like puppy dogs, mocking me the whole way.

"Why can't you two have anything helpful to say?" I asked.

"I can be helpful!" Yokel yelled as he burst through the entrance out of breath. "But first, you'll never guess who's coming to dinner tonight!" Before we could answer, he continued, "The p-prince! It's, it's the prince!"

"The prince of what?" Roc and I both asked.

"THE prince. The High Queen's son."

"Since when does she have a claimed son?" I retorted smugly.

The High Queen ruled the entire continent, allowing kingdoms and queendoms and cities like Starfall to operate with a certain degree of autonomy, and it'd been that way for centuries. The High Queen had reigned longer than any person in known history, due to her divine gift from the Nine Gods. Long ago they had given her everlasting life to rule over the continent. She was our high priestess, our singular connection with the gods, and our way to spiritual immortality.

But I had always liked the rumor that she was secretly an elf who would paint her skin every day to hide her markings. It was silly, but the South had less regard for the High Queen than the rest of the country did. It was mostly due to the fact that she had never, in her entire time as ruler, visited the Southern peninsula. To have one of her children here was very peculiar.

The doors opened behind Yokel, and a royal coterie of attendants entered, followed by a boy who looked about as old as we were.

An attendant announced, "Your Royal Highness Prince Kitanchulee Amuka—"

"Please, you can call me Kit," the prince said, bowing his head and awkwardly avoiding eye contact. He was a decently handsome boy with sharper features than my own and short, meticulously kept black hair. He wore a midnight-black suit jacket with a black shirt and black pants. This was the Southern style alright, but even that was a lot of dark tones for any outfit.

"The pleasure is ours, Your Highness," I replied in a courteous reflex.

"Oh, no please, it's Kit." He waved his hand in an apologetic manner. I caught his gaze ever so briefly. There was something strange about him, but I couldn't quite understand what it was.

"I'm sorry, Your Highness, forgive me," I replied, unwilling to give ground with the comfortable formal distance between us. The prince's head shot up, staring me down with a commanding air. Why I had decided to disobey a direct order from a high royal was beyond me. Something inside me screamed against him, willing me to contradict everything he said, but I held a simultaneous urge to trust him, as if we had met an understanding neither of us knew anything about.

He turned and took Reagan's hand, kissing it gently. "Lady Quartermaine, thank you for the invitation. I am curious how you knew I would be visiting Starfall."

"I think you'll find I know a lot of things," Reagan said flirtatiously.

We moved into the dining hall even as the Black Prince dismissed all his attendants and guards. Wanting to get a measure of this prince who sat in front of me as we ate, I decided to take stock of him. "I see Your Highness has chosen the Southern style of formal wear tonight. I believe I can speak for all of us here in Starfall City when I say we thank you for your thoughtfulness."

He didn't answer for a moment, and a silence lingered a moment longer than was comfortable. I battled against his expression, not wanting to lose the staring contest for reasons I couldn't understand. I felt as if my soul had met its mirrored image, and that feeling was pushing me to subconsciously reject this boy through a petty game of titles and politics. My mind wavered for a moment and I blinked. The Black Prince turned back to his food.

"Yes, you are most welcome. I find the Southern style quite comforting, although with this heat I would have expected something a bit more breathable." He paused to accommodate the polite giggles before turning to Roc.

"You are Lord Roclan, yes? Your description precedes you, as does your reputation in the joust."

"I am, Your Highness, but I'm sorry, I'm not a lord," Roc said without any of the bitterness that normally accompanied the reply.

"Please, m'lord, call me Kit."

Don't fall for the trap, Roc, don't do it.

"Apologies... Kit. But I am not a lord. My uncle is but a simple hedge knight."

A short-lived smile disappeared from the Black Prince's face as he turned again to his meal. "No apologies necessary. I'm sure that you will be elevated to lordship soon enough. You do plan to compete in the World Championship in Romir? The rightful Starfall representative was sorely missed last year." The Black Prince was talking to the table, but Roc answered anyway.

"That is the plan, Kit, but first I have to win the Starfall City Tournament."

"But you will win, won't you? From what I've heard you may very well have won the World Championship in Romir last year if you had competed. Why didn't you make the trip to the Iron Kingdom?"

Embarrassment and anger washed over Roc's face and I could see his hand turn white squeezing his spoon.

"The Institute didn't afford me the leave I needed to compete. But I have no plans to lose either tournament this year, and you can put money on that," Roc said firmly.

After winning the Starfall Tournament last year and having to see the runner-up leave to compete in Romir, we had sworn to find some way to attend this year. For Roc, that meant the prospect of losing out on his education and a means to rise above his station, but I hoped we might yet find another way.

Reagan gracefully changed the subject. "So, Your Highness, tell us more about yourself. Here in the South it came as a bit of a surprise that the High Queen even had a claimed son and then for us to find out you were visiting the South."

The prince kept his eyes averted as he answered. "I never knew my father, and although you are correct that normally my mother's children wouldn't have claim to title, my mother has taken a particular interest in me." He sounded both happy and contemplative. Over so many years, he must have had brothers and sisters, nieces and nephews, and Nine knows how many cousins. None of them were afforded titles, though they did enjoy a modicum of fame.

"That sounds like it could cause quite the problem during family reunions, Your Highness," I said. It was true that over the hundreds of years of the High Queen's rule, rebellions would arise with usurpers to her throne, but they were always quashed by her Imperial Army.

"Kit," the Black Prince corrected, boring into me with his eyes. I didn't know why my defiance was so important, but a strong uneasiness had entered my mind like a cloud, urging me to keep a solid foothold.

Perceptive as always, Reagan spoke up. "So, Kit, why all the interest in jousting? Are you contemplating taking up the lance?"

The prince broke eye contact with me after a moment of hesitation and stared off past Reagan's head at a portrait of an ancestral Quartermaine on the wall.

"Actually, I must admit, I am purely a fan. The lance was never an area of strength for me. I'm partial to the sword myself. My interests in my visit are purely selfish. I seek to find the best, and the rumors of Lord Roclan's skills reach even the ears in Land's End."

Roc gaped. "You came here to see me?"

"One of the reasons. The other is to chase down another rumor." He looked at me. "I know a knight from Mercyhold who told me a tale of a fighter from Starfall. The only one who had ever bested him in a match. A fighter whose training came from the famous Workshop."

I immediately looked at Reagan and gave her every sign with my face to not mention anything about the Workshop, but she disregarded all of them.

Nine Hells.

"Oh, is that so? Well, it just so happens Oliver here is a Carpenter, one of the highest-ranking Carpen—"

"Carpenters do not have ranks," the Black Prince and I said in unison, catching me off guard.

"Sir Declan did not disappoint in his tale, Lord Quartermaine. You truly are interesting." He paused for a moment. "Would it be an imposition to go to the Workshop?"

"Anything for you, Your Highness, just name the time," I replied, hoping to stall. This entire night was getting out of control.

"Now."

"Uh, sure, I suppose that works, although I doubt there will be any Carpenters there at this hour." Why did he want to go all of a sudden? What was I missing?

"There will be at least one," he said, motioning to me with his hand. "But we can wait until after we have finished our meal." He continued eating and I looked at Reagan who only shrugged as the servers approached.

"Oh, my favorite, dessert!" the Black Prince exclaimed.

The Black Prince accompanied me to the Workshop by foot. It was an awkwardly long journey, given we had to travel across the entire city and into the Narrows. It started out in silence, but I quickly became bored of that. Even with the Black Prince in my company, all I could think about was Iris and what to do.

"Is there anything particularly interesting on your mind, Lord Quartermaine?" the Black Prince asked, acknowledging the absence of my full attention. I tried to think about any number of interesting topics, but in the end, the thought of Iris overwhelmed me.

"Actually, I was just thinking about a girl," I blurted out. I stopped in a panic, staring at the Black Prince. Had he somehow tricked me into saying that?

"Oh, matters of the heart. Yes, I am familiar with such preoccupations." The Black Prince stared off into the city and then continued walking. "Please, regale me with tales of your romance. Maybe I can help."

I was stunned, but for some reason, I began to tell the Black Prince all there was to know about my romantic quandary. The more I talked, the more I divulged, until I was sure I had told the Black Prince everything, including her dress measurements.

What power did this Black Prince hold over me?

Strangely, he listened attentively, and when I had finally run out of breath, he offered up some advice.

"If I understand this Iris as you've described her, it seems she wouldn't be opposed to a greater display of your affection."

"What do you mean by that?" I asked as we slipped into the Narrows.

"I find a song is always appreciated," he replied as we approached the door to the Workshop.

"I'll take that into consideration, thanks," I said with all sincerity as I pulled a key from my pocket and unlocked the door. Inside, I lit six lanterns along the pillars, illuminating the floors and the practice weapons lining the walls.

"So, this is the Workshop. I've heard tales of this place, but nothing can quite adequately describe its…" He trailed off, searching for a word along the walls and ceilings.

"Simplicity I believe is the word you're looking for, Your Highness," I finished for him.

He clapped in approval. "Yes! That's it. It's so simple, but so perfect, perfect." His demeanor was different. He seemed less shy and a little more… affable?

The Black Prince walked over to a wall and grabbed two practice swords, making his way back to the center of the room and tossing one to me. He nimbly spun his in his hand until it rested in a ready position. I took the cue and readied my sword as well.

What in the Nine Hells was going on right now?

Slowly and exaggeratedly, he swung his sword in a long overhead motion toward me and I easily parried as the two of us went through an improvised warmup.

"They say you truly learn about someone in the ring. I've found you truly learn about someone when they aren't pretending to be who they are not," The clink of our swords started to speed up, creating a rhythm to his words. "So, tell me, Oliver Quartermaine, who are you?"

"I don't believe I understand, Your Highness," I replied as his slashes and thrusts started to become more pronounced and with greater speed and strength.

You want to play tough, let's play tough.

"See! Right there, I told you to call me Kit. You want to call me Kit, I know you do. Deep down, you desire so much to follow my commands, and yet you don't. Why is that?"

The Black Prince started to step in a circular pattern, and I moved to compensate. We locked eyes, not looking at our feet but knowing right where to move.

I grinned. "I don't know, Your Highness. I may just be a bit stubborn." This was as much a mental exercise as it was physical, and it was just another series of games I didn't care to lose tonight. Not against him. I felt no contempt, nor did I want to see him fail. I respected him, but I felt as though his success would be my failure.

"No, no, I don't think that's it. Tell me, Oliver, who are you?" With every word he spoke, a slash came at me.

"A leader?" Clink.

"A killer or a scholar?" Clink, clink.

"A beast? A soldier? A force of nature? A villain? A savior?" Clink, clink, clink, clink, clink.

"What are you?!" He yelled this final question and launched into a full-on assault, flowing in and out of different offensive and defensive forms. His technique was perfect, and he compensated for every form's weakness with the perfect counter of the next. He wasn't lying when he said he was partial to the sword, and what an understatement that was. He was almost as good as I was.

Almost.

I broke into a flurry of counters and attacks equal to his, but after lulling him to a state of acceptance that our techniques and knowledge were equal, I feigned a thrust, waited for the parry, and dropped the tip of my sword down, creating a fulcrum with my left hand, slapping the pommel down as hard as I could and expertly disarming the Black Prince in exactly the same fashion that Pathfinder had disarmed me. Without the romantic tension.

The metal of the sword made a dull impact on the dirt floor as it landed, and the tip of my sword was resting just under the Black Prince's chin.

"Yield, Your Highness."

I wasn't losing this fight, nor any other tonight.

"The stories about this place did not disappoint, nor have the stories about you." His arms were raised, yielding his position, but I refused to lower my sword.

How many stories exactly had he heard, and what were they?

He lowered his eyes to my sword, and I snapped out of thought.

"Glad I could live up to expectations. But if you'll excuse me, Your Highness, what exactly were those expectations?"

"I believe you'll find out in the spring. The next time we meet, I expect, will be in the Ring of Fire, and I'll be sure not to fall for that little trick again." He shook his head. "Ah, so simple yet so effective."

"Much like the Workshop."

He chuckled. "Tell Azel, my most gracious thanks for the invitation." He walked toward the door, turning at the last moment and looking past me. "Oliver, you never did answer me. Who are you?"

It was a question I didn't know how to answer. I was Oliver, I was a student, a son, brother, and a friend—but none of those things, I thought, was what he was looking for.

"I don't know… Kit."

I'd give him one win.

"A champion, I dare say, but we will see."

He left and the door closed behind him loudly. I felt as though my mind had just been trampled by twenty horses. The mental energy of the fight and the conversation had left me exhausted. A creak of a door sounded behind me and I turned.

"I think it is time you learned the final form," Azel said, slowly walking with her stick out in front.

"I didn't know you were here, Carpenter," I responded, superfluously bowing my head. "What final form? I know all twenty-four already."

She stood in front of me, the flickering of the lamps casting odd shadows on her face.

"The Original Form," she stated, as if I was supposed to know what that meant.

"The Original Form?"

Azel held up a fist and then unfurled her fingers, showing an empty palm facing toward the ceiling. "Form Zero. Empty hands."

"Empty what?"

# LOVESICK

"This has got to be either the most brilliant idea we've ever had, or the stupidest," I proclaimed to Whiskey Danger as we huddled near the edge of the dining hall at the Institute.

"Oh, this is absolutely the stupidest thing we've ever thought of," Roc answered.

"Yes, there is a zero percent chance this works," Yokel calculated.

"Not going to lie, Oliver, I've heard of better plans," Po admitted.

"Thanks for the votes of confidence, guys."

Roc slapped my back heartily. "That's what friends are for!"

Today was the day I would win Iris back, with an elaborate display of embarrassment for myself and love for her. I was going to show her she was worth fighting for, and the Black Prince had given me the idea.

If this doesn't work, I'm walking off a cliff.

Iris and her friends had seated themselves directly in the middle of the hall for lunch, just as we had planned. Everything was lining up perfectly, and perfection is exactly what we needed. If we didn't execute everything precisely, it would blow up in our faces. My face. I only had one chance to make this right.

We'd stayed up all night planning, and miraculously Po had taught the entire First Year Class the drum beat Yokel had created all within a single morning. He'd even secretly given each of them a pair of wooden sticks Roc had been gracious enough to cut. The orchestra Yokel played in had set up on the stage at the end of the hall, but as per usual, no one paid them much mind. This would either be the single greatest musical show the Institute had ever seen, or more likely than not, Yokel, Roc, Po and I were going to get detention, literally forever.

"Okay, boys, sound off, how are we looking?" I asked, ignoring their negative comments.

"The freshies are ready to go, Oliver, just waiting on the signal." Po bobbed his head back and forth to the beat he'd learned this morning. He smiled at a couple of freshie girls sitting at a table. He was enjoying his newfound popularity for joining Whiskey Danger.

Yokel was the second to answer. "The orchestra is ready. I've had this melody written for quite a while, and if I must say, we may be even better than the Imperial Orchestra. Did you know, last year I.O. tried to play —"

"We get it, Yokel, calm down. How we looking, Roc?"

"Just waiting for our honored guests! They should be here any minute."

"Excellent. Everyone get into position. See you on the other side!"

On that, we all raised our hands, and without a count, clapped in unison.

I love you guys.

As we approached our positions, a group of professors entered the dining hall. Not a moment after they crossed the threshold, Roc walked directly into them, not slowing his pace. His large mass bowled them over and back out into the hallway, and as luck would have it, right into Ridhan and his Sharks. A tapestry was cut down by a freshie and they were all entangled in the kerfuffle.

Perfect.

Two freshies closed the doors behind them and near silence descended on the room as everyone turned to see the commotion. Whispers darted around the small groups of students as they waited for a cue to resume their teenage deliberations. The moment had finally arrived, and I could feel my heart racing. What in the Nine Hells was I doing? This wasn't going to work.

Don't think that way. You can do this.

I sighed, remembering all that my friends had done to help me get to this moment, right down to Roc holding off the professors.

I spoke to myself under my breath. "You've got this, Oliver, now knight up and let's do this crazy thing." I nodded to Yokel and then to Po. They were ready and waiting, and there was no turning back now.

I jumped on top of one of the tables in Iris's row and yelled as loud as I could without sounding unintelligible. "Hello? Hello everybody! As many of you may know, I'm Oliver Quartermaine."

A few laughs rose, but most of the students just stared at me.

"I, uh, I have something very important to say, and I need you all to hear it."

The entire room fell silent, and I could hear my heartbeat through my chest.

An anonymous voice from the crowd yelled out. "I have something important to say as well." A loud explosion of flatulence accompanied his heckle as well as laughter and a few students who evacuated the blast radius. But the moment when I could have forfeited my plan had passed, and the room was once again mine to command.

And here, we, go.

"I LOVE THIS GIRL!" My finger pointed directly at Iris. "I love her! I do. I'm not ashamed to admit it. And I want everyone here to know!"

The sound of a fork falling on a plate echoed through the still air. My breath felt as heavy as lead while I looked around for any sign that this wasn't the stupidest thing I had ever done. Iris could have been mistaken for a ghost given her embarrassment, but I had already started and I needed to get it all out.

"I also want you to know one other thing. I am an idiot. I'm an idiot and I've done some dumb things, said some dumb things, but I'm hoping… well, I'm hoping that this will make up for all of that."

I looked at Po and gave him a wink. On cue the freshies took out their sticks and Po yelled out, "One, two, three, four" and in unison, they all started to drum away at the beat. After a quick succession of taps on the table, the orchestra joined in with Yokel on guitar accompanied by an assortment of violins, cellos, a double bass, and even a scattering of flutes and reed horns tootling along to the intro. A melody started to play and on the downbeat of the final bar of the intro, I started to sing.

> "I was stupid I'm so sorry
> I was acting a little crazy,
> I was a little bit hazy,
> Haven't any decent excuse."

I started to walk down the table, avoiding cups and food with each unconscious step. I let myself fall into the beat of the song and lyrics, doing my best impersonation of Roc when he accepted the adulation of his fans.

After a few more down beats the melody continued.

> "Kissing you has blown my mind
> I feel like I am already dying,
> I feel like I could go flying,
> I wonder if you are feeling the same.
> If you do, please stop me right now."

Iris's cheeks colored, but she quickly gave way to a smile when her friends started to giggle.

Oh, ladies, I've barely even started.

I spun around quickly to face the crowd, singing to them as if they were fans of a famous bard, and that bard was me. If I was to embarrass myself in front of the whole of the Institute, I was going to do it in style. With background vocals singing, I continued.

> "I'm lovesick and I'm not well
> And I can't stand how far I fell."

I jumped off the table and onto the floor between the rows. The crowd started clapping along a steady beat with the freshies, and I turned around and started slowly shuffle-dancing forward, throwing my shoulders in rhythm to the beat as I made my way toward Iris.

> "Many women in the world
> But none of them are who I am dreaming,
> You know you give me that feeling,
> And I can't get you out of my head."

I jumped in a zigzag pattern with both my feet timed perfectly to the quick change in tempo, and landing on the final beat, I fell to my knees with my hands cupped in front of my body.

> "Let me tell a story it begins
> With me, being shortsighted,
> And then you felt a bit slighted,

You got me down on my knees why won't you please forgive me"

Popping up and landing on my feet on the last word, I backtracked toward the stage and away from Iris. Her face was now scarlet, but she was tapping along to the song with everyone else in the hall.

I just needed Roc to hold off a little longer. As I made my way back to the stage, I sang the chorus again.

> "I'm lovesick and I'm not well
> And I can't stand, how far I fell.
> I'm lovesick and I'm not well,
> It hurts so bad, I'm in Nine Hells."

As I sang the added bars of the chorus, I grabbed an extra guitar from the stand, threw the strap on, and jumped up onto the stage.

Yokel and I exaggerated each beat of the bridge, leaning back to back on each other for support as we milked the emotion of the words. In full dramatic flair, we inched down closer to the floor of the stage, climbing back up with the tempo for the final verses.

> "I want to hold your hand,
> I want to be your man,
> And I don't care who knows.
> I just want you to feel the same,
> I'm sorry I'm so lame,
> Please won't you be my dame,
> Did I say dame?
> I just said dame."

I pulled the lute off my body before the last word, throwing it into the hands of a waiting freshie and flying off the stage. Landing emphatically on the first word of the next verse, and walking casually to Iris, I continued.
> "Please forgive me, please forgive me
> I know I'm running out of excuses,
> All this singing is useless,
> I think I'll try and go with a dance, please give me a chance."

Iris was now laughing and whooping, her hair flowing freely around her shoulders and over her face as she bounced to the beat. I started dancing instead of walking forward, making even more of a fool of myself. It didn't matter; the rush and euphoria of the entire event had taken over. It was contagious, and various students on either side of me stood up and danced in place, framing my performance. My face hurt from the strain of smiling and singing loudly, but I could feel the pulse of the crowd, willing me to continue into the final verse.

Time to take it home, Oliver.

"You're the best thing in my life
And somehow never cease to amaze me,
It makes me a little crazy,
So could you please decide before we run out of time, woah!"

I was still a bit away from Iris, but she began running toward me, excitement in her eyes. I caught her with both arms, and her lips were instantly on mine, the crowd of students cheering for us as I spun us around. The backup singers finished the final chorus for me, the students singing and dancing along with the words they had picked up.

"I'm lovesick and I'm not well,
And I can't stand, how far I fell.
I'm lovesick and I'm not well,
It hurts so bad, I'm in Nine Hells."

As the song ended, the entire dining hall erupted in excitement and cheering. I felt what I assumed were congratulatory slaps on the back, but with Iris in my arms, the rest of the world melted away.

"You're crazy, you know that, right?" she yelled as the other students danced around us.

"Crazy for you," I said and snuck a kiss. She laughed and tickled my neck in embarrassment. Everything was perfect. I was with the perfect girl, in a perfect world. We were the only two people and there was nothing that could bring me down. Suddenly, the crowd silenced, and I snapped out from my love coma to see what was wrong.

Professor Lortho was holding Roc by the collar.

"Everyone in this hall, out!" he yelled, and a riot of students evacuated through the doors. In the rush and chaos, I had lost Iris and all my other friends, and the only ones left in the hall were Lortho and I.

"Impressive display, Mr. Quartermaine."

"Uh, thanks?"

"I believe this may be cause for expulsion, for you and your co-conspirators."

I gasped. I didn't care so much about myself, but Roc and Yokel and Po, matriculating from the Institute would open doors for their lives that nothing else could. Po may become the Lightning Knight, but he would still need the social status the Institute would provide.

"Professor, please don't. This was all me, they had noth—"

"You may be correct, Mr. Quartermaine. Possibly a suspension then. Say for one month. Enough time for you all to think about what you've done, maybe even go on a trip north. I hear Romir is particularly dreadful this time of year."

Professor Lortho smiled at me before turning to walk away. We now had our cover for a leave of absence from the Institute, so all we still needed was a reason to go to Romir. It was up to Roc now.

# THE STARFALL CITY JOUSTING TOURNAMENT

The Marshall of the Field pulled up the starting flag and Roc spurred his horse forward from our recess with incredible speed. His opponent had done the same, although he was half a moment slower, which was all the time Roc needed.

Jousting was as much a sport of precision as it was about strength and speed. Preparation was paramount, but more important was the ability to predict and react simultaneously. There were jousters who were strong and those who were fast. Some were even accurate, but rarely were they all three. There were so many variables to consider, all within a matter of seconds, that amateurs would more likely miss their target altogether. The speed at which the horses ran, the balance of the lance, the position of the rider, the weight of the armor—everything had to be considered, calculated, and recalculated each second.

For all that Roc lacked in his academic studies, he made up for with an uncanny ability to do the impossible on the field. In fact, the last time he missed a target was when he was twelve, and even then, it was Yokel's fault.

But now, not even Yokel could distract Roc. In the seconds between when his horse jumped to start its run and when his lance hit, Roc naturally saw each part of the field and calculated it to his advantage. It was truly a sight to behold, and I had the best seat in the place.

Mere seconds passed before the thundercrack of a hit and shards of splinters flew through the air. Cheers erupted from the grandstands to the cheap seats as Roc cantered back to Whiskey Danger and a blue flag was pegged to the scoreboard, sealing his victory.

"We're going to the finals! I can't believe it!" Po yelled as he grabbed the broken-tipped lance from Roc.

"I don't care," Roc said with a scowl. "We're going back to the Anvil."

He bumped past Yokel and back to our tent to undress as Yokel rubbed his own shoulder.

"You two stay here and watch the next semifinal match. I suspect Ridhan will be the winner, and we'll need all the intelligence we can get if we want to defeat him," I commanded.

We all knew why Roc was in a mood, but it still stung when he treated us with such disregard. I needed to confront him now, or else who knew where his head would be for the finals.

In the changing tent, Roc was struggling with the laces on his armor. After a moment, he yelled out in frustration when he spun and tripped over a stool, falling to the floor with his arms wrapped awkwardly around his body. I bent down to help and he once again yelled and turned away, kicking his feet in a tantrum.

"Go away!" he cried, uncharacteristic tears streaming down his face. I had never known Roc to cry except once a year on the anniversary of his parents' deaths. Given his uncle's own health, it now made sense.

"You need help!" I screamed back, pinning him down and undoing the laces.

"Not from you!"

I didn't let his comment deter me and while I untied the laces, I decided to speak my own mind.

"We're not having this discussion again. I told you before, you're as much my family as my actual family. I'm sorry I'm me, but the best chance your uncle has is at the Anvil and with our apothecary. You don't owe me anything, family never does."

This was a battle I wasn't letting my friend win. Sir Roclan had been on the decline for months, but just as the Homecoming Tournament had started, his health had fallen off a cliff. It was only after the biggest fight we'd ever had that Roc finally relented and the old knight was taken to my home to be cared for by our own apothecary, who happened to be the best in the entire South.

"Fine." Roc hated the charity, but when it came to his uncle, even his ego couldn't stand in the way. The walk back to the Anvil was silent, and when we arrived, Roc immediately ran to his uncle's bedside. Sweat drenched the old knight's forehead, and Roc desperately tried to cool him with a cloth and bowl of water. The apothecary took me aside in the hallway.

"I'm afraid Sir Roclan is in worse shape than I originally thought. I'm surprised he's lasted this long, to be honest, but his body is quickly failing him now. He won't make it to Black Sunday." Her advice was sharp but her expression was solemn. "Should I tell his son?"

My answer caught in my throat. "He-he's not... No, I'll tell him, thank you."

She left and I walked into the room, quietly listening as Roc recounted his most recent joust.

"You wouldn't believe it, a clean board! He couldn't hit me if he wanted to! You should have heard them, Uncle. They yelled and cheered... it was... You would have been so proud."

The old man lifted his head up. "They cheered for you? Did they yell your name?"

Roc slouched back into his chair. "Well, no, they kind of just hollered. But one day, they'll cheer our name, I promise you. You're the greatest knight this city has ever seen, and they know it." We all may have wanted that sentiment to be true, but the Roclans were from the Narrows, and even if Sir Roclan was a knight, the elites in the grandstands and boxes would never chant their name.

Or maybe they would.

A plan started to formulate in my head even as Sir Roclan beckoned me to his bedside. "Please, my lord. My nephew I'm sure has much to prepare for, and I would have a word with you, if you grant me one."

"Sir, whatever you request will be yours. And please, again, call me Oliver."

Roc kissed his uncle's forehead and left us alone.

"Of course, m'lord, old habits from an old man." He laughed. He still had that hedge knight charm, even like this.

"The apothecary has seen you. She's a family friend and the best in the South," I began, unsure how to look a man in the eye to tell him the news.

"A waste, m'lord, but appreciated nonetheless. I do not need an apothecary to tell me what I already know in my bones. I am dying."

He stated it so matter of factly that I almost didn't know how to respond. How could a man be so casual about his own mortality?

"It is alright, m'lord," he said as he reached out for my hand. I seized it gently and he squeezed it in response. "I have lived a life many could only dream of, serving lords and ladies, low-born and kings alike. I have no regrets in my life because of that young man you call your friend." My throat seized up as I stood, utterly speechless. "You know, I've loved that boy since the day my sister by law bore him into this world. Everything I've ever done was to make sure he had a good and safe life, so he could become a man with honor."

"You've done that, sir. He is one of the best people I know."

"Thank you, that means a great deal coming from you, m'lord, but apparently I can't live forever. Riley is at an important part of his life now, and I will not be there to guide him. He's a stubborn boy but there's much good inside him. He is going to need people to help him along. Do you think you can do that for me, m'lord? I know it's a lot to ask from someone such as myself—"

"Sir, it would be my honor." I watched as a tear fell down his ruddy cheek.

"Now, what exactly did the apothecary have to say?" His body may have been failing him, but Sir Roclan's mind was as sharp as ever.

"Sir, she said that you don't have much longer. Possibly to Black Sunday, maybe less." The words pierced my own heart like a knife.

"Ahh, I see. Well, not many of us are lucky enough to know when our life will end." He stared up at the ceiling, his eyes empty.

I opened my mouth only to close it again, unsure of what to say or how to comfort him. I had never been half as courageous as Sir Roclan, and I wasn't nearly as brave as his nephew, but I wanted to know how to be. I sighed, asking the only question that made any sense to me.

"Sir, are you scared? Scared of death, I mean."

Sir Roclan turned his head and smiled at me. "When you've lived the life I have, death is an old friend."

I furrowed my brow, and Sir Roclan replied, perhaps noticing my confusion. "I think you mean to ask a different question, m'lord."

I felt small and scared and was reminded of when Po first met Azel months ago. I remembered the question he had posed, and seeing this wise old knight in front of me, I thought of no one better to answer.

"How can you be brave all the time, sir?"

Sir Roclan relaxed, visibly melting into his bed with a knowing smile. "You don't have to be brave all the time, you only have to be brave once."

I repeated the phrase over and over in my head, willing the words to blossom into understanding. Sir Roclan coughed into a handkerchief, leaving a dark stain on the fabric and pulling my attention back to the present. His fingers were still wearing his three rings; one for each Knightly Act. He looked to me again, his gaze hollow, a chilling sadness washing over his expression.

"There is so much in a life that remains unfinished." He took off the ring on his third finger and held it out to me. "I am fondest of this ring. An Act of Honor, where I dared defy a lord's treatment of his subjects."

I smiled at the memory of Roc retelling the story to Yokel and me of how Roc's uncle had defeated an obnoxious lord in a duel, in front of the High Queen herself. Sir Roclan placed the ring in my hand.

"Now I must ask you to do me an honor, but it is a rather large thing, if I may ask it of it, m'lord?"

I looked at him. "I can't take your ring, sir."

"The ring is a symbol, Lord Quartermaine. A symbol of acknowledgment that I recognize all you have done and all you will do. For looking out for my boy for all these years and looking out for him for the years to come. And for accepting one last request from an old and dying man."

I gripped the ring tightly, letting my head sink to my chest. "Anything you ask, sir, I will see that it is done." I listened to his next words intently, nodding. "You have my word."

The following night was the final match of the tournament, and as predicted, we would be facing Ridhan for the title. As we sat in the tent preparing, an uneasy silence prevailed.

Roc broke the quiet. "Okay, Whiskey Danger, let's get started. Po, lead us off." He sat heavily on a stool as I shifted his armor and Po squeaked his rundown of the tournament.

"Right, so as we know, Ridhan may be the worst person ever, but he's been really making up for that with his jousting. I've watched every single one of his runs, and he hasn't been hit, for the entire tournament." Po's face turned sour as he searched for the words. "I've been watching all the runs, Roc, but I just don't see any weakness Ridhan has."

This was true, and also our worst nightmare. We had never seen anything like Ridhan in this tournament, and unfortunately, there were no clear paths to victory for us to take.

"Yokel, assessment?" Roc asked, hoping for better news from our eagle-eyed friend.

"Po is right. Ridhan s-seemingly has n-no weakness. His technique is flawless, he rides with speed and power, and his aim is true. Truer than should be possible. He hasn't m-missed a mark he's aimed for all tournament, and furthermore, no one can seem to even graze h-his armor."

Roc scoffed. "What do you mean by that?"

"I mean, he literally c-cannot be hit with a lance. Not this tournament anyway. I've n-never seen, seen anything like it." Yokel stuttered, avoiding Roc's questioning gaze.

"So, I can't hit him, and he never misses."

"Exactly!" Yokel and Po exclaimed together. Roc stood, taking up several poses as he moved around us, stretching his armor to move more freely at the joints.

"We have an opponent who is seemingly invincible and also unhittable. How exactly do I beat that?"

Silence fell over our group again, with each of us looking to another for the elusive answer. In all our time spent at the joust, we'd never come upon a problem like this.

A sharp knock on the shield outside the tent sounded, accompanied by a soothing voice.

"Hi, boys, is everyone decent in there?" Iris walked in with Reagan in tow. She gave me a quick kiss on the cheek and, noticing us all deep in thought, her expression turned from jovial to confused. "Are you all prepared, Riley?"

"Physically I am, but my brilliant strategists here"—he motioned to the room, sighing heavily—"nothing. We've got nothing. Any thoughts?"

Iris pinched my cheek playfully. "Oh, little lord, why don't you just sing them a song. That ought to make Ridhan go drown himself in the ocean!"

"Hey! I wasn't that bad, right, guys?"

Roc, Yokel, and Po each nervously turned away to avoid giving an answer.

My gaze landed on Reagan who was never shy to speak her mind. "Oh, you already know what I think about your singing, Ollie. But speaking of a plan, I actually do have one." She turned to Iris mischievously. "I believe some help is needed in our box. Could you meet me there?" Iris winked at me and left while Reagan pulled out a necklace from under her collar.

"A gift, from the prince."

"Why is the prince giving you gifts?" I asked pointedly.

"Oh, I don't know," she replied coyly, and I just about melted to the dirt floor in a puddle of brotherly embarrassment and rage. "But there's something peculiar about it."

"More peculiar than a prince giving you a necklace?"

"Ollie, I'm a big girl. Anyway, Yokel, put this on and do me a favor?" She put the necklace over Yokel's head as he did his absolute worst to avoid staring directly where he shouldn't have been staring. The necklace was a black oval tied by a simple brown string, nothing that would signify any wealth or status. Regan walked to the other side of the tent, picked up a rock, and hurled it at Yokel as hard as she could. Yokel had no time to react, but what should have been a dead-on hit glanced away at the last second.

We gaped at each other.

"Do it again." Roc handed Reagan a gauntlet without looking.

"Wait, don't I get a say in—"

But Yokel was interrupted by the flying piece of armor. Again, what should have been a sure strike glanced away, leaving Yokel unharmed.

"Holy Realms, what is that?" Po asked.

Reagan took the necklace back from Yokel. "I believe it's called a Relic? Like your ring, Ollie."

Stunned, I instinctively put my hand behind my back. "How do you —"

"I flirt and I know things," she replied pugnaciously. I hated her so much. And I loved her so much. I had a lot of feelings about my baby sister. "But, really, Iris told me about your night at the Shears. I don't know why you all don't come to me with your problems more often. I obviously know more than any of you."

"Obviously," Roc responded. "That must be why he's never been hit. He must be wearing one of these necklaces."

"Interesting, very interesting," Reagan repeated to herself.

"Welcome to our problem," I responded. "The question is, now that we know he's cheating, how do we beat him?"

Reagan began to simmer like a pot of water, pacing as she tapped her nose frantically with her finger. "I know what to do. Roc, if I get you one chance, you think you can hit him?"

"What is one hit going to—"

"You'll probably only get one, better make it count!" she yelled, racing from the tent.

"How in the Nine Hells am I supposed to win with only one hit? The only way that could happen is if—" His gaze drifted to mine and we both connected on the thought instantly.

"Yes!" I yelled, putting the last piece of the puzzle together in my head. "It's so simple but so incredibly difficult."

Po looked confused. "What's, what's simple?"

Yokel had figured out our plan and began to protest. "Oh no, there's no way this will work."

Roc laughed before replying gleefully, "Oh yes it will, Yok, and do you know why? Because it's just crazy enough to."

Yokel stopped his protest and smiled mischievously. "I like crazy."

We made our way to the entrance of the stadium and trumpets sounded as Roc and Ridhan crested into the crowds, people cheering and hollering loudly. Half the stadium was adorned in different shades of black, a nod to the house sigil of the Shipwights—a large sail ship being pulled by three black sharks. The other half of the stadium was adorned in the browns and reds of the Roclan coat of arms—a brown rooster in front of a rising red sun. Some of the students at the Institute had made banners and signs for people to hold and chant, but as the sun finally set and the planet above came out of hiding, a darkened dusk light fell upon the roofless stadium and the crowd became silent.

I bent down to Po and put my hands on his shoulders. "Now this is where it gets really fun." The night sky suddenly became illuminated by large colorful explosions, startling Po and many of the people in the stands.

"Nine Hells!" Po yelled, barely audible over the sounds of the fireworks.

"Language, kid!" Roc called, giving us all a wink and throwing his visor down with a clang.

I bent down to talk into Po's ear. "This is nothing. I've heard the World Championships are even crazier, and that the Circus puts on quite the show with fools and jesters and even wild animal tamers."

The fireworks died down, giving way to the black of night and soft crackling of torches. Suddenly, as if by magic, rings of fire exploded into existence around the stadium, lighting each of the four levels of seating along the walls. Lamps and large basins followed, illuminating the entire stadium and magnifying the forms of Ridhan and Roc, rearing their horses to a gallop around the ring, their house banners waving proudly in their hands. Amid the cheers and screams of the crowd, a gong rang to signify the start of the championship bout. An orator walked to the center of the tilt. He projected clearly in the direction of the nobles' boxes, completely disregarding the rest of the stadium, but the design and acoustics of the structure allowed everyone to hear his words.

"Lords and ladies, may I present to you, on this finest of evenings, the final two contenders for the Starfall City Jousting Tournament. For your consideration, managing to make it through to the final round with a tournament record of no lances against, Lord Ridhan Shipwight!" In response, all of the darkly clad "Shark Heads" in the crowd redoubled their efforts to split the night sky with their deafening roars, cheering on their young lord. I laughed, mindful of the surprise Po had prepared with help from many freshie girls, all of whom were thoroughly convinced that Roc was the most attractive boy Starfall had ever seen. When the Shark Heads' bellowing lessened, the orator turned again to the nobles' boxes.

"And to my right, the defending Starfall Champion, Riley Roclan!" Upon hearing the name, all the "Roosters" in the crowd donned their newly feathered caps, crowing in a single voice louder than anything the South had heard for a hundred years.

"Do you hear that, Roc? That's for you. They're all here, for you. They're all cheering for *your* house, *your* name, *your* uncle's name!" I pointed toward my family's box, and standing next to Iris, clapping along in his full set of armor, was Sir Roclan. His face beamed with pride. It had been his final request that he might see his nephew joust one last time.

"Oliver…" Roc gasped.

"He's here for you, Roc. We're all here for you. You're the one we chose to follow."

He looked at me, his face flushed and eyes determined to keep his composure. "I'd punch you right now I wasn't mounted," Roc responded with a laugh.

I smiled. "I'll punch Yokel and we'll call it even. Hey, Roc"—I stuck out my hand and he grabbed it—"I believe in you."

Roc nodded and squeezed my hand before moving into ready position. Po checked Roc's saddle straps and Yokel checked the flanks of the horse's armor. I handed the lance up to Roc. "Don't forget, we only get one chance at this. You ready?"

"Ridhan won't know what hit him," Roc replied with a wink. "See you on the other side!" Roc's horse reared and spun around, anxious to start. I could feel my whole body tense up, and as Yokel stood next to me, I punched him in the shoulder, instantly releasing all my anxiety.

Yokel yelped. "Hey! What was that for?"

"For Roc," I answered without looking.

"Ah, that makes sense."

The Marshall of the Field stood in the middle of the tilt, holding the Starfall City banner horizontally across both lanes. Trumpets sounded in a long blast, and at the moment they ended, the flag lifted and Roc spurred his steed toward Ridhan.

The plan hinged on every single thing going perfect, and that started with the horse. Roc was going full speed, pushing his horse faster than I'd ever seen it go. Ridhan hugged his side of the tilt, spurring his horse forward to meet Roc's assault well into his own half.

"But what if he goes for my head?" Roc had asked in the tent.

"Then you better hope your new helmet was worth it," I had replied.

Now that they had begun their run, it seemed that worry was needless, for Ridhan's aim held steady and true, the tip of his lance poised to make contact with Roc's chest piece. It was a gamble of a tactic for us, but we knew Ridhan would aim for the easier target when given the chance.

Bullies always do.

With Roc's speed and Ridhan's aim, we had accomplished two of the three parts of our plan. The only variable was whether Reagan had accomplished whatever it was she was going to do. Within moments, Roc was just a few lengths from Ridhan. Suddenly, my Carpenter training kicked in unprompted and time stood still.

Illuminated in my vision was a necklace, a small stone hanging from around Ridhan's neck, similar to the one Reagan had shown us. As time sped back up, I saw it fall from his breast and onto the dirt track.

Roc lowered his arm to tilt the lance upward, aiming for Ridhan's helmet and leaving his own torso square and open, an inviting target. Ridhan took the bait, moving his lance slightly to aim straight at Roc's heart. The next moment stretched out forever, like the last drops of honey dripping from a jar. Ridhan adjusted his position in his saddle, squaring up his chest and crouching down at the last minute. At a mere half-length from Ridhan, Roc raised his arm with incredible speed, dropping his lance tip to make contact with Ridhan's now-exposed chest as he leaned into the blow from Ridhan's lance, accepting the force and absorbing it throughout his body. At contact, both lances shattered, throwing splinters in every direction, accompanied by the flying form of Ridhan who had been knocked from his horse to the ground where he rolled violently before sliding to a stop in the loose dirt.

Silence fell as the crowd stood in awe of the prowess they had witnessed, but as Roc turned his horse and cantered back to his starting position, the stadium erupted in a deafening roar. We rushed Roc, helping him dismount while taking hugging and slapping his back, jumping and screaming in joy.

"We did it, Po!" Roc yelled, lifting him and spinning him around in a giant bear hug.

"I can't believe you... I don't think I've ever heard of someone..." Po struggled, unable to get the words out of his mouth.

"It was our only chance to beat him! The only way to win was to knock him off his horse. I dismount him, and it's an instant win!" Roc explained, catching Po up on the strategy. We walked slowly back to the center of the pitch, my eye following the line of the tilt intently. I stopped, bending my knee as if to fix my shoe but instead scooping up the small glimmer that had caught my eye and stuffing it into my pocket.

Trumpets sounded and the stadium slowly hushed as the head of the City's Elders spoke.

"Thank you, thank you all. This has truly been a tournament that will go down as one to remember. I give you our winner and once-again champion, Riley Roclan!"

The crowd again cheered, and fireworks exploded into the sky as Ridhan sat in the dirt, unmoving and utterly speechless.

Roc ran to his uncle, embracing him in a hug as the sounds of the people of Starfall rang in our ears, chanting the old knight's name.

"Roclan! Roclan! Roclan!"

# HOMECOMING

"Why are you yelling?" I moaned from my seat in the dining hall. I was trying not to puke on my plate, my head feeling as though a thousand tiny smiths were all hammering on my skull at once.

"I'm not yelling." Reagan laughed as she continued her conversation with Iris.

"You're definitely yelling," Roc said, his face hidden in his large arms.

Yokel had his head sideways on the table and arms dangling from his seat. "I've never been this hungover," he whimpered.

"I think… I think I'm still drunk," Po added, curled up in his chair in an attempt to block out all light and sound.

The party in the streets of Starfall had lasted the whole night, but all that had transpired during those hours was a blur and a mystery for Whiskey Danger; even I had a hard time remembering. Iris and Reagan were all too willing to recount the previous night, but for some reason chose to do so with the loudest voices in the history of humankind.

They were literally the worst people I knew.

But there would be no excuse for us from the parade and the banquet. Traditions cared not for hungover teenagers, and there wasn't a former champion alive that had ever missed the Homecoming Banquet, which meant we would need dates.

Yokel had convinced some third-year student to accompany him, and although Po wasn't a noble and shouldn't have attended, being part of Whiskey Danger had its advantages. His popularity at the Institute was such that, between Whiskey Danger and getting suspended for my performance, he snagged a second-year girl to go with him.

Good for him, dating above his year.

Iris was accompanying me in an amazingly cut black dress that sparkled when she walked.

Nine Hells, can she wear a dress.

We arrived at the Institute's Grand Hall where the Homecoming Banquet was held, our arms folded together in a formal entanglement. We made our way through the lords and ladies, each of whom bowed and offered some formal platitude. Catching the orchestra at the beginning of a song, I pulled Iris's hand to lead her to the center of the room.

"So, who shall we make jealous tonight?" I whispered in her ear, pulling her body close to begin a waltz amongst the other dancers.

"We don't have to make anyone jealous, Oliver, it's just us," she replied as I spun her out before pulling her back in for a dip. I felt her hesitation as we flaunted our routine amongst the other dancers, and I let us fall back into the subdued rhythm with everyone else. It felt uncomfortable holding back, but she hated these parties more than anyone I knew. I never understood why.

If you got the girl of your dreams on your shoulder, why not show off?

Yokel joined us in the dance circle and pointed to Po, who stood by the entrance as scared as a duckling who had just lost his mother, nodding awkwardly to the tall lords and ladies offering him congratulations on the week's events. To my dismay, Iris took this opportunity to end our dance, moving me off to the bar to find some quiet respite over a glass of wine. Just as we were served, thunderous applause broke out as Roc entered the room with Reagan shimmering on his arm in a blue silk dress.

Baby sister, you sure can turn an eye.

Gross.

Reagan had offered to accompany Roc, who had planned to spend the entire day and night at home with his uncle. He agreed to attend only after a few rounds of arguing and the insistence of Sir Roclan himself. I watched as Roc was swiftly surrounded by lords, each offering him a cigar. Reagan slipped out of the circle, making her way to Iris and me.

"How's he holding up?" I asked, handing her a glass of wine.

"He's holding," Reagan answered before downing the entire glass in one gulp. "More, please," she urged, tapping her finger impatiently. Once the glass was filled, she raised it in a silent toast. With a soft clink we sipped, and Reagan planted a kiss on my cheek before leaving to pry Roc from his new fans. Iris turned to me with a soft expression.

"Your sister is one in a million."

"I know," I said, feeling slight disgust at the thought of dealing with my growing sister's future suitors, who were bound to be many in number.

Lords and ladies walked up to Iris and me, making small talk about nothing particularly interesting. I didn't mind the attention, but Iris never let go of my hand as she eagerly searched for an escape.

"Maybe we should head back to your place," she suggested, pulling me closer to her after a particularly talkative lord left us to go mingle with a lady he had been eying from across the room. "And we can take Reagan and Roc with us and save them from this craziness," she finished abruptly.

The moment when I thought we might actually have some alone time quickly dissipated. I nodded begrudgingly, and we walked over to Roc and my sister, pulling them aside with our apologies to their surrounding menagerie.

"Roc, how about we ditch this place and head home? Grab a few drinks, play a few games?" I offered with as much hopefulness as I could muster.

Roc let go of a deep breath and a release of tension and anxiety flowed through his body as he threw his arm onto my shoulders. "That sounds perfect." Turning, he nodded toward Yokel and Po. "What do we do about those two?"

I turned, watching as Yokel entertained several willing victims with his strategic recount of the joust. Po stood nearby, embellishing the tale with gusto, much to the delight of his date.

"Leave them. They look like they're having the time of their lives," I said, smiling. Our harmless voyeurism was interrupted by a familiar voice bellowing through the hall.

"Lord Roclan!" The Black Prince, still adorned in Southern-style garb but this time in charcoal grey instead of midnight black, walked up to us. "In all my years, I have never seen anything quite like what you did. Unhorsing Lord Shipwight? Just amazing." He approached us with his hand extended, but all four of us had already committed to a formal bow. Roc noticed his hand after a sharp jab from Reagan's elbow and stepped forward to grab the Black Prince's hand.

"Thank you, Your Highness, but again... I'm not a lord."

The Black Prince's previously averted gaze darted upward to find Roc's bright green eyes. "Of course, but again, I have no doubt that one day you will be." Amid the soft exclamation murmuring through the room, the Black Prince quickly changed the subject. "You must tell me how you came up with that strategy! It was utter perfection."

"Humbly, Your Highness, it was a group effort, though I feel I must inform you, you provided a bit of inspiration." He turned his head toward Reagan.

"Oh, I did?" The Black Prince said, staring at Reagan's neck. "So interesting a thing, inspiration, I mean. But alas, I must leave you to your night, my lord. Congratulations!" The Prince extended his arm for another embrace and Roc took it heartily.

"Thank you again, Your Highness, but I'm not a lord."

The Black Prince stared into his eyes and smiled, turning away to make a path into the sea of lords and ladies.

"He's so intense!" Iris exclaimed, turning to Reagan.

"You don't know the half of it," she replied.

What have you been up to, baby sister?

At that moment, Ridhan walked in accompanied by a stunning girl, a crazy grin carved wide into his face.

"Q!" he yelled out, as if we were the best of friends.

"Ridhan," I replied coolly, catching sight of Po and Yokel making their way over at the sound of his voice, abandoning their girls at the bar.

Ridhan unhooked his arm from his beautiful date. "Tck-tck-tck, oh Q, I don't know how you did it, but I must commend you. A job well done indeed!" He clapped and patted my shoulder.

"So, no hard feelings?"

"Hard feelings? Oh, you mean that bit of business with threatening your lives and what not. Of course not, Q, of course not. No, I must say I am a man of my word. I'm more impressed than anything. Big plans for you and all that. A storm is coming, and the winds of change are upon us, and I could use some men like you three. Tough, smart, willing to stare down a lance and not flinch. Tck-tck-tck, you can even throw in the little freshie as well." He waved vaguely at Po before turning back to me, shaking me by the shoulder playfully. "What do you say, Q? I could use a giant like this one," Ridhan finished, caressing Roc's chest salaciously. I looked at Reagan and then at Iris, whose expressions were warning me not to engage. I twisted the chain of the Relic in my pocket, contemplating my next move.

Ridhan was manic one moment and calm the next, but I still held out hope for the good inside him. If he could turn that good out, he'd be a valuable asset and maybe even a friend. At the very least, I had to try.

"You know, Rid, there was the other part of our bet, if you remember."

"Yes, yes, I am quite upset I was unable to retrieve my family's heirloom," he replied as I waved to one of my butlers by the entrance.

They came over and handed me the Staff of the Seas. I held it above my head, letting the light do its work to illuminate the staff.

"This is a fine weapon, don't you think, Roc?" My goal was to win Ridhan over, but that didn't mean I wouldn't make him suffer just a little more.

"One of the finest I've seen, and I work at the Forge," Roc acknowledged.

I spun it around and landed it in front of Ridhan, extending it toward him in a peaceful offering. "Eh, you know, it just doesn't quite feel right. I think I'm more partial to the sword myself. Besides, a Staff of the Seas belongs with a family of the seas, not one from beneath a volcano."

Ridhan wore a genuine look of shock, and I'm sure that for all his plans and machinations, he never thought this would happen. I doubted kindness came to him easily, if ever. That was the plan I hatched this morning. Butting heads with Ridhan from now until the end of time would never serve us well. With everything we were up against, we would need more friends than enemies.

I pushed the staff closer to him. "Here, it belongs with you."

"But I lost. We had a fair bargain," Ridhan protested.

When was the last time someone did something nice for you, Ridhan?

"A bargain, yes, but fair, probably not so much. Besides, I don't think it would match any of my outfits."

Ridhan actually laughed, and accepted the peace offering. "I don't know what to say, Q," he muttered, staring at his family's prized heirloom.

"How about we all just start over, Rid. Clean slate."

"I…"

Was his world so bleak that he couldn't recognize the situation?

I offered my hand. "Friends?"

He took my arm and shook it. "One day." Ridhan took his date and his staff and left us.

Po turned around with his mouth open wide. "I can't believe you just did that. After all he's said and all he's done. I thought you were going to rub it in his face for the rest of his life!"

"Bud, if there's one thing Roc, Yokel, and I have learned over the years, it's this: Why have enemies when you can have friends?" I winked at Po and he barreled into me with an unexpected hug.

Yokel and Roc joined in and beneath the piles of bodies, I heard a muffled, "I love you guys."

The overwhelming affection we felt for each other suddenly was too much and we pushed each other away, turning awkwardly and looking for an escape.

"Uh, uh, let's get back to our dates, Po," Yokel suggested. Roc and I stood still, neither one of us knowing what to do next.

"Aww, you boys are too cute," Iris said, breaking the awkward tension.

"No, we're not!" Roc argued back.

"Yeah, we're men!" I added and Roc and I both nodded.

The girls didn't seem all that convinced and waited for us to express our undying love for each other. Instead, I punched Roc in the crotch.

"Yeah, okay," he groaned.

"I will never understand men," Iris said, shaking her head.

Reagan took her shoulder. "These are boys." She surveyed the room and posed a question. "Elven goodbye?" We all nodded. Without saying anything to anyone around us, we slipped through the door, heading back to the Anvil and away from the banquet.

Iris accompanied Roc to Sir Roclan's room as I walked my baby sister to her own.

"Ollie," she said before crossing the threshold.

"Yeah, Rea?"

"Tonight is a big night."

"It's been a crazy couple of months, but the night is almost over."

She leaned on the doorframe. "No, I mean… ugh, never mind." With that, she went up onto her tiptoes and kissed my forehead.

It wasn't the strangest interaction I had ever had with my sister, but it ranked up there. I was too tired from the day, the week, the month, and even the year to try and decode her cyphers. Another night maybe, but not tonight. Tonight, all I wanted to do was lie in my bed and sleep for a week.

I walked into my room and stopped dead in my tracks.

"Hi, little lord." Iris was sitting on the edge of my bed, looking at me like the first time we met. She quickly got up and clutched both my hands.

"Hi, my love, what are you doing here? I thought you would have headed home after seeing Sir Roclan."

"Not tonight," she responded, pulling me in close for a kiss, and for once in my life I stopped thinking and just let the moment take over.

We kissed and kissed and in between taking breaths for air, kissed some more. She would pull me in close, pressing up against me, regardless of how uncomfortable that made certain pieces of my clothing. Other times I pinned her arms against her sides as I enveloped her in a strong hug.

Somehow, we'd traveled around the room and landed on my bed. My soft, soft bed in which I so desperately wanted to sleep. But there was no way in the Nine Hells was I going to stop kissing Iris. Taking a brief pause, she looked at me, her eyes wide and her smile wider. She pulled on the strings of her blouse, tugging it free from under the weight of my body.

"Hi," she said simply.

Her arms were above her head as she lay under me, the flicker of candlelight dancing across her face and bare skin. I blew out the candle, thinking of nothing except the beautiful girl in my arms, letting the night and our love take over.

"Hi," I replied.

# THE LILYTHORN

"**N**ow the" last time I left you on a platform like this, you didn't come back for six months," Iris said after kissing my cheek. I wanted to retort that it was she who had ended up courting someone else when I finally returned. That it was me who had turned down MULTIPLE advances from girls in Kandaheart, and that after Homecoming night, there was no way I could even think of another girl.

But a little voice that sounded suspiciously like Reagan whispered in my mind that that would be a bad idea. "It'll barely be a month and then I'll be right back in your arms," I said instead. I held her tightly, kissing her neck as she squirmed at my tickle attack.

"Break it up, lovebirds, the train is here," Roc said as he walked through us rather than around. A week since the end of Homecoming and also a week since Sir Roclan had passed away, and he was still grieving, but in his own way. To everyone else, he was the same old Roc. But in quiet moments, I could see the sorrow on his face and hear the despair in his voice. I could only hope that a trip out of Starfall might help him come to terms with the death of his father figure, as I had hoped a trip would do for me when my mother died.

I pulled Iris back into me and spun her around. "So, what exactly will you do with us gone? You won't be bored, will you?"

"You know, I had a life before your silly song, and I still have my classes at the Institute, unlike you delinquents."

"Don't you worry about a thing, Ollie. I have loads of plans for Iris and me," Reagan said as she cut into my dance and took Iris as a partner.

"Since when did you two start spending time together?" I asked.

"The sisterhood has to stick together!" Reagan replied, letting Iris out into a spin.

"Girl power," Iris added, bumping a fist with Reagan and giggling much too hard for my liking.

"Oh no, they've teamed up," Po said as he dragged his luggage to the platform.

"You're telling me, kid." I shook my head and helped him with his bags.

The train came to the platform and unloaded its passengers, and we said our final goodbyes to our family and friends and embarked on our journey north. Typically, this would be the final train out of Starfall until the spring, its only passengers being prisoners headed for the Floating Isles. But when your family was the one that built, owned, and operated the railroads and trains, there was always an entire private train car available. The trip would take us through the heart of the South, up the Neck where we'd have to travel by foot and steed through the Floating Isles, and back onto a train as we entered the Kingdom of Romir and made our way inland toward the kingdom proper.

Although Roc, Yokel, and I had taken the Iron Caravan a few times, it would be Po's first and he was asking a thousand questions. Luckily for us, Yokel loved to answer, and it would help pass the time.

"I don't even understand how this works," Po stated.

"No one does," Yokel answered. "It was invented by the Quartermaines, by Oliver's grandfather Wiggin. But there are only so many in all the world, and he never revealed the schematics to anyone. I don't even know if Oliver's own father knows."

"He does not," I answered, staring absentmindedly out the window. Leaving Starfall felt like some type of renewal, but my heart also yearned for what I had left behind. When I came back, would Iris be waiting for me or would she have found a new suitor once more? My gaze shifted to Roc, who likewise was watching the fields and groves go by. His thoughts would surely be on the loss he was feeling and the void it left in his heart. He needed someone to help him heal, I thought, but the inevitable slew of girls who would throw themselves at him in Romir would never be what he really needed. He needed what I had with Iris.

"Oi, now this is something else!" Pathfinder said as she snuck in through the door connecting train cars. Windrunner came in from the other end, and the five of us were once again together.

Maybe Roc and Windrunner would be a good match.

Given what I knew about Windrunner, which admittedly wasn't very much, I knew it wasn't the right fit. The perfect match for Roc was obviously Pathfinder, and I knew that deep down inside. But something wouldn't let me contend with that thought. Yes, I had Iris, and yes, I loved her very, very much. She was my whole world. Nothing could compare to her.

But I couldn't quite let go of Pathfinder, not in my heart of hearts. Not even for Roc.

"Yokel was just telling me about this train!" Po said as he got up and gave a big hug to the Knight Angels. They'd become something of older sisters to him. Secretly I hoped he would feel the same about Iris and Reagan one day, and then all the people I cared about most in the world would be family.

"Oh, was he now, please continue." Windrunner took up residence next to Roc. Pathfinder sat next to me, and I swear everyone could feel the awkwardness hang in the air. Everyone, that was, except Yokel.

"As I was saying, there are only so many of these in the whole world! The Lilythorn Train that we are on and that will bring us to the Neck; Big Thunder, which is the train that travels North to Land's End and the Northern Tribes; Splashwater, which runs east and west along Starfire Bay and travels to Mercyhold and Kandaheart; and Spacefarer, which travels through the heart of the continent and all around Romir. Each train comes with its own personal security force, mostly to dispel bandits and pirates from trying to steal its secrets. Oliver, do you even know how Wiggin Quartermaine even conceived the idea?"

"Wiggin Quartermaine the First, and no, no one does. One of the greatest technological inventions in the history of the world, and he never even told my father. I think it was one of the big reasons for their fight and my grandfather's eventual exile. No one has seen him in years. Reagan wasn't even born when he left."

I turned to Pathfinder as Yokel continued his history lesson for Po.

"So," I started.

"So," she replied.

"I, uh, I have some news." I had no idea how to tell her about Iris. I hadn't seen Pathfinder since she left me on top of the Shears with that glorious kiss.

"Oh, news, have you? It wouldn't happen to be about that girl of yours, would it?"

So perceptive, so in tune with me. If this were any other life, any other time, I thought we might be together. But my heart was for Iris and Iris only.

At least that's what I told myself repeatedly.

"Yes, exactly. Iris and I are, uh, together now. And I know we, uh, well, you know."

"Kissed?" Pathfinder said casually.

"Yes, that. Well, I just wanted you to know that you're amazing and awesome and I love working with you and all this."

"But?"

"But..." I wavered. Something inside me didn't want to let go of... whatever it was we had. It was nothing, really. But I didn't want to lose her.

"But, I mean, you know, Roc over there is pretty sad."

What was I doing?

Pathfinder tilted her head and studied him. "Oh, yes, I can see that."

"And I mean, he's pretty great, don't you think?"

Nine Hells, stop this, Oliver!

"Quite wonderful."

"And you're great. And he's great. Both great. Great, great, great," I repeated like a buffoon.

Pathfinder grabbed my hand. "You're great too."

I pulled away instinctively, like a moron. "Yes, yes, we're all great. I'm just saying maybe you and Roc could, uh, get to know each other."

Pathfinder smiled understandingly at me and I hated every moment of it.

"If that's what you think is best, little lord." She stood up and joined Windrunner and Roc in a conversation while I sat by myself, stunned at my actions.

"You'll find that history is littered with these kinds of inventions by the Quartermaines. Trains, printing presses, and not to mention all the weapons, architecture, all manner of machines. It's truly quite astounding. Must be something in their blood," Yokel said. He was right about one thing: we Quartermaines were astounding.

Astoundingly stupid. Surprisingly foolish.

Foolish.

I jumped out of my seat and raced around the car to find the itinerary for the World Championships. After rummaging through Yokel's belongings, much to his protests, I pulled out the flyer.

"I found it!" I yelled.

"Found what?" Windrunner asked.

"Find the fool." I handed her the flyer. It was for the traveling circus, who would be in Romir during the Championships.

Windrunner handed the flyer to the rest of the group and finished the thought. "He will be your guide."

# THE PRINCE OF ROMIR

The Kingdom of Romir was the largest and most prosperous kingdom in the world. It was also the worst. In the geographical center of the kingdom sat the City of Romir atop three intersecting rivers. Romir had at its disposal the landmass for a booming agricultural economy and would use it judiciously to get whatever it wanted from other kingdoms. What it lacked in raw materials, it traded for, and over the years, as the population of the world increased, so too did the royal Romirian family's appetite for extravagance.

There was also the small problem of slavery that existed north of the South. Whereas Starfall and all the other towns in the southern peninsula had outlawed slavery centuries ago, the same could not be held true for the other kingdoms. Romir was the biggest advocate for slavery, using slaves to sustain their farms and build their famed city. It was a city that had seen massive changes over the last few generations, taking inspiration from none other than my own family's aesthetics and machinery.

"I've never seen anything like this," Po yelled as the train crested the hilltop to put the Iron City in full view. "What's with all those weird-looking clouds?"

Yokel, being ever the student of the world and history, obliged Po's curiosity. "That is the Iron City, and unlike cities and towns anywhere else, they've embraced an industrial renaissance. It's all quite fascinating."

"More fascinating than what we just had to go through with the Floaters," Roc complained as he gathered his belongings. Our journey north had been anything but unexciting. When we reached the Neck and the Floating City, we'd run into a problem with some bounty hunters looking for a particular Southern prisoner on our train. Now that was a story I would be retelling for a very long time.

The train pulled through the gates of the walled city and into a large bustling station. Being the epicenter of the world meant that most trades passed through here, regardless of their final destinations. Raw materials were imported from the mines, sent to Romir to be turned into finished products, and sent back into the world. Taxes on all those goods funded most of the kingdom's expenses and also their tribute to Land's End. If ever Romir wanted to turn against the High Queen, they'd be the only kingdom who could put up a decent fight. The soldiers in the Imperial Army would be hard pressed to fight the very people whose taxes paid them.

"I am so ready to be off this train," Po said as the train rocked to a final halt. We all felt it was time to leave after the week we'd had and the adventures with the Floaters. All around us in the station, people moved like schools of fish, occasionally bumping into each other but never stopping. The five of us headed to a carriage, and as slaves loaded our luggage, Po peered out the side door and began to bombard us with questions that didn't stop even as we began to travel through the city proper.

"Why does everyone look the same?"

"Romirians aren't too keen on foreigners. In Starfall, you can see every shade of person in the world, but here in Romir, they hate anyone who doesn't look like them, especially Southerners like us," Roc explained as the hard stone and metal buildings passed us by. Unlike Starfall, which had a myriad of people from all around the world, Romir was more isolated and nationalistic; many different people came to the city but rarely stayed.

We were heading to the far side of the city to a towering building that was paid as tribute to my family for their architectural work in redesigning Romir. It was situated in the area designated for foreign travelers, and soon enough Po started to feel a bit more at home. Romir's xenophobia might have been prevalent within the walls of the city, but if they wanted to do business with any of the other kingdoms, they needed to allow the "other" people a place to lodge at least.

As soon as we came to the entrance of our building, I noticed a rather unusual character dressed in royal garb standing nervously in front of the doorway. That meant we were being watched by the Royal Romirian Family.

"Everyone stay in here, we have company," I said. They were expecting four of us, not six, and we didn't want to give away the Knight Angels.

The messenger bowed and held out a scroll. In his Romirian accent, he said, "Hello, Lord Quartermaine. You and your entourage have been invited by the First Prince Froderick to dinner tonight." I'd met the First Prince of Romir once when we were younger, and the memory had left a sour taste. I had no desire to see him again, especially given we were here on a mission.

"Thank you," I said, taking the scroll, "but it's been a long journey and we would very much appreciate a chance to rest."

The messenger straightened up, tugging on his coat with a look of disgust. "Southerners," he spat. "This is a direct request from His Highness. Your absence will not be tolerated." With that, he turned and stalked away, scoffing at the other travelers milling about the streets.

Roc poked his head out of the carriage. "Is it safe to come out?"

I sighed. "Yes, but don't get too comfortable. We're off to see the First Prince for dinner tonight."

"Oh, no we're not!" Roc yelled as Yokel stuck his head out too.

"This will be wonderful. I was hoping I would have a chance to see my new wardrobe in action." Yokel, always fashion forward, had been procuring Romirian-style outfits for a few years now and was excited to finally be able to show them off without the accompanying jokes from Roc and me.

"We weren't exactly given a choice," I said, returning to the carriage. I looked at the Knight Angels. "You two were obviously not invited. I suggest you stay in our suite tonight until we return."

Pathfinder looked at Windrunner and waved her hand. "Or how about we search the city for clues for this Fool or the codex. Savvy?"

Savvy? Was she a pirate now? Nine Gods I hate this.

"Fine, do what you want, but when you need rescuing—"

"I'll be sure not to send for you," Pathfinder teased back. She sure knew how to pull every one of my strings, but I'd be lying if I didn't admit I liked our verbal sparring.

We walked into the tower, the Knight Angels taking the carriage around the back so as not to be seen with us. In the lobby, Po looked up in amazement at the finery and decor. Along with the tower, my great-uncle's family owned a Romirian forge that was responsible for the conversion of raw materials into everything. Not only were we wealthy in the South, but we were also wealthy in the biggest kingdom in the world. Sometimes being a Quartermaine had its advantages.

Po turned to look at me in pure bewilderment. "Sometimes it's dumb how rich you are."

"You don't even know the half of it, kid," Roc said.

We made our way down a long hallway, meeting up with the Knight Angels as a door in the far wall opened to a small room, quickly cramped by the six of us and the tower's staff following with our luggage.

Po looked around the room apprehensively. "What is this thing?"

I signaled to the bellhops that we wanted to go to the suite named for my great-grandmother. "Quartermaine Penthouse, please."

Two sets of doors closed, and the lift propelled us toward the top of the tower. The quick start of the lift startled Po, and he stumbled and fell, Roc catching him mere inches from the floor. With another sharp jerk, the lift stopped, its doors opening for Roc to push the still reeling Po through.

"What was what!" he yelled, unable to contain his excitement upon reaching steady ground.

"That was a lift, operated by a pulley system of ropes and levers above and below. The invention of Oliver's great-uncle," Yokel commented.

"Is there anything your family hasn't invented?" Po asked as we entered the suite. Roc, Yokel, and I looked at each other, trying to ascertain the answer. It seemed that, in one form or another, Quartermaines had been at the forefront of most if not all the technological advancements that we could think of.

Later that evening, we dressed. Roc wore his Black Sunday suit as usual, and I wore a colorful blue suit fit for a Summer Solstice party in Kandaheart. Po wore a fine but plain suit his grandmother had sewn for him, and Yokel, being Yokel, came out of his room in an emerald-green Romirian suit complete with a top hat and brass spectacles.

"Okay, gentleman, you ready?" I asked.

"Don't you all look dapper," Windrunner said, straightening Po's shirt.

"Yes, quite the look, boys," Pathfinder said as she walked dangerously close to me, adjusting my collar and peering into my eyes. I could get lost in her gaze so easily, and being so close to her sent a rush of excitement through my body.

Why was I like this?

She patted my chest and walked away, assuredly not thinking the same thoughts I was currently having. Thoughts of being alone in a room together. Thoughts of ripping off her mask. Thoughts of continuing the kiss we started on top of the Shears.

"Try not to get into too much trouble," Roc said as he grabbed his scabbard and sword.

"Why do we need our weapons?" Po asked, following his idol.

I glanced at him. "We're foreign travelers in a foreign land. Better to be prepared."

We decided to walk most of the way, the idea of being back inside a carriage of any type outweighing the possible dangers of the city. Our confidence was helped by the fact that we had swords on our hilts and a very large Roc leading the way. But even as we neared the castle, it seemed we could not escape adventure.

In the middle of an alleyway were three armored Royal guards flanking a cloaked figure.

"I told you, mate, I don't know what you lot are talking 'bout, I swear on me mum's grave," the cloaked figure pleaded as he conspicuously patted at his sides.

"Your little knives aren't going to be any use to you, bugger, not against our swords and armor. Now, you're going to pay for what you've been carrying on about with the prince," one of the guards said.

Whiskey Danger hurried behind a merchant stall along the street, out of sight of the scuffle that seemed about to ensue.

"What's the plan?" Yokel asked Roc as I peered over the top of the stall.

"I count only three, unsure what to make of the guy in the cloak," I relayed.

"We need to save that guy, whatever else happens," Roc instructed. He was always so courageous in these moments, always so sure of what to do. He glanced at Po. "Po, you remember what I said at the Floating Isles?"

Po nodded. "Being a knight means helping those who need it."

Roc nodded back. "These guards are a disgrace. They aren't protecting, they're inciting fear. It's time to put an end to that."

Po smiled at his hero and we stood, hopping over the barricade behind him and brandishing our swords.

"I'm going to ask you again, scum, what were you and the prince discussing?" The guard's sword was dangerously close to the chest of the cloaked figure they had cornered, pressed up against the wall.

"Mate, I'm going to tell you one last time, I have no bloody idea what ya going on about!"

"Ack, ahem. Hello there, what seems to be the problem?" Roc yelled, gaining the attention of the three guards. Even in the dusk light with the lamplights on the street lit, it would still be hard to make out our faces.

"Piss off!" one of the other guards responded as he unsheathed his sword in our direction.

"I'm sorry, took a piss earlier. Now, again, what seems to be the problem here?" Roc teased with his long sword at a low angle across his body, glinting off the lamplight.

"I'm going to tell you one last time, piss off or you'll end up like this piece of street filth," the lead guard shouted, turning his body away from the cloaked guy to face us.

"Have it your way," Roc said, confidence in each word. He took a step back and motioned toward me, muttering, "You got this."

Roc's confidence lifted my spirits, and while the scene was familiar to me, I knew it would end very differently.

"Okay, boys, who's first?" I asked, parrying the incoming slashes and thrusts from the two guards. Within a minute they were both crumpled on the ground, unconscious. The final guard started to approach, and I waved a finger in the air back and forth. "I wouldn't do that if I were you."

He stopped, looked around at his fallen colleagues, and ran off. Every kingdom may have had their own training centers, but nothing would ever match the Workshop.

"Where'd the cloaked guy go?" Roc yelled, turning his head every which way.

"He left as soon as the guard turned his sword away!" Po exclaimed.

"It doesn't matter, we're going to be late," I said, not bothering to spend any more mind power on the cloaked guy. We left the two unconscious guards and continued on to the castle.

Castle Romir was located in the heart of the city, a towering spectacle of stone, flanked by a city of iron. The redesign of Romir had been done with only one stipulation: that the castle stay intact and undisturbed. It sat upon an island between two rivers where they conjoined to flow east to the ocean.

Its outer stone walls were segmented by tall towers with connecting walkways to the center structure that stood another six levels high. We approached the river and signaled an attendant to lower the drawbridge. After a long cacophony of clunking chain and groaning wood, the bridge settled flat, the castle itself looming before us.

We crossed through the yard and entryway and moved up a long staircase to the large dining hall that already contained milling Romirian nobles. We were stopped at the doorway by a slave, to whom we reluctantly relinquished our weapons. Inside, we tried our hardest to stay by the wall and avoid attention, but the attention seemed to find us.

"My guests, thank you for joining me on this lovely evening, not that you had much say in the matter." Laughing, Prince Froderick turned from us and eyed the room, the nobles laughing uneasily along with him. "Regardless, let us all have a bit of fun tonight, shall we! Ahh, look, we have an honored guest here, the Southerner! What was your name again?"

I watched as Roc became more agitated, but he held firm with a forced smile.

"Riley Roc—"

"Ah, but not a lord, so it doesn't matter, now does it? I didn't know we even allowed you folk into the city, let alone the tournament!" The prince laughed again, this time harder and more pronounced. The other nobles joined in ceremoniously but immediately stopped when the prince did.

"Honored to be here, Your Highness," I replied, given Roc was about to explode.

"Oh please, please, no need for such formalities. You can call me Champion, if you prefer." The prince took a smug sip from his goblet, malice radiating across the room toward Roc. "To think you dare to challenge me for the victory this year!" He laughed once more.

I was pretty sure he was insane.

The prince abruptly ended his laugh by spitting out, "You stupid sandeater." The slur was for someone poor and from the coast and was Roc's least favorite word.

It was at this point that I began to think of the various ways we could escape the castle without dying. I was confident that Roc was going to murder the prince here and now, which would have been a boon for our chances at the World Championship but less so for our lives. The plan to escape quickly only had one small hiccup. I could navigate through the castle easily enough, up until that stupid moat. It was too wide to jump, and there were rumors that it was filled with spiked rocks and lances lodged just under the surface of the black water.

As I stood thinking, Roc replied. "You sound scared, m'lord."

Yokel and I exchanged glances. Roc was not only taunting the prince but outright insulting him.

And Prince Froderick knew it.

"You forget your place, you worthless cur. Or did that sorry excuse for a knight uncle of yours not teach you your manners," he snarled, his gaze intensely focused on Roc. An uneasiness fell over the room. Before we could stop him, Po did the most insane thing I had seen someone do since Yokel's famous experiment with Southern Isle hot peppers. Under his breath but echoing through the quiet room, he muttered contemptuously.

"Better a sorry excuse for a knight than a sorry excuse for a prince."

I watched as the most curious expression overtook the prince's face.

Roc broke the horrified silence. "What I think he meant to say was —"

"What did you say to me?" the prince interrupted coldly.

"He's just a young squire, Your Grace," I added, knowing it was too late.

"Silence!" Prince Froderick slammed his cup onto the table, shattering it. Blood started seeping from his hand. He smeared his hand on an unsuspecting noble's face, eyes still trained on Po. "I asked you a question, you worthless little sandeater! Now answer me!" His eyes were burning a hole through Po, but Po didn't seem fazed.

"I said, you're a sorry excuse for—"

Yokel snatched him up, clasping a hand over his mouth and backing toward the door.

I finished for Po as Roc and I made our way to them, creating a human shield between Po and the rest of the guests. "I think this one has had enough wine for one night, Your Highness! If you'll excuse us…" I looked around at the guards posted at the door and several moving around the room, knowing the final problem of our escape was still the moat.

We had to make it out of the room first.

Suddenly, every torch and lamp in the room fell dark and the doors to the hall burst open as a stream of entertainers flooded the room. They swarmed the guests, fire spitting from their mouths and their juggling sticks, throwing shadows to dance along the walls. An announcer called out into the dark room.

"Your Royal Royalness! May I present the Jesters of…"

But Whiskey Danger didn't stick around to listen to the announcement. We took full advantage of the fortuitous diversion, slipping through the doors and running through a labyrinth of rooms and hallways before unintentionally plowing into an unaware guard rounding a corner.

"Hey! What do you four think you're doing?" he yelled from the floor, fumbling to simultaneously pocket a large skeleton key and unsheathe his sword.

"Afraid of jesters, sir," I mumbled, moving my head quickly as Roc's fist hit the guard straight in the face. He collapsed and the clank of his armor and sword against the stone rang loudly in the empty walkway.

"I'm not sorry. I said what I—"

Roc cut him off sharply. "Not now, Po. Right now, we have to make it back across the city."

"And get our gear," Yokel added.

"Well, I wonder if this will help?" I said, stooping to pick up the fallen sword and key.

"Oi, what are you boys going on about?" The strangely familiar voice came from behind us. I spun around quickly, pointing the sword at the stranger as he lifted his arms passively.

"Woah there, mate, I'm not one of them. I'm just looking for a bit of fire to light me pipe is all. You Southerners and your 'swords first, words later' and all that."

Where did I recognize him from? He seemed to be about our age, and there was something oddly familiar about his presence.

"Who are you?" I asked, sword still pointed at him. He edged closer, eyeing the tip of the sword before brushing it down to pass us, and for some reason, I let him. Looking down at the unconscious guard, the strange boy continued to talk.

"Oi, would you look at this bloke. He's not going to feel good in the morning, I can guarantee that. Who did that, the big one or the skinny one?" He bent to search through the inner pockets on the guard's tunic, pulling out a small matchbox. "Here you are, just like always," he mumbled before striking a match to light his pipe. He turned back to us. "Now, where are you lads off to, this go around?"

"That's none of your concern," Roc replied. The stranger hopped gingerly onto a table on the wall, sitting with his legs crossed and staring at the four of us.

"Interesting, it was him last time," the boy said, pointing at me. "But I'm not looking to cause any trouble here. Oi, you're a big lad, aren't you?" He nodded at Roc. "Well, it seems you gentlemen are missing quite the party back in the main hall." Not liking his tone, I pointed my sword tip back toward the boy who sat unfazed. "You need to learn not to point sharp things at people, you know that?" he said.

"We just want to leave, we don't want any trouble," I said sternly.

"Like I said, I'm not looking to make trouble for ya. See, I'm part of the troupe back there, but it seems someone's upset the prince. He's taking it out on the jesters instead of... oh how did he put it, 'the little shite I'm going to lock in the dungeons until he rots.' Oi, you look like a little shite, don't you?" he said, pointing his pipe accusingly at Po. I swiftly brought my blade back up to the boy's neck.

"I don't think anyone needs to know we came through here, do they?" I said.

"No, they never do," he retorted, blowing smoke into my face. I turned to my friends and we moved down the hall, the stranger yelling to us from his table. "Oi, if you're looking for your swords, you might try that door on the left. And don't forget about the torch this time."

The boy was correct about our gear but wrong about any torch. After recovering our gear from a closet in the room, we moved across one of the walkways leading to the outer wall. As we reached the wall tower, an alarm sounded to signal more troops being called to the main castle behind us. In our relative safety on the wall we looked down at the faintly reflected planet light on the surface of the moat. We could see our freedom but had no good way to get there.

"We could jump," Yokel offered, trying to look at the water from a new angle.

Roc shook his head. "We'd never survive the fall, let alone whatever's underneath the water."

I searched the surface of the moat for an escape, finding nothing.

"Oliver, go to your temple place. There has to be something you're not thinking of," Po said desperately. In answer to my raised eyebrow, he explained nervously. "Windrunner told me about it when I was having trouble with my own thoughts jumbling around in my head."

Maybe he was right.

I stepped back from the wall and put my two forefingers at the sides of my head, thumbs lining along my jaw. Roc and Yokel stared at me curiously as I closed my eyes to enter my mind temple.

I race into the temple, searching for anything to do with Romir.

"I need the Kingdom of Romir," I call out in my mind, and stacks of books encircle me with a familiar flutter. "Architecture of the buildings of the City of Romir," I say once more, and the stacks shift vertically. "About Castle Romir," and the stacks vanish.

Disappointed, I press on.

"Architecture of all buildings," and a whirlwind of scrolls and maps fly about me like birds caught in a storm. "Tower defenses of ancient castles." But again, I am left without answers.

My eyes snapped open and I moved along the battlement to the storeroom on the edge of the tower, my three friends following me closely.

"What are we looking for, Oliver?" Roc yelled out from behind me.

"I don't know! Something! Anything!" I yelled back. From the corner of my vision I saw Po linger at an out-of-place unlit torch holder on the wall and give it a tug. Suddenly, a loud groaning release sounded, and we scrambled from the room to see what had happened.

A long rope was waving between a notched window in the tower and a large iron building some hundred yards away across the moat. I reached for my belt buckle, motioning to the others. Yokel wrapped his belt on the rope and jumped, followed closely by Po and then Roc. I stood with my belt around the rope ready to jump, looking back to make sure we were in the clear. Oddly enough, I saw the strange boy from earlier, in the courtyard below, casually striding along and smoking his pipe. Looking up to me, he motioned with his pipe before moving across the yard. Baffled, I turned and jumped, meeting Whiskey Danger and our freedom at the bottom.

# THE ERRANT KNIGHT

"This is insane!" Po yelled, dodging flowers being thrown at our procession by young girls on either side of the road. The opening ceremonies for the Tournament of Romir were a spectacle like nothing he had ever seen. As we made our way under the shower of petals, I looked for our stealthy compatriots.

Really, I looked for Pathfinder. Being away from Iris and around Pathfinder had muddled what I thought to be true in my heart. I yearned to spend more time with her, but we were on a quest. Multiple quests, really. As I searched, I couldn't help but notice that the King of Romir had spared no expense this year in celebrating the reigning champion, his son. What a sight it would be if Roc actually defeated that jerk.

Whiskey Danger made our way along the procession, waving at the thousands of fans in attendance and moving to our designated area of the stadium.

Roc turned to Po, motioning him to a chair. "Just watch, kid, it's something you'll never forget as long as you live. Trust me."

We'd seen the World Championships only once before when we were just kids visiting my cousin, and being in the middle of the celebrations was an entirely new experience for us all. Cauldrons of fire were lit all around the stadium, shadows dancing in the night air as the crowd in the stadium clapped and stomped in unison to a beat.

Stomp, clap clap, stomp, clap.

A series of explosions sounded to accompany the fireworks whistling upward to illuminate the night sky. All the fireworks we had seen at the Starfall City Tournament were nothing in comparison to the display tonight.

Colors from every section of the rainbow filled the stadium with light as the crackle of the fireworks spread across the sky, disappearing as quickly as they had been born.

A large consortium of trumpets sounded, and through the main entrance burst a flood of performers dressed as fools, knights, and all manner of characters. Some did cartwheels and flips while others walked on large stilts through the crowd. They danced throughout the stadium, moving suddenly to form a large circle around their Ringmaster who was wearing a very large hat. He waved and gestured at the crowd who answered him with screams of jubilation. As quickly as they had entered, the entire circle of performers stopped, dropping to a knee and lowering their heads as the crowd hushed to a knowing silence. The Ringmaster removed his large hat as he began to speak into it, his words amplified somehow so all could hear.

"Lords and ladies"—he paused, waving loftily to the crowd before continuing—"and all you other miscreants and ne'er-to-do people!" The crowd began to roar once more, as if the jokes about second-class distinction were a badge of honor. They settled, and the Ringmaster continued. "Tonight, we are honored and pleased to present a very, very special show for you all!"

The beat of drums began to pound their way through the stadium as the cauldrons were simultaneously extinguished. The darkness lasted mere seconds before flames shot up from the circle as large torches were lit, blinding us all. In this moment, the circle of performers disappeared with their Ringmaster, though his voice remained.

"We give you, the Errant Knight!" he called out, and the stadium cheered for the beginning of the show. My focus however was not on the empty circle, nor in search of the voice's location. Four of the fools had surrounded Whiskey Danger during the darkness, miming to each other as they pointed and judged us silently. After a few moments of visual arguing, they seemed to settle on Po, who had been sitting, transfixed by the spectacle. Before I knew what was happening, the jesters grabbed him and escorted him to the center of the ring. The crowd cheered in ignorant excitement as Po was given a small shield and an even smaller wooden sword.

"What are they doing?" Roc asked furiously, trying to make his way to the ring. Yokel and I held him back with all of our strength.

"It's all part of the show. It must be. He'll be fine," Yokel argued.

"Yeah! Besides, we're here if anything goes wrong," I added.

After a moment, Roc relented and stood watch, clearly unhappy. The four pillars of the ring that were on fire were extinguished, and we once again plunged into darkness. A single torch blazed awake in the hands of the Ringmaster as he stood alone next to Po.

"And what might your name be, my boy?" Once again we could all hear as clearly as if he were standing next to us.

"Hugo," a quiet voice replied.

"Hugo! Well, Hugo, we need your help. See, this gentleman over here has lost his way. He's supposed to be a knight, but he keeps going on these foolish adventures, looking for trouble in all the wrong places."

At this, a single pillar lit up and a fool dressed in a poor imitation of an armored knight paraded around in comedic drunkenness.

"Will you, Hugo, save us from this knight's foolery?"

The crowd cheered wildly, chanting Po's true name in encouragement. Po stood frozen, not entirely understanding what was being asked of him. He looked out into the stadium, calling for Roc, but we were completely hidden from him by the darkness.

"It looks like our Errant Knight here needs some encouragement. What do you say, who wants to see Sir Hugo here put an end to this foolishness?" the Ringmaster asked, stoking the mob into a frenzy.

Po muttered something that went unheard in the wild stadium, but the Ringmaster bent to lower his head to hear, raising his hands for silence from the mob. He stood, turning back to the crowd.

"Young Hugo here has just informed me that he is not a sir." The mob began to boo as they simultaneously cheered for Po to fight.

"Hugo, may I call you Hugo? I guarantee, if you help us out tonight, you will be a sir, you have my word as Ringmaster." On his last word he shoved Po encouragingly toward the fool knight, and Po reluctantly took a step forward. The strangeness of this false fight clearly confused him, and all his Carpenter training fell from him as his wooden sword hung pointed down, leaving him defenseless.

The fool knight was spinning around in place, stopping only to keep from falling over in dizziness. Po approached him slowly, looking up and then around at the crowd. I could never have expected what he did next.

He stopped, then threw his sword and then his shield onto the ground in front of the fool. His lips moved as he said something I could not hear, and all four pillars were suddenly lit. During a momentary blindness from the flash, Po was surrounded by more fool knights, all holding something. Taking turns, they threw pies at Po and his small body curled into a defensive posture. I looked sharply at Roc who turned to Yokel, and without one word we broke into a dead sprint.

The first fool couldn't have known what hit him when Roc plowed over him. The rest of the fools saw me and Yokel, but it didn't matter much as our momentum took them to the ground. We made a tight circle around Po and readied ourselves to fight, but the fools retreated and the Ringmaster emerged once more.

"Well this is a sight to see! The Errant Knight has some squires!" The mob roared in laughter, but our resolve kept our focus on searching for any more sneak attacks. Roc knelt swiftly next to Po, wiping remnants of pie from his face, yelling at him over the din of the crowd.

"Are you okay?"

Po looked up at him before plunging into his chest, crying violently. I looked from Po to Roc, whose expression was now screaming that he was about to murder each and every fool he could find.

"It looks as though our little knight isn't having a good time, folks!" the Ringmaster announced, and the crowd awwed in sad agreement. Anger and rage were boiling inside me, and suddenly my head cleared to focus on my target. I started walking toward the Ringmaster, catching the wooden sword with my foot and flicking it up to my hand in one motion, spinning it around intimidatingly. The Ringmaster cheered on his mob, noticing me only at the last second. I watched his expression change from vile happiness to shock, and I swung the sword with as much force as I could muster.

Clink!

The sword was knocked from my hand to land abruptly on the ground, a knife sticking out of the wood. I traced the throw back to its source, a fool with a painted face who looked curiously at me. I stared defiantly into his eyes and found them strangely familiar.

I'd seen this boy before, but where?

"Sorry, mate, this never works," the familiar fool said.

Before I could react, the stadium was plunged into darkness and just as quickly the cauldrons along the walls were once again lit. Whiskey Danger was alone in the circle, no sign of the fools or their Ringmaster. I walked back to the group as the crowd began to cheer and laugh, throwing food and garbage onto the ground around us. Po pulled his head away from Roc, tears in his eyes as he fought to catch his breath.

"I said I wouldn't fight him... that it wasn't right! It's... not what a knight would do..." he stuttered, trying to breathe through quivering lips. Roc held him tight, looking at me with hatred and vengeance blanketing his face. I looked up quickly, searching for the royal box and finding Prince Froderick grinning maliciously inside. I snapped my head back to Roc who had followed my line of sight and nodded curtly. Pulling Po tighter, Roc bent to put a word in his trembling ear.

"Don't worry, kid, we're going to kill them all."

# THE FOOL

Back at our suite, Pathfinder and Windrunner helped Po clean up while Yokel and I tried to calm Roc down, but he took his large sword from his room and headed toward the lift.

"Where are you going?" I yelled, sprinting to get in front of him.

"Out of my way!" he yelled back, juking to avoid my block. Luckily Yokel came to my aid and between the two of us, Roc couldn't get past, although that didn't stop him trying.

"You can't do this," Yokel said, struggling against Roc's large frame.

"Yes, I can. Did you see what happened? They're going to pay for what they did to Po, and I'm going to make them!"

A final shove as I kicked against the wall sent Roc sprawling backward.

"We were all there. We're all angry, Roc!" I yelled, trying to catch my breath.

"Oh yeah? Then why aren't you doing anything about it!"

I walked straight up to him and pulled him by the collar. "If you think you're the only one who cares about that kid, think again, my friend. But tonight is not the night for this."

I let go of Roc and he slid his back to the wall, accepting defeat. Pathfinder and Windrunner joined us in the hallway.

"He's asleep," Windrunner said. "But what are we going to do?"

"Why don't you ask our fearless leader. Apparently, he has all the answers!" Roc spat. I knew he was angry and that I was the most convenient punching bag, but it still hurt. Our friendship had always teetered on a delicate balance of power. I was a Quartermaine and he was a poor kid from the Narrows, but I always deferred to his leadership, knowing there were unspoken rules to our friendship.

"What do you think we should do?" Pathfinder asked Roc.

"I say we make them all pay for what they did."

"And when would you like to do that?"

"Tonight!" He stood up with a newfound sense of urgency.

"Oh, is that right? And where are you planning on finding them?"

"Well, um…"

Pathfinder pulled him in for a hug and a small part of me shuddered in jealousy. Unfounded jealousy, but it was there, nonetheless.

"The circus begins tomorrow, so how about we wait until then? We need to find the Fool so how about we kill two birds with one stone, savvy?"

She is definitely a pirate.

Roc relented, composing himself through elongated breaths. "Fine, but we bring Po with us. He deserves to see justice himself."

The following night, we headed out into the city in our best attire. Upon reaching the circus we entered the enclosed tent and I moved to the front of our group, my outstretched hand holding a note sealed with my family crest for the usher to inspect. "The Quartermaine Box, please."

"Lord Quartermaine, so nice of you to join us! And who might your guests be?" He looked conspicuously at Pathfinder and Windrunner who had donned dresses but kept their faces concealed under headscarves.

"That doesn't matter," I replied.

"Of course, my lord. Please follow me and I'll show you to your box." Upon reaching my family's box, the usher quickly added, "If there is anything at all you require, please do not hesitate to inform our staff."

"We only require privacy, thank you."

He bowed briefly and I joined my friends to choose from the many plush seats, tables of food and wine, and any and all comforts my family could require.

"Sometimes I hate you, you know that, right?" Roc said, talking through the appetizers he had stuffed into his mouth at one of the tables. "Like… really, really hate you."

I returned the sarcasm, replying coolly, "Yes, I realize that."

All six of us moved to sit in a circle on giant pillows, the boys eating and the girls drinking. I looked out into the center of the tent where a showy spectacle of acrobatics was taking place.

"So, what's our plan?" Po asked between mouthfuls.

"We're going to get revenge!" Roc interjected.

"No," I stated.

Roc was resolute. "Yes."

Pathfinder put her goblet down. "We're here because Haralabos said we needed to find the Fool, so that's what we need to do. We're on a quest, boys, don't get distracted."

"Oliver, they deserve to be punished for what they did," Roc argued.

"If that's their fate, I leave it to the one they humiliated," I snapped, turning to look square at Po. "Po, if a time comes when we can help you get revenge, it'll be up to you what you want to do."

"That's a bit much to put on the kid," Roc protested.

"He's going to be the Lightning Knight. He can make the decision, right, Po?"

Po nodded again. "I can do it."

"Good. Now, let's find our fool." I stood, strapping on my sword.

"But we still don't know how," Windrunner said as she also stood.

"I have an idea about that." I disrobed from my finery to reveal my vigilante outfit. Everyone else did the same and we snuck out of the private box and into the maze of the circus. Before long, after asking around for the fool who smoked from a pipe and liked knives, we had narrowed it down to five.

A few hours later, the fool we wanted sat bound to a chair in the middle of a dark room, lit only by a single candle. His still form stirred slightly, and he opened his eyes, shaking his head to clear it from the cloudiness of being knocked unconscious. He blinked rapidly, moving his sore jaw to measure the swelling. Finding himself bound tightly, he began to struggle.

"Oi, what the hells is this?" he cried out, and realizing his struggles were futile, began to search the dark room. He jumped slightly at Roc's low response, the six of us invisible to him in the shadows.

"We'll be asking the questions."

"And who might you be, mate? One of the prince's cronies? I told you all before, I haven't seen him since—"

Roc cut the Fool off, his frustration growing.

"We're not with the prince, you moron." I could sense Roc stewing as he fought to control his voice. He wanted revenge for Po so badly, but he knew the stakes and tried his best to keep it to himself. The Fool looked up in his direction.

"Aye, I suppose not. This is new." The Fool looked out into the darkness of the room. "So, what can I do for you? If you're looking for a performance, it'll be a bit hard to oblige what with these binds and all. I'm not saying it can't be done, but it'll cost you extra if —"

"Enough talking! Why did you help us at the castle?" Roc asked furiously, but the Fool did not immediately respond. "Answer me!"

"Sorry, mate, you told me not to talk, just following orders…" Sighing, he nodded to where the rest of us were standing hidden in darkness. "I don't know how you all do it, this one's mighty confusing."

Unwilling to allow this spat to progress to a physical confrontation, I moved into the light before Roc could respond, addressing the boy calmly.

"Who are you?"

"Nobody of consequence, mate. Do you have a pipe on hand?"

"No, and stop being a wiseass. Listen, the quicker you answer our questions, the sooner we let you leave. Now, why did you help us in the castle?" I kept my tone steady, hopeful that he would be reasonable and answer me.

He replied calmly, peering into the darkness behind me. "I was bored. Figured it'd be a bit of fun. Never liked performing for the prince."

"What do you know of magic?"

The Fool looked at me in disbelief and then looked around the rest of the room anxiously.

"So, that's what this has all been about? Blimey, it took long enough. Who are you people? Are you with the imps?" He seemed nervous.

"No, we're not," Pathfinder said, stepping out of the shadows. "Tell us about the Codex."

"The what?"

"The Th'aumaturgy Codex. Haralabos sent us to find you. You're supposed to be our guide."

The Fool sat quietly thinking. Roc was about to explode with impatience. When the Fool finally did speak, we all listened intently.

"I don't know no Haralabos, nor whatever Elven codex you're talking about."

My heart fell at the dead-end we had come to. Then again, maybe this boy knew something he didn't realize was valuable.

"You know Elvish?" I asked in the clicking language of Elvish. The Fool lifted his eyebrow.

"Aye, enough to get by," he replied in our language of Sorayian.

"A dead language mustn't have much use, unless you have some Elvish texts?" I asked in Sorayian.

"I've been known to read a tome from time to time," the Fool replied, his hands now free and searching the inside of his jacket. Pulling out a pipe, he crossed his legs and motioned for us to continue.

Po stepped out of the shadows and the Fool placed both his feet back on the ground suddenly, a ghostly look on his face. Undeterred, Po said, "Look, we're on a quest, and that quest has led us to you. Please, tell us where the Codex is." His voice was sincere and genuine, as if this fool had never wronged him in any way.

No wonder he was chosen to be the Lightning Knight.

"Hey, kid," the Fool said, staring at Po intensely. "I'm sorry about that business with the pies. It always happens when you escape the castle. Orders from high up and all." Po unsheathed his sword and pointed it a hair's width from the skin of the Fool's neck.

"Oi! I told you it was orders from high up!"

"How high?" Po asked coolly.

"The highest point you can think of!" the Fool said, leaning back and away from the blade at his throat.

Po sheathed his sword once more and moved closer to the Fool, peering deep into his eyes. "Please, help us."

"I can't."

"Why not?"

The Fool looked around, letting his hands drop to his lap. "I don't know what will happen, we've never made it this far before."

Po didn't move but let the moment linger in the air. I wanted to jump in and force the Fool to answer, and I could see Roc's muscles twitching. But we didn't give in, and soon enough, a single tear fell from the Fool's eye.

"I gave it to a priest at the temple." The Fool's shoulders sank under his confession. Po moved away but the Fool lunged at him, turning Po back around. "Be careful, kid! This never ends well for you."

Po shrugged off his hand and looked away. "Next time someone orders you to do something you know is wrong, don't do it." Po looked at our surprised expressions. He could have exacted his revenge against this boy, a justified act, but he didn't. "Why make enemies, when you can make friends?" He turned to walk away, but suddenly stopped and lowered his head, sighing. Without warning, he looked up and punched the Fool square in the face, knocking him out once more.

He shrugged. "He did throw a pie in my face."

# THE TEMPLE OF ROMIR

The Temple of Romir was a large building located in the northwest section of the city. It was at one time the oldest building in the kingdom before being torn down and replaced during the endless rebuilding of the city. My great-uncle had designed the new temple in the style of the modern buildings surrounding it while retaining the aesthetic from the original stone temple. The synchronous application of modern efficiency and ancient detail was among his proudest accomplishments.

A smaller church would typically not have as many levels either above ground or below, but the prestigious temples that populated the main cities were built in accordance with the heavens and hells of the religion. Nine levels above the ground, each signifying a different god of the Nine in their respective heaven, and nine levels below the ground for those gods' corresponding hells. Starfall held more secular beliefs than the heartlands, and the Northern Tribes worshipped different gods altogether, but they both still had their large Temples of the Nine, as the High Queen had commanded.

Luckily, the temple was one of the few places in Romir where even foreigners were not uncommon, and we could easily blend in. We made our way to the temple's side entrance and stopped to go over our plan. "Okay, we split up in groups of two. Yokel and Windrunner will enter first, followed by—"

"I call being on Roc's team!" Po yelped.

Roc's smile engulfed his whole face as I continued happily. "Po will go with Roc next, and Pathfinder and I will be the rearguard." I took a stick and drew in the dirt a crude schematic I had seen once in my father's study at the Forge. "Let's meet here," I said, pointing to a sketched hallway deep within the bowels of the temple. "Everyone follow your routes and if you find anything, send someone to the rendezvous point and we'll all meet up. Clear?"

Everyone nodded and we broke out into designated entrance points. Yokel and Windrunner entered through the front, pretending to be two young lovers in search of confession. Roc and Po entered through a side door and melted into a crowd of less fortunate folk looking for help. Pathfinder and I tarried for a few minutes before heading inside, waiting to see if any of our companions were being followed.

"Just like old times," Pathfinder joked. My heart fluttered at having some alone time with her once more. But even in these quiet moments with her, my guilt would speak Iris's name and I would unconsciously suppress that voice.

"Wouldn't have asked for a better partner," I flirted.

What the Hells was I doing?

"Well, I'm no Yokel," she joked.

I burst out into an uncontrollable laugh. "Pathfinder, I just want to say—"

"Looks like we're clear, let's move!" she whispered loudly as we flanked the temple walls and entered through a window.

Our journey took us through rooms and corridors, with no sign of the priest we were looking for or the Codex. A few times we were almost discovered but were able to avoid detection by a combination of hiding and pretending to be wayward lovers. I hated to admit that the pretending was all too easy with Pathfinder, and in moments like this I was glad Iris was safely back in Starfall.

Pathfinder and I came up empty and moved to the rendezvous point, where we found Po using Roc's abdomen as a punching bag.

"No luck either?" I asked.

"Oof. None."

"Where are the other two?" Pathfinder asked.

"Haven't seen them yet," Po said between heavy breaths. Before we could respond, Yokel came crashing around the corner. "I th-think we f-found something!"

We raced behind him, keeping to the shadows and avoiding contact with anyone we came across. Yokel led us to a hall that stopped at a dead-end, but no Windrunner.

Pathfinder looked around anxiously. "Where is she?"

"I've got a bad feeling about this," Roc said.

"No escape if we're found," I pointed out.

"Yes but look at this." Yokel was pointing to a single brick on the wall that bore the nine-pointed star sigil that matched the lock on Haralabos's book.

"Where's Windrunner?" Pathfinder asked once more.

"Why is there a dead-end here?" Po asked curiously, tracing my schematics from his memory into the air. He was right. I sifted through the blueprints in my mind temple; there should be another room here. I ran my hands along the stone wall, pressing my fingertips to glean any unusual or useful detail, but I needed more light.

"Grab that torch, Yok."

Yokel walked over to the torch but slipped and grabbed at the torch's bracket to halt his fall. With a metallic scrape the torch shifted down, throwing Yokel face forward to the floor. Roc and I bent to pick him up as the torch shifted back into place, and the sound of grinding stone resonated from the dead-end wall. With a crack, the stones broke open a seam, revealing an open doorway.

Roc patted Yokel on the back heartily. "Good job, Yok!"

"Anything I can do to help," Yokel responded, rubbing his nose.

"Wait! Where is Windrunner?" Pathfinder yelled as she stood in front of the door.

In our excitement we had forgotten about her and now were torn between two paths.

"Pathfinder, you go search for her, meet us back outside, and we'll check out the room."

She hesitated but reluctantly agreed. Whiskey Danger carried the torch through the door and into a large room, more cavernous than I had anticipated. In the middle was a rectangular table and chairs placed haphazardly across the floor, and in the corner of the room stood a desk with papers and ink wells.

"Yokel, check out that desk. Oliver, you and I will search the rest of the room. Po..." try not to punch anyone in the face," Roc instructed with a wry smile.

Po punched him in the stomach instead and then wandered off into the room. I walked along the table, trying to imagine all that was talked about in this secret room. Roc was staring at a series of nine portraits on the far wall, five men, four women. Each face had been desecrated with marks and tears, and nothing could be ascertained about their identities. One of the men held a sword hilt in his hand that I didn't recognize, but it looked powerful, and that power called to me.

"You guys are not going to believe what's here," Yokel called out from behind the desk. I looked to Roc and we moved toward Yokel when all of a sudden, bells started to ring and trumpets to sound.

"What's going on?" Roc yelled, covering his ears. From the ceiling, a shelf was being lowered with an object in the middle of it. On the far side of the room, we could see Po pulling on a book on a bookshelf that didn't want to come out.

"Po! What are you..." Roc yelled, rushing toward the kid. I ran to the entrance and pulled the lever on the wall, causing the hidden door to swing back into its original position.

"I just wanted to see what this book was about. It says The Knights of Nine on it," Po responded nonchalantly.

Roc raised an eyebrow at him. "You can read Elvish?"

Po squirmed in embarrassment. "Only a little. I'm only in my first year at the Institute."

"Shhh!" I put my finger to my lips and pointed to the wall where the door once was. I explained further with Hand Language to Yokel. (*Someone is on the other side of the wall, we need to find another way out.*) Roc got the gist and immediately began a silent search for an alternate passageway.

Yokel, on the other hand, was teetering on a stack of furniture, trying to reach the shelf that had stopped its descent midway. The voices on the other side of the wall were getting louder, and I assumed that guards of some sort were making their way to the dead-end. We didn't have much time.

Po was staring at the portrait of the man with the sword. Running up behind him, I whispered, "Po, we need to find a way out. Keep looking!"

He kept staring at the portrait. "That sword looks out of place."

"Yes, I know, I was looking at that earlier, but we don't have time for..." I trailed off, noticing that the sword had a strange tilt, leaning... the wrong way? I handed Po the torch and jumped on a chair, reaching up to put my hand on the image of the sword. I pulled away in surprise when I felt its raised profile. Curious, I pushed at the sword hilt, moving it to what I felt was the correct angle.

Click.

Suddenly, a stone in the floor by the desk receded, revealing a darkened staircase. At the same time, the stone caused Yokel's leaning tower to come crashing down, leaving him hanging precariously from the shelf, swinging erratically.

"No way they didn't hear that!" Roc yelled as he scooped up Po and put him on his shoulders. The torch landed on the ground and rolled under the shelf Yokel was so obsessed with. With Po on top of Roc's shoulders, the two of them managed to grab hold of Yokel, who was still stretching for the prize in the middle of the shelf.

He groaned. "I can almost reach it!"

"We don't have time for this!" Roc yelled as he tried to balance two people on his shoulders.

"Yok, catch!" I yelled as I threw him my sword. Taking it, he ran the sword over the edge of the shelf and swept the treasure to the ground.

"I got it!" I said, picking it up.

Yokel let go of the shelf and dropped to the ground, catching Po as he descended off Roc. Roc ushered Yokel and Po and we bolted for the secret staircase. As I ran down the steps behind the others, I brushed along the tight walls for support. My hand hit a protruding brick that I accidently pushed inward, which moved the staircase stone back to its original position and plunged Whiskey Danger into complete darkness.

"Anyone have a light?" Yokel asked gruffly, but the torch had been forgotten in our haste. "I can't see an inch in front of me. There's no telling what we'll walk into."

The sound of a striking match and a blast of sulfur wafted toward us to expose a figure in dark clothes not unlike our own, holding the light to her face.

"Fancy meeting you here, boys," Pathfinder said in her metallic voice.

Yokel exhaled loudly. "Thank the Nine you're here!"

"I thought I told you to wait outside," I said, now concerned for her safety as well as the rest of Whiskey Danger.

"I found Windrunner, she's waiting for us. She led some Spider's Web folks on a wild chase through the temple, but then the bells started to ring and we knew we had to double back. Follow me." She spun and her tiny matchlight wavered in the narrow tunnel.

After running for several minutes, a sliver of light shone in front of us, promising freedom. We approached the end of the tunnel to find ourselves looking out from a hole in the cliff face, high above a mist-laced and swiftly rushing river.

"So, our options are, stay here and hope nobody finds us, or jump and hope we don't die," Yokel grimly summarized.

"Or we could climb the rope to the top," Pathfinder pointed out. The rope was dangling down the cliffside, albeit farther from us than any one of us could reach. "Windrunner is waiting, but she's exposed so we have to hurry."

We grabbed each other's hands, creating a chain anchored by Roc. Po stretched to his full extent, leaning out along the cliff face and just catching the rope with the tips of his fingers, but not before slipping a few times and scaring us all nearly senseless. Roc directed us as we pulled Po back into the tunnel.

"Yokel, you'll go first. Po, you follow, then me, Pathfinder, and Oliver, you follow behind."

Yokel looped the rope into his belt, but before he could ascend, I strapped his prize to his back. "Take this, Yok, you earned it."

"I think we all earned it," Roc said as he prepared Po's belt. "It better be worth a lot of money." He turned to me before starting his ascent. "Don't you two do anything stupid, you hear?"

I pushed him away over the edge and he pulled his massive body up. I grabbed the rope to hand it to Pathfinder but at the same instant we both noticed a flickering light in the tunnel.

"The guards must have found the entrance," I whispered. Voices began to echo, accompanied by the familiar ting of swords and scabbards. I looked up the cliff to see that Yokel had reached the top, but Po and Roc were still climbing.

They needed more time.

I looked at Pathfinder. "If you hurry, you can make it."

"We can make it."

"No. If they find the edge and they find the rope, we'll all be caught. I can hold them off. Just go." I brandished my sword and moved into Form

Sixteen, which would afford me movement within the confines of the tunnel.

I heard another ting of a scabbard but this time from behind me. Pathfinder had taken her sword out too.

"Do you trust me?" she asked.

"What?"

"Do you trust me?"

My heart pounded and my breathing became erratic. My skin caught fire but it was like some kind of frozen fire from an Ice Dragon. I didn't know if it was the impending fight or just knowing I was going to spend what were possibly my last moments with someone I cared so deeply about, but for a brief moment, I felt free.

"Yes," I finally said.

Pathfinder swung her sword along the cliff's face, splitting the rope. Its tail twisted and fell into the mist below. She sheathed her sword and I did as well. Pathfinder pulled at my tunic and put one of my own hands over my eyes. Once more I felt the sweet lips of my vigilante heroine, but as quickly as it had come, it was gone again and she stood, teetering at the edge of the tunnel.

"See you at the bottom, little lord," she said, and then she jumped back and down into the dark mist of the river below.

"No!" I muttered, but I could hear the guards getting closer. Going against all my better judgment, I took a deep breath and leapt over the edge and into the dark abyss, waiting for the icy cold of death to follow.

But death did not follow, just the river.

# THE WORLD CHAMPIONSHIP

"Easy, Yok, it's just us," I said as the tip of Yokel's sword pressed gently against my soaking tunic. He threw his sword to the ground of the suite and grabbed both Pathfinder and me in a hug so tight, I thought he might never let go.

"We're okay," Pathfinder said in a muffled voice.

"Where have you been!" Roc yelled as he rushed over, grabbing me up in a hug.

Pathfinder walked past us to meet Windrunner. "We jumped into the river. There was no other choice, we couldn't let them get to you."

Yokel gaped at us. "And you survived?"

"I have no idea how," I answered. "Once we hit the fog over the river, we slowed down. It felt as if we were falling through a jar of honey. Then, we gently plopped into the river and made our way here."

Po barreled Pathfinder over as she tried to explain further. "I'd heard rumors about those mists, and it turns out they weren't rumors at all."

Windrunner went into another room and returned with the prize Yokel had so earnestly worked for. "You two won't believe what this is," she started. Pathfinder and I looked at each other and then back at Windrunner. "It's the Codex. The damn thing we've been looking for!"

Yokel took the book excitedly and began to flip through the pages. I dropped to the floor with my back to the wall.

"I can't believe it. We did it. We actually did it." I couldn't process my emotions, for they were too many and too strong. I had kissed an impossible girl. Survived an impossible fall. Completed an impossible quest. I had found magic. It was over.

Relief washed over me and yet, also sadness. So many paths had brought me to this point. So many obstacles. Now all that was left to do was train

Po to be the Lightning Knight, something none of us knew anything about. But now, now we had hope. We had the Codex, which would help him become the hero we all needed.

"There's just one small problem," Yokel said, handing me the tome. I flipped through the pages of the book, recognizing the Elvish markings, but none of it made any sense.

I looked back up, puzzled. "I don't get it."

Yokel bent down to point out his findings. "It's Elvish alright, but either in a dialect we don't understand or, more likely, it's encoded."

"So, we can't read it?" Roc looked encouraged. He may have devoted himself to Po's cause, but he still for the life of him hated the idea of being involved with magic. Some things would never change.

Yokel shook his head. "Not unless we find the key to unlock the cypher. Until then, no one can read it. Even the pictures aren't all that useful."

My brain itched. Not my mind, not my thoughts, but my actual brain. I could feel it, which was weird because I had never felt anything like it before. Po took the Codex and began to finger through the pages, pretending to read it. But suddenly, his head started shaking and his body trembled uncontrollably.

Windrunner looked at him in concern. "Po, what's happening?"

"I don't know. I'm not doing it on purpose. I'm starting to freak out here!"

And he did indeed begin to freak out. Roc smacked the book out of his hands and Po collapsed, heaving heavy breaths while he lay on Roc's and Windrunner's arms. I crawled over to pick the Codex up, hoping to find an answer to our young friend's reaction.

"We've got a big few days ahead of us, with the World Championship, so how about we worry about the Codex when we get back to Starfall?" I offered.

Everyone nodded in agreement, although secretly, I was hoping to steal moments when I could examine the Codex myself. I knew Po was supposed to be the Lightning Knight, but it didn't make me want to learn about magic any less.

Over the next three days, Roc was astonishing in the tournament. He was in rare form, even better than he was in Starfall. He'd doubled down on his tactic of unseating his opponents and it made him famous. Although at the beginning of the tournament the crowd had chanted the slur encouraged by Prince Froderick, it had quickly turned to a new moniker Roc wore proudly with each and every victory. He'd come to realize the quickest way to defeat a bully was to take away his power.

Words had power, and Roc knew that better than anyone.

"You ready, Sandman?" I prompted Roc as he settled into his armor. He sat, anxiously fidgeting with his breastplate. The Knight Angels had used the tournament time to search Romir for any help with the Codex, and Po and Yokel had already gone to secure Roc's horse.

"Do I have another option?"

I'd never seen him this nervous and watched his face spiral through waves of emotion. I knew that if he remained this vulnerable and it carried into his match, the night was as good as over. All color drained from his face and he turned to look at me.

"I don't know if I can win, Oliver..."

I knew what I had to do.

"Why don't you think you can win? You're the jouster who unseats his opponent nearly every match! Sounds like a good reputation to have," I said frankly, trying to guide him into a better frame of mind. He was about to face Prince Froderick, and I needed him to focus on his strengths rather than everything that could go wrong.

"You know as well as I do that it's all useless. It's just good entertainment. They can scream and shout all they want, but the fact is it's that damned prince running opposite me, and I just can't beat him." Roc stared at the floor, his shoulders in a defeated slump.

Prince Froderick was as old as my brother but had a jousting reputation of someone ages older. As much of a jerk as he was, he was still a prodigiously talented jouster. I looked at my friend. His face was furrowed into as close to a pout as he could muster, the steadfast champion I knew and loved having been pushed to the side as he argued himself into his own defeat.

"What's he better at than you?"

Roc sighed in frustration. "Everything, Oliver. He's faster than me, stronger than me, more accurate, hits harder, smarter, sturdier..."

"Sturdier?"

Roc rolled his eyes at me. "You know what I mean! He's a brick wall that I can't get through. I just can't beat him. He's the best."

"I see... Although, he's never unhorsed a rider..."

Suddenly, Roc's posture changed and he looked up at me, his left eyebrow raised slightly.

I continued. "And he's never won three straight matches by unhorsing his opponent. In fact, nobody has ever done what you have. Nobody."

Roc stood, his eyes brimming with proud understanding. I stood in front of him, yelling as I pushed him forcefully in the chest.

"Who are you!?"

"I'm Riley Roclan," he replied steadily, color returning to his cheeks.

"I said, WHO ARE YOU!?" I screamed back, throwing more force directly to his chest and pushing him a few steps back.

Roc's eyes lit up and he stared back, moving his feet to a sturdier ready position.

"I'm the Sandman!" he yelled, rapidly hopping from one foot to the other.

I began to jump in place, intoxicated by our growing energy and emotion.

"What are you going to do?" I cried out and Roc yelled an indistinguishable answer.

"And what are you going to do?" I repeated.

"I'm going to put him to sleep!" Roc yelled.

"And why is that?" I asked, and Roc stopped jumping to stand perfectly calm in front of me.

"Because *nobody* can do what I can do." His eyes were resolute, and we stood for some time staring at each other before I nodded in affirmation. After a moment, Roc's expression changed from excited determination to slight panic and he gestured toward the tent door.

"Erhm, should we... go out now?"

"Uh, yeah, let's go."

"Oliver, when we tell people this story, let's leave that bit out."

"Yup."

Our pace was brisk as we made our way to the stadium gate, the cool night air catching the beaded sweat on my neck and resulting in a shudder that ran swiftly down my back. Roc mounted his horse and settled into place, pulling tight on the reins and shaking out his stirrups in practiced routine. He turned, looking down on us from his seat, nodding to Yokel as he spoke.

"Yokel, you know all those times I said to shut up?" He watched Yokel's expression turned from defensive to confused.

Yok quietly responded with a shaky "Yes?"

Roc grinned wildly. "Let 'em have it."

Clasping his hands together sharply, Yokel called out gleefully. "Finally!"

Suddenly, the sound of thousands of cheering people blasted through the slowly opening gate, momentarily obliterating any semblance of coordination our bodies held. We held position and acclimated, trying to grasp the magnitude of our surroundings before Roc reared his horse gallantly and galloped into the deafening stadium, making sure to pass directly by Prince Froderick who stood at the ready, the reigning champion having been announced first. The crowd of foreigners went wild, chanting Roc's new nickname as the Roclan crest flew on banners high above their screaming faces. If there was ever such a thing as a homefield advantage, there was no evidence of it here; more than three-quarters of the stadium were Romirians, but they couldn't match the excitement of the non-Romirians.

Roc completed his lap of the stadium and galloped back to us, dismounting as Yokel made his way to the center of the stadium. Silence crept over the crowd, and I was sure they could hear the groan of leather lashes against steel as Po and I made last-minute adjustments to Roc's armor. We turned to watch as Yokel began his herald.

"Lords and ladies! Your Highness, and all of our great noble houses!" he cried, waving up to the nobles' boxes before turning around sharply on his heel. "And all of you! The fishermen, farmers, the cobblers and smiths, woodworkers and low-borns, sandeaters and treejumpers!"

The crowd roared, and for the first time I realized that the crowd was made up mostly of non-nobles. In fact, every crowd we'd ever competed in front of, be it in the joust or the sword ring, had been low-born. I'd spent my entire life surrounded by the wealthy minority, when these were the people who mattered. Roc was one of their own, Romirian or not, and he was their hero.

Yokel waited for the crowd noise to subside before turning around in place, addressing the entire stadium. "My friends! I present to you a man who needs no introduction. He is not from a high house, he is a jouster born of the Narrows of Starfall, and he jousts for you, all the people of this world. I present the only man to unhorse every opponent in the World Championship, the Starfall City Champion, a man feared by opponents and fans alike, and the best man I know... I give you the Sandman, Riley Roclan!"

The already rowdy crowd erupted into a cacophonous frenzy, screaming as Yokel announced Roc's name. Yokel made his way back to us, grinning widely. He reached Roc and the two slapped each other's shoulders before Roc mounted his horse once more. I called out to him as I handed him his lance, "See you on the other side!" and he nodded, slapping down his visor to stare down the tilt at his opponent.

I looked on as the Marshall of the Field approached center track, holding the flag of Romir flat over the tilt as the crowd hushed to a quiet murmur. The horses' hooves thumped against the ground in anticipation. He looked to each side before looking at the flag as he jerked it up from the tilt. Both riders spurred their horses forward, furiously trying to gain ground over their opponent's approach. They met in the center, each rider making contact with the other's breastplate and shattered lances splintering in every direction. The crowd sent up a mix of groans and cheers. The riders brought their horses back to their respective recesses, and as Roc moved back to first position, he lifted his visor to breathe more easily, groaning quietly as he raised his arm.

"He hits like a hammer! Ugh, it's perfect technique," he gasped, his chest rolling up and down heavily. I nodded but responded calmly, reiterating our strategy.

"But so do you. Keep pace with him and don't let up. He may be hitting you, but you are hitting him right back. He'll break before you do. People like him aren't used to being hit."

I was unwilling to abandon the plan we had come up with yesterday. Yokel's study of the prince's runs had given us one visible crack in his otherwise insurmountable technique. He had run through the Championship with relative ease, racking only four lances against him. Our strategy was that of attrition; if we kept pace, we could outlast him... theoretically. Before I knew it, the Marshall had signaled the second run, each rider once again dealing a direct blow to the other's chest.

"I can't breathe..." Roc gasped from the starting position. Po hopped onto a block to loosen his armor.

"Look, I know what our plan is, but we didn't anticipate the fact that I may not survive until the end," Roc said glumly as he peered down the tilt. I followed his gaze to see the prince yelling at his squires and kicking one in frustration. I smiled, turning back to Roc.

"Look at him. He's flustered. He's never been hit like this before. We have him just where we want him, just keep holding strong!"

"You're not the one getting hit!" Roc cried, followed by a sigh. He knew full well that it was far too late to change our approach now.

"Po, lace him back up," I yelled as I noticed the Marshall walking up to the tilt again.

"I can't breathe!" Roc cried in protest.

"No time for that!" I replied with a quick slap to his horse's haunch as the starting flag was drawn up.

The horse sprang forward and Roc's body fell into its rhythm, aiming his lance directly at the prince's chest once more. I looked on, noticing the prince's shift a second too late. Instead of countering Roc's approach with another blow to his chest, the prince moved to make full contact with Roc's head, hitting it square on and throwing Roc backward on his horse. His body hung strangely off to one side as his horse made its way back to the starting position.

"Roc, can you hear me?" I yelled, watching his head bounce from side to side as his horse trotted toward me. "Po, water!"

"You want a rag?" Po asked, but I grabbed the bucket from him, throwing its entire contents into Roc's face. He blinked rapidly, shaking his head clear.

"I'm here, I'm here. What's the score?"

"Four lances to three," Yokel reported.

"New plan?" Roc asked in a low voice, staring at the prince.

I nodded slowly, talking through my thoughts as we worked out the next move.

"He's scared. He knows you can beat him, and he's hurting. He won't try the same thing twice. He's going to go for the safe play against the chest. You match him, and we lose... You know what that means?"

Roc nodded. "Lance!" He swiftly cradled the lance I handed him and spurred his horse into a tight circle, energy exploding from its body as it read the resolve coursing through its rider. If this didn't work, if we lost this match, all we had worked so hard for all year—really all our lives—would be for nothing.

It all came down to this.

Roc settled his horse into the starting position, and the flag was lifted for a final time up and away from center tilt. Both riders raced forward, and as expected, the prince's aim was directly for Roc's heart. Roc made the only move he could, dropping his handle down at the last minute to score against the prince's helmet. He rode back to us, and we looked on as the flagman signaled the start of sudden death.

"This has to be the first time in history that the World Championship match has gone to sudden death!" Yokel exclaimed loudly as Roc dismounted.

"What does that mean?" Po yelled over the noise of the screaming crowd.

"Get this off, I can't, I can't…" Roc gasped heavily as he sank to his knees, gesturing nonspecifically to his armor. I hurried to undo laces and Yokel quickly explained our predicament to Po.

"Whoever scores the most lances first wins, no matter how many runs it takes. We get five minutes before it starts. Roc, what are you thinking?"

"I'm thinking if I take another hit like that, I won't survive." He turned his head to cough, a gobbet of blood hitting the dirt as he held himself up on his knees with both hands on the ground. The three of us looked on gravely.

Yokel began to fidget and motioned for Po to help him. "Only two minutes left, we've got to fix that armor."

I stood gripping Roc's helmet and turned from my friends, taking a moment to look at the prince. I could see him shoving his squires around in angry frustration; he hadn't expected such a complicated match and had never been hit on every single run before. Roc's last hit to his helmet would make him reckless, and that was the opportunity we needed.

"Stop! Don't put the armor on!" I yelled suddenly, throwing Roc's helmet to the ground and tearing Yokel away.

"Are you insane?!" Yokel screamed, trying to make his way back to Roc.

"Oliver, I'm not giving up," Roc said flatly. "I can win this."

I smiled, leaning forward to speak to him. "I know you can. Don't put the armor on. Don't put the helmet on. He's going for your head regardless. Look at him. He's never made a mistake in any joust, but he's about to make one now. He hates you. He hates the position you've put him in. He hates that you've hit him so many times because he thinks he's better than you, better than us. He thinks we're going to play it safe, but he wants to win, and he wants to win on this run. Roc, he's going straight for your head."

Po's expression was a mix of nerves and confusion. "... okay, so then shouldn't he be wearing his helmet?"

"No, we should let him think he's got the upper hand. You come down the track with no armor, no helmet, not only is he going to be distracted, he's going to try for your head even harder at the insult, and that's where we'll get him. He'll think that he's going in for the kill, but he can't do what you can, Roc."

"Nobody can," Roc replied simply.

"Nobody can," I repeated with a smile.

Roc nodded sharply. "Okay, help me on my horse." After he settled into his saddle he looked steadily down the pitch. "This ends now. Lance!"

I could hear my heartbeat even over the crowd's screams, and I felt as if my whole body might convulse in the anticipation of this next run. I trusted Roc now as I had trusted him with Ridhan's terms, but I couldn't help fearing I had just condemned my best friend to death.

Roc winked at me and turned to Po just as the Marshall readied his flag over the tilt. "See you on the other side!"

Po looked up at him in awe, flashing the Whiskey Danger hand signal proudly. We waited in suspense, and each of us jumped when the flag was jerked up and Roc spurred his horse, gaining ground swiftly without the added weight of his armor. Roc met the prince several paces into the prince's own half, taking Froderick by surprise just as Roc and I had predicted. The prince hesitated, unable to get his lance tip up in time to meet Roc's head accurately. Froderick threw every bit of his remaining strength and momentum toward Roc, but his missed lance thrust caused him to fall forward just as Roc's lance shattered into him, throwing Froderick from his horse and into the wooden tilt with a splintering crash. Freed of the weight of his rider, the prince's horse jumped forward through the newly formed gap in the tilt and galloped by us in a startled blur.

Roc turned and rode as quickly as he could back to us. He reared his horse to a stop in first position, and the crowd began to scream louder than they had ever threatened as the streaming white banners next to the scoreboard were replaced with brown ones, embroidered with the Roclan sigil. Roc slid from his horse and looked up at the board, falling to his knees. The three of us rushed him, tackling him onto the ground in a tangled pile of limbs. I grabbed Roc by the face.

"You! You crazy little—"

"LITTLE!?" he roared, embracing me warmly in a big hug. He let me go and looked me straight in the eye. "For real though, Oliver, I couldn't have done this without you."

"Yes, you could have!" I pressed, shaking in utter joy at my friend's momentous victory.

"Well... yeah, maybe I could have, but it wouldn't have been nearly as fun!" he joked as he shook me by the shoulders. I took the ring Sir Roclan had given me from my pocket and held it out to Roc.

"Here, this was your uncle's."

But Roc closed my hand around the ring, shaking his head. "No, it belongs to you. Thanks for being my friend, Oliver."

I smiled and squeezed the ring tightly. Suddenly, a group of people from the crowd rushed us, scooping the whole of Whiskey Danger onto their shoulders and out to the middle of the stadium. At one point, I heard Yokel exclaim, "Someone grabbed my butt!" to which Roc, Po, and I all in unison replied.

"Shut up, Yokel!"

# A QUEST ENDS

"Cheers, mates!" Pathfinder yelled above the noise of the party. The six of us clinked our mugs. The first floor of our building was packed with people from all over the city and especially the Foreign Quarter, celebrating Roc's victory. Everything was falling into place, and for once, life seemed to be utterly perfect.

I hopped up onto the bar and sat, surveying the rave in front of me. An orchestra played as people gyrated and jostled for position on the dance floor, which was the entire floor. For the briefest of moments, I took stock of everything that had led to this point.

The quest Professor Lortho had set me on months ago was completed. We had found the Th'aumaturgy Codex, essentially finding magic, or so we thought. Maybe we couldn't decode it yet, but it was a victory nonetheless. Po had become a Carpenter and was on his way to becoming the Lightning Knight, or so we hoped. I was finally courting Iris, and Ridhan was no longer a threat and maybe even an ally. I'd even made two new friends in Pathfinder and Windrunner. Everything was perfect, and I could feel the sadness of the end. For so long my path had been set and my focus homed in on these quests. I may not have been the hero like in the stories, but I felt accomplished. I felt completed. I felt at peace. I didn't know what the future held, but I knew that I had made an impact on the world. Like the end of a great story, it was bitter but still sweet.

Po climbed on a stool, then onto the bar and sat next to me, his legs crossed in a meditative form. "How did you know what the prince would do?" he asked between sips of wine.

"I didn't, Po. I just trusted my gut, and I trusted Roc." I paused, turning to laugh and wave at Roc who had found himself surrounded by girls. I turned to Po again, trying to explain myself. "My family has a saying, ironically enough for a bunch of ironmongers: 'Put your faith in people, not metal.' It has generally held true for me."

"So... Roc must put his faith in you too."

"That's what friendship is, Po. It's trusting each other, even when it might be crazy. It's putting away your own doubts and trusting their judgment. We're stronger together than we are individually," I said, suddenly aware of the depth behind my awkward words.

Po's expression turned solemn, and his voice. "Oliver, I still don't know how to be brave like that. Like Roc was, or like you. How do you do it? How are you brave all the time?"

I paused to think about his question, the noises of the party fading away. This was the same question he had asked Azel and that I had asked of Sir Roclan. I had never thought of myself as very brave, never truly believed that I would have the courage required in a truly desperate situation. I stymied a wave of self-doubt and looked at my young friend, his questioning mind yearning for an answer. I inhaled slowly, repeating the answer the wise knight had given me.

"You don't have to be brave all the time, you only have to be brave once."

Po looked at me, a smile slowly forming. "Only once?"

"Here's a secret, Po. I'm not brave either. I want to be, but I'm not. I'm still trying to find my courage too."

"How will we find it then?"

I reached out my hand and he instinctively grasped it as I answered, "Together."

Po looked down at his wine, scowling at the remaining amount as he processed what I had said. "I hope I can live up to it. To be what you all want me to be," he said finally before draining his glass.

"You will. You'll be the hero we all need. The hero the world needs. The Lightning Knight. I have no doubt about it. All we have to do is figure out how to read that stupid Codex." I watched a small tear break his lashes and start to roll down his cheek. He wiped it away and replied quietly.

"Thanks, Oliver."

"You're welcome, bud. Now, I'm going to go try my best to save Roc. You okay hanging out for a while?"

Seeing him nod, I grabbed my drink and weaved slowly through the crowd, approaching Roc, but Pathfinder took me and spun me around, making me crash into party goers.

"Oi, where are you off to, love?" she asked, practically falling over herself.

"Well, I was planning on helping Roc with—"

"Oh, bollocks, he's fine. Look at him, in all his splendor and women. But what 'bout yoouuuuuuu," she slurred as I caught her in my arms.

"You're very drunk," I said, dropping my own glass to the floor.

"Nope. Nope, nope, yep. I mean, nope, bollocks!" She giggled before pulling me in closely and whispering in my ear. "I have a secret, hehe."

"Oh, do you now?" I said, caught in the euphoria of the spell she somehow put on me. "And what might that be?"

"Shhhh," she whispered loudly, putting her finger to her masked lips. "It's a secret. I'm not allowed to tell!"

"Who said?" I asked, playing with the choker necklace that held an ordinary looking stone in the middle, trying to hear her true voice.

'Nah uh, love, nooooooo cheating."

"We could dance instead," I said, swinging her around and crashing into another group of people.

"No, no, no, I hate dancing. We could find a place more quiet." Her eyes sparkled. My heart pounded as Pathfinder pulled me away from the party, down the hall, and into the lift. I put my hand over my eyes in anticipation, and my invitation was met with her lips on mine for the entire ride up.

We arrived at the suite, my mind intoxicated. Inside me were two Olivers, neither fighting for control. I knew that what I was doing was wrong, that I was betraying Iris and that I was betraying myself. But I also knew I couldn't stop. Didn't want to stop. There was no justification, no trying to talk myself around the situation. Instead, there was just acceptance. I was going to give in to these feelings and live with the consequences later.

The door of the lift opened and neither of us paid it any mind. Our passionate kissing took us along every side of the lift until we fell out of the opening, tripping over a pair of small boots and crashing onto the floor. I took my hand away from my face and found Pathfinder's mask was once again over her own.

"What was that?" I yelled in rapturous laughter.

"I don't knooooooowwwwww!" Pathfinder giggled back, walking the small boots with her hands.

"Those are Po's fancy boots," I responded, grabbing one and walking it myself. "But he should be wearing these downstairs." A moment of panic and shame coursed through me. If I'd been able to see Pathfinder's face, I'm sure I would have seen my feelings mirrored. In our euphoria, we had both given in to feelings we shouldn't have had. Po would never forgive us if he found out.

I put my finger to my lips and motioned for us both to survey the suite, hoping not to be caught by our innocent friend. We tiptoed loudly, Pathfinder hanging on my shoulders and trying to stymie her whispering laughter. I slowly opened the door to his room, a creaking echoing in the empty chamber. I turned to Pathfinder, wide-eyed. She ran to check the other rooms while I ran to check mine.

"The Codex is gone!" I yelled.

"Po's outfit is gone too," Pathfinder confirmed.

My heart stopped. Why would he leave without us? Where would he go? I thought about the last conversation I had with him, about being brave and becoming the Lightning Knight. I thought about Po's reaction the first time he held the Codex, and my breath caught.

"We need to find Po, now!" I yelled as we raced through the suite and down the stairs, jumping and skipping many of them. Pathfinder ran to update Windrunner while I bolted for the door. Yokel and Roc must have noticed my panic because even as I ran through the streets, I could feel Roc's long strides catching up and hear Yokel's questions.

We rushed through the streets without regard for anyone in our way until we heard a scream ring out, turning our attention toward an alleyway. A crowd of people blocked the scene, and as I pushed through, I felt as though I had been hit by a sledgehammer.

The street was painted with small pools of blood trailing from a barely moving supine figure. Bruises were forming over his face and arms as he crawled along the wet stone, his hand outstretched to a smaller body lying motionless several feet away. Roc rushed by me, screaming in agony as he slid to his knees to clasp the still form tightly against his body.

"No! No! No, no, no, no, no, don't do this, don't do this…"

"Give him space, let me, let me see!" Yokel yelled, his voice cracking with urgency as he checked the body for pulse and breath.

"Oh, Po…" Yokel whispered, releasing Po's bloodied and bruised head. Roc pulled the small, broken body closer to him and wept uncontrollably, rocking back and forth and pleading earnestly to ears that could no longer hear.

"Don't do this, kid, don't do this. Don't be like this, wake up!"

"His pulse is weak, death is close now," Yokel said quietly to me, barely able to muster the words. We put our hands on Roc's shoulder who jerked away defensively, turning to snap at us.

"He could come back! He could! You don't know him like I do. He's stronger than you, stronger than any of you. Please… Please, Po, please!"

All Roc's bravery was gone as he knelt there shaking, more vulnerable than I had ever seen him. All his pride and confidence had melted into grief and despair. I looked for Yokel's usually logical presence, but in all his intelligence he could not see the sense in this moment. He too was spiraling into emotion and sorrow. Pathfinder and Windrunner had finally arrived, falling to their knees in anguish, weeping ferociously in each other's arms.

As for me, I felt hollow, like an old dead tree. The grief, the anger, the guilt all washed over me in an instant, and in lieu of being overwhelmed by them, I instead extinguished all feeling.

My mind was empty for the first time in my life, and I could no longer feel my heart beating in my chest. I felt death from within myself, from a place I once thought held my soul. But I was alive, fixated on my young friend's limp body, on my oldest friend losing all his logic, and on my closest friend's grief as he cried out in a pain I had never witnessed before. Roc continued his pleas quietly, begging shamelessly. "Kid, no… don't. Please, Po… I'll do anything."

I turned, barely registering the voice of the battered boy as he moaned. I moved toward him, controlled by an emotion I couldn't understand. It was more than hatred, more than rage; it was as if the inverse of love had taken me over, filling me with this new presence.

It was unlove.

"What happened!?" I screamed as I turned the boy onto his back. The Codex lay under him where he had crawled, and he was battered nearly beyond recognition, but still I knew him. The Fool stared back at me, moaning and spitting out blood.

"Kid… not again. Leave him alone…"

"Who did this! Answer me!" I yelled, gripping his shoulders and shaking him.

"Prince… no… I didn't… Prince… stop… kid, don't…"

The unlove took over fully, telling me what needed to be done. Retribution to the person who had taken everything from me.

I stood up, blood coursing through my body with a power I had never felt before. Any question of how I felt incinerated into a burning tempest, honing my devastation to a dangerous, volatile point. I looked at Po's broken body, fueling the rage that now burned brighter than the sun.

Po was murdered. And it was the prince's fault!

I felt a bloody hand grab hold of my ankle and looked back at the Fool, who had snapped a vial from a string he wore around his neck. Pulling the stopper off with his mangled teeth, he drank some of the liquid with the last of his strength. Pathfinder came up behind me, bending down to examine the vial.

She muttered something to the Fool, but I couldn't make any of it out. All I could see was red, and the anger I felt overwhelmed me. A single word repeated over and over in my head: prince.

"Where are you going?!" Roc yelled, transparent in his despair, but I didn't answer. I couldn't answer. I wasn't thinking, just feeling. I let go of all reason and logic and allowed the unlove to be in control.

Passage into the castle was easier than I cared for. One part of me wanted a challenge, to perhaps stop me from doing what I knew I would. But there was nothing to stop me, nothing to stop what was about to happen. A servant's door allowed me unfettered access to the prince's chamber, where I saw Prince Froderick standing alone, unbuckling his sword belt. I opened the door silently, quickly unsheathing my sword and walking up behind him, placing the blade across his throat.

"What is the meaning of this?!" he spluttered furiously.

"This is for tonight," I said, ready to kill him there and then. But I kept my blade steady, wanting to hear his confession before I exacted judgment.

He seemed genuinely surprised. "What the Hells are you talking about?"

"I mean for the young boy you murdered!" I yelled, my rage pushing my blade slightly, drawing blood from the prince's neck.

"You'll have to be more specific. I've had a lot of people killed!" Prince Froderick hissed. Even with my blade to his throat, with blood trickling onto his shirt, he still thought he was in control. My breathing labored as I felt myself losing control of the situation.

"He was my friend, and you killed him," I whispered into his ear as I pressed my blade tighter against his neck, "and now it's your turn."

"I don't know who you are, but if he was your friend, I'm sorry… sorry he's not alive to be killed again!" the prince spat, turning his face as though to headbutt me. My rage was undeterred and my focus remained clear, pushed by the vengeful hatred that had brought me there. I punched him in the face, sending him reeling backward onto his bed. I grabbed him by the collar and threw him to the floor. I hit him over and over in blind rage, numb to any pain in my own knuckles.

I cried out, trying to find power again. "How could you! He was just a kid! He was a good kid! You don't deserve to live. You're going to pay for this!" Tears began to stream freely down my face, and my hands moved from his face to his ribs, punching them over and over with a speed I didn't know I possessed. I cried out over and over, expecting an answer I never received.

"How… could… you… he was the best of us!"

The prince's face seemed to laugh at me, to say that Po deserved it. With every one of the false smiles from the prince I hit him harder and harder, desperate to exact my revenge, to bring justice for my friend.

My dead friend.

This last thought rang in my head, throwing me into convulsions between hits. I felt lost, as if I were drowning at sea… a sea of blood, and I was unable to float or swim. Suddenly, a pair of arms wrapped around me, pulling me off the prince. I gasped as the ringing in my ears subsided and a familiar voice called out to me.

"Ollie, you need to leave! The guards are coming! Ollie, can you hear me! Oliver!" It was Windrunner, shaking me furiously. She led me to the balcony and pointed to a pair of ropes dangling over the river.

"Take the rope. Leave now, they're almost here," she implored.

"I failed! Po's dead," I cried.

"No, he's not! Po's alive, but we have to leave!" she shouted as she grabbed a rope and rappelled down from the balcony. My hands held the rope loosely, incapable of knowing what to do. Could it be true? I saw his broken body in Roc's arms. How could he be alive?

The image of Po's face smiling at me leaped into my mind and hope returned to my heart. But there too was the stain of what I had just done. I looked back. The prince lay unmoving on the floor of his chamber. Blood dripped down my boots, none of it mine. The clashing of metal armor and the sound of heavy running feet came from the hallway, snapping me into action.

What had I done?

The unlove dissipated and reason returned, and it threatened to overwhelm me. My quests were at an end, and I had failed. I jumped onto the ledge to rappel down to the river and to the unknown future.

# THUNDERCLAP

The journey back to Starfall was long and arduous. We'd taken the carriage south to a riverboat that would take us to Starfire Bay and then back home along the coast. The journey was also mostly silent. A combination of anger, frustration, worry, and most of all sadness befell our group. We had lost in the most spectacular fashion.

After I had gone after Prince Froderick, the Fool had told Pathfinder to use the vial on Po, which she did after much protest from Roc. Po had come back from the brink of death, but without the use of his legs. It seemed whatever was left of the magical potion wasn't enough. Regardless, we were glad he was still alive. The Fool had conveniently disappeared without a trace and with the Codex. So not only was our future Lightning Knight now lame, we had no Codex to train him with.

I felt the weight of it crashing down on me heavier than a wave in the riptide. I had failed at my quests, and I honestly didn't know what to do. I had failed to protect Po, and now he was crippled. I had found magic only to lose it within a matter of days.

Then there was Pathfinder. I held such resentment toward her, but really toward myself. My selfishness had caused a momentary lapse in judgment, and I couldn't help but think that it was a reason for Po's current situation. If I hadn't been flirting with Pathfinder, been following her up to our room, I might have stopped Po. He might have avoided his fate.

Worse was the thought of Iris, back in Starfall, none the wiser to my wandering eye. Ever since I had met Pathfinder that night in the Shears, I knew I was playing with fire. I knew it would eventually burn me. But still I continued to pursue her. Still I put myself in situations that could jeopardize everything I had with Iris.

And still I yearned to be in Pathfinder's arms, or Iris's arms, or anyone's arms. I felt utterly alone, even surrounded by my friends. Roc stared at me seemingly the entire trip back, seething with anger and rage. I deserved it. We had played with magic, and Po had paid the price. The worst part was that I was the one who had pushed for it. I was the one consumed with the idea and intoxicated with the feeling.

"Oliver," Roc said as we passed through the Outer Gate of Starfall, finally home.

"I know," I answered, trying not to engage in a long-awaited debate.

Roc pulled me around by my shoulder, yelling, "No you don't know!"

"Yes, I do!" I snapped back. I held out Haralabos's book. "This ends tonight. Get Po out of here."

"No," said a small voice from the pushcart we had acquired in the Floating Isles. "I'm coming too. Whatever it is, I'm coming too. We're all in this together."

I grimaced and looked away into the close quarters that were the Narrows. Po was correct; we were in this together, even if it was all coming to an end. So, we headed to the ocean and to the beach. Black Sunday offered no reprieve from the darkness, but it didn't matter much. I dug a small hole and placed driftwood in it. A small torch lay on the ground, barely illuminating our faces. I took out Haralabos's book and threw it onto the pyre. I took Po's ring off my finger and went to throw it on the pyre as well but was stopped by a small noise from Po. His eyes were watering, and I sighed, placing the ring back on my finger.

"A few months ago, we started out on a journey. On a quest. My quest. We were wrong. Magic was never ours to play with. We're just kids, and we messed with things that were beyond us. Roc, you were right."

I paused, surveying the group. Roc looked steadfast and Yokel still looked to be in shock. Pathfinder and Windrunner traded glances, but I didn't care. Not anymore. Lastly, I looked at Po, who was staring at the pyre, his grandfather's book lying dangerously at the bottom.

"Oliver, you don't mean—" Windrunner started.

I struck a match. "Yes, I do! Look what happened! None of us have had the courage to say it, but I will. We failed. Po was supposed to be a hero and we were supposed to be his protectors. Now look at him, he can't even—" My throat caught. Roc looked at me in a panic, as if I was about to say something taboo.

"You can say it, Oliver. I'm crippled," Po stated without looking away from the book. "I can't be the Lightning Knight like this. I can't be the hero. I can't be anything."

I fell to my knees, tears streaming down my face and my lips quivering as the match burned, inching closer to my hand. "I'm so sorry, Po," I finally choked out.

Po looked up, and the flame wavered in a slight breeze that rolled off the ocean. "It's okay, Oliver. It's okay. I should be angry, or I should be upset. At you, at the world, at those guards who did this to me. But I'm not. You once told me Carpenters see what others can't handle, and we fix it. I have to believe that."

Roc knelt next to the pushcart. "How can you believe that?"

Po looked at his hero. "Because if I don't, then I'm just another crippled poor boy from the Narrows. I may not be the next Lightning Knight, but I have to believe I can serve some purpose."

I looked at him. He was everything this world needed. He was everything I needed. But something was holding me back. Something inside me, like a knot within my chest. Then I felt a burning sensation on my hand. I yelped and dropped the match onto the pyre. The pyre was set ablaze impossibly fast, and a small concussive force blew heat against our faces.

"No!" Windrunner yelled as she lunged, but Pathfinder held her back.

"Good riddance!" Roc proclaimed. "Magic is what did this to us, to Po. Better to be done with it. We should be eradicating magic and those who use it, not becoming one of them."

My heart pounded at what I had done. Haralabos's book was turning to ash and I didn't quite know if that's what I wanted. A part of me agreed with Roc, but a part of me also felt loss. Magic was something I had yearned to learn more about, and the thought of cutting ties so cleanly felt wrong. I was upset, confused, and angry and tired. I wanted Po to blame me, to hate me, but he wouldn't. I wanted to hate myself, but I couldn't. Not fully.

I could hate Haralabos though. I could hate him for putting us on this path. For putting Po in danger. For giving me purpose and then taking it away. I felt lost.

Like a soldier without an army.

Like a ship with no cargo.

Like a book with no words.

Thunder sounded and I reacted as if Haralabos were taunting me directly with the weather. I stood and walked toward the ocean, seeing lightning strikes in the distance. Rain began to pour down, soaking my clothes and giving my internal struggle the fuel it needed to rage. Another flash of lightning in the distance was followed by a thunderclap, and I looked toward the dark horizon in angry defiance.

"What do you want from me!" I yelled into the void, to any god that might hear me. "Why did you allow this to happen! He was innocent."

"Oliver! What are you doing!"

I didn't turn. My fight was with whichever one of the Nine wanted to listen. "He was the best of us, and you let him suffer!" I yelled again. Lightning struck closer now and the thunder quickly followed. I yelled up into the rumbling darkness, fists clenched at my sides, all the tearing emotion I felt in my soul thrown into my voice. I searched deep within me, looking for that feeling darker than hate and more powerful than anger.

I found it. The unlove. I fell to my knees, gasping for air and blinking rainwater and tears from my eyes as I questioned the divine. "What do you want from me!" I waited for an answer that would not come. I raised my hands to my face, breathing deeply before standing once more without answers. I turned to see my friends by the hissing, smoldering fire.

Then the strangest thing happened. The unlove that had enveloped my very soul dissipated in quick fashion, and I was at peace. The air around me paused, and the hairs on my arms stood up. I looked out at the dark horizon once more, but a snapping jolt of energy coursed like fire through my body and a flashing light blinded me before all fell to quiet darkness.

I never heard the thunderclap.

# THE DARK MIND TEMPLE

"I can't breathe…" I grumbled as I opened my eyes to a nest of hair on my face. Iris jumped and yelled much louder than I would have liked.

"He's awake!" She lunged into the bed once more, hugging me tightly.

"Still can't breathe…" I muttered, but her enthusiasm did not relent.

"You can breathe later," she said as she repeatedly kissed my cheeks over and over. If I had to choose between kisses and breathing, the choice was obvious. But even as she kissed me, my stomach turned. Even in this moment with the girl of my dreams, all I could think about was Pathfinder and our would-be affair. It sickened me to the core, how I was treating Iris, but even so I tried to either justify my actions or not think of them at all. That became much harder with Iris's kisses as they reminded me so much of Pathfinder.

A commotion out in the hallway heralded the rest of Whiskey Danger. Yokel and Reagan stormed into the room, followed by Roc who was carrying Po in his burly arms like a baby lamb.

"Thank the Nine you're alive!" Yokel said, gesturing his hands in the sign of Nine of Nine. I tried to sit up, but my body felt strange and exhausted.

"What happened?" I asked.

Roc looked at Yokel and then Po. Reagan sat on the bed and grabbed my hand.

"They said you were on the beach, Ollie, in the middle of a thunderstorm," she said with so much parental disappointment my mother would have been proud. "What were you doing there?"

"Yelling at the ocean." I was sick of telling lies, but I still couldn't tell her the whole truth.

"And what did the ocean ever do to you?" She snuggled up under my arm for a hug.

"You don't know the half of it," I said, staring at Po. "But how did I end up here?"

"Y-you were..." Yokel stuttered, unable to finish his sentence.

But Po's eyes were wide with excitement. "You were struck by lightning! It was the coolest thing ever!"

"Don't say that!" Iris reprimanded.

"What! It was! It was like, bloosh!" Po reenacted the explosion of lightning that must have crackled through my body and added a generous involuntary shake for good measure. "And then he was all like, blitksk, and then it was just sand and glass and Oliver and it was so cool, right, Roc?"

"It wasn't not cool," Roc replied with a teasing wink at Iris.

"But what if he'd died!" Iris yelled back.

Po looked down. "Well, I didn't think of that. But he's not! He's alive and, and..." His energy had nowhere to go, especially now that he couldn't get around on his own. I was so relieved to see the old Po filled with curiosity and eagerness again, but I was also dismayed at his condition. A condition I still felt responsible for.

I started to touch and feel all over my body, looking for tell-tale signs of the lightning strike. It was good odds that if a person was stuck by lightning, they would live to tell the tale. If they did, it always came with fractal pattern scars called the "tree of life." But I felt nothing, no markings, no anything. I pounced up from my bed with speed and strength I wouldn't have thought I'd have, and made my way to the mirror, inspecting my skin.

"Are you sure I was struck?"

"We were there, Oliver. We know what we saw," Roc answered.

I paced around the room, unable to contain my thoughts. I tried to enter my mind temple, to retrace my steps and calm my nerves, but I was forced out by a storm of thoughts and anxieties. It seems the lightning may not have affected my body, but it definitely affected my mind. I started convulsing as my body reacted to the new sensation within my mind. My brain itched, under the skin of my skull, and everything felt like fire.

"Ollie, what's happening!" Reagan whispered. Or did she yell? I couldn't tell. There was something happening to me on the inside. I couldn't stop it.

"I... can't... mind... temple..." I said before falling to the floor.

I was suddenly in a dark room, a place familiar to me although I couldn't quite place it. Light flashed and thunder roared as I saw the outer walls of my mind temple. The temple beckoned me, but I was too afraid to go in.

"Hi, big brother," a voice said next to me.

"Reagan? What are you doing here?" I was completely confused.

"This is all in your head. You need to face whatever is in there," she said, pointing toward the temple steps.

"I can't, I'm too scared."

"Yes, you can. You must. It's the only way."

I took a single step forward, and the ground lit up in a blaze of light before retreating back to its dark form. I knew this place. I had been here before, in a long-forgotten dream.

Po.

Magic.

I stopped, and the unlove began to spread its roots over the temple walls like an invasive vine. "Not again. I failed once, and it almost cost Po his life. I won't. I can't." I turned and ran away from the temple, away from the darkness that was consuming it and away from Mind Reagan.

I woke up to a puddle of drool on the floor. Iris was standing over me and Roc was holding a belt in my mouth. "I won't do it!" I muffled as I spit out the belt. "I'm done. Get out!" I yelled at everyone around me. I could feel the tendrils of the darkness rising through my body, and I screamed once more at my friends. "Leave!"

They looked shocked, but they left. I could hear them conferring outside in the hallway even as I sat alone on the floor. I wanted them back so desperately, but I didn't know how to say it. Every emotion I had ever felt was coming to the forefront. I felt a mountain of devastation for what I had caused Po, and an avalanche of shame for how I was treating Iris. The spark of jealousy for Roc's bravery was only surpassed by the inferiority I felt to Yokel's intelligence.

And then there was Reagan, whose disappointment had washed over me in wave after wave. Mind Reagan was correct, but I had chosen to run. Real Reagan didn't deserve me yelling at her, or the small amounts of resentment I had shown her for years. I was finally alone, and it crushed me. Every moment now was like trying to breathe underwater. I was suffocating in my solitude, afraid to close my eyes for fear of returning to that dark mind temple. I needed my friends and I needed my family. I needed my sister, who was just outside the door but may as well have been outside the world. I needed my brother, whom I wanted to punch for leaving us and hug for coming back. I wanted to hear my mother's voice, but that would never happen again. I wanted to feel my father's warm breath on my head as I buried into his burly smith's arms, but he was as absent as my mother.

"Hello, my son," I heard from a dark corner of the room.

"Father?" I said, as I tried to make out the man through my watering eyes. "Is that really you?"

He walked out of the shadows and toward me, stopping by the vanity to tidy the accessories. He bent down and cradled my face within his bearpaw. "What's wrong, my boy?"

I flew into a tirade. "What's wrong? What's wrong? You ask me this now? Where were you? Where have you been? I needed a father and you weren't here! What's wrong? I'll tell you what's wrong." I jumped up, unable to control my anger any longer. Years of turmoil and pent-up resentment at a father who loved my brother more, filled my mouth. "What's wrong is you. What's wrong is this family. What's wrong is I'll never be good enough. I'll never be Wiggin. I'll never make you proud. I failed! Did you know that? No, of course you didn't. You don't know anything about me. You never cared about my life. Just your perfect little soldier and your perfect little forge. Well I had a chance to do something great, and I messed it up. I had a chance to be with someone great, and I'm pretty sure I messed that up too. Now I have no friends and I never even really had a family. So, you want to know what's wrong, it's you. It's me. It's being a stupid Quartermaine."

I fell to my knees, fists balled up in the most intense anger I'd ever felt. I don't know if I'd ever talked to my father like that, and I wasn't about to head into the dark mind temple to find out. I sat there, my vision turning blue and then perfectly clear as I lifted my head and stared at the man who would call himself my father. I could hear a crackle of energy and I knew if I held on to this fury any longer, I'd be consumed by it.

Po's small voice echoed in my ear. "Carpenters see what others can't handle, and they fix it." I unclenched my fists and the crackling subsided. I felt, for some reason, at peace. As if a weight had been lifted off my chest and suddenly, now that I had finally made my feelings known to my father, I felt free.

My father curiously enough, stood there with a strange grin. I would have burst into anger at his expression except I was utterly confused. He tapped his forefingers together three times and rubbed his palms as if some great epiphany had struck him. Bending down in front of me, he grabbed hold of both my shoulders, and for the briefest of moments, I felt comforted like a son would.

"I know I haven't been the father you needed, but I have to go now. When I come back, we will talk once more. I… You may be the answer to what I've been searching for, my son." He kissed my forehead and left me alone in my room once more. The open door allowed me to see Iris standing just outside, with Po sitting at her feet.

My chest was heavy again, and the vines that wrapped around my mind temple were slowly making their way down my neck and into my heart. The rejection from my father coupled with the remorse I felt to the two people I'd hurt most in this world consumed me. I sprang up and locked eyes with Iris, willing myself to go to her. But instead I escaped to the balcony and fled into the night.

# AZEL'S STORY

The tunnels beneath the Workshop were vast and abandoned. It was easy enough to avoid other Carpenters if I wanted to, and I did want to. Just as I had months before, I had run away from my friends and family to find refuge in this place.

For weeks, I had succeeded in avoiding Po and Reagan. I'd also avoided Iris, Yokel, Pathfinder, and Windrunner, and most of all, Roc. He would never understand. He would never see me the same way again. I didn't want to lose my best friend.

For weeks, I wandered listlessly, trying to come to grips with my inner turmoil. I couldn't escape to my mind temple, the most sacred of my sanctuaries. The darkness still waited.

For weeks, I searched for a way to understand my place in this world. To understand what I was meant to do, meant to be. But I found no answers, only loneliness. It was killing me to be alone, but I was drowning in my own depression, with no way out. So, I wandered through the dark tunnels without a light, knowing the way nonetheless. I ran the obstacle course, polished plate mail, sharpened steel, carved wooden practice weapons, and pored over training books that I'd read hundreds of times. I had come here once before because I was a murderer, and the Workshop had saved me.

But I feared it couldn't save me now.

It was late, or early, maybe midmorning, I couldn't honestly say, but I made my way up to the main training room, finding it empty. I sat in the practice circle, my feet crossed, preparing for a meditation. Focusing on my breathing, I let my thoughts flow through me, not allowing myself to latch on to them. My mind temple was barren, and I was standing in a dark room, surrounded by images and words and thoughts. They encircled me and I sat in the eye of the tornado, letting them rage without me.

A storm brewed above me and I shuddered at the sound of crackling and thunder. The tornado around me was struck by brilliant streaks of lightning, turning the images and words and thoughts to sand that showered down around me. The tornado subsided and the sand dissipated, leaving me alone and anxious for what would happen next. Every day I came to meditate, and every day this was the end of the road. I needed to know what was beyond the tornado, and the loneliness.

A moment longer and I would have wavered, but this time was different. This time, a figure made of light, no, lightning wrapped into a shape, approached me from the darkness, bending its head curiously. It looked like a person, but its body was undefined. Maybe it was a woman, or maybe I just missed my mother.

"What are you?" I asked, reaching out my hand to touch her. The lightning figure looked at my fingers and reached out with her own. Soon, our fingertips were connected by lightning that bounced back and forth between us, creating a strange melody.

"Odd," the lightning figure said in a staticky voice.

"What's odd?" I asked defensively, pulling back my hand.

"I am not yours," the lightning figure said. "This should not be possible, unless…" She dissipated into nothing, leaving only sparks in the air where she once stood. I looked around, hoping to find her once again, but she was gone. A sharp pain punctuated my chest.

I opened my eyes to see Reagan standing in front of me, with a sword tip held to my chest. I stared at her, infuriated. "I was trying to meditate."

"Tough," she said as she backed away and twirled her sword. I walked to the armory and pulled out a newly sharpened sword. Carpenters of our level didn't train with blunted weapons.

"You don't want to do this, Rea," I said as I swung the sword in a stretch. At first, I was sure the lightning strike would have caused some type of temporary or permanent damage to my body or skills. Instead, the opposite had happened. For weeks I had been training in secret within the Workshop, and during that time I never tired. My body felt amazing, my focus was perfect, and my speed was faster, both physically and mentally. The most advanced set in the obstacle course was now as easy as the simplest. But still, all of that couldn't have changed who I was now: a coward who ran away from failure.

Reagan stood into position, taunting me with her hands. "You forget, big brother, that I'm the one who brought you back last time."

"You lost last time," I countered, readying myself.

"Did I?"

And we began. The sound of clashing swords reverberated off the walls. Reagan's sword skills had vastly improved since the last time we sparred. She was no longer overly aggressive, and her tactics hinted that she was exercising restraint. All those nights I spent with the Knight Angels and Whiskey Danger, she must have been practicing here.

I wasn't trying as hard as I should, and it showed. I kept her at a distance and countered every move, but she could tell I was holding back.

"That all you got?" she gloated.

"You can't begin to imagine what I got," I replied, looking to take my internal frustrations out on her. I executed a quick few slashes in the air, demonstrating a flurry of dazzling techniques.

We met in the middle of the circle again, this time moving in and out of forms quickly, unable to find the weakness in each other's defenses. But my tempo quickened, and her reactions couldn't keep up. I used Form Twelve, an overhead striking attack form designed to present a false weakness to the opponent, causing them to change from defense to offense. Her fatigued mind fell into the trap and as she pivoted into a new form, I used my momentum to fly into a barrage of slashes and thrusts, causing her to lose balance.

I backed away, hopping on my feet as blood coursed through my body. "What's wrong, baby sister? Still a bit rusty, are we?" I had missed this. I had missed people. I had missed my sister and my friends. For the first time in a long time, I felt the seed of what might be happiness.

That seed wouldn't have time to grow. Reagan's expression changed quickly from worn and tired to angry determination. She launched into a new series of attacks that I parried easily, but as I raised my arms to deal a final blow, she dropped swiftly to the floor, spinning around with a leg outstretched to sweep both my feet out from under me. I fell backward as I watched her continue to spin, throwing her leg up at the end of the turn to kick out sideways, making direct contact with my sternum. My fall shifted abruptly, and I flew backward, landing some ways away from her. I lay there, unwilling to move as I worked through the forms, trying to pinpoint my mistake. Reagan walked to the wall and calmly placed her weapon on the bracket.

She came over to me, bending down. "You done being mopey now?"

It was blunt and hurtful but also the truth. I couldn't help but lie there stunned. This was the first time she had beaten me.

This must be it. The end of the world.

"Again!" a familiar voice said from behind us.

Reagan bowed to Azel and walked over to the armory, picking up a staff and spinning it around to get a feel for its weight.

I stood and began to pick up my sword when Azel spoke again.

"No."

I tossed my sword to the side and pushed my open palms together, turning them as if unlocking something within me and then pulling my right hand back as I jetted my left forward.

"Where's your weapon?" Reagan asked.

"I am the weapon," I said braggadociously. As far as I knew, I was the only one Azel had taught Form Zero to, and Reagan was about to get a taste of what that meant.

"Fine, I'll try not to hurt you too badly," she said as she moved into an assault. I moved and dodged her attacks easily, parrying them without giving ground. With each parry, I punched and kicked her lightly, just enough to be annoying.

She screamed in frustration when she couldn't land a hit on me, even with her assumed advantage of a weapon, and she retreated to the armory to trade her staff for batons. It didn't help. Reagan traded the batons for a blunted sword and once again, I had the upper hand.

Upper hand. I'm hilarious.

My laugh must have been visible because her frustration gave way to grunts and yells. "I hope you fight like this at the Southern Tournament in two weeks!"

"I'm not competing," I said, dodging an overhead slash. She stopped dead in her tracks, staring at me incredulously.

"What do you mean you're not competing? You've been training for this for years. The whole reason you went away this summer was to grant you a high seed. You won't be able to go to the Dragon Championship if you're not the Southern representative!"

I didn't know what to say. I couldn't tell her the real reason for my sojourn last summer. I couldn't tell her that I didn't trust myself anymore. Not after everything I had done this year: the guard at the Bluefish Tavern, Po losing his ability to walk, almost killing Prince Froderick, and the fear of my own mind temple.

Then there was the lightning.

"I just don't want to do it, okay?" I finally responded.

"No!" she yelled as she lunged into more attacks. "Not okay. You're the best fighter in the South, you have to compete!"

"I'm tired of fighting!" I screamed as I disarmed her and tossed her sword away. She was determined to keep the argument going and retrieved tonfas as her next weapon of choice.

"Well, I'm tired of you. We all are! You can't just run away every time life gets hard. You can't just—"

"Give up?" I interrupted as I bent backward to avoid the spinning weapon. "Why not? I can't do it anymore, Rea, I just can't."

"Can't do what?"

I fell to my knees in forfeit and she locked my head between her weapons. "I'm sick of destinies and trying to save the world and be the person you want me to be. I can't do it. I failed. You don't understand, you're just…"

She glared. "I'm just what?"

"I was the one! I was the one who was supposed to protect him. To guide him. To find magic and help save it." My voice broke and she dropped her weapons along with her knees. It felt good to finally let her in on the quests, even if she didn't know the full story.

"Ollie."

"I'm just so tired, Rea. I wanted to be the hero, but I wasn't meant to be. I was meant to find the hero, to help him, and I didn't. I failed my quest."

"Carpenter!" Azel yelled. "Form Zero!"

"What?" I said, snot starting to drip from my nose as I held back tears. "Form Zero! Now!"

I got up and started into the form, moving my body to an intricate choreography. I let my emotions pour out now, for the first time in what seemed like forever. I let my guilt, my sadness, my anger, and everything else flood out of me and into my form. The ferocity of my movements gracefully melded with the minute details of the dance, and the weight of my sorrows evaporated.

As I moved, I saw glimpses of my mind temple and the darkness and tendrils receding. My heart felt empty but not corroded as it had been. I could feel my body turning and stretching, and my hands began to feel warm and I looked down in absentminded curiosity.

I'm… glowing?

Without warning, I was overcome with an intense pain as my mind raged through all my emotions, until I couldn't take it any longer. I didn't want to feel this way anymore. I didn't want to be sad. I needed to forgive myself. I needed to let go.

I screamed out and a huge force emanated through the room, causing a cacophony of sounds from the weapons on the walls and in the armories. Small bolts of lightning crackled between the steel weapons on the walls and ground. I looked down at my hands and gasped at the small circlets of the same lightning coursing around each finger, growing and moving up my wrists and forearms. I brought my arms up in amazement, completely confused. The snapping roar in my ears dulled enough for me to hear Reagan approaching, her hands clamped defensively around her head.

Azel removed her shaded spectacles and put both her hands on my shoulders. Instead of cloudy, her irises shone a deep shade of purple.

"It is time. Follow me." She turned and proceeded to leave the Workshop. Reagan looked at me.

"Ollie?"

"I don't know what's happening, Rea."

We caught up with the Carpenter as she began to speak without care for who might be listening.

"I know you have many questions, and I will do my best to answer as we walk, but there are many things I am still in the dark about, so to speak."

My mind raced at the possibility of answers. Answers to what little I actually knew about Azel and answers to what just happened. As always, Reagan was quicker to the draw than me.

"Is your name really Azel?"

I of course knew the answer was yes and wondered why she would waste Azel's time.

"Yes, but only because I was not given an Elven name," she replied, jarring my attention.

"What do you mean, Elven name?" I asked.

"I am a M'ordykhai," she said in Elvish, complete with the clicking vowels.

My jaw dropped. "Child of human?"

"Yes. My mother was an elf, and my father was a human."

"But all the elves are extinct," I posed to the she-elf. Elf-she? This couldn't be real.

Azel stopped to turn to me. "Not all of us." She continued her journey west through the Narrows. "Many years ago, I journeyed over the Sunrise Mountains with my half-sister, your ancestor Satine. We made our way through Kandaheart and Romir, smaller kingdoms then they are today, until we happened upon a small fishing hamlet at the edge of a peninsula. We named it Starfall and founded the queendom we walk through tonight."

Reagan and I were silent. All our questions were inconsequential next to the story Azel was telling us. We continued through the Narrow Gate and into the city proper, unwilling to interrupt her spectacular tale.

"We met our friend Minka, and together the three of us ruled." She stopped suddenly and stared at a set of buildings. "That's where we…" But her memory drifted off into a smile.

We continued through the city toward the Shears and Azel continued her story.

"Satine was gifted with her father's knack for invention and married a smith, founding a house named after our father, Quartermaine, and building the Forge with the help of some friendly dragons. I founded the Institute so that I could pass on my knowledge and give our new queendom a chance to flourish."

Our journey ended in front of the monolith that was the Shears. "And my Minka… After I taught her to read, her lust for knowledge became insatiable, and she married a wealthy Kandaharian noble named Shearson, forging an alliance between our two nations and building this library."

We opened the door and headed down into the sublevels and beyond any areas I had ever known about. Finally, we came to a dead-end and a brick with the nine-pointed star on it. Azel placed her hand over the brick and smiled at a memory. She held out her hand to me.

"Your ring, Oliver."

I tried to take the ring Po had given me off my finger, but I couldn't. Interestingly enough, I could spin it around my finger just fine, but when I tried to dislodge it past my knuckle, it was as if the ring itself fought against me. I looked at Azel in a panic, but she smiled and took my wrist, placing the ring still attached to my finger on the brick.

Her voice became more intense. "It was the most exciting time in my life. The three of us had all we could desire: wealth, power, station, fame. But most of all, we had each other. Kingdoms big and small curried favor with the three Queens of Starfall. Sometimes those relations were good, other times they were hostile. Even then, we were victorious. No one could defeat us."

"So, what happened to you three? Why aren't you still Queen of Starfall?" I asked.

"We were defeated by the most powerful enemy of all, time. We ruled for years, but although I was cursed with the Elven grace of immortality, they were not. Minka lived a long and prosperous life, seeing great-great-grandchildren in her house. I was there by her side when she—" Azel caught a tear and sniffled.

"What about Satine? What happened to our ancestor?" Reagan asked.

"Satine's family blossomed and spread throughout the world and the Quartermaine name lives strong today through you two and those relatives you have in other kingdoms. As for Satine, one day she left for the Forge and never returned. We searched and searched the ocean but found nothing. No shipwreck and no sign of her. There was no note, no ransom, and no other kingdom laid claim to her. She simply disappeared." I could feel the heaviness of her memory in the air.

"Once they were gone, I turned Starfall over to its people. I never wanted to rule it without my two loves. So, I taught at the Institute, and when I grew tired of that, I opened the Workshop. While the Quartermaine family grew like a large tree, the Shearson family was not as fortunate. Its numbers dwindled and dwindled until there were only two left. Then, over three hundred years ago, they too were gone."

Azel pressed my hand firmly, and the brick underneath shifted, revealing a false wall similar to the one I had encountered in Romir.

"This room doesn't exist," Reagan whispered.

"Strange," Azel said, "for a room that doesn't exist, it seems quite real to me." Her smirk would have been infuriating if it hadn't been accompanied by a mysterious chamber in front of us.

"What happened three hundred years ago?" I asked as we walked in. The room stretched out in front of us, brimming with books, scrolls, and stacks of tomes. Littered among them were a multitude of treasures, weapons, and bejeweled artifacts gleaming in the low torchlight. Ancient art adorned the walls, and I was afraid to touch a single thing lest this brilliant mirage disappear.

This can't be real...

"I assure you, your eyes do not fool you," Azel stated flatly from a corner of the room. She was staring intently at a painting of a man holding a strangely familiar sword. Reagan and I stood next to our queen and looked on.

"Before the High Queen's reign, there was magic in this world. Mages, wizards, warlocks and witches... They had many names, but they all had one thing in common: They were magicians. But magic isn't easy, it must be earned and honed and practiced. We elves knew this, and it is why we never shared magic with humans. But that all changed when Satine and I came to this land. We unleashed magic to this country and for a time, humans flourished. It was a golden age of discovery and prosperity. Yet, it wasn't enough. It never is with humans.

"Soon, wars aided by magic and for magic were waged, and every kingdom and queendom suffered, including our Starfall. Then, three hundred years ago, nine knights used their magic to help save the people of this land, and every land they could. They were heroes, and we knew peace once more. A peace that wouldn't last.

"An enemy arrived they were not prepared for, from a distant land beyond the sea. She defeated the knights one by one, until only two remained. The Lightning Knight and the Blackfyre, or as I knew them, the Shearson twins, the last of Minka's family. They left Starfall for one final confrontation with the foreign invader, and that was the day I lost my sight. That was the day we lost magic."

I looked at my hands, knowing in my heart what I didn't want to be true. Azel walked to another door that led us into a large room with a giant metal birdcage in one corner.

"As I'm sure you've surmised by now, magic is real, and it is back. You have the lightning magic, Oliver. You are the new Lightning Knight."

I shook my head in disbelief. "No, no, this can't be true. I wasn't supposed to… Haralabos said…"

Azel turned sharply to me. "What did you say?"

"Haralabos, we, uh, we found his journal. Or book, or something. I wasn't supposed to be the Lightning Knight. Po was." My heart sank.

"Regardless of what Haralabos said, you have the magic now. For the first time in three centuries, we have hope again. Use this place to train, as he once did. Use the knowledge in here to learn more about magic, so that you might save it. Magic is in a fragile place, Oliver. It needs you."

I looked at Reagan, who was smiling wide.

"This is your purpose, Ollie. You can be the hero you wanted to be."

I looked around, suddenly eager at the untapped knowledge now at my fingertips. Then I thought back to Romir and all the trouble and pain magic had caused us. Had caused me. Magic was seductive, but I resisted. I didn't want it. I didn't want any of it. It was supposed to be Po's. I was never meant to be the Lightning Knight. I was meant to be his follower.

"I'm sorry, Azel, but I can't. I'm not meant for this. I can't be the Lightning Knight. I won't. Maybe magic was gone for a reason."

"Magic was stolen from us! Stolen from me!"

"Regardless, that was someone else's war, not mine. I tried to get involved with magic, and someone ended up hurt because of it."

"You can't be seri—"

"He almost died, Reagan! Don't you get that? Magic isn't some answer, it's the problem. It couldn't save Po, and it can't save us either. I'm sorry, Azel, but you've got the wrong guy. I'm not a hero, I'm a failure."

I turned and left them both in the secret chamber, resentment building in my soul and unwanted lightning coursing through my body.

# THE MERITS OF MAGIC

I knocked three times on the simple wooden door and waited each and every excruciating second, hoping no one would answer, but footsteps on the other side of the door proved me wrong. The door opened and there stood Po's grandmother, a stout lady dressed in her kitchen robes, holding a baby nearly a year old.

"Oliver Quartermaine? The Nine bless us with your presence, my young lord!" Her voice was cheerful and without contempt, even though she had every right to hate me. This must have been where Po had gotten his positive demeanor.

"A pleasure, m'lady. Is Po here? He wasn't at the Workshop barracks."

"Oh, you flatter me, but you know I'm not a lady. But yes, he is, one moment," she replied as she escaped back into the Kentaro kitchens. She pushed Po to the door on his wheeled contraption, and for the first time in a long time, I felt a smile work the muscles on my face.

"Hey, bud."

"Oliver! Is that really you?"

"Yeah, it is. Do you think we could take a walk?" As soon as I spoke I gasped at my poor choice of words.

"Don't worry about it, Oliver. We can go for a walk, as long as you promise to push." He smiled wide, showing his oversized teeth.

"Of course." I pulled his chair into the street and we made our way along the gardens, winding through the city and toward the Shears. We didn't talk but rather enjoyed the quiet comfort of each other's company. I racked my mind with how I could tell him what I had become and what I had taken from him. He deserved to know the truth about magic, and Azel and this city, and me. But I was so afraid of losing him, of losing my friend, that by the time we reached the overlook next to the Shears, I still was at a loss for words.

The sun was making its descent toward the edge of the world, and the clouds above us were painting a picture only the Nine could make. With the winter storms almost at an end, the breeze was soft and the air had only the tiniest bite.

"So, what do you think of my new ride? Roc made it for me!" Po said proudly.

"It's something alright," I responded.

For all of Roc's struggles with his prescribed work at the Institute, there was nothing that boy couldn't make or build at the Forge. If I hadn't known better, I would have sworn he was my father's son.

"It works alright, unless I get to the stairs. Then I have a problem." Po was so matter of fact about it all that I found myself holding my breath like I had seen him do so many times. He looked up at me. "Oliver, where have you been?"

I was too ashamed to tell him, and the silence between us said more than I ever could.

He looked up at me awkwardly. "It's okay, you know, Pathfinder isn't here."

"What do you mean by that?"

He laughed and I relaxed, letting my heart do the talking instead of my head.

"I was scared, Po. I thought I had failed. That's why I left. It's what I do when…" I couldn't finish for fear saying the words aloud would make it real.

"Failed at what?"

"Failed at protecting you. Failed at finding magic. Failed at life. Po, when we found you in Romir, it broke us. Each and every one of us. Seeing you like that, we thought you were gone." I began to choke up once again.

"But I'm not gone, Oliver. I'm here. You didn't fail." He turned to gaze back at the ocean. "It's okay to be scared sometimes."

"Where did you learn that?" I asked as I swiped at a tear on my cheek.

"From you. We don't have to be brave all the time, which means sometimes we can be scared. I'm okay, I promise."

"But look at you!" I yelled, moving toward the stone ledge protecting us from the cliffs below. I leant my back against the half wall and sank down, unable to stand any longer. Po looked down at his legs, and regret overwhelmed me once more.

"I know you think this is your fault. So does Roc, and Yokel, and Pathfinder and Windrunner and everyone. But it's not. And it's not my fault either. I'm supposed to be the Lightning Knight, so either we find a way to get my legs back, or I learn to fight from this chair."

He was so determined and so strong, stronger than I would ever be. It made all the sense in the world that he should be our hero. Even with everything against him, at the edge of death, he came back, and he hadn't given up.

Not like me. I would never be the hero. I knew that now.

Po looked out into the bay once more with a determined look. "Magic saved me once before. It can save me again, and you, and everyone."

"How do you know that?"

"I have to believe it, Oliver. I have to." I let our conversation settle into a quiet reprieve. I still hadn't said what I came here to say, but I knew now that Po could take it.

"Po, I need to tell you something." He looked up at me, twelve years old going on thirteen and already more mature than I would ever be. "When I was struck by lightning—"

"Oh, geez, that was so cool! I was telling everyone at the Institute about it."

"That's great, bud, but let me finish. When I was struck by the lightning, I don't think it was by accident. It made me... It turned me into... Ugh, just, look at this." I stuck out my hand and tried to will the lightning magic to my fingertips.

"Uh, why are you waving at me?"

"No, I'm not, just look!" I concentrated my whole being into my hand but nothing, not a spark appeared. Po couldn't handle the excitement any longer and slapped my palm with his own, laughing the entire time.

I gave up in frustration but continued my confession. "Po, I have magic now. Lightning Magic. I'm the Lightning Knight."

Po's face dropped and he wheeled himself back away from me only so slightly, but it might as well have been on the other side of the world.

"I'm so sorry, Po. I didn't mean for this to happen. I don't even want it. If I could, I'd give it to you, I swear!" I fell to my knees and begged him to forgive me.

His face contorted, and what once looked hurt and scorned now had an air of excitement and enthusiasm. "Do you know what this means?"

"No?" I answered in confusion.

"Don't you get it? You were supposed to train me. How else could you do that if you too didn't have magic? It makes perfect sense! You have lightning magic now, and you can learn how to use it and then you can train me. You didn't fail, Oliver, and neither did I!"

It was now me who backed away, overwhelmed at his oddly sensible rationale. "No, you don't get it, Po. I don't want it. I never did," I lied. It was a lie I kept telling myself, over and over. I didn't want the magic; it was meant for Po. Every time the truth threatened to sneak to my conscious awareness, I would tell myself the lie.

"Oliver, please. You have to help me. I know this is my destiny. I know I'm meant to do this, I just need your help," he pleaded, and for the first time his optimistic attitude broke. He desired all the things I did but was too humble to say so. He wanted the magic, and he wanted to be a hero. He wanted purpose, like me.

"Po, look where magic got us," I protested. "You in a wheelchair, and me—"

"With all your friends and family and Ms. Iris upset at you?"

"Yes! Wait, how mad is she?"

"Remember when she hated you a few months ago?"

"Yes?" I did not want to hear the reply.

"It's worse now."

"Wonderful." My breathing became erratic and I moved into Form Zero to find my balance. After a quick few successive moves, I opened my eyes and saw Po reaching for my arms, which were now coursing with visible lightning magic. I quickly shook them and he recoiled in awe.

"Nine Hells!"

"I told you, bud."

"How, how did it feel?"

I was afraid to tell him, but there were now no secrets between us. "Amazing," I said flatly. "Like nothing I've ever felt before."

"Not even when you kissed Ms. Iris?"

"Better than that," I admitted.

"Better than when you kissed Pathfinder?"

"Better than— Wait, how did you—"

"I like girls too, Oliver. Sometimes I stare at them and Pathfinder is pretty cute. Or at least I think she is. But I've seen the way she stares at you. Like how Ms. Iris stares at you when you're not looking."

I chuckled. For all his maturity and strength, he was still just a kid. "It's like finishing a puzzle, but instead of completing the puzzle, you are the puzzle, and magic is the final piece that makes you feel whole. It's a rush of energy and calmness and…"

"It's everything," he added.

"Everything," I confirmed. It was addictive and seductive; the more I used it, the more I wanted it. The more I needed to have it. It was powerful and fragile and fleeting. But these things I didn't explain to Po. These feelings I kept for myself.

"We can't tell Roc," Po said.

"No. We can't tell anyone."

"Tell anyone what?" Pathfinder said as she snuck up behind us. "Oi, where the Hells have you been buggered off to?" She punched me in the shoulder. She bent down and stroked Po's cheek familiarly. "And how's our wee hero doing today?"

Po looked at me, but I shook my head. "We're doing fine. Out for a roll."

"Oh, are we? Where'd you find this one?" She thumbed at me.

"Hiding in the Narrows, like he always is."

"I'm standing right here," I said in annoyance. Po had known where I was this whole time but never sought me out. This kid was full of surprises.

"Hiding in the Narrows? Figures a little lord like that would be there."

"I'm not a little any—"

She turned to me with a stern expression. "Only a little man would run away when his friends needed him most. When I needed him most." She tugged on my hand and the sadness in her eyes spoke the rest.

"I'm sorry." It was the only apology I could muster.

"I am too, little lord. I really, truly believed in you. You let me down, and you let him down."

"No, he didn't, he actually—" Po started.

"I know. I was a coward and I screwed up. I'm sorry, for leaving Po, for leaving you. I needed time, but I'm back now."

"Oh, just like that, a snap of your fingers and you're back and we're all supposed to, what? Hmm? Throw you a party or something? See, while you were hiding, we were out there doing what we set out to do!"

"I said I'm sorry."

"That's not good enough!"

"Well then what is?" I yelled, unsure why I was so angry. I was ready to make amends, I was ready to try again, but she wouldn't let me. Why did I care so much about what she thought?

She turned and paced away, muttering incoherently. "You, just, you, agh!" Pathfinder stormed back up to me, a finger in my face and a grim expression. "You hurt a lot of people, Oliver. Me, Windrunner, Yokel, Roc, Po.'

"My sister and Iris and Azel and—"

"Blimey, it seems like every name in Starfall. You want to prove to all of us you're back? You want to prove that you truly are sorry? Well it better be something bloody spectacular and not some juvenile little song."

We heard a scattering of pebbles along the walkway and before I had even turned around, Pathfinder had disappeared.

"Tck-tck-tck, my sweet Q, what brings you out on this lovely evening?" Ridhan walked behind Po and pulled on his chair, spinning him around jovially. "So sorry to hear of your accident, little sandeater."

"That's enough, Ridhan. What do you want?" I said as I pulled a dizzy Po to safety.

"A hug?" Ridhan opened his arms and approached. "I've missed you so, my Q. This city is such a bore without you." He pulled me in and whispered in my ear. "Remember our plans."

I pushed gently away, looking for an escape. He had no Sharks with him, no bodyguards, no anyone. He was alone. But he also wasn't our enemy anymore, although not quite our ally.

"I remember, but I don't think that will be happening. I'm not competing in the Southern Tournament, which means I won't be going to Dragon's Treasure."

"You're not competing?" Po and Ridhan said simultaneously. It was eerie to hear them together, two diametric opposites of a human being.

"No, I'm done with fighting."

Ridhan turned on his heel and scraped his fingers along the retaining wall, turning only when he was a good distance away. "This was not the plan!" he yelled. He searched along the ground but didn't find what he was looking for. "You were supposed to bring me magic. You were supposed to give me the power to…" He trailed off and regained his composure in an instant. He adjusted his collar and looked out into the ocean. "Do you know what magic is?" he asked.

"Magic is peace," Po responded.

"No, you naive child, magic is passion!"

"No, it's knowledge."

"It's strength and power and victory!" Ridhan spit out in rapid succession.

"Magic is harmony," Po responded deftly.

Ridhan moved to Po and bent down to his eye level. "Magic will free me."

"Magic saved me," Po ended.

Ridhan stepped away, turning to me. "I was counting on you, Q. You disappoint me."

"I've been getting that a lot."

He looked at Po, and his thin smile crept along his face. "Sandeater, how would you like to walk again?"

I rushed to Ridhan and picked him up by the collar. "Don't you dare joke about that!"

Ridhan tapped me slightly on the nose and I let him down. "I would never. Not to you, Q. You know what it's like at Dragon's Treasure. There's the High Queen's Dragon Championship, with all the banquets and parades and such. Then there are the other, more illicit events. Events where more nefarious things are bartered, traded, and gambled, without the High Queen's knowledge. Things like magical items."

"What's that got to do with Po?"

"Tck-tck-tck, you're not listening, Q. I just so happen to know there will be a particular magical item there, an elixir. It will give him his legs back."

"And you'll get this item for us?"

"Of course, as long as you get something for me. Win the Dragon Championship, bring me the key to magic, real magic, and I will give you the elixir you need to fix your mistakes."

"That's just a fairytale poem, Ridhan. The kind of magic you seek is a myth."

"So is surviving a lightning strike without a mark to show for it, but we both know better than that, don't we? Find me the key, and the little sandeater will walk again." Ridhan patted Po on the head, and left us alone, gaping at each other.

"Do you think it's true?" Po was obviously hopeful, not only because of his faith in magic but also his faith in me.

"I don't know, bud. It could be a lie or a trick. But either way, even if it's a long shot, if it means you might walk again, I have to try."

Po yelped in excitement and I spun him around as we celebrated the possibility. Sparks flew from my hands and Po tried to catch them, his hair frizzing up whenever he made contact.

I stopped before we both became dizzy enough to puke, and I sat on the ground in front of him, my heart racing.

"So," Po said, "how do you become Dragon Champion?"

"Well, the Dragon Championship is in less than a month, and in order to be the South's representative, I need to win the Southern Tournament first. But I have no team, and everyone is mad at me."

"You have me!"

I patted his leg. "Thanks, but I meant like Yokel and Roc are mad at me."

"And Pathfinder and Windrunner and Ms. Iris."

"And Reagan. Looks like it's just me and you, bud."

Po looked at me curiously. "I think I have an idea for how to win back our friends, but…"

"But, what?"

He looked away shyly. "It's a little bit crazy."

"Po, have you met us? All we do is crazy."

# THE EASY PART

"I take it back, this is never going to work," I said, propping myself up on my hands and knees.

"It's gotta work. You just need a new suit, so you don't die," Po said, wheeling around to the front of me.

"Johanous promised it would be ready by the start of the tournament tomorrow," I panted.

"Then the plan will work! I just know it. We'll all be friends again!"

The Carpenters around me readied their practice swords and I stood wearily. Every day for a week we had practiced, and every day I had come out with more and more bruises. Every Carpenter was helping me train, Azel's voice echoing regularly along the chamber: "Again!"

One by one and often teaming up, the Carpenters engaged me. Although the tournament would be like any other I had competed in, I was rusty, and we had decided on an accelerated training regimen meant to prepare me for the South's best warriors. I parried and danced my way through, receiving less of a beating than before and signaling that I was returning to form.

As with most of our insane plans, it was actually fairly simple. I would fight in the Southern Tournament with no armor, save for my new vigilante suit courtesy of Johanous. Even with the dulled weapons used during the tournament, without the protection of typical metal armor, I would be exposed to all sorts of blunt injuries. Given that points were scored by hitting your opponent, I'd have to make it through the entire tournament with minimal points against me if I was to survive. It was dumb but it had its purpose.

"He's going to break every bone in his body," a voice from the entrance said as the other Carpenters returned to a holding position. "I thought you were done fighting?"

"I was, but"—I looked to Po—"things changed." I groaned as I stood up. "Rea, I'm going to be fine."

"Let's see it then," she mocked, picking up my sword and tossing it to me. She took two batons and tossed a staff to Azel, who caught it gingerly.

"What is this?" I protested as Reagan nodded her head to Azel. Every Carpenter in the room sat on their knees, laying their practice weapons in front of them. Po was spinning himself in his chair, unable to contain his excitement and narrating his thoughts for all to hear.

"I cannot believe this! This will be the most epic sparring session in the history of sparring sessions!"

Reagan spun her batons around. "You weren't here for it, but Ollie and our older brother could put on quite a show." A quick flicker of anger at the thought of my brother subsided as Reagan pounced, executing blow after blow. Azel joined and they worked in tandem, calling out signals of combination forms to each other.

"Eleven and Four?" Reagan yelled.

"The Carpenter will not fall for it," Azel said, and sure enough she was right. The combination was meant to throw me off balance by occupying my upper body while the second attacker worked on my legs. It was easy enough to defend against, as long as I kept moving away and putting one of them in the path of the other.

"What is going on?" Po said, flabbergasted.

"There are teamwork forms," I yelled as I kicked Reagan away to focus on Azel's spinning staff. "It's meant to help coordinate fighters rather than everyone working alone. There's strength in numbers, but only if used together." I was growing fatigued and knew their combined strength and skills would soon beat me if I didn't finish this quickly.

After pushing Azel back, I turned quickly to an approaching Reagan.

"What's wrong, Ollie, can't handle us both? And here I thought you were the best fighter in the City." Reagan spun her weapons for an attack.

Time stopped again and I saw the paths to victory, smiling as the most fun one presented itself.

"Oh no," Reagan muttered.

"Oh, yes," I said as I flew into a variety of attacks intended to hide my final play. I tossed my sword at Reagan, handle first. Her instinct was to try and catch it, but given both her hands were already occupied, instead of batting the sword away, she ended up fumbling all three weapons. I came with a front kick to her sternum, sending her into a pile of other Carpenters as they broke their silence and groaned in sympathy. I whipped myself up from the ground and grabbed the two batons to face Azel.

"Push, push, push, baby sister. That's what you do, isn't it?" I said as I circled Azel, trying to see her approach now that it was one on one.

"That's what family does, Ollie. We push," she said as the Carpenters helped her to her feet. "We push each other until we break, and then we push some more."

A flurry of attacks came from Azel, but I easily avoided each one, my teacher testing my defenses.

"Why do you hold back, Carpenter?" Azel asked, dragging her staff along the ground. I didn't answer, just spun my batons, and she continued. "Always afraid of outshining others, you dim your light. It's time you let go, Carpenter. Be the person you were meant to be." She continued a more advanced assault, and I defended again, without counterattacking. "Stop holding back!" she yelled, pushing harder and harder with each swing of her staff. She was flowing in and out of different forms so quickly, I had a hard time keeping up. But I did keep up, and soon began to see it all more easily. I'd never fought against an opponent of Azel's skill, but was this all there was? Was there more to Azel, and more to my own self?

"What do you want from me!" I asked, frustrated by the intensity of the attacks.

"I want to see you, Carpenter, for the first time," she said, backing away. "It is time to live up to your name." Azel threw her staff aside and moved into the beginning position of Form Zero. I tossed my batons to the side, and we stood there, waiting to begin.

"Carpenters, leave us!" Azel commanded, and after disappointed grunts, everyone left the room, save for Reagan and Po.

"Become who you were meant to be, Oliver." The sound of my name from her voice in this place gave me goosebumps. She pushed to the attack, her hands and feet moving in quick succession. I defended, countering and launching my own attacks. Each kick and punch were blocked by a forearm and shin, neither of us able to gain the upper hand.

Then it happened. Power coursed through my body, and I felt a surge of energy run down my arms and into my hands. I moved into attacks so fast and powerful, each hit burst like a firework upon impact. After only a few moments, Azel was on her back. I pushed my palm forward, and a burst of bright light exploded in the air and sent sparks of lightning jumping from the various weapons on the ground and walls before they dissipated.

Reagan looked over at Po, whose hair was sticking up from touching a stray bolt.

"It's okay, he knows," I said as I offered to help Azel to her feet. I looked at my arms; no lightning any longer.

"That... was... so... AWESOME!" Po yelled.

"Yes, yes, awesome, but you can't go doing that at the tournament. That's a fast way to get the Black Sun Battalion to take you away."

"Got it, no magic," I agreed, even as my heart soared. Without magic, the world seemed gray and dull, not vibrant and alive as it was when I was in its midst. I turned to Azel and posed a question to my longtime mentor. "So, do you think it'll work? Can I win the tournament?"

"Oliver, you might be one of the best students I've ever had. There's nothing left for me to teach you. You are a Carpenter no more, but I suspect you'll have a different moniker soon enough."

"Like Dragon Champion!" Po hollered excitedly.

Reagan piped up. "Like the Lightning Knight?"

"Like none of that matters if I don't win the Southern Tournament. So, you gonna help?" I asked her.

"Only if you promise to tell me why you're not using armor."

"Oh, uh, that was my idea," Po answered. "It's the only way to show Roc and Yokel and Path—"

I interrupted. "To show all our friends that I'm sorry. I have to do what Roc did in Romir."

"That is the stupidest thing I've ever heard," Reagan said as she walked toward a bag by the door. "But I suppose I understand the sentiment. Good thing Johanous sent this." She pulled out the new suit, handing it to me with a wry grin.

The suit was a marked improvement from the last one he had made. It didn't lose any of its flexibility and was still lightweight, and after a few hits by Reagan, we confirmed that it could take a beating without me taking a beating.

A beating my suit and I took throughout each match of the tournament. Even as skilled as I was, the South had proven to have many a great fighter. By the Nine's grace or by luck I had survived four rounds of the tournament with minimal damage to my body, and now the final match was upon us. For once, things felt like they were going our way.

"I can't breathe," I coughed as Reagan adjusted the laces on my suit. The sounds of the stadium were louder than they had been for the Homecoming Tournament, and while I felt the relief from the suit on my lungs, I rubbed the silvery emblem on my chest.

The story of my run through the tournament had reached every part of the city because no one had ever heard of a fighter attempting even a single match without protection, let alone four. Although it was my name that was gaining the glory and reputation, it was really Po and Reagan who deserved most of the credit. They'd spent the entire tournament in my corner, giving me suggestions and scouting the fighters. If it weren't for them, I'd have been fighting blind, and there was absolutely no way I would have won, let alone survived.

"Are they here?" I asked, hopeful for a better response than I had been given throughout all my other matches.

"Ollie, you need to focus. This fighter you're going up against, we've been watching his matches. He's nothing like you've ever faced before. If you're not careful—"

I cut Reagan off as I walked to the tent's opening, pulling the flap to stare out into the stadium. "Are they here, Rea?"

"I don't know."

My heart sank at her answer. "Will all of this have been for nothing?" I asked myself aloud.

Po wheeled in. "This wasn't for nothing."

I walked over and grabbed him by the shoulders, understanding his reference. "I know. I wouldn't be here without you. Both of you. Thank you for sticking with me." I leaned in to whisper into his ear. "Do you know if our other friends are here?"

He looked at Reagan before hiding his answer in a shrug. I took a breath and decided to focus on the task at hand. Regardless of whether Roc and Iris or Pathfinder and Windrunner were here, I wasn't just doing this for them. I was doing this for Po, for Reagan, and for me.

"I'm ready. Who am I facing?" I asked. Reagan and Po looked at each other, and a brief moment of panic set in at their hesitation. "What is it?"

Reagan winced. "Oliver, the fighter you're going up against, he's... well he's better than you."

"What do you mean better than me? Have you seen me this week? I've never felt in better form." It was the truth. I was more focused than I had ever been, and the paths to victory were so easy to see, I barely even questioned them anymore.

"Big brother, listen to what we're saying. We've been scouting him all tournament. He's a monster, like nothing we've ever seen before. He's even better than Wiggin was." It was hard to hear that name, but if Reagan was talking about our brother, then she was as serious as she could be.

"I wish Yokel were here," I said. "If anyone could find his weakness, it'd be him."

"True, his insight would have been nice," Po said with a big smile.

"Did somebody say they actually needed Yokel?" a deep voice said as a large silhouette filled the entrance to the tent. Following behind him, our master tactician squeezed in, and Whiskey Danger was once again whole.

"How did you..."

"It was Po," Roc said. As if nothing had changed between us, we went into our unique handshake and he continued. "He told us what you were doing." Roc paused for a moment then yelled, "ARE YOU INSANE!"

"Well, you all were mad at me and..."

"And what? Saying sorry didn't occur to you?"

"Um, no. No it did not." We both laughed at my stupidity and I grabbed Yokel for a tight hug, so glad to have him back in my life.

Roc slapped me on the back, wincing at the new suit's sturdiness. "So, Yokel, tell us about this fighter."

Yokel cleared his throat and began his breakdown. "He's faster than you, even with armor on. He moves like a train and hits like one too. His technique is flawless, and Reagan says he moves in and out of forms better than even Azel. He finds an opponent's weak point and then breaks down every other strength until that weak point is all that remains. He doesn't just beat his opponent, he obliterates them."

"Who the Hells is this guy?" I asked incredulously.

Reagan answered. "His name is Corbin Drinkwater and all we know is he's from somewhere deep in the South. We don't know who he's trained with, but he fights with an intensity I've never seen before. It's like, if he doesn't win, he might die. That's not a fighter you want to be in front of, because he's not just fighting for pride or money, but for life."

So, a fighter that no one knows about. Someone seemingly impossible to defeat. Wonderful.

"How is it we've spent this entire year facing people who are seemingly invincible? Like, who has that kind of luck?" I asked.

"The Nine always test their children in ways we can't understand," Po recited dutifully.

"Perfect," I answered, grabbing my sword and spinning the handle in my hand. "So what's the plan?"

Reagan looked at Yokel who looked at Roc who looked at Po who looked back at Reagan. A sadness crept over her face. "We don't have one, Ollie. We don't know how you can win, let alone survive." A trumpet sounded, and we all looked toward the stadium. We had no plan and we had no time.

"Well, you guys got me this far, I guess it's my turn to do the rest," I said as we exited the tent.

In the stadium, lights danced along the walls and throughout the night sky. A large nine-sided ring sat in the middle of the grounds, with chairs surrounding it in addition to the seating of the stadium itself. The crowd erupted in a frenzy when I waved to them, most of my supporters waving the banners of my house—the sword in the mountain, with a dragon flying out of it. I looked around, peering through the crowd in search of the three people I most wanted to be there.

But I couldn't find them. I let out a sigh of disappointment and looked across the ring at Corbin who was already in his corner of the ring. He had no team behind him, nor any herald, and there was something about the way he stood, waiting for me.

He wasn't afraid at all, and I was just a little terrified.

Unlike other tournaments, the Southern Tournament had special scoring rules, because of course we just had to be different. Nine Gods, I hated the South sometimes. Five rounds of three minutes each were all that separated me and victory. The fighter with the most points after the final bell would be the winner. Just survive and get a few hits in, and I'd be on my way as the Southern representative for the Dragon Championship.

Easy.

The tournament herald talked through his large horn as I disregarded him and began my routine. I closed my eyes and focused on my breathing, allowing the sounds of the world to fade. After a few moments, I opened my eyes and searched for the path to victory, just as I had each previous round. But without a proper plan, my paths were limited, and in the end, I couldn't see a way to win.

Nine Hells.

I panicked and turned quickly to Reagan, gesturing for them to come to the ring. I knelt down.

"What's wrong?" Reagan asked.

"I can't see it. I don't see the path to win. Every one of the possibilities leads to me losing. Some of them lead to something worse. But none of them lead me to a win."

They all looked at me, then back at the herald who had finished and was exiting the ring.

Reagan started. "Just make it through a few rounds. We'll figure something out, won't we, boys?"

"Uh, uh," Yokel stuttered before Reagan hit him with an elbow to the side. "Yes, ow, yes we will, just m-make it though in one piece!"

"That's easy for you to—"

I was interrupted by a large gong, signaling the beginning of the first round. I whipped around and Corbin moved forward with sure steps. We circled each other. I moved in for a testing attack and he parried the strike easily, not countering.

What was he up to?

I moved in once more, changing up my forms and flowing into a few combinations that were fairly advanced but well known. As I expected, he performed the correct counters and I slid back, waiting for an attack. But none came. We danced around the ring, with me mostly attacking and him defending every mix of combinations I threw at him. A loud pounding of a drum sounded, signaling thirty seconds remaining, and that was when he moved in with blinding speed, pushing my defenses to their limits as I reacted to the array of strikes and slashes I'd never seen before. The drums sounded for a second time, letting us know there was only ten seconds left, and Corbin spun his sword around and hit my pommel, sending my sword flying across the ring. His sword pointed at my throat, and for a moment, he could have ended my life right there and then. But the toll of the gong sounded, ending a scoreless first round.

The crowd booed at the lack of points scored. Corbin retreated to his corner and leaned against the post, hanging his arms over the ropes as he stared directly across at me. I walked over, picked up my sword, and sat in my corner on the small stool Yokel had provided.

"Why didn't he go in for the strike?" Reagan yelled over the deafening crowd. Roc dabbed my forehead with a wet rag, trying to get the sweat out of my face.

"You said he likes to break a fighter down, right?" I replied between breaths. "He wanted to show me that no matter what I did, I couldn't touch him. That at any point he wants, he can disarm me. He didn't score because he didn't want to."

"Well, let's hope he keeps that up," Reagan said as she moved my hair from my face. "Stay safe, big brother," she said and exited the ring as the gong sounded for the second round.

For the next round, I decided to take a defensive approach, allowing Corbin to show his plan of attack. It wasn't my brightest idea, for every strike he landed sent me flying back against the ropes. It took every ounce of my strength and skill to avoid more devastating hits, and as the drums alerted us to the final ten seconds, Corbin raged into a series of attacks that resulted in a damaging hit along my left forearm, scoring a point. My sword dropped for a second time as my arm went limp and the gong sounded once more, ending the round.

"Oliver, are you alright?" Yokel yelled as I slogged back to my corner.

"I think so. The reinforcements Johanous put in my suit saved my arm. I felt it, but it's not broken. I'm okay, but have you found anything I can use against this guy? I don't know how many more rounds I can take."

Yokel looked at Reagan who looked at Roc who looked at Po who said with a shrug, "Uh, maybe try hitting him back?"

"Thanks, I'll work on that," I said as the gong sounded once more.

I was really starting to get sick of that sound.

I changed my tactic for the third round and decided to put Corbin on the defensive. He countered with moves I had never thought of, scoring point after point on my legs, torso, and back. After the first minute, my attack turned back to defense, and I was lucky to get out of the round without a strike to my head, though it wasn't for lack of trying. I had to sacrifice my body to protect my exposed head, and it has cost me five points alone.

I coughed out blood as Reagan checked my suit for any structural weaknesses. "It's like being hit by a train. How many points did I let up?"

Yokel reluctantly replied. "Fourteen. The score is now fifteen to zero."

"Only fourteen? It felt like thirty."

"Two more rounds to go, Ollie. You need to do something or else you're going to lose this in spectacular fashion," Reagan said as she pushed me back into the ring.

The fourth round started, and I could barely move in a cohesive way. I was bumbling around and Corbin saw the opportunity and attacked with a rage I had never seen before.

No. Wait. I had seen it before, in myself. I'd felt that same rage, that unbridled anger. I knew how to beat that.

As he attacked, I used his own energy and motion against him. He missed many of his strikes, but in my current physical state, he landed enough to send me to the floor of the mat a few times. The gong sounded and I stumbled to my corner once more, unable to stand. I looked at the scorekeepers, squinting to see the score through the sweat and blood running into my eyes.

Twenty-eight to zero.

"Oliver, are you there?" a voice said, but I was in a daze. My head was spinning and my body felt broken and bruised. I closed my eyes and could feel every muscle in my body rejecting every impulse my mind sent.

"Oliver, it's me, Iris."

I heard, but I must have been dreaming. I looked over and there stood Iris, tears streaming down her face.

"Are you, are you real?"

"Yes, you idiot. What the Hells are you thinking? You're going to get yourself killed!" she yelled as she grabbed my hand. A jolt of energy coursed through me and I felt as though it was the beginning of the match again.

What's happening?

Coughing up some more blood, I responded. "Well, we thought if I could win without armor, maybe you'd appreciate the gesture and forgive me?"

"That's the stupidest thing I've ever heard!"

"To be fair, it worked with Roc and Yokel," I said, a small smile trying to form.

"Oliver, I forgive you, please just stop. Don't put yourself through this anymore. You have nothing left to prove." She was giving me an out, and I so very much wanted to take it. But she wasn't the only one I was trying to make amends with. Even with Iris here in front of me, I still searched the darkened crowd for Pathfinder and Windrunner.

"I can't, Iris. I have to win."

She pulled me in for a kiss, our first real kiss in what seemed like forever. I'd forgotten what it was like, to have her in my life. She gave me hope and strength and courage and the will to win, all with a simple kiss.

Iris let go and whispered in my ear, "Don't hold back, little lord."

I jumped off my stool with renewed vigor. I could feel the magic inside me giving me a power I had sorely lacked during this match with Corbin. I closed my eyes and found my balance once more, and suddenly I found a path to victory. It turned out finding the path was simple, once I had love back. Love from my family in Reagan, love from my friends in Roc, Yokel and Po, and love from Iris. I knew Pathfinder was watching, and Windrunner too. I could feel it in my heart, and together, the support from everyone who loved me unlocked the magic within me. A smile crept across my face and for the briefest of moments, I felt sympathy for Corbin.

He stood alone in his corner without a soul who loved him. He stared back at me from across the ring, taking off his helmet.

"Don't recognize me, do you, Oliver? No, you wouldn't, now would you, Oliver? He always said I took after Mother."

I looked at him and crumpled my brow, unsure what he was talking about.

"You killed him. My father, that night in the alley. The other guards heard your name, and how you fought. You of all people should know of your reputation. You left him there to die like some gutter rat. Now is my chance to avenge my father. To take away everything from you. These people will see you for who you truly are when I defeat you. The worthless little rich brat you are."

"I... You don't understand. I didn't mean to... I..."

"I understand enough. Prepare to lose everything you care about." He pointed his sword at Iris while still looking at me. "I'm going to kill you right in front of her."

The gong sounded and the final round commenced.

I didn't know what to do. Corbin was on a path of destruction, my destruction. He didn't just want to win the tournament, he wanted to destroy my life and then take it. I wanted to feel rage and anger but instead felt only pity. He was so lost, because of me.

No, he made his own choice, I reasoned. He could have chosen to honor his father's memory. He could have chosen to come to me, to talk to me. Instead, he chose a darker path, like I had once done for Po. I had my friends to pull me back, but Corbin was lost to his vengeance. He was the enemy in front of me, and I needed to defeat him, for Po, for me, and for him.

I hoped everyone was paying attention, because this was going to be a fight no one would ever forget.

"You want me, you got me. Come on!" I yelled as I ran toward Corbin. I dropped my leg and slid under his oncoming strike, hitting him in the torso and sending him stumbling back.

"That's one," I said as I pressed the attack. Suddenly a combination of moves and forms flowed from my body without any conscious thought. My instincts took over and I let them, allowing my body and mind to become one without hesitation. Within two minutes, I had successfully scored nineteen points and taken none.

I could hear my friends, and my love, screaming in my corner and over the crowd as they cheered me on. I circled back, sizing up Corbin for one last flurry of attacks. He stumbled around, trying to gather himself, spitting out blood.

"This can't be happening. I'm not letting you win. Ahh!!!" He screamed, coming in for his final attack. I glanced at my corner, hearing Reagan above all others.

"It's time, Oliver, show him who you really are!"

The drums sounded: thirty seconds left.

I turned my focus back to Corbin and muttered to myself, "It's over."

I threw my sword into the air above him, causing Corbin to look up for only a moment. But a moment was all I needed. I used the distraction to kick his sword out of his hand and into the air. I continued my spinning kick and sent him falling back into the ropes, catching both swords in my hands as I landed. He leaned against the rope, his eyes wide with shock.

The drums sounded again: ten seconds.

I launched into a series of strikes and hits with both swords that he was unable to defend.

Twenty. This one is for Roc, I'm sorry I wasn't there for you.

Twenty-one. This one is for Yokel, who has been the truest friend I could have asked for.

Twenty-two. This one is for Iris, I don't deserve your love.

Twenty-three. This one is for Reagan, who's never doubted me even when I doubted myself.

Twenty-four. This one is for Pathfinder, who's always had my back.

Twenty-five. This one is for Windrunner, who's always the voice of reason.

Twenty-six. This one is for Po, the greatest hero I've ever known.

Twenty-seven, twenty-eight. Each hit a thought coursing through my head. For all the people who loved me, who stood by me, who never gave up on me.

Azel. This city. They all believed in me when I didn't.

The final seconds were closing in, and we were tied at twenty-eight points each. Corbin was barely standing.

"And this one, this one is for me," I said as I spun around, putting the broadside of my sword against my leg and sending a spinning kick that connected with Corbin's head. He fell to the ground, unconscious but alive. As I came out of my kick, the sound of the gong reverberated throughout the stadium.

Twenty-nine.

Screams came from all over the stadium, and my team rushed up onto the ring, hugging me with such excitement I thought I might fall over. Roc lifted me up onto his and Yokel's shoulders and walked me around the ring for all to see. I searched the crowd for Pathfinder and Windrunner, but my heart told me once more they were cheering for me, out there in the darkness.

"Put me down, put me down!" I yelled as I tapped Roc's head.

Reagan ran over to me, embracing me in a hug. "Big brother, that was insane, and I can't believe, and, Nine Hells!"

I kissed her forehead and walked over to Iris, my love, who was standing in the middle of the ring waiting for me. I picked her up and spun her around, kissing her at the landing.

"Oliver, I—"

I put a finger on her lips and looked at her with all the love and sincerity I could. "Thank you, Iris. You saved me, again. I love you."

Before she could reciprocate the affection, Whiskey Danger and Reagan tackled us both to the mat in celebration.

"Now what?" Roc yelled enthusiastically.

If only he knew the whole story, the whole plan. He would never approve of our mission, of working with Ridhan, or even of the magic I knew I had inside me. I hated having to keep him in the dark, but if I wanted to get Po his legs back, it had to be this way. I looked at Po and he nodded back.

"Now, the hard part begins," I answered.

"You mean that wasn't the hard part?" Roc yelled back, laughing.

I smiled. "Not by a long shot."

# THE STAFF OF THE SEAS

"Ah, Lord Quartermaine, right this way," the attendant said as he ushered me onto the *Kelani IV*. The sea breeze beat on my cheeks as I leaned against the railing, waiting for everyone else to arrive. We had planned out our trip to Dragon's Treasure over the three days since my big victory, and I still felt uneasy.

It would take two days to get to the chain of islands, which sat south of Starfall. The five islands had been gifted to the High Queen as a tribute and peace offering by the dragon lords of old. The legends told that the islands served as the arena where dragons would fight for supremacy and lordship, but now it only served as a reminder of their lost power. Now, the only fights were among humans for an ironic title.

Ever since forever, the High Queen had hosted the tournament every fifth year, and every fifth year the Dragon King would crown the winner as Dragon Champion, though that meant nothing to the reptilian ruler. Dragons and humans held a tense peace with each other, with skirmishes arising mostly from the Northern Tribes, who lived closest to the Dragonlands. But to win the honor meant you were the greatest fighter in the known world and could receive any station you chose. Most champions would either join the Imperial Army at a rank far beyond that of a mere soldier, whereas others would court high positions for a king or queen of Kandaheart or Romir or the like. It was a title that came with station, privilege, and wealth, but it also meant there was a target on your back. Everyone wanted to take down a Dragon Champion, which meant they were just as likely to end up in a brawl as they were to get a free drink.

Yokel was the next to arrive, and he joined me by the railing where we watched the various lords and ladies who were lucky enough to obtain a ticket to travel on the luxury ship named after my mother. Yokel and I began a game we had loved to play as children during parties at either of our homes.

"Okay, okay, this one, this one is a middle-aged lady who has recently come into some money, because she found out about her husband's mistress, who is also secretly the luggage courier!" Yokel pointed to a lord and lady making their way onto the ship, followed eagerly by a lesser dressed woman carrying their luggage. The lord and lady seemed to be engaged in some sort of quarrel.

It was now my turn to fill the story with voices. "I can't believe you brought that tramp with us," I said in my highest pitched and most annoying voice. I switched to a lower voice, much lower than my normal one. "If it weren't for that tramp, you'd be carrying your own luggage, you insufferable—"

Yokel joined in with his own version of the lady. "Insufferable, you know what's insufferable, that thing dangling between your legs you think actually pleasures women."

I added, "Oh you didn't seem to mind all those years when you were —"

"I was faking it," Yokel said, loudly enough for the passing lord and lady to hear. They stopped talking, gave us both a disgusted glare, and then continued on. Yokel and I looked at each other with held breath, then burst out into loud laughs.

"Yok, there's a few things you need to know," I began, seeing this as my opportunity to fill him in on my and Po's alternative quest. After I had finished telling him every piece of the story, the lightning magic, the history of Starfall, Ridhan's claim, all of it, he looked out at the people gathered on the docks.

"I knew there was more to Starfall than what we'd been told," he finally said, fixating on history instead of anything else.

"Yok, did you hear what I said? I have Po's magic now..." My voice betrayed my shame. I knew Po was meant to be the Lightning Knight, but that didn't mean I was ready to let go of the magic.

"Yes, yes, but think of the history books and how they are all wrong!" Yokel never ceased to surprise me, but it was refreshing to let him in on my secret without the judgment I had been expecting. He looked at me, blinking rapidly. "You haven't told Roc yet, correct?"

"No."

"Oh, thank the Nine. The way he's been going on about magic and such, I don't think he'd take it well."

"What's he been saying?"

"He, he, well, he's been saying a lot of d-dark stuff, like that he w-wants to get rid of anyone associated with magic, especially after what it did to Po."

"But it saved him."

"N-not in his eyes. He sees m-magic as the thing that almost killed Po in the first place."

My heart sank. I was hoping to spend the two-day sail to try and convince Roc of the merits of magic, of the good it could do. Of the good it was doing me. But if half what Yokel said was true, Roc would never look at me the same way again.

Yokel tapped me on the shoulder. "Do Pathfinder and Windrunner know?"

"Not yet. I was going to tell everyone below deck, but now I might have to change those plans. I'll wait until we reach Dragon's Treasure, but this is really going to screw with my plans for the trip. Do you think you could…" I struggled to find the right words, but Yokel, as always, was already working out scenarios in his head.

"Keep Roc from finding out? You can count on me, Oliver."

"Thanks, Yok. I can always count on you."

"We both can," Reagan said as she snuck up behind Yokel and tapped his shoulder, hiding behind the other one as Yokel spun around looking for her. "But what are we counting on Yokel to do this time?"

Yokel widened his eyes and I answered his nonverbal question. "She knows. Roc thinks we're going on this trip for the sole purpose of the Dragon Championship, and Yokel will make sure to keep him none the wiser. For the four of us, we have our other quests."

Reagan turned her head. "The four of us?"

I panicked. She didn't know about the Knight Angels, and I didn't know if they were comfortable with Reagan being involved. "We've, uh, we've made some new friends who will be helping us. You'll meet them at Dragon's Treasure. They're taking a different ship."

"Oh, and who might these new friends be? Anyone I know?"

I laughed awkwardly. "No, no, I don't think you know them. They're the Knight Angels. There's two of them! I know, I know, it's crazy but it's true and they're totally awesome and you'll love them and—"

Before I could continue, Yokel elbowed me in the ribs. "Oliver, look!" Below on the docks were Iris and Roc, pushing Po in his chair. Po waved to me, and I ran off the ship to meet them.

"Thanks, Roc. Enjoy your trip!" Po said.

"We'll come back with the trophy for you, Po!" Roc yelled as he finished our hand gesture and made his way onto the ship. A horn sounded, followed by a man yelling for the last call of passengers onto our ship.

"Po! What are you doing here?" I asked after giving Iris a hug and kiss.

"I wanted to see you off, Oliver. And…" His little voice got lost as the horn sounded once more, this time with a bit of urgency.

"It's okay, bud, I'll get that elixir, I promise."

"That's just it, Oliver. If you don't, or if something happens, just… I'll be okay. You've changed my life so much already, and I know you'll win the Dragon Championship. I just, I just wanted to thank you. Thanks for believing in me, letting me be part of Whiskey Danger, letting me be a Carpenter, all of it."

"Po, I didn't let you do anything. You earned it, each and every step of the way," I replied and Po leaned over for a hug. "I'm going to win and we're going to fix your legs. You're going to become the Lightning Knight, I promise," I whispered into his ear.

Po smiled wide and tugged my sleeve. "Oh! I forgot to tell you. My baby sister's name day is soon, and I picked a name." He looked at Iris, who winked, then he turned back to me. "We're going to name her Olivia."

My stomach dropped at the gesture. "Bud, that's… that's really nice of you," I finally mustered.

"I figured we'd name her after the best person I know," Po said proudly.

Iris hugged me and gave me a kiss on my cheek. "I couldn't agree more."

"You'll look after him, right?" I asked my love.

"Yes, yes, silly. Now be off before you miss your—"

She was cut off as the final horn sounded and the ship began to drift away. Yokel waved awkwardly at me while Roc punched him, yelling something inaudible to my ears. They raced away from the railing and I was left on the dock with Iris and Po.

"Tck-tck-tck, Q, my love, isn't that your ship?" Ridhan said, suddenly materializing next to me.

"Hello, Ridhan. Yes, yes it is."

He looked around at Po and Iris, then back at me. "Won't it be difficult to compete in the Dragon Championship if you're not there?"

"Why, yes, yes it will."

"And if you don't win, I don't get magic."

"No, no you don't."

"And if I don't get magic, my sweet Q, then your little friend here doesn't walk again."

"Do you have a point, Ridhan?" I could kill him now, make it look like an accident. Tie some rocks around his ankles and toss him into the ocean. Hells, I could fry him with my lightning magic; wouldn't that be a bit of irony. Oh, here you go, Rid, you wanted magic, you got it.

But my daydreams were vanquished when Ridhan answered. "Tck-tck-tck, that's no way to speak to your savior, Q. Here, you will come with me. The *Tiger Shark* hasn't left port yet."

Iris pulled at my hand and I gave her a shrug, kissing her goodbye and giving the Whiskey Danger hand signal to Po. Ridhan and I boarded his family's yacht and set sail among the dozens of ships heading to the islands. The seas were relatively calm, given the winter storms had recently subsided, and although the ship wasn't as big as the *Kelani IV*, it handled what waves there were with grace and speed.

As the evening came upon us, I was invited below deck to dinner with Lord Shipwight, Ridhan, and a few other lords I didn't quite recognize.

"... and then she said, 'It may not be the size of the ship, but it sure does take a long time to get to Dragon's Treasure in a skimmer,'" I said while all the men around the table laughed at the crude joke. The nighttime seas had calmed just enough for us to enjoy a dinner without having to nail down our plates.

"So, Lord Quartermaine, my son has told me of the exciting final match of the Southern Tournament. Some are calling it the fight of the decade," Lord Shipwight said, cutting his food with a loud screech as his knife moved across the plate.

"I don't know about the decade, but certainly the tournament. Were you unable to attend, m'lord?" I asked before sipping my wine.

"Away on business, but word reached me very quickly of the match. Did you know of your opponent beforehand? Some were saying he was quite a mystery."

I looked down at my food, suddenly feeling full and pushing the plate forward to indicate I was finished. "No, I had never met him before. He was a tough fighter, great footwork."

Ridhan excitedly jumped in. "Great footwork is an understatement. The betting markets had Q down as a seven hundred and fifty to one underdog going into the final round."

Lord Shipwright banged his utensils on the table loudly, sending a shiver down my back at the noise. He made a stuttering ticking noise before scolding his son. "I thought I told you not to speak of those gutter rats you consort with."

"I'm sorry, Father," Ridhan said, shame and embarrassment covering the hint of anger in his voice. That ticking noise sounded so familiar but wasn't exactly what Ridhan did.

Strange.

The dinner was suddenly quiet apart from the groaning of the wooden ship.

Ridhan spoke up. "He's everything I've told you about and more, Father."

"That will be enough of that! I have already told you—" But the lord stuttered into a tick again, unable to finish his reprimand.

Ridhan stood up quickly, his chair falling to the floor with a loud bang. "You never could see past your own nose, you old…"

But the lord stood as well, a knife in his hand pointing directly at Ridhan. The young Shipwight pushed his plate forward in anger and stormed out of the cabin.

"I think I'll be heading to my room, big days ahead and all," I said. "I thank you for your hospitality, my lord."

Lord Shipwight waved me away without speaking. I found my way to the upper deck, where Ridhan was holding his family's Staff of the Seas.

"Well, that went better than expected," I said sarcastically.

"He'll never understand," Ridhan said, staring out at the black ocean.

"I thought my joke came off fairly well."

"He's always been too weak to take the risks needed. Not like us, Q. Not like me." Ridhan's grip on his staff grew tighter, and lightning in the distance illuminated the bleak horizon. There was something primal and fantastic about the lightning. Skyfire, moving quicker than my eye could comprehend. So fast it seemed as though it couldn't possibly be real.

But it was real, and I was in control of it now, or at least something like it. Each strike sounded like an orchestra playing a song only I could understand. The bright light flashed against the underside of the clouds and a crackle forewarned of the loud explosion of sound that would immediately follow. The dance between the sky and its destination, never moving in a single line but zigzagging throughout its route.

If the Tree of Life was real, as the elves believed, then lightning most surely was the flame that gave the world its soul. I stood there on the top deck, letting raindrops wash away all thoughts and feelings and putting me at ease. I could feel when the clouds gathered, getting ready to send the strike to the ocean, and for a moment, I thought I could almost will it to happen.

"You can feel it, can't you?" Ridhan said ominously, and for a moment I thought he knew my secret. How could he know? Was he spying on me? Was I careless? Ridhan continued. "You can feel the winds of change. A storm is coming."

The clouds above us rumbled as the lightning struck closer and closer. He spun his staff and twisted its shaft, letting two prongs jut out from its primary blade. He held it with both hands above his head, and the waves rolled, and the wind blew harder.

I grabbed the railing as the ship rocked back and forth. "The winter storms are supposed to be finished!" I yelled as rain and saltwater spit into my face.

"Don't you see, Q, I control the seas now!" His face was maniacal, but I couldn't help but think he was speaking the truth.

"Ridhan, you have to stop! You're going to kill us all!" I yelled as another lightning strike hit the ocean.

Ridhan laughed and laughed, hitting his staff to the deck. "They'll never understand, Q. Not like you. Together, we can achieve more than they ever dreamed!"

I lunged at Ridhan, grabbing both his shoulders as he continued to laugh. "Ridhan, this isn't you! I can help you, I can save you. We can take down the Spider's Web together!" Another strike hit the ocean, this time closer.

"Don't you see, Q. Magic is the answer. Magic will free us. It will free me. This is the only way!"

I shook him again. "Ridhan, I can't let you do that. I won't. You can't have magic. You don't know what it can do!" My eyes betrayed me in the light of the strike next to the ship.

"You have it, don't you, Q. You have it and you are keeping it from me!" He dropped his staff and the winds subsided, but the waves kept heaving. "I thought you understood. No one understands! I thought you were like me, but I was wrong. No one is like me, no one understands me, no one sees what I see." He dropped his staff to the deck. "Fine, I'll just do it myself." He pulled me in for a strong hug and whispered into my ear. "Tck-tck-tck, goodbye, Q."

I slipped on the wet deck as Ridhan shoved me over the edge of the railing. I flailed around helplessly and plunged into the dark waves below. Holding my breath, I swam in the direction I thought was up and emerged into the air above the water, gasping. Before I could catch a new breath, a wave engulfed me and I tumbled through the water, unsure which way would lead to freedom.

I struggled to find my bearings, trying to swim in earnest with my lungs burning in rage and pain. The saltwater hurt my eyes and, in the darkness, the only thought I had was that of fresh air. Suddenly the water erupted in a flood of light emanating from far above me and dissipating through the ocean. The surface seemed leagues away directly above me; however, my body kept moving away from it. I stretched out for help, for relief, but it was folly. Something was grasping at my legs, or maybe that was all in my air-deprived mind.

I closed my eyes, thinking of my friends and of failing Po. The water pulled me deeper and deeper and a final thought streaked across my mind as I opened my mouth to breath the final watery breath. "This isn't the end."

I moved into Form Zero, hoping the lightning magic could do something impossible. With each movement, my body convulsed. I thought the lightning magic would save me, but my eyes grew heavy and the darkness overtook me. I would die in this watery grave, and not even magic could save me.

# PART II
# THE LIGHTNING KNIGHT

# THE IN-BETWEEN

Oliver lay on his back against a cold, marble-like floor. He had a strange sensation, as though he was now watching his life from without, instead of from within. He opened his eyes, seeing only darkness, and a brief sense of panic washed over him.

"Oh no, I'm blind," he said aloud. Instantly, light appeared, silhouetting his body, and he relaxed. He sat up, taking inventory of his body. He was wearing the clothes he had drowned in, excepting his boots, but they weren't wet and neither was he. His arms moved when he wanted them to, and while he wiggled his toes, he took large breaths, coughing up dribbles of water.

"Well, this is unexpected." Sarcasm had proved, on more than one occasion, to calm his nerves.

Oliver turned his head in either direction, but beyond the faint glow underneath him, the darkness was total. He stood, wobbling to his feet and coughing up more drops of water. He took a step with his bare foot and the ground glowed under the pressure he exerted.

"I've been here before," he said, putting his hands to his head and trying to recede into his mind temple. But it was locked to him, and his body physically jerked at the expulsion from the sacred space. Oliver took a breath and began to walk, hoping to find an end to wherever he was. Voices echoed from above and around him, screaming and moaning.

As his right foot stepped on the ground, the light from below grew and grew into an image of Starfall on fire, with smoke billowing from the Narrows and the outer wall crumbled into rocks and dust. He stepped with his left foot and out from it came an image of the high noon sun blotted out by a cloud of dark arrows that stretched across the sky. Another step and another image, a volcano exploding, then wind hitting his face as he fell from high on a cliff, and then a fire raging through a forest. The images of carnage and death mortified Oliver, and he ran and ran to escape them. More and more images followed him, each worse than the last. An image of Po lying dead next to him transposed into an image of Iris kissing a shadowed stranger. Finally, he saw his sister, bound to the floor and surrounded by bodies formed into an intricate design.

Oliver stopped and yelled out into the void. "Please! I'm begging you, make it stop!" With each vision came a cacophony of emotions. With death came grief, with the kiss came betrayal, with destruction came helpless devastation. He fell to his knees and saw all the kingdoms and queendoms of Soraya crumbling to ash, armies falling by the thousands, people suffering and bloodied, and a personification of magic uncontrollably devouring the world.

Then, nothing. No light from beneath him but only the surrounding darkness. Oliver curled up with his head by his knees, rocking back and forth. The screams of hundreds of thousands, maybe millions of people crescendoed in his ears and Oliver wished for death, if this was not already death.

The sounds stopped and he felt a hand on his shoulder. "Everything is alright, Po," a somber voice said.

Oliver looked up over the ridge of his arms to see a handsome man standing over him. He emanated light from within. He glowed.

But the man's expression grew cold. "You! Why are you here?" he asked.

"Am I dead?" Oliver knew he was dead, and he knew he had drowned. He remembered it all so clearly, the fight against the pull of the ocean, the struggle to resist the urge to breathe even as his lungs burned. Fighting to have the lightning magic save him and failing. But this place was certainly not like any afterlife he had ever read or heard about. This wasn't one of the Nine Heavens and neither was it any part of the religion the Northern Tribes followed, nor the ancient Elvish myths. Maybe this was one of the Nine Hells, but even that seemed incorrect.

"You're not supposed to be here. Where is Po?"

Oliver unfurled his arms to reveal a terrified face, but the man scoffed and grabbed Oliver's hand.

"Why do you have this ring?"

"Uh, Po gave it to me," Oliver answered, snatching back his hand. The man buried his head into his hands and screamed while Oliver scampered backward along the floor and into the feet of another person.

"Hello, my child," a woman said. "You're quite unexpected, young one. How exactly did you end up here?"

Oliver froze, unable to decide his next move. In front of him stood a man muttering curses at himself, at Oliver, and at the floor. Behind him stood a lithe woman who kind of reminded him of his grandmother.

"I, uh, I think I'm dead," Oliver finally responded.

The woman laughed. "Yes and no, young one. But that still doesn't answer the question, now does it." She looked up at the angry man and shook her head. "He doesn't take new circumstances well." She moved to stand in front of Oliver and extended a hand. Oliver took it and was pulled to his feet, and they walked as the room spun up around them, leading them to the secret chamber within the bowels of the Shears. Oliver sat down in the familiar room, next to a fireplace that inexplicably radiated warmth.

"Where are we?" he asked as the woman sipped on a cup of tea that manifested from nowhere.

She looked into the fire before taking a final sip from her cup and addressing her new companion. "We are… in-between. That is to say, you are not dead, but you are also not alive. It is a place few know about and even fewer have been to. A place, Oliver, that you should not be."

"You know my name?"

"I know everything that is," the woman began, and the floor transformed into a river of stars and heavens, flowing in constant motion. Oliver had seen this once before, in a wayward dream months before.

"I know everything that is," the woman repeated, and certain stars lit up within the river, creating ripples in the stream that bounced off other stars, lighting them up as well.

"And everything that is to—" She suddenly rose to her feet. "What is this?" she said as the stream fell into what Oliver could only surmise was a waterfall into nothingness. The woman looked at Oliver incredulously. "What have you done?"

Oliver looked around the room, wondering who she was talking to. After turning back to her, he finally pointed at himself. "Me?" Before she could answer, a lumbering slam of door echoed within the room and the angry man barreled in.

"He has my ring!" the man yelled, gasping for air. Oliver held up his hand to show the woman, and she sank back into her chair looking dismayed.

Oliver glanced at the river of stars on the floor, tracing the waterfall backward. Certain stars waxed and others waned while even more were steady and strong. There was a whirlpool not very far from the waterfall that didn't look like it belonged there.

"Can one of you tell me what's going on?" Oliver asked, pointing to the whirlpool. But he was ignored as the man and woman argued, often pointing fingers at one another and sometimes saying Oliver's and Po's names. Oliver decided to inspect the river himself. He stood within it, the gaseous flow reaching up to his knees. He put his hand into it and felt the same sensation as a thick fog on top of Nobleman's Hill. He touched one of the solidly bright stars and a rush of images flooded his eyes. He yelped and jumped out of the stream, which did get their attention.

"What was that?" Oliver asked, panting.

"What did you see?" the man asked.

"I saw," Oliver began, trying to remember without the help of his mind temple, "that night on top of Roc's roof. When we learned who Po truly was."

"Ah, yes," the man replied. "I used quite a bit of magic that night."

Oliver looked at the man, furling his brow and letting his mouth sink open. "You're Haralabos."

"Yes."

"But that's impossible," Oliver argued. "You'd have to be hundreds of years old."

Haralabos waved around the room and the ceiling transformed into a vision of the space and stars, of planets and moons. "We are in-between, or out of time. It's the place elves commune with for their everlasting life."

"Elves are extinct," Oliver countered.

"So are you," Haralabos replied with a sneer.

Oliver sat and watched the man as he took a seat next to the woman, drinking from a cup that never seemed to empty. Haralabos seemed content in silence, and Oliver felt pressure on his chest, as if someone were pushing on it repeatedly. A boom of thunder sounded from farther away, followed by a gust of wind. Haralabos began to anxiously check the room, searching for something.

"No, no, I'm supposed to have more time with him!" He grumbled at the woman, but she simply pursed her lips.

"I'm confused. I thought you said we were out of time?" Oliver asked.

Haralabos looked back with disdain at Oliver and muttered, "Quartermaines." He sprang up and walked over to a row of books, pulling them out one by one and discarding them to the floor in annoyance. "Not this one, not this one. Nine Hells, you would have thought I was more prepared for this." Haralabos paused to stare at Oliver with disgust. "Then again, it wasn't supposed to be you."

"Um, what exactly is happening?" Oliver asked, falling to the floor as his chair disappeared from beneath him.

"Here it is!" Haralabos yelled before abandoning his search and crouching next to Oliver. Another boom of thunder, this time closer, and a stronger gust of air hit the two of them. Haralabos grabbed Oliver by both his arms. "Listen! It was supposed to be Po, not you. He was the one who was supposed to become the Lightning Knight."

Oliver looked away, ashamed. "I know, I failed."

"Yes, and we don't know why," Haralabos said, looking back at the woman. "The future is malleable, Quartermaine, but"—he pointed to the river behind him—"there are certain points that are keystones to the timeline we chose, and they ripple throughout all of eternity, both forward and backward."

"I don't understand," Oliver said, his head growing heavy and water continuing to dribble from his mouth.

Haralabos continued. "We chose the future, she and I, and for hundreds of years we have steered history into those keystone moments. For instance, you defeated Sir Declan and—"

"No, I didn't," Oliver corrected.

Haralabos stopped talking and looked again at the woman, who was now knee deep in the river searching for stars.

"You didn't... But you were supposed to..." Haralabos looked at the waterfall and held his hand to his mouth. "The future is unknown now. Everything we worked for. Everything I gave up." He sat back on his butt and his hands dropped to the floor.

Oliver looked at him, then at the woman, but couldn't make sense of any of it. "What's the big deal?"

The woman rushed over to Oliver, grabbing him by his shirt and lifting him slightly. "You were supposed to win! That was the path we chose and now everything has changed. We don't know the ripple effects of…" But she trailed off to move back into the river and inspect the whirlpool.

Haralabos snapped out of his dismay and grabbed Oliver himself. "We can still make this work. Yes, yes, we can. Po is the key. He can still save magic and save us all from the High Queen."

"No, he can't! He's… there's no way for me to help him now," Oliver revealed. "I can't do anything for him anymore."

"The High Queen must be destroyed. That is the only way I can be… There is an evil coming to this world, Oliver Quartermaine. An evil I failed to stop centuries ago, but now, now we can! We can save magic once and for all, but we need Po Pondarion to do it."

"What does that have to do with the High Queen? From what I can tell, the world is doing fine with her in it."

"You are a FOOL! Magic is at a tipping point. It could easily be lost forever or devour this world. The High Queen rules with tyranny and fear, and soon she will unleash pain. You've seen the visions! You know what is to come." Haralabos stood and paced away, scowling. He opened a drawer and searched through a pile of junk as Oliver contemplated the visions he had witnessed.

Starfall on fire.

The world consumed by magic.

Oliver broke down crying. The thunder sounded even closer now and both Haralabos and Oliver were blown over by the wind. The woman braced herself within the river, then pushed through the wind gusts and extended her hand once more to Oliver.

"Who are you?" Oliver asked as he pulled himself up.

"I am Satine. Satine Quartermaine." Oliver almost fell over again, this time from the weakness in his legs. His own ancestor, the beginning of his family name, and one of the long-lost original queens of Starfall was in this place, with Haralabos.

"Easy, my child," Satine said. "The future is unknown now," she said as she pointed to the waterfall. "It is up to you to write it."

"I can't. I'm not the hero, I'm just a dead boy."

Haralabos stood up furiously and took hold of Oliver's hand, trying to pull the ring off. A lightning bolt from above struck between the three of them and Haralabos was sent backward while Oliver and Satine were unaffected.

"He stole my magic!" Haralabos yelled.

"I didn't steal anything!" Oliver screamed back.

"It was meant for Pondarion, not you! It was meant for the owner of my ring, and you stole it."

"Po GAVE me this ring, you moron. Besides, Po can't even walk. He's a cripple and will never be the Lightning Knight. Is that what you want to hear? I didn't ask for your magic, I didn't ask for any of this!"

"But you like it, don't you! You want to keep the lightning magic, thief!" Haralabos threw a journal to the floor at Oliver's feet; the same journal Oliver had burned on the beach. But it was unscathed. Haralabos once more grabbed Oliver's hand, trying to remove the ring, this time with the aid of his journal. "Give it back! Return the magic and I might give it to Po!" But instead of a lightning bolt from above, it came from within Oliver, and it wasn't a lightning bolt at all, but rather the amorphous being of lightning Oliver had once communed with during his meditation.

The lightning magic figure took Haralabos by the collar and lifted him into the air, speaking in a crackling and hissing voice.

"I am not yours, pretender." Haralabos's eyes widened and he grew quiet. He was thrown to the ground by the lightning figure who turned now to Satine. "I warned you not to meddle with that magic. They always were quite unruly."

Satine bowed to the figure. "No more unruly than people, I have found." She glanced quickly at Oliver, who was standing with mouth agape. Haralabos tried to move and the lightning figure hissed a crackled static in his direction.

"Please come back to me," Haralabos pleaded.

"You broke our covenant long ago and look where you arrived. Still, you learned nothing and now you've tried once more and failed," the lightning magic replied.

"I didn't fail," Haralabos retorted. "He stole you from me!" Thunder ruptured the room, splitting the ceiling into a thousand different cracks of glass, and Oliver felt the pressure on his chest once again.

The lightning figure bent down and grazed Haralabos's face with her hand. "No, I am not his magic." Haralabos tried to grab her hand, but before he could, she dissipated into nothing. Oliver recognized the expression of sorrow and yearning on Haralabos's face, for he wore it now too, thinking the lightning magic was gone forever.

Suddenly his hand shot up toward the ceiling, being pulled by the ring, and a lightning bolt shot through it, turning the glass into sand that rained upon them all. Oliver could feel the lightning magic once more within him, but it felt different this time. He didn't feel whole but rather like he only had one piece of the puzzle and that there were still more pieces out there. Lightning magic flickered along his fingertips and Haralabos flashed a strained but accepting smile at him. Oliver looked to Satine for guidance.

"If the magic has chosen him, it is his to keep, for now," she said.

"But how will Po get his magic?" Haralabos argued vehemently.

A thunderclap struck and the rush of the wind's concussive blow pressed them all to the floor and kept them pinned.

"We will figure out another way!" Satine yelled, reaching out for Haralabos's hand. She grabbed Oliver's hand too and held it tight as the wind pushed them down. "The future is now uncertain, my child, but we will do our best to help you. Po is the key magic, but now you are just as important." She looked at Haralabos, who nodded in agreement.

He looked at the whirlpool and back at Satine. "We will get the Codex to Dragon's Treasure, but you'll need help."

Satine scowled. "That is a risky future, with uncertain ripples."

Haralabos argued back. "Everything is uncertain. It's up to Oliver to create the future now, not us."

Satine turned her head to Oliver. "You will need help." A devious grin grew upon her face. "Nine should do." Haralabos let out a snort of amusement, and Oliver couldn't help but wonder if these two were here by accident or by choice. Satine continued. "Find it and help Po become the person he was meant to be. As for you, my child, you will need to become a hero. To become a legend. To become more. Good luck, Oliver Quartermaine. Please tell Azel, I'm sorry about dinner."

Haralabos grabbed Oliver's other hand and yelled above the wind. "Tell her I'm sorry as well. Tell her, tell her I tried my best."

Oliver panicked, wishing against all hope for more time in this timeless place. "I can't do this alone!" he yelled.

Satine smiled at Oliver, and a spark of lightning jumped from Oliver's hand to her own. "You are not alone."

A final thunderclap sounded, and the pressure of wind picked Oliver up and threw him into the air. Then he fell and fell and fell some more, descending into darkness even as he seemed to rise toward light.

Oliver jerked, spitting water from his mouth. The sounds of waves gently moving along the shoreline flooded his ears even as a high-pitched ringing battered his eardrums. He opened his eyes to see a blurry image in front of him. Coughing, he pushed himself up to sitting as the strange person helped.

"Ah, aak, what, where am I?" he asked, blinking rapidly to clear his vision. A stunningly beautiful, golden-haired girl knelt before him. Her violet eyes, deeper than the ocean itself, stared directly into his while a wide smile indented her cheeks. Freckles lightly dotted those cheeks and hints of laugh lines could be seen at the corners of her eyelids.

"You're on Dragon's Treasure," Oliver's savior said, sarcasm starting to tinge her words, "and that's one."

# A GRAND ENTRANCE

"One what?" Oliver asked, still taking in the scenery. It was daytime and the sun was high, midway to its peak. He blinked rapidly, shaking his head and trying desperately to remember where he had been.

Unlike his previous experience in the in-between back in Mercyhold, he could remember everything so clearly. Almost too clearly.

Something was different inside him; something was unlocked. He looked at his rescuer, waiting for an answer even as he felt his soaking wet clothes harden the soft sand underneath them.

"I saved you, so you owe me one. A life debt that is, it's pretty simple," the beautiful girl said with a smirk as she sat back on the beach, allowing the waves to kiss her boots. They sat there, letting the warm sun dry their bodies as Oliver regained his breath.

"Who are you?" Oliver asked after what seemed an embarrassingly long amount of time. This was quite possibly the most beautiful girl he had ever laid eyes on, and his heart fluttered at the mere idea of talking to her.

She wrung her hair of water and brushed it to the side of her head as she turned to Oliver. "My name is Kiara, and what kind of fish might you be?"

"Fish?"

Kiara pointed. "I pulled you out from there, so you're a fish. It was a joke..." She slapped a hand to her forehead and rubbed it down her face, stretching it in the process. "You hoomans have no sense of humor, I swear."

Oliver rubbed the back of his neck. "Sorry, drowning will do that to you, I suppose." He tried to stand but stumbled and held himself steady with his hands on his knees. "I'm okay, I'm okay. Just getting my land legs back, being a fish and all." He cracked a smile and looked up at Kiara, who was now standing as well.

"Oh, he's got jokes, everybody," she said aloud to no one. Oliver looked at her, perplexed, his mouth slightly open. He was absolutely enamored with this girl, his savior, and his usual sharp mind was completely and utterly useless.

She continued to take inventory of her clothes and continued. "So, does the fish have a name, or do I have to make up one for you?" Her arms were on her hips as she posed, causing Oliver to briefly freeze.

"It's Oliver."

"Oliver, huh? That's a cute name. Oliver. Oliver, Oliver, Oliver. Really just gets stuck right there in your mouth, doesn't it?" She talked fast and it seemed as though her mind was racing from one point to the next. Oliver relished the idea of chasing her thoughts from subject to subject and knew instantly this was a person he wanted in his life.

He went to run his hand through his hair and stopped in shock.

"What happened to my hair!" He rushed to a trapped pool of seawater to glimpse his reflection. His hair was short. It had been shoulder-length.

"It wasn't always like that?" Kiara asked as her head popped into the reflection next to his.

"Noooooo, my beautiful hair. It took me so long to grow it out."

"Oh, Oliver, vanity is wasted on hoomans. But as a matter of point, I think I quite like your look, Oliver."

His infatuation had quickly subsided into annoyance. "Please stop doing that?"

"Doing what, Oliver? Saying your name, Oliver? Don't you like Oliver, Oliver?" Kiara giggled as she started to circle him.

"You're a peculiar one," Oliver said as she spun around, falling to her butt. Kiara had an oddly playful energy, unlike anyone he had met before. She laughed at her own clumsiness and Oliver smiled.

Kiara stopped laughing and a mischievous look came over her face. "Here, come join me." She swept Oliver's legs, sending him to the flat of his back once again. She lay opposite him, their heads next to each other as they looked up at the sky. Oliver thought he saw an odd dark wisp of a cloud streak quickly along the blue canvas, and Kiara's breath stopped.

"What's he doing here?" she whispered.

Oliver turned his head in the soft sand, wondering what she was talking about, but decided to let it rest as he fawned over her. Before long, his head started to throb, something he brushed off as part of dying and coming back to life, but the pain soon became unbearable.

"Here, let me," Kiara said. She sat on a rock next to Oliver and applied pressure to the back of his neck with her fingers. Suddenly, the throbbing subsided and he felt clear again. He looked at her in astonishment. "A trick I learned from my mother." Kiara sat, looking out at the ocean as the sun ascended and became hidden behind a cloud. "You know, there's a story going around on the big island that some dumb little lord went and found himself overboard on a ship out here. His name was Oliver, too. You wouldn't happen to know him, would you?"

"It's a long story," Oliver answered, touching his back waistband to find the outlines of a book.

"Ooo, I love stories." Kiara placed her elbows on her knees and propped her head on her hands.

Oliver breathed in, letting the air fill his lungs, but coughed once more as some water sprinkled out of his mouth. He closed his eyes and tried to calm his body, and suddenly, he found himself meditating quietly within his mind temple. There was something different now, an odd sensation he'd felt a few times before. Hope sprang within him, filling his entire being, and a smile crept along his face.

"Are you okay?" Kiara said, patting his back gingerly to help with the coughing.

Oliver sprang to his feet with boundless energy. "I feel, I feel great. I don't know, I just feel... like really positive right now."

Kiara sprang to her feet as well and linked her arm with Oliver's and spun around. "You are the most interesting fish, Ollie. Can I call you Ollie?"

Oliver embraced the spin and also this new feeling. Had the lightning magic changed who he was on a fundamental level? Or was this a result of death and rebirth? Or the in-between? Or Kiara? A thousand and one ideas rushed through his mind, and he absentmindedly answered Kiara.

"Only my sister calls me that." He thought of his sister and his friends who all must have been heartbroken to hear of his supposed death. Ridhan must have sold everyone a story of bad weather and unsure footing. "Wait, she's here on Dragon's Treasure. As are my friends. I need to find them."

"Well, that shouldn't be too difficult, seeing as everyone will be at the

Opening Ceremonies soon."

"What Opening Ceremonies?"

"For the Dragon Championship," she replied casually.

Oliver stopped spinning. "But that's in three days?"

Kiara booped him on the nose. "That would have been true three days ago."

Oliver grabbed Kiara by the shoulders. "I've been gone for three days!"

Kiara shook Oliver back. "You've been gone for three days!"

"When are the Opening Ceremonies?" Oliver asked, looking around for his belongings but seeing only his butt print in the sand and three sets of footprints.

Kiara looked up at the sun. "Oh, pretty soon I would guess."

He still had time, he thought. If he wasn't there for the Opening Ceremonies, he would be forced to forfeit. He just needed to get there, and fast. Oliver began to dart in different directions, unable to get a bearing for the correct one.

After a few false starts, Kiara giggled. "It's this way, follow me."

They ran through the woods and up toward the center of the island. Goldenflower was the biggest island in the string of Dragon's Treasure, and named for the yellow flowers that grew abundantly there. In the center was a small town flanking a large structure built from melted stones and dragon fire.

Oliver could hardly keep up with Kiara's brisk pace, given he had recently returned from the brink of death. Or maybe she was just faster than him. Either way, Oliver's intrigue in his new companion propelled him along as the sun journeyed to its zenith.

"Hurry! We're almost there!" Kiara yelled as they both tumbled over boxes and into the main street of the small town. Kiara was hustling as though she had some stake in whether Oliver arrived in time or not.

"Thank you so much, but I have to ask, why are you helping me?" Oliver yelled as he stopped abruptly, not willing to walk any farther until he received an answer.

Kiara looked at him sternly. After seeing Oliver's resolve, she relented. "I had heard of this crazy boy in the South who fought with no armor and did impossible things. I heard he was the best fighter the world might ever see. I want to see him. I want to see if what I was told is true."

"And what exactly is it that you were told?" Oliver asked, moving closer to her.

"I was told you could do anything," she said, booping him on the nose before turning and sprinting again. A fire lit inside Oliver and he followed her, outpacing her. They raced, knocking over various stands and vendors, until they arrived at the back gates of the Coliseum. They blazed past the two guards at the gate and met with no resistance, eventually reaching the final entrance door.

Oliver stopped, trying to catch his breath and thoughts. "Okay, ah, okay," he said as his lungs burned. "Well, this entrance is for fighters only. I'll see you in the stands. Uh, I didn't get a chance to say this before, but thank you for finding me in the ocean."

Kiara pulled down her tunic and adjusted her hair, which changed instantly from golden yellow to a brilliant blue. "You're welcome, but I never said I found you." She began to make for the entrance door. Oliver tried to walk in front of her and protest, but she pushed by him.

"This entrance is for fighters only, you insane girl!" he yelled as the open door started to close.

Kiara turned in the tunnel with an annoying smirk on her face. "I know. See you on the battlefield, Oliver." Then she disappeared into the darkness of the catacombs.

"Lords and ladies, I am pleased to announce this year's eight fighters!" The muffled voice snapped Oliver out of his surprise and he began to run through the catacombs of the Coliseum. Various tunnels ran beneath the main floor of the battleground, allowing for underground rooms to house fighters, smiths, animals, and any manner of workers.

Oliver raced through the dimly lit hallways, trying to find the room for the Southern Champion. Each champion was afforded a private room in which they would spend the duration of the tournament. The rooms were designed to create a circle around the inner ring of the Coliseum, with a trap door that would raise a platform up into the fighting arena.

"Sir, you're not allowed to be here," a guard said at the intersection of five tunnels. Oliver, having no idea if he was even going the right direction, stopped to talk to him.

'I'm a fighter, and I'm late. I need to get to—"

"Sir, if you are a fighter you need to speak with…"

A loud voice above them described the fighter from Kandahar, which meant Starfall City would be announced in six fighters.

"I don't have time, I just... look. Okay, what is your name?"

"Deckard, m'lord," the guard said with pride, straightening up.

"Look, Deckard, my name is Oliver Quartermaine, and I need to find the Southern Champion's room before the gentleman above us gets to it on his list."

"Oliver Quar— You're supposed to be dead!"

"Yes, well, clearly, I'm not, and if I'm not on my platform by the time they call my name, you know what will happen?"

"How do I know that you—"

Oliver spun around and pinned the guard to the wall with his boot.

"Second tunnel to your left, fifth door, my lord," Deckard croaked from under a crushing windpipe.

"Thanks, Deckard!" Oliver yelled as he raced down the tunnel.

As Oliver entered the room he heard the cheers for the Northern Tribes champion. A solitary figure was on one knee, holding a banner staff with an all-black banner hanging from its top.

"Oliver?" Yokel said as he looked up from his vigil. "I don't, it can't be..."

"It is, Yok, and we don't have time for—"

"I knew it! I freaking knew it! They all laughed at me, but I swear, I swear, I knew it!" Yokel jumped off the platform and tackled Oliver to the ground.

"Nice to see you too, Yok, but there's no time to explain. They're already at Land's End."

Yokel jumped up quickly and ran to a chest in the corner. "Right, of course. If you're not on the platform when they call your region, you'll be disqualified. Here, put these on!" Yokel threw a bag of clothes to Oliver.

"What are these?" Oliver opened the bag and began to undress.

"Johanous left you a new outfit for the tournament, said he made a few 'tweaks' that you would find interesting. Would have found. Will find. Ahh, hurry!"

Oliver put the new suit on, which had an emblem of a dragon flying up toward a ring on its chest, and threw on the cape and hood. As usual, everything fit perfectly, but nothing seemed out of the ordinary.

Oliver jumped onto the platform, throwing the banner to the ground. He put his hood up and bent to a knee, hands pushed together in front of his stomach, as if in a trance.

"And lastly, it is with great sorrow that I announce the fighter for the South," the announcer said as the crowd came to a hush. The roof moved away, flooding the platform in a cone of light, particles of dust floating in the beams.

"Oliver!" Yokel yelled as he ran to the cabinet in the wall. He grabbed a sword and threw it to Oliver, who looked up quickly at the sound of his name.

"Thanks, Yokel," he said as he regained his pose. He was brimming with confidence and positivity. "They love a good show, so I'll give them a good show. I'll give them something they've never seen before." And as his head peeked out of the hole, he finished his thought. "A legend."

The sun hit his hood and the warmth of its rays give him a burst of energy. As his platform rose into place, so did he. His cape moved lightly in a meager wind, and he opened his eyes, twirled his sword in a fashion befitting an entertainer, and unclasped his cloak. It fell to the ground by his feet and the same rays that had heated his hood now kissed his face. He raised his sword and the silent crowd burst out into loud cheering.

Oliver looked around at his opponents, sizing up his competition with what little he knew. He had no scouting reports, no idea what their names were or even what weapons they preferred. The crowd started to chant Oliver's name, and the fighters stepped off their platforms and made their way into the middle of the stadium, waving their hands. Over one hundred thousand people filled the stands of the Coliseum, and the deafening sound made any talk between the fighters impossible.

He looked around the stadium and found his family's private box. Roc and Reagan were hugging and hollering, as amazed as the rest of the crowd at Oliver's appearance. In the box next to them was the High Queen who sat on her throne, unmoving. She was flanked by four of her Black Hawks, whose red capes hung vibrant against the blackened armor they wore. The High Queen motioned one of her Hawks over, pointing to the field. Oliver was hoping against hope he wouldn't be interrogated for his sudden and miraculous appearance.

Oliver felt a tap on the shoulder and turned, seeing the Black Prince standing next to him. But the tap did not come from the Black Prince but rather Kiara, who was flanking the prince's right.

"Show off," she yelled.

Oliver responded with a smirk, continuing to wave to the crowd. "You haven't seen anything yet!"

Kiara hung off the Black Prince's shoulder, whispering in his ear as they both looked at Oliver. The Black Prince murmured back, and Kiara laughed, sending a pang of jealousy through Oliver's chest.

Soon, trumpets sounded and all the fighters returned to their platforms and descended into their respective rooms. As Oliver walked off his platform, he could hear the banging of armor against walls and the protests of guards at a trespasser. Roc burst into the room, with Reagan shortly after him.

Roc barreled Oliver over, trying to catch his voice even as it cracked. "We thought you were lost!"

Reagan joined the pile and soon after Yokel did as well.

"You wouldn't believe me if I told you," Oliver answered from under the mess of limbs and bodies. The group of friends settled into a circle on the dirt ground, taking a moment to gather themselves.

Roc was the first to speak again. "Ridhan said you'd fallen overboard. We searched for days, Oliver, we really did."

"Ridhan is a big fat liar," Oliver said as he struggled to change into more formal clothes. "He pushed me, threw me, really, overboard during the storm."

Reagan gasped. "What do you mean he threw you overboard? Why? He said you had a bit of wine at dinner and then slipped and fell over the railing."

Oliver stood and went to the door, making sure there weren't any lingering ears in the hallway. "Ridhan caused the storm, using the Staff of the Seas. He wanted me to give him magic, and I refused. That's when, that's when he just lost it."

"Why would he think you would give him magic?" Roc accused.

"He thinks it's here on the island. He thinks it's part of the Dragon Championship," Oliver answered, trying not to give too much away. He wanted so desperately to tell them all that had transpired in the in-between, but he couldn't with Roc present.

Roc huffed and paced around, and Reagan tried to change the subject. "How about we head back to the estate? I'm sure we could all use a rest after these last few days."

"No!" Roc demanded. "Not until we get one thing straight. Why are we here?"

"To win the Dragon Championship," I answered.

"Why are we here?" Roc demanded once more.

"I told you. It's what I've been training for my whole life. It's what we planned for last summer." It still wasn't a lie, which Oliver was happy about. But he didn't know how much more he could have said without crossing that line. Roc seemed to be a willing participant in the ruse and didn't press the matter any further.

They made their way out of the catacombs and hopped into a carriage, taking the often dangerous Queen's Road all the way to the Quartermaine estate. Goldenflower contained three long roads that stretched along the coasts, each a different journey in their own right.

The High Road stretched along the northern coastline of the island and was lined with cottages and mansions belonging to high lords and ladies from all over Soraya. To own a house on the island was the most impressive way to show one's power and station, but given the size of the island, the houses and estates tended to stay within the same families for generations.

In the middle of the island ran the Queen's Road, aptly named for the High Queen herself. This was the primary road for all intents and purposes, and two major cities punctuated the road at the center and southern end. The islanders lived along this road, and if you weren't careful, you were bound to be robbed when you traveled through the forest from the Coliseum to Dragon's Eye.

Along the cliffed southwestern coast was Starfire Road, which only the daring traveled on. The southern coast of the island was plagued by rocky terrain, cliffs that fell precipitously to the ocean below, and the most beautiful scenery in the world. Smaller islands made up the rest of Dragon's Treasure, and together the islands created a series of hills above the flat ocean.

During the journey of a couple of hours to the Quartermaine estate, Oliver recounted all that had happened on the ship with Ridhan. He left out his conversation with Haralabos and Satine, along with his recovery of the book, as he wanted to have those conversations with Pathfinder and Windrunner, if he could find them. Oliver also kept his chance rescue with Kiara a secret as well, although he didn't know why. Maybe, he thought, some things he could have all to himself.

"But what I don't understand," Reagan asked as Oliver finished his story, "is why the haircut?"

"Don't even get me started! I woke up on the beach like this."

Yokel and Reagan laughed and continued prodding Oliver for more information, but Roc stayed silent, looking out the window of the carriage as they came up to the front entrance of the estate. To call it an estate was a courtesy to the other lords who lived on the High Road, because this was much closer to a castle, clinging to the cliffs on the western shore. It was an imposing sight, with spires and towers that ignited the imagination. Stories were told of screams and bellows from within the dungeons from ghosts and haunted souls who still roamed the halls. Those stories were often perpetuated by jealous families who coveted the large estate. In actuality, the Quartermaines had been gifted this keep long before the rule of the High Queen, and now that Oliver knew the true history of Starfall, he wouldn't have been surprised if it was sometime around then.

Yokel and Reagan exited the carriage, leaving Oliver alone with Roc, who was still staring out of the carriage in a daydream. Oliver sat back in his seat and closed the door, the sound jarring Roc awake to notice the emptiness of the carriage.

"Oh, uh, are we here?" he asked, beginning to move toward the door. Oliver threw his foot against the latch, unwilling to let Roc leave so easily.

"Spill it."

Roc sat back and looked at Oliver with a grim expression. "You're back. It's just a lot."

"Not something you were expecting?"

"Don't do that. I'm happy, I am. It's just, I spent these last few days thinking you were gone. Now, now it's like a miracle and I can't help but think..."

"Think what?"

"Just promise me something. If Ridhan is correct, that the Dragon Championship has something to do with magic, and we find it. Promise me that we'll destroy it."

"Roc, I can't—"

"Look what it did to Po! It nearly killed him. He's a cripple, and what can be expected of his life now? Huh? A beggar on the streets of the Narrows?"

"You know I would never—"

"Never what? Would he live a life of pity and charity? He'll never be a knight, all because we had to do exactly what I said we shouldn't."

"Roc, we're here for the Dragon Championship, nothing more. I promise." It was the first lie in what Oliver was sure would be a long list of lies, but he saw no alternative. Once Po got his legs back, Roc would understand, Oliver just knew it.

Roc nodded. "Okay. Let's get out of here, shall we? There's someone here to see you."

In Oliver's room, a solitary figure stood, back to the door, staring out the balcony over the beach and ocean below. For the briefest of moments, Oliver thought it was Iris and his heart fluttered. But the figure turned around, cape swinging through the air and revealing the familiar disguised face of Pathfinder. They both rushed to the middle of the room, embracing as if it was the last time they would ever see each other.

Pathfinder cried into Oliver's arms as she punched him lightly. "Oi, who said you were allowed to die?"

Oliver laughed and pulled her in tight. "Oh, you know, I figured it would give me something interesting to talk about."

"Oh, because your life is so uninteresting?" Pathfinder looked up at Oliver, her expression turning serious. "You don't get to leave me like that again, savvy?"

"Aye, aye, captain."

Pathfinder's eyes narrowed at being teased but Oliver could tell there was a smile underneath her mask. She composed herself, adjusting her mask that had become crooked. "So, you ready yet?"

"Ready? I just got here! And if you hadn't noticed, I was recently almost dead."

"That's a good point." Pathfinder waited a moment. "How 'bout now?" She laughed and punched him again before leaving.

Oliver sat on the edge of the bed and pulled the book from his back, unlocked the book, and opened it, seeing the name of its owner on the first page. He turned to the next page, seeing his previous conversation with the jealous knight. He turned the page once more, and it was blank. He sighed in relief. But then ink appeared on the page, scribing the words of Haralabos once again.

I'm back.

Oliver slapped the covers together immediately and tossed the book behind him like throwing off a spider from his hand. He still didn't know what to make of the old Lightning Knight, and his experience in the in-between only caused more confusion. Oliver didn't fully trust Haralabos and until he knew more, he would keep the man out of time, in the dark.

Pathfinder popped her head around the doorframe playfully, interrupting Oliver's thought. "Oi, how 'bout now?"

# THE FIFTH BEST FIGHTER

"So, what were you up to while I was on my..." Oliver paused, searching for the right phrasing.

"Underwater holiday?" Pathfinder finished as they walked down the hall toward the lower levels of the castle.

"Unintended escapade."

"Undead adventure."

"Unexpected..." But Oliver failed to come up with an answer and lost at their game. "But you never answered the question."

"Yokel filled Windrunner and me in on the original plan. We had hoped to get the elixir for Po but hadn't quite figured out a plan yet."

Oliver thought through the different quests as he and Pathfinder entered the dungeon halls. "We have three objectives and not a lot of time. You and Windrunner head into town and see what you can find out about these other events Ridhan mentioned, and maybe we can help Po without needing Ridhan."

"Sounds like a plan, but what will you be doing?" Pathfinder asked as they stopped at the dimly lit door.

"There's a Dragon Championship to prepare for. You know, no big deal."

"Oh, of course, that silly little thing." Pathfinder bounced up to her tip toes and kissed Oliver on the cheek through her mask. "Thanks for not staying dead." She left Oliver alone in the hallway.

"You're late," Reagan said as she opened the door to him.

"Does nobody care that I was dead?"

"This place seems a bit smaller than I remember," Yokel said, walking into the practice room. It was located within the cliff under the castle, well below the main entrance. Another entrance was accessible by a long winding staircase leading to a small beach cave opening. When they were young, the Quartermaine children would swim from the top of the cove all the way to the hidden beach, where they could ensure no adults would find them.

Reagan looked around the room, touching various objects. "We haven't been in here in what, five years?"

"Just about," Oliver answered as he lit some torches and lanterns.

The first round of the Championship was the next day. Oliver grabbed a sword and started to warm up with swings and stretches. Yokel laid out a portfolio with loose pieces of paper falling out and organized them into eight separate piles.

"Okay, I've gathered all the information I could on the opponents. If I had to guess, I'd say this will be the best group from top to bottom that Soraya has seen in almost one hundred years."

"And when you say top, you obviously mean me, right, Yokel?" Oliver joked as he moved quicker and quicker, building up a sweat.

"Actually, no."

Oliver stopped mid-swing, losing control and hitting himself on the head. "What do you mean, no?"

"I mean, if we are being objective, you're the fifth-best fighter of the eight, although given your name and the story of how you won the Southern Tournament, you've been ranked third."

"What do you mean fifth-best fighter! You're supposed to be on my side. Fifth-best fi— I'll give you fifth-best fighter!" Oliver worked into a flurry of movements that were meant more to impress than to land a strike.

"I am o-on your side, wh-which is why I'm telling you the truth. I have reports on each of the fighters, and if my analysis is correct, which, I mean, of course it is, then you are the fifth best. Plain and simple."

Oliver and Reagan joined Yokel and studied the dossier he had created. Yokel, for all his quirks, was going to make the greatest City Watch Captain Starfall City would ever see. Years of burying his head in books and watching tournaments all over Soraya had given him an eye that could hardly be matched. If there was a reason Oliver was ranked as high as he was in the eyes of Yokel, it was most certainly due to the team that backed him. That notion gave Oliver every confidence.

"You created a scouting report on me?" Oliver asked in surprise, thumbing through the papers.

"Of course. I had to be objective. It's how I was able to figure out where you truly should be ranked."

Oliver reviewed his own report, which if he had to be honest with himself, was accurate to the letter.

- Fighter will sometimes become arrogant about his own abilities
- and underestimate his opponent
- Fighter's primary weapon is the sword but is skilled enough to hold his own with other weapons
- Speed is not the fastest but can outlast most opponents
- Strength is average
- Reaction is based on anticipatory movements; if caught in an improvised attack, will falter
- Holds back full range of abilities

Oliver put the report down. "Yokel, you're absolutely right about everything you wrote here. Except you forgot one important thing. Do you have a quill and ink?" He took the quill from Yokel and added a new line.

- Has the best team

Oliver handed the report to Reagan, who looked at it and smiled. Yokel grabbed it, wondering what would be so important to add to his perfect report.

"I think that vaults me to the top, don't you think?" Oliver asked, an amused smile on his face.

"I suppose you're correct. But the Tournament Committee has ranked you third, behind Aasar, the son of a chief from the Northern Tribes and High Prince Amukamora. After you is Princess Kiara, daughter of the Dragonbender, Samaje the Spectacular from Kandahar who we met this past summer at your uncle's, Tyvis from the Floating Isle, Glover Danson from Mercyhold, and HaHa Dix from Hamstead."

"Wait, his name is HaHa?" Oliver asked in disbelief.

"Yes, and don't let his name surprise you. Any other year and he'd be a top four ranked fighter. This year is insane fo-for talent." Yokel was bursting with energy, finally able to share his thoughts and feelings about the subject he so passionately loved. Oliver looked over the rest of the reports and concluded that Yokel was correct about every hyperbolic notion he was having. This year's field would be once in a generation, and Oliver was a part of that. Still, it was peculiar that all the champions were around Oliver's own age; Tyvis was the eldest at nineteen years old.

Oliver looked over the additional reports, trying to inconspicuously find the one he wanted. As he read it over, the face of the fighter shining in the sun against the ocean backdrop came into his memory.

Princess Kiara of the Dragonlands

- Use of dual dragon-hook swords
- Expert in all sword forms
- High speed and strength
- Prefers to improvise rather than plan
- Use of acrobatics to confuse opponent
- Will try to finish the fight quickly instead of outlasting the opponent

As Oliver continued to read, Reagan walked over, and he quickly picked up another report to hide his curiosity. Reagan pulled the Tyvis report and started to read it with greater scrutiny.

"Well," she said, "we don't have to worry about all of them, just the one you're fighting next. Tyvis, is it? Yokel, you didn't put his family name."

"That's because he doesn't have a family name."

"What kind of person doesn't have a family name?"

"Everyone who comes from the Floating Isles. They don't have the same family constructs that, well, everyone else does. When a child is born, they're integrated into the society at a naming ceremony. Then they're raised by their village, in some sort of communal upbringing. It's actually quite interesting, but it does add one distinct advantage for him as a fighter."

"Lovely, what is it?" Oliver asked, starting to rub his head with his hands. In all his time for preparation, which was very little, he always assumed he would just get by with his natural ability. He was starting to doubt whether he was particularly special at all.

"Tyvis was raised by an entire village, heck, an entire kingdom, as they all were. When he fights for his family, he fights for them all, and that kind of purpose drives him. When others would quit, he will remember whom he is fighting for, and push on. This will not be an easy first round for you, Oliver."

Oliver looked around. "Where's Roc?"

Yokel pulled out Aasar's report, pointing to the weapon. "Roc is working on a special task for us. This will occupy his time here, I guarantee it." He winked and Oliver slapped him on the back. With Roc preoccupied with forging Aasar's weapon, he would have little time for the more magical aspects of their trip.

"Great job, Yok."

Oliver walked over to Reagan and peered over her shoulder at the report. He patted her on the back and retrieved his sword, ready to train. He looked at Yokel, who was standing there, studying him. "It won't be an easy first round for Tyvis either, I guarantee it. We're going to win."

Reagan picked up the double-bladed battle axe that Tyvis would most likely use, spinning it on its buttress before readying herself. "What's got you so confident?"

Oliver smiled, spinning his sword as lightning magic kissed his eyes. "I'm not alone."

# THE STRANGER

T he town surrounding the coliseum that sat in the middle of the island was alive with people from all around Soraya, except of course, Romir. Romirians never participated in the Dragon Championship, let alone crossed the borders of their kingdom.

After a grueling training session with Reagan and Yokel, Oliver had slipped away and taken a horse down to the town, hoping to find Pathfinder. He wanted to tell her about the in-between, about Haralabos, about it all. He wanted to tell someone, anyone.

Would he tell her about Kiara, now known to him as the Dragon Princess, or would he keep that to himself again? He was confused, wandering around the small town on his horse, when he opened Haralabos's book with the ring and thumbed the pages. He still felt uneasy about the curmudgeon of a knight, but his options were to wander around aimlessly or ask for help.

"So, Haralabos, where should I go now?"

The response appeared as it always had, only now Oliver had a grumpy face to imagine along with the words.

Do you plan to shut me out again?

Oliver chuckled. "Maybe. How does this work now?"

My lightning magic has provided more power for this conduit. We can speak freely now, without restraint.

"You mean my lightning magic." Oliver pondered. This new development excited him and was a new resource of knowledge and information, albeit one he didn't fully trust yet. He looked down at his hands, imagining the lightning magic wrapping around his fingers. "You were the original Lightning Knight, correct?"

Yes.

"Can you teach me how to use my lightning magic?"

My lightning magic. It was meant for Po.

"Yes, but I have it now, and if I'm going to train him, I'm going to need to know how to use it myself."

Find the Th'aurmatology Codex, it has the answers you seek.

Frustrated, Oliver jumped off his horse, tying it to a post in front of a tavern. "We had the Codex, and we lost it. Besides, we couldn't read it anyway." Oliver couldn't tell for sure, but he thought that Haralabos might be yelling.

It is here on this island, you moron.
Did you not pay attention?
Gods, I hate Quartermaines.
Find it.

"You were serious? How did you... Where is it? Since when? Never mind, it doesn't matter, we can't read it."

Po is the key.

"Po is the key? What does that even mean? Nine Gods, you're insufferable." Oliver slammed the book closed, grunting in anger. "Come on, horse, we're leaving." But the horse neighed and hip-checked Oliver rather than be taken away from his new trough of food. Oliver sighed. "Fine, I could use a drink anyway."
"Hello and good evening, what can I get for... young Lord

Quartermaine? By the Nine, I haven't seen you in years. You're so much taller. Anything you desire I will make!"

The middle-aged barkeep wore a broad smile. Oliver had been coming to this tavern every fifth year since he was born, most times with his father, then his brother, now alone. It wasn't the busiest tavern in the town, nor the best, but it was the only place that served every kind of drink, not just wine and mead.

"Dealer's choice," Oliver replied.

"Ahh, well, I have just the thing for you." The barkeep began to mix a concoction of drinks. "Here you are, my friend. I'm sure you will tell everyone you meet of the special drink I have prepared for you."

Oliver was astonished by the smooth flavor of the liquid, with a hint of alcohol that gave it a kick as soon as he exhaled. "This is delightful, what do you call it?"

"Dragon's Breath, my friend."

"Cheers to the inventor of Dragon's Breath!" Oliver yelled, and the rest of the tavern cheered along, not knowing what they were cheering for but cheering, nonetheless.

"Cheers, cheers, cheers… What's there to celebrate anyhow?" grumbled a boy at the end of the bar, covered by the shadow of his cloak and banging his stein. "Oi! I'm empty over here!" He was obviously drunk out of his gourd.

Oliver walked over to the tables, looking for an open seat where he could sit and think. Between the Dragon Championship and Po's elixir and now Haralabos, everything seemed to be in motion, but nothing seemed to be going anywhere. To top it all, his feelings about the girls in his life were threatening to tear him apart from the inside. A drink might help solve some of his dilemmas.

Oliver had grown up drinking some of the finest wines in the Southern region, where the climate and soil produced the best grapes in the country. He never enjoyed getting drunk though, preferring to enjoy good wines with a meal. Mead and wheat beer never appealed to his palate, and the one time Yokel, Roc, and he had tried to spend all night seeing who could drink the most beer, it had ended up with all three of them naked on the beach, surrounded by vomit.

Thus, Oliver had gravitated toward mixed drinks, where there was an element of sophistication and creativity. One could not just simply put potato alcohol and an orange slice in a cup and call it a mixed drink. There was an art to it, finding the combination of ingredients that would not dilute the alcohol but also not obfuscate the other ingredients. The spiced rums from the Southern Isles were a thing of pure artwork, but getting the drinks to cross the Red Seas without pirates capturing the cargo was always risky, even for a Shipwight vessel.

He finally found an open seat in a booth opposite a petite, lean figure in a hood. "Is this seat taken?" he asked politely, already making his way to sit.

"Yes."

"Great, I love company," Oliver insisted as he sat and put his drink on the table. The Stranger, as Oliver was already calling her in his head, was drinking a goblet of wine with some bread and cheese to accompany it.

Then, an odd thing happened. A shimmer of sound and a wave of thoughts threatened to subsume Oliver's own mind. He was once again vaguely aware that his point of view was from without and not within. But beyond that feeling, he got the sense that he could feel this stranger's point of view.

"You need to leave," she implored, not wanting to miss the opportunity she had been waiting months for.

"Nah, that's okay, I'm good," Oliver said with the most braggadocious tone he could muster. He didn't know why he decided this was the fight he wanted to pick, but he was itching for one regardless. Maybe he was tired of arguing with a man in a book. Maybe he was tired of being alone. Maybe he just wanted to talk. "My name is Oliver, and you might be?" he asked, taking a sip of his drink, increasingly surprised at how good it tasted.

"No one. Now please leave."

"Hi No One, so very uncomfortable to meet you. Tomorrow is a big day for me, do you, do you mind if I talk? Thanks. So yeah, tomorrow is a big day, first round of the Dragon Championship and all that. I'm sure that's why you're here. You might recognize me from the opening ceremonies, but in case you didn't, I'm the Southern Champion."

"Do you always talk this much?" she asked, clearly agitated by this distraction.

Oliver continued as if the interruption was preordained. "As a matter of fact, yes, yes I do. Anyway, I didn't come all the way here to talk about the

Dragon Championship."

"Then why are you here? Please leave, I'm begging you."

"I haven't finished my drink but thank you anyway. What I wanted to talk about is, well, how do I put this. I think I'm in love with more than one person."

"I hate you so much," the Stranger said. She had come to this tavern on a mission of her own, and this odd hooman was threatening to destroy months of work.

"I get that a lot. Look, I know how it sounds, but I'm not trying to be sleazy. It's like my heart is being torn in two directions and I don't know what to do. I need help."

"Will you not leave me alone?"

"Nope, it's your lucky night."

"If I listen to you ramble, then will you leave?"

Oliver smiled. "Maybe." Her stare bore through Oliver, melting every muscle in his chest. Oliver knew this stare, for he'd felt it before, from his sister. Oliver felt oddly at ease now and confessed his soul.

"So, there's this amazing, wonderful, magnificent girl back in Starfall. Her name is Iris and—"

"Like the flower?" the Stranger asked, a hint of curiosity in her voice.

"Uh, I suppose so. Anyway, we've known each other for years now. Nine Hells the time goes on. So, she comes from a high family, I'm obviously from a high family—"

"Obviously," the Stranger added flippantly.

"—and it's literally a match made in every romantic tale ever."

The Stranger took a sip of her goblet and put it down. "But…"

"But there's just something, I don't even know, something wrong. I can't put my finger on it, but there's something off about it all. Like the puzzle is incomplete and the final piece will tell me the real answer. I love her, I truly do. I thought about her all summer and swore she was what I wanted. All I ever wanted, but, AHHH, I don't know. We make total sense, I know we do, it's just…"

Oliver's sudden change from lighthearted banter to sharing his feelings caught the Stranger off guard. She stopped looking around for her bounty and focused on Oliver, whose gaze was now wandering past her to a picture of a dragon on the wall.

The Stranger offered up a suggestion. "Just she's not the one?"

"Of course she's the one! We're meant to be. How could you say such a thing, you barely even know us!"

"So, tell me about the other girl?" The Stranger was trying to understand what exactly this boy-hooman wanted from her. This was not her plan tonight, but it seemed he would not leave unless he was able to come to terms with his feelings. If this was the only way to get on with her night, she would play relationship apothecary.

"You mean Pathfinder?" Oliver asked.

The Stranger slammed her goblet to the table. "My patience is running thin, hooman."

Oliver cocked his head. "You have an odd way of speaking. Anyway, there's this other girl. I've only known her for a short time, but we just, I don't know, we just click. When we're together it's easy and fun and exciting. She's smart and intelligent and powerful and funny and…"

"Beautiful?"

"Actually, I don't know what she looks like. Honestly, I really don't know much about her. She wears a mask whenever we're together—"

The Stranger shook her head in disgust. "Nope, nope, nope, I don't need to hear the weird things your kind is into."

"Not like that, it's a long story."

"I'm starting to think there's no such thing as a short story with you."

Oliver laughed and nodded. "Fair enough. Short-long story is that we have this natural… I don't know what to call it, alchemy!" He felt his stomach tussle at his internal struggle, or maybe it was the Dragon's Breath finally catching up to him. "I don't know what to tell you, she's just sending my stomach three ways to Black Sunday and I have no idea why. I mean, I have a little bit of an idea," Oliver said, remembering the times he had blinded himself with his own hand. "But it's not fair to Iris for me to even be thinking of another girl in this way, let alone spending the kind of time with her that I am. I'm scum, I know it."

The hooman was fishing for sympathy and the Stranger knew it, but there was a hint of truth to his feelings. Her culture's views on love and relationships hadn't prepared her for this odd hooman's problems, and her own experience was minimal and full of heartache, something she could relate to at least. There was something about this hooman that caused her heart to stir, but she didn't recognize the feeling. It wasn't infatuation, or lust; he was not her type in the least. But something about him clung to her, like they somehow needed each other.

"Listen, you're a good hooman, and good hoomans are hard to come by."

"I'm not a good— What did you call me?"

"Stop that," the Stranger scolded. "You can't help who your heart likes. Trust me, I know. But you can be honest with yourself."

"I can do that."

"And you can be honest with them. Both of them."

"I liked the first part better when it was just myself," Oliver joked, but the Stranger wasn't laughing.

"What did you think would happen?" she asked.

"Honestly, with all that's been on my mind, it's not something I've been trying to think about."

"And yet here you are, sitting in a booth in a nondescript tavern, talking to me."

"And yet here I am, sipping a drink with my new friend… I never got your name."

"So, what will you do? Who will you choose?" The Stranger was now invested in this odd hooman's story, for reasons she couldn't quite understand. Did he have this effect on everyone he met, or was it only her?

Oliver drained his drink and slapped his hands down to the table. "I will… ah, I don't know!" He banged his head onto the table over and over. "This isn't like it is in the fairytales."

"What's a fairytale?"

"You know, fairytales? Made-up stories you tell children?"

The Stranger was perplexed. "Why would fairies make up stories?"

"Uh, fairies aren't real?" Oliver asked, unsure how this conversation had wandered to this point.

"Oh no, fairies are real, and fairies are jerks."

"What are we even talking about!"

"You're the one who sat in my booth!"

"AGOOBWAH!" Oliver yelled and the rest of the tavern fell silent, every eye on the crazy boy.

The Stranger lifted an eyebrow. "Agoobwah?"

"I think it pretty much says it all," Oliver said, begging his cup for more of the drink.

"Looks like you're finished."

"Looks like I am." Oliver began to slide out of the booth when a different argument made its way to his ears.

"I told you, mate, I gave it to the priest at the temple in Romir, just like I was supposed to." It was the drunkard at the bar, arguing with an inconspicuously dressed man. The man left in a hurry and Oliver stood up instantly, causing the Stranger to turn around.

Oliver made his way to the drunkard. "What did you say?"

"Oi, get your bloody hands off—" But the words caught in his throat as Oliver stood face to face with the Fool from Romir.

"You…" Oliver lifted the Fool by his collar into the air. The Fool dangled helplessly, willingly submissive.

"You're the reason we lost it!" Oliver hissed.

"Lost what?" the Fool squeaked. Oliver headbutted him. "Ow! Yes, I remember now. It's like I told you in Romir, mate, I gave it to the priest."

"We already took it from the temple in Romir!" Oliver said, his anger boiling at the image of Po lying on the ground near death.

"There is more than one temple in this world, mate."

Oliver rushed the Fool to the wall and put his forearm across his throat. "Do you know what you've done?" The Fool grabbed Oliver's forearm and twisted it around, reversing their positions and pinning Oliver against the wall.

"Look, mate, you don't understand what I've been through. I'm finally out and I was told to do one thing and now I'm finished." His face was ghastly, and Oliver could smell the drift the Fool must have been drinking. Drift was a potion no addict could kick.

"I suggest you put him down," the Stranger said from behind the Fool's back.

The Fool turned around and in one swift movement he had a pair of knives aimed directly at the Stranger, who had an arrow aimed directly at his left eye. Neither one was willing to budge, until Oliver literally stepped between them.

"We don't have time for this! You said it's at the temple?"

"Aye," the Fool confirmed, unwilling to drop his weapons. Oliver left, flipping a few coins to the barkeeper and stepping into the night air. He thought about finding Pathfinder and Windrunner, or Yokel or even Roc, but he had no time. Oliver needed to gain his bearings of the town and find an inconspicuous way of traveling to the temple. Stars dotted the planet-lit night sky while lamps illuminated the main street as well as many of the side streets. But the rooftops could provide the cover he required and so he climbed the side of the nearest building and pulled himself up onto the roof. The temple would be located in the Northern section of the city, which meant Oliver had to travel over a generally easy rooftop path.

As Oliver stood at the edge of the rooftop, he heard a sound and quickly pulled his sword out as he spun around looking for his attacker. His sword met the tip of a metal arrowhead and the metallic sound vibrated through the air.

"What are you doing here?" Oliver asked.

"I could ask you the same question."

Oliver eyed the Stranger. "Look, I don't know what you think you're doing, but this is a dangerous game I'm in, and I don't want to see you get hurt."

"Then you best be out of my way."

"Look, you can't come with me," Oliver reasoned, but the Stranger had other ideas. In one fluid motion she holstered her arrow into her quiver, swept Oliver's sword aside, and flipped him onto his back, the string of the bow trapping his head.

"No, *you* can't come with *me*. I've been hunting for this longer than you know. Stay out of my way, pretty hooman."

"You think I'm pretty?"

The harsh snap of the wooden bow ricocheted off his head and he yelped out a laugh.

"What is it exactly that you're hunting?" Oliver asked as he used his legs to wrap around the Stranger's torso and pull her off him. They both sprang up, ready to engage in combat.

"Who are you?" Oliver asked.

"Who are you?" the Stranger repeated.

"Someone's having a bit of an identity crisis," a metallic voice interrupted. Windrunner had her staff aimed directly toward the Stranger's heart. Oliver dropped his sword and hugged Windrunner, forgetting his opponent.

"You two know each other?" the Stranger inquired.

Oliver picked up his sword and jerked back into a defensive posture, ready to interrogate the Stranger once more. "Are you part of the Spider's Web?"

"Do I look like a spider to you?"

"That's exactly what a Spider would say!" Oliver was heated and hated himself for letting his guard down. He should have known better than to trust anyone he met on this island.

"I am not a spider, you dumb hooman."

"Why do you keep calling me that?"

The Stranger ignored him. "You don't understand."

"Then make me understand, because you're not going anywhere as long as I'm around."

"We're around," Windrunner corrected.

"Yea, what she said." Oliver held out his fist for Windrunner to bump. Oliver felt elated to have at least one friend with him.

The Stranger huffed, agitated at the delay. This was the most solid lead she'd had in weeks, and it was all going to be foiled because of some stupid mad-hooman and his metal girl. The only way out was through, and the only way through, she reasoned, was honesty. If he was willing to spill his heart out to her, then she could allow him some small bit of truth.

"I'm hunting a book that belongs to my family. If I cannot retrieve it, I cannot go home."

"The Th'aurmatology Codex belongs to your family? How can that be?" Windrunner asked.

"How do you know its name?" the Stranger asked.

"Because we're looking for it too. So is the Spider's Web," Oliver answered.

"Why would spiders be after a book?"

"No, not actual spiders," Oliver answered. "It's a group of... Well, they're more like a... They're the bad guys who wanna do bad things with that book."

"And you want to do good things?"

Oliver paused, not knowing what the truth of the answer was. Sure, Haralabos had told him to find it, and sure, he was supposed to use it to train Po and take down the High Queen, but at what cost? Were they the good guys?

He told the truth. "I don't know."

"Honesty. How interesting from your kind. You are full of surprises, hoo— Oliver Quartermaine. This Codex, it means more to my people than you realize. Please, I need to find it if I am ever to return home."

Oliver studied the girl, who was probably no older than he was, and started to reach for Haralabos's book to ask for advice but decided against it. "What do you think?" Oliver asked Windrunner instead.

"I think we can trust her."

"We'll help you get the Codex," Oliver said. With Windrunner along for the adventure, Oliver had the beginnings of a plan to solve multiple problems; he just needed more time. Time they didn't have, so he would have to improvise.

"You will?" The Stranger was surprised by this hooman's selflessness. "Why?" In the time since she had been banished from her home, from her people, she had rarely received help of any kind. Even when she did, ultimately, she would be let down. She expected to be let down by this Oliver Quartermaine too, but she had no other choice.

Oliver sheathed his sword and hopped to the roof's edge. "Because we're friends and that's what friends do. They help each other."

"I don't have friends," the Stranger said, saddened by the harsh reality and stepping to the edge of the roof next to Oliver.

Oliver and Windrunner flanked the Stranger, each putting a hand on her shoulder.

"Now you have two," Oliver said.

The Stranger felt an odd sensation she couldn't quite describe. The closest she could liken it was to when she would read about her mother and look at her painting hanging in the halls of the throne room. She smiled. "Which way?"

"Follow those buildings," Oliver said, pointing the way toward the small temple.

"Try not to slow me down," she replied with a small laugh.

"You never did tell me your name."

"No, I never did." And she jumped to the neighboring roof.

"Oh, I like her," Windrunner said as she followed.

They jumped from roof to roof, blazing a path through the town.

"Karen?" Oliver asked, his fourth guess.

"No," she replied, losing her amusement at the game with each guess.

"Tilda?" Windrunner offered up.

"Stop, you two!"

"Catlin?" Oliver asked.

"Do I really strike you as a Catlin?" the Stranger yelled back, offended.

"No, but do I strike you as a Dragon Champion?"

"Not particularly," she replied, amused once more.

"Not cool. And what are you laughing at?" Oliver asked Windrunner.

"She got you, Ollie." Windrunner giggled, sliding down a roof onto a wall.

Oliver snapped his fingers. "Robin!"

The Stranger rubbed her face in disappointment. "That's a bird's name."

They approached the temple's front door and looked at the building, taking in the architecture. Although smaller than the other temples in Soraya, it still stood high and grand, a testament to the High Queen's righteousness.

"I'll scout the area, meet you on the east side," Windrunner said as she took off.

From their experience with the temple in Romir, Oliver and Windrunner assumed that there would be a similar secret room with a secondary escape route. If they were lucky, that escape route would rarely be used and could provide the perfect way for them to sneak in.

"I was thinking about your dilemma," the Stranger said as she and Oliver approached the underside of the temple's east wall.

"Which dilemma? I've got a few hundred."

"The one in regard to your heart." The Stranger slid down an embankment.

"Oh, that one. What about it?"

"I think you should leave the flower."

"You mean Iris? I can't leave Iris!"

"Then leave the other one."

Oliver stopped her from walking any farther. "I don't want to leave her."

"Sounds as though you've made your decision," the Stranger said, pulling her shoulder away from his grip.

Oliver stood there, confused and anxious. "What do you mean I've made my decision? I'm right back where I started!"

"Shhh, keep your voice down." The Stranger grabbed hold of Oliver's arm and they both dropped down in the stream. By the look of the banking, this stream was man-made and most likely used as a flood release. They approached the iron barred grate and looked around every crevice for any type of mechanism to open it.

The Stranger continued as they searched. "What I mean is one of them you can't leave and the other you don't want to. Seems to me you know your answer already, you're just too—"

"Cowardly to admit it. You might be correct, thanks. Tesmeen?"

"You will find I am always correct, and no."

For the first time in a long time, Oliver felt a small respite of relief. Maybe this Stranger was correct; maybe his dalliance with Pathfinder only solidified his feelings for Iris.

"I think I found it," the Stranger said as she pointed to a rope on the inside of the tunnel.

"Well it makes sense that the escape route would have the latch on the inside. But I can't reach it, I'm too muscular," Oliver said as he tried to force his forearm through. He looked back with a smirk on his face as the Stranger slapped the back of his head.

"Let me try." The Stranger pushed him out of the way. Her slender arm fit but was not quite long enough to grab hold of the rope. She stretched as far as she could, and when all seemed lost, her eyes closed tightly in concentration, she felt resistance in her hand and pulled. The far side of the gate slid down into an opening in the ground and they were allowed entrance into the tunnel.

"Nice work, Ketara."

"No," the Stranger replied as she walked into the tunnel. Oliver laughed, and in the planet-light he glimpsed her face, committing it to memory. She was prettier than average, but there was something about her that didn't stir his feelings the same way even someone like Kiara did. Her petite figure was slender and nimble, and on a few occasions while traveling over the rooftops, she had demonstrated a hidden strength and speed he wouldn't have otherwise assumed.

Windrunner arrived as the gate opened and took the rearguard as she descended into the tunnel after them. "You two work fast."

"We aim to please," Oliver joked. The light in the tunnel grew dim until complete darkness enveloped the three. Oliver grabbed the Stranger's cape as Windrunner grabbed his, creating a train.

"Why does your family want the Codex?" Windrunner asked, probing for more information.

"I'm sorry, but who are you again?" the Stranger inquired, trying to change the subject.

"Her name is Windrunner," Oliver offered up.

The Stranger stopped dead in her tracks, turning to faces that couldn't make out her expression. "You're who?"

"Windrunner!" Oliver repeated. "You know, made-up folk hero of the ancient elves."

An audible slap to the Stranger's forehead followed by a muttering of the strange name she had for Oliver reverberated through the tunnel. The Stranger turned back around, shaking her head at the insult. Hoomans taking the moniker of the legendary hero, the nerve! Her temper flared for only a moment as she thought more about the personality of these two companions and their zeal for helping her. Unsure exactly why, she decided to trust them.

"I know what it is, it is a book of magic, the only one of its kind in the world. From what I know, magic is outlawed on this side of the Sunrise Mountains, so why exactly are you searching for it?"

Oliver was blind in this tunnel but somehow the Stranger had not led them into any walls or obstacles. "You mean Sunset Mountains, and magic isn't so much outlawed as it doesn't exist anymore."

"And you believe that?" the Stranger said, pulling her hooman luggage at a fork in the tunnel.

Oliver smiled a smile that would go unnoticed in the darkness and Windrunner touched her pendant choker as he answered. "Not anymore. Someone I know, well, kind of know, they told us about the Codex. We're supposed to help save magic and all that." He was stunned by just how open he was with this information. For all he knew, she could have been a spy for the High Queen, or worse. He didn't know what was worse, but he was sure there was, just as he was sure he could trust her.

"Well, it would be difficult for you hoomans to do anything with the

Codex, given how my family encoded it when they wrote it."

Oliver stopped in complete shock. Her family's book? Not just owned, but written? "You mean, your family wrote the Codex?"

The Stranger turned, now under a grate that showed small beams of light. "Shhh, look." She pointed through the grate and Oliver crouched to look up at two men standing above them in a room not unlike the secret one in Romir. Although the two men's identities were unknown, there was no mistaking what one of them was holding.

The Stranger stood quickly, prepared to engage in a fight to retrieve the Codex. The quest she had spent months pursuing was now mere meters from completion. She was denied by the combined efforts of Windrunner and Oliver as they restrained her.

"Are you crazy?" Windrunner whispered. "There are Spider's Web guards everywhere! At least fifty of them throughout the temple."

As they struggled to contain the Stranger, the Spiders above continued their discussion. "Lord Shipwright, what an unexpected surprise."

"Tck-tck-tck, what a web you have woven, isn't it? Thinking you could keep this hidden from us?" Ridhan said as he covered the Codex with a fine cloth.

"Oh no," Oliver whispered.

"Oh no what?" the Stranger asked, looking around for immediate danger.

"Did you know I recently came back from the dead after falling overboard?"

"I heard rumors."

"Well, that's the guy who threw me overboard."

It was now Oliver's turn to spring to his feet, itching to repay the favor Ridhan had so generously given him on the *Tiger Shark*. Windrunner and the Stranger were now restraining him as he fought against them, hoping to even the score with this wannabe murderer.

"Oh, my young lord, merely rumors and lies. I was just on my way to see your father and inform the..." the older man said, reaching out for the book. Ridhan quickly snatched it back and started to pace around. From what Oliver and the Stranger could see, it seemed the two men were the only people in the room above.

"Tck-tck-tck, you are either foolish to think you could have gotten away with it, or stupid to think it would have curried favor with the other Spiders."

"No! You will hand that book to me, m-m-my lord." The older man screamed and stuttered as he clumsily pulled out a sword that looked as though it was made for a man twice his size.

"Tck-tck-tck, my lord. You of all people should know, once you are caught in the Spider's Web, there is no escape." Ridhan pulled out his own sword and quickly disarmed the older man, sending him to his knees. "I'll ask you once, who is your spy? How did you know this would be here?"

"I am a lord and I will not be treated like some—"

The old man's words were cut short by the slash of steel to his neck. He crumpled to the grate and blood started spilling into the tunnel, between Oliver and the Stranger. They both silently moved around it to see Ridhan once more as he opened the book, trying to understand what was in front of him. After a few minutes of frustration, he left the room.

The Stranger and Oliver made for the grate, but both were held back by Windrunner. The Stranger shoved Windrunner, trying to climb onto Oliver.

"What are you doing, I need to retrieve the Codex!"

"Remember the bad guys? The Spider's Web? Well that's them! If we storm out of this tunnel and attack Ridhan now, we'll be ambushed. No, we need to backtrack and get the book some other way," Windrunner explained, being the only one in the small tunnel currently with a clear head.

The Stranger tried to ignore the protests. Oliver, coming to his senses, pulled the Stranger back down to the floor of the tunnel. "Leave it!" he implored.

"I won't!"

"But you can, which means we live to steal another day. There's only one place that book is going, and I know exactly where."

"Besides, he can't read it anyway," Windrunner added.

The Stranger pushed Oliver away, knowing they were correct in their assessments of the situation but feeling betrayed all the same. "Given enough time and resources, he could."

"What do you mean by that?" Oliver asked, not understanding.

As they made their way back through the tunnels, the Stranger explained. "The book is coded, but if he finds a key, he will be able to unlock its knowledge. We cannot let that happen."

"Po is the key," Oliver muttered.

"What was that?" the Stranger asked.

Oliver shook his head. "Nothing. So, who else knows where to find this key?"

After a few moments of silence, she answered. "Only my family."

"Okay, so who is your family, Teha?"

"No," she replied. Her emotions were livid, and she thought over and over to herself how she had once again been thwarted from her quest by people who claimed to be her friends. They didn't know what she was going through; how could they? Dumb hoomans with their dumb ideas. She couldn't count on them; she couldn't count on anyone.

The three exited the gate and ran to the corner where the front door of the temple could be seen. Ridhan came out, flanked by ten guards all with a Spider's Web insignia on their breastplate.

"Not real subtle," Oliver said, trying to make his point.

"I need that Codex," the Stranger muttered, agitated at the thought of losing it once again.

"We'll get the book, trust us. The Shipwights have a home on Silverfox Island."

"There's no house on that island, only a fortress," the Stranger corrected.

Windrunner continued Oliver's thought. "That's what he meant. It's near impregnable and heavily guarded. It's where the Shipwights stay, and if I had to guess, it's crawling with Spider's Web guards also."

Oliver added an ending. "We'll get your book back, I promise."

"We promise," Windrunner said.

The Stranger straightened out her cloak and put her hood back up. "I work alone, and I don't need your help, or anyone's. This is my hunt, and I will retrieve my family's Codex and return it to my home. Thank you for your help tonight, and best of luck with all of your relationships."

The Stranger disappeared into the darkness and Oliver slouched back onto the ground, bemused. The feeling of having the thoughts of two people in his head dissipated and Oliver felt once more alone with his own thoughts and feelings. "Oh, I'm sure this isn't the last we'll see of each other... Donna." Oliver looked over at Windrunner, whose eyes betrayed a smile under her mask. "What are you laughing at?"

Windrunner winked at Oliver. "I like her."

# AN UNEXPECTED GUEST

"I still can't believe you defeated Tyvis like that!" Yokel said, writing information on a large slate board that had been installed in the practice room per his request. In four separate columns were listed the four remaining fighters, each the top ranked.

"So that's what they mean by chalk," Oliver said.

"It's even more surprising given you were out all night," Reagan said, looking over the information as Yokel wrote it.

"Oh, you know me, never could sleep before a match." Oliver shoved his sister with his shoulder, and she returned the favor.

Yokel continued his summation of the match. "I thought his use of the double-sided battle ax would throw you off our plan. I know you practiced against it but still, he was quite skilled and full of surprises."

"But what he gained in surprise he lacked in speed. His technique was flawless however," Reagan said, admiring the detail of Yokel's notes. "Yokel, do you ever sleep?"

"I can sleep wh-when I'm dead. Oliver, your next match will be against Prince Amukamora, who I must say, I am a huge fan of." Oliver gave Yokel a sideways look. Yokel shrugged his shoulders and continued. "And Aasar will be going against Princess Kiara, which should be a match for the ages."

Reagan and Oliver shared Yokel's excitement for the other match. In the first round Aasar had handily defeated HaHa but had shown a slight vulnerability to dual-wielded weapons. Aasar used a standard shield and warhammer, which he wielded as nimbly as if it were a short sword. Kiara's two dragon-hook swords would be a wrinkle he might not be prepared for.

When Kiara fought in her first-round matchup, Oliver was entranced. It was as if he was watching a professional ballet. Every movement and stance was accentuated by the sun radiating off her. A few points during the match, he even found himself cheering for her, though he quickly hid it before anyone noticed.

Oliver moved to stand in front of the Black Prince's column, trying to ascertain an advantage. The Black Prince was a perfect copy of Oliver in every way. A pure swordsman, who could move in and out of any form with grace and speed. He never made mistakes, and it seemed as if he forced his opponents into moves they wouldn't normally have made.

"So," he said, "where does that leave us with the Black Prince? How do we defeat him?"

"With a stick, to the knees, while he ate. But in a ring, with a sword? There's no beating him," Yokel concluded, his voice becoming lower. Oliver looked at Reagan, a small smirk on his face. She nodded and walked over to the armory, retrieving two sets of kali sticks and handing one set to Oliver. Much like baton fighting, these sticks were lined with metal, giving them weight and the ability to deflect other hard metal weapons.

"Yokel, have we ever had an easy match?" Oliver asked, warming up with his new weapons.

"Come to think of it, I don't th-think we have."

Oliver smiled at him, locking his two kali sticks together at the end to create a staff. "If it was easy, it wouldn't be us."

The prospect of yet another invincible opponent energized Yokel, and his mind raced at the possibility of the tactics at hand. "We go with the element of surprise," he yelled as Oliver and Reagan entered into a warmup, clanging the sticks together at a rhythmic pace.

"Exactly," Oliver yelled over the sounds of the weapons.

"You want to fight the prince with those?" Roc asked.

"Ask the nerd. I don't match up with him. At least not with the sword." Oliver backed away, getting ready to enter into a full sparring session with Reagan. "So maybe I should stop trying to match him and be something different. He's the best pure swordsman in the championship, I'll grant him that. But that doesn't make him the best fighter." Reagan was unusually acrobatic in her assault, but even with Oliver trying to explain the tactics to Roc, she was still no match for him.

"Tyvis had the upper hand on me for the beginning of the match, but after I understood how he fought with his double-sided ax, I was able to defeat him. I won't give the prince that opportunity. I'll start out with a staff and then switch to kali sticks."

"And if that doesn't work?" Roc looked unconvinced that Oliver would survive.

"Then I'll have to think of something special, now won't I?"

"Maybe something special like this?" Roc yelled, unveiling his newest weapon. It was a pair of kali sticks, just like those in Oliver's hand. Yet, instead of only one transformation, they had a second. They could combine into a single staff, or a single kali stick could also break apart once more, to become chainsticks. As Oliver marveled at the new weapons, Reagan swept his legs, putting him on his back.

"Roc, these are amazing! Is this what you've been up to?" Oliver asked.

"Sure is. I've got something else special cooking up for you, but it's taking me a bit longer to complete." Roc was brimming with pride. For all his failings at the Institute, he was by far the best smith in Starfall, beside Oliver's own father. Given enough time, he might even surpass his mentor.

"Thanks, Roc, this means a lot," Oliver said, looking at his friend. Emotion overwhelmed them both, so Roc punched Oliver in the crotch, doubling him over.

Oliver had always gravitated to one primary weapon, like most fighters did. His was classic: the sword, the weapon of most fighters. But even as he was drawn to it, he made it a practice to discover and train with other weapons. This was a trait passed on to him by his brother, who would challenge him with impossible situations and only a non-sword weapon to help him. Oliver reconciled the fact that it was his own brother who probably made him into the well-rounded fighter he was today, and the bitterness he held toward the man slowly began to wither.

Very slowly.

Roc walked to the beachside door and turned the knob. "Oh, there's also this," he said, opening the door to reveal the silhouette of Iris.

"Iris?" Oliver dropped his fancy new weapons and ran to her. "Is it really you?"

"Sure is, wonder boy," she answered as he picked her up and spun her around, landing with a kiss.

"What are you doing here?"

"I came to see you, silly!" She hugged him tightly, and all his trepidations and worries about how he felt about her vanished. The Stranger was right: He had made his choice and nothing could change his heart.

Iris's hug turned into punches as she berated Oliver for his recent undersea adventure. "Don't you ever try and die like that on me again, or I'll kill you!"

Her anger was belied by a wide smile, and Oliver felt that all was right with the world. He had his girl, he had his friends, and he was two matches away from being crowned the Dragon Champion. What could go wrong?

"Oliver," Iris said as she swung from his neck, "can we go outside and talk?" Oliver's happy ignorance obliged, and he and Iris took a walk along the beach, leaving their boots by the dry sand and letting their toes kiss the tide.

"How's Po?" he asked anxiously. This silence between them as they walked was confusing. He had made his decision between Iris and Pathfinder, so how could she not be as excited?

Oh right, because she hadn't a clue about any of it.

Iris flicked a shell back into the murky waves. "Po is doing fine. He's with Azel, surely having the time of his life."

"Surely," Oliver agreed.

"Oliver?"

"Yes, my love?"

"I love you, you know that, right?"

Oliver stopped walking. "Where is this going?" He watched as the waves ate at their feet, sinking deeper and deeper into the sand.

"Nowhere. I just wanted to... I don't know. Everything just seems so..."

"Awkward?"

"Yes! How did we get here? This feels like..."

"That night in the Shears, when we kissed. We were just kids."

Iris pushed him lovingly. "That was only months ago, you acorn nut!"

The laughter was back, and Oliver felt confident they were in a good place. This was the person he was choosing to love, possibly forever, and he couldn't have chosen a better girl. He pulled her in close. "I choose you, Iris."

"What do you mean you choose me?" Iris asked, her ear to Oliver's heart.

He was feeling relaxed, without a care in the world. He had everything he wanted in his arms at this very moment. "I mean, I choose you. You're chosen." His voice sounded flirty, but her expression hardened as she pulled away slightly.

"Chosen over who?"

"Whom," Oliver corrected, immediately regretting it.

"Who are you choosing me over, Oliver? Who are these other women in your life?"

He stuttered a response as the ocean water sank his feet deeper and deeper into the soft sand. "Well, I mean, it's not so much other women, per se."

"What do you mean, per se?"

"I mean... I don't know what I mean. Can we just go back to the kissing and I love you parts?" Oliver floundered. When Iris first appeared, he thought it might mean a bit of alone time for them, but this was not the alone time he had envisioned.

Not by a long shot.

"No, I want to know. Who are they?"

"It's not they..." If his feet weren't buried at the moment, he swore they would have been in his mouth.

"But it's a her? Who is she? Who am I unintentionally competing against?"

Iris's temper was abundantly clear by her assault on the sand pebbles beneath her toes. Whenever Oliver was in a fight, be it the ring or in real life, he was always able to somehow just slow everything down and play out every scenario. It was a trick all Carpenters had, though when Oliver really thought about it, his brother seemed to do it better than anyone else. But that trick never seemed to work in situations like these. Situations that didn't require fists or steel, but words and feelings. Rather than time slowing down, it seemed to speed up, and if Oliver had any chance of keeping up, he would have to blurt out whatever was on his mind.

Even if it was the stupidest thing to say.

"It's nobody, just… You don't have to worry about it because I've decided, and I've chosen you! You won!" He was sure bards would look back on this day and sing of his poetic prowess, how he could soothe any hard feelings in a girl with mere words. Oliver was proud of his work, and his expression showed it.

But he was wrong, like he always was. Oliver remembered that night in the Shears, not the fun night nor the night he was saved by Pathfinder nor any other ordinary night. He remembered the night when he'd made a fool of himself and Iris had slapped him. That memory flooded his mind's eye because suddenly, Iris looked exactly the same. Same expression, same twitches of her brow, same mumbling to herself. He knew what was about to happen; he didn't need special skills to see that path.

Slap.

"When are you going to get it through your thick skull that I am a person! I'm not a trophy and neither are you. I'm not trying to win, and this isn't a contest! Do you even… grrrr… Do you even know what love is, you lousy…" Iris turned to walk away but immediately came back to dole out more verbal punishment. "You just don't get it, do you. Oliver Quartermaine, you're always the same. I love you. Nine Hells, I don't know why, but I do. I came to this island to help you. To support you, and for what? To be *chosen* by you over some hair-changing hussy!"

"Hair changing?" Oliver was more confused than ever. "Do you think… Are you talking about Kiara?"

"Yes! It's all over the taverns, how she saved you, how you two had a moment during Opening Ceremonies. I didn't want to believe it, but… AHHH!" Iris turned once more to leave and once more she whirled back. "You better figure your life out, Oliver. You better figure out what we are, and what you want. I thought you wanted this, a relationship, but I just don't know anymore. I don't know you anymore." Iris turned and ran, and this time she did not stop.

Oliver followed, albeit at a slow trudge. By the time he arrived back at the practice room, Reagan and Yokel were talking about different forms and Roc was nowhere to be seen. Barefoot, Oliver picked up his new kali sticks and stood waiting in the middle of the floor for his opponent.

He was so angry, but he didn't know at who. Iris was being entirely unreasonable, but also, was she? He knew he was being stupid but also, was he? He needed to talk to someone, but the only person he wanted to talk to was nowhere to be seen. Pathfinder had been gone since just after the Opening Ceremonies, searching for clues for Po's elixir.

So, he figured he'd hit something instead. "Where's Roc?"

Reagan walked over, grabbing a sword similar to the one the Black Prince would wield. "He and Iris went to the island forge. Soooooo, how are things with you and Iris?" she asked, dropping down for an easily seen leg sweep. Oliver froze for a second, and in that second fell feet over head to the flat of his back.

"Just peachy," he grumbled.

"Seems that way?" She helped him back to his feet. They continued their sparring, the Quartermaine way.

"I just can't do anything right with her." Oliver parried a slash from Reagan's sword and backed away, seeing the follow-up thrust. "It's like I can't be myself with her anymore."

"Well, you love her, right?" Reagan asked, unrelenting in her attack.

"Of course I do," Oliver responded, slightly annoyed by the accusation.

"And she loves you?"

Oliver went into a full-on assault, pushing Reagan back and giving her an array of moves that were mostly sword forms, a few sai and tonfa moves as well, but no kali forms.

"Yes, we love each other," he said as Reagan sued for peace.

"Ollie, do you realize what you just did? I've never seen anything like that."

"What do you mean?" Oliver asked as he went over to get a drink of water.

Yokel chimed in in awe because Reagan was out of breath. "You just mixed in three sword forms, two sai forms, and a tonfa form for good measure. No one does that. No one can do that. Not with kali sticks. Not with any weapon. I don't even know how you just did that, and I saw it happen."

"Oh, well, I uh, I don't know. Reagan made me upset."

"Well whatever it is that Reagan said, have her say it again."

Oliver snapped his sticks together to create the staff once more, and

Reagan took her place as the Black Prince. They began to spar again, and once again, Reagan began to talk.

"And you're sure she loves you?"

"Why are you harping on this?" Oliver spun his staff in a vertical motion.

"What does Pathfinder think about it all?"

Oliver was feeling distressed now, and instead of pushing the attack, he backed up in a defensive manner. Had Reagan read his mind? How could she know? Iris blamed his hesitation on Kiara, Reagan tugged at his heart with Pathfinder, and Oliver was left in the middle, dying a slow and painful death by heartache.

But Reagan's misstep was reading his mind one too many times. "Maybe we could get Kiara in here to help—"

At that, Oliver pushed an attack once more, moving in and out of various forms for the staff, battle-ax, longsword, and even a mace for good measure.

"Why did you say that?" Oliver asked, pinning her to the ground with his staff.

"Just the silly rumors around the island," Reagan said, forfeiting. She stood up, panting heavily. "Ollie, while that's amazing and we just figured out how to defeat Kit, I think there's something we need to talk about."

"No, no, there's not. There's something I need to think about, is all." Oliver tossed his staff to Yokel and walked back out onto the beach. His heart was pounding, not from the practice but from anxiety. Oliver was in turmoil, and the rage he felt could set fire to the entire ocean in front of him. He loved Iris, he knew it. He also cared for Pathfinder. With one, he knew they were meant to be together. With the other, it was easy to be together. One made sense, the other just was sense. One was his dream girl, and one was a dream.

Then there was Kiara. Oliver was sure he didn't have room in his mind or his heart to even contemplate her. She would stay at the fringes, where he couldn't get into any more trouble.

He needed balance, and he needed peace. He would never defeat the Black Prince feeling like this. "Damn you girls!" he yelled into the dusk sky. Why did Iris have to come to the island? It was only to be a week apart, and it would have been a week when he didn't have to worry about her. He could have spent his time with Pathfinder and completed his quests. But no, she had to come.

"This is all Ridhan's fault. If he hadn't thrown me overboard, none of this would be happening. Damn you, Ridhan!" he yelled once more, the wind answering his call with a high-pitched howl.

Oliver moved into a stance, letting his arms trace a circular pattern, calming his heart and regulating his breathing. Form Zero would bring him the balance he needed, and if he was lucky enough, a taste of the magic he so desperately craved.

He found rage and anger inside his body, deep within his soul, like a dark cloud squeezing the life from his spirit. It was the turmoil and self-loathing at his situation, like a stain on a white shirt. He saw a bright spark within the darkness of the cloud, the spark of lightning magic, and willed it to come alive. Immediately it came to him, eradicating the cloud and burning brightly within him.

Peace followed, and elation. It was tangible grace that filled him to the brim and overflowed. Oliver opened his eyes and found the lightning enveloping not just his arms but his entire body in a cocoon of energy. He could feel the air reacting around him, the fibers of every muscle twitching in unison, and suddenly a vision of darkness and stars. Stars everywhere, flying by him through a sea of midnight. Then they stopped and rotated around him, and he was suddenly thrust into the ocean once more, swimming and swimming, desperate to reach the surface.

He took a deep breath of the sea water and he was back on the beach. This time the cocoon of lightning had formed into a person, standing in front of him and mimicking his every movement. Oliver put his hand up and the mimic did the same, the pressure of the lightning hand creating an odd sensation. As Oliver tilted his head to the side, trying to adjust for a better viewing angle, the mimic followed suit, as if Oliver was staring into a mirror. Oliver then moved his hand to his heart, and the mimic waited, looking down at his hand with a curious expression. Instead of touching its own heart, it placed a palm on Oliver's chest and evaporated into his body.

Oliver fell to his knees, feeling as though his body, mind, and soul had been cleansed once more. He breathed heavily, looking around. The sand around him was a circle of glass that shattered into dust as he stood. He looked out at the ocean, seeing creatures break the plane of the horizon as they leaped and played. The sound of falling rocks turned his attention to the cliffside above, and he saw a dark creature in the diminishing light. The creature retreated and for a moment, Oliver panicked. Suddenly the beast flew overhead, with wings of a bat and the head of a serpent.

Oliver smiled.

He hadn't seen a dragon in a very long time.

# THE ELIXIR

"Y ou're sure this is the place?" Oliver asked Pathfinder as she led Yokel and Windrunner down a set of stairs on Blue Ivy Island. The trip across the Long Bridge had been silent, but not for Oliver's lack of trying. Whereas Yokel and Windrunner seemed content to discuss their competing knowledge of the island chain, Pathfinder had been unusually quiet.

"Yes," she said shortly. She knocked on the door in rhythmic fashion, and a slot opened up, revealing a pair of beady eyes.

"Password?"

Pathfinder looked around and leaned in. "Donkey butt."

The slot closed and the door unlocked and opened to a wave of heat from the cauldrons that were flanking each side of the entrance. Pathfinder extended her hand to the three others. "After you."

Oliver took her invitation and as he passed questioned, "Donkey butt?"

"You don't want to know what I had to do to find that out," she responded, and the moment of levity lifted Oliver's spirits. The four of them entered the large hallway, all dressed in their vigilante outfits with their identities hidden from the world. They would have stuck out if not for the fact that illicit events such as this one meant everyone else dressed similarly with masks and hoods.

"Okay, now what?" Oliver asked as Pathfinder hooked his arm and Windrunner did the same to Yokel, carrying them off into the crowd of other unidentifiable people.

Pathfinder took a cup from a passing waiter. "Now we mingle. My sources say this is the place where all the black market items, magical or not, will be."

Music played in the background as the two couples split up, trying to learn as much as they could without giving away their intention. Oliver had a bounce to his step, feeling progress was finally being made on the quest for Po. The bounce led to a hop and a step and before he knew it, he had pulled Pathfinder into a dance.

"What are you doing?" she protested, trying to pull away.

Oliver pulled her back, unwilling to let her get away without a dance. "We're mingling."

"Stop, everyone is staring," she said.

"Exactly," Oliver said as he pushed her out for an elaborate spin. The music waned and transitioned to a new song, while the people surrounding them clapped and began walking up to them, trying to curry favor.

"Well done, my lord, well done. May I interest you in some particular items for your mistress here?" asked a rotund man draped in long striped robes and an elaborate peacock mask.

Before Oliver could answer, Pathfinder interjected. "If anyone is a mistress, it's him," she said.

The man cocked his head curiously and then without hesitation moved his stubby fingers quickly to Pathfinder's neck, touching her choker. "Ahh, I see you already mask your voice with a particular item. You are not new to this game."

Pathfinder recoiled at the grubby man's hands, touching her choker to make sure it was still there. Oliver stepped between them, pointing his finger into the man's chest. "What do you know about particular items?"

The man took Oliver's finger and shook it aggressively, "Oh, you have come to the right person. I know of everything and anything you might need. A new voice for yourself, my lord? Or maybe something a bit more powerful?" He looked Oliver up and down. "Maybe something to help with injuries you might sustain during your travels."

Oliver glanced at Pathfinder, betraying their intentions, and the salesman jumped at the opportunity. "Ooooooh, yes, of course, a man of your travels would be very interested. Please, follow me. Raul will not lead you astray, my promises." Raul the salesman grabbed Oliver, who grabbed Pathfinder, and led them through a maze of people all trying to trade and sell their supposed items and knowledge.

"Right this way, right this way, my friends," he said as Pathfinder took ahold of Windrunner, who yanked Yokel. They walked down a stairwell to another catacomb of rooms, with hollering noises bouncing off the walls.

They were introduced to a crowd of people who formed a circle around two large fighters, each with their shirts off, knuckles wrapped in cloth, and no one keeping score. The two fighters engaged in a box, bloodying each other relentlessly until one was on the ground and one was still standing.

"What is this?" Oliver yelled over the crowd as they walked to the bar and Raul ordered them all drinks.

"This, my friend, is where you will find the best items you desire. Those people above, they know nothing of value and worth. Here, here the best items of a nature you seek are gambled. All you need do is enter!"

Oliver huddled with the rest of the group, trying to decide on their next move.

"Obviously we have to enter the fights," Windrunner stated.

"No, no way we can do that, we'll be killed!" Yokel said, taking a gulp of his beverage and peering over to see the fallen boxer's bloody body being dragged away.

"It's only worth it if it's for the elixir," Pathfinder countered.

Oliver popped his head up and turned to Raul. "What is the next item up f—"

"Ladies and lords," a herald announced, "I give you our next prize. From across the Sunset Mountains, this elixir is said to give you the gift of the elves: an everlasting life!" A small, skinny, bespectacled man who looked like a more annoying version of Yokel whispered to the herald who then raised his hands once more to clarify. "Excuse me, ladies and lords, but everlasting life seems to be a different vial!" Everyone laughed and he continued. "This will, however, heal any ailment, sickness, injury, or otherwise, I've been assured." The crowd cheered, and various lords and ladies pushed their way to the long end of the bar to sign up their contenders.

Oliver dropped back down to the group. "Well, I guess that settles it." He began to disrobe before he was stopped by Pathfinder.

"What are you doing?" she asked.

Oliver's arms became stuck inside his suit and he almost tumbled to the floor before Yokel and Windrunner caught him. "What does it look like? Someone has to win that elixir for Po."

"You have a match against the High Prince tomorrow. You can't possibly think you're going to—"

"Yes, I can! This is my fight and my responsibility!" Oliver was heated. He was within reach of fulfilling his promise to Po, and nothing was going to get in his way.

"No, it's all of our responsibilities." Pathfinder tripped Oliver to the ground, his arms still bound within his suit. She leaned over and whispered into his ear, "It's my turn." She shoved him down and removed her cape and tunic, revealing her naked torso save for a battle brassiere. She walked over and entered her name onto the list, keeping her mask and choker on but removing her hood.

"We can't let her do this!" Oliver protested to Windrunner and Yokel as he flailed around like a fish on dry land. But they didn't move.

"I think we just did," Windrunner said as a makeshift bell rang, and Pathfinder found herself facing off against a man even taller than Roc. From the looks of his lord and lady behind him, he most assuredly was a slave, but from which part of Soraya, Oliver couldn't tell. The crowd cheered and waved their betting tickets in the air as they all supported the obvious frontrunner.

They were all quickly disappointed.

The slave had thought this would be an out-and-out boxing match but realized his folly when Pathfinder spun around low and swept the legs out from under the large man, who hit the ground much harder than he had expected. She followed up with a destructive kick to the man's face, who was then out for the count. Silence fell over the crowd, many of whom had lost their wager, and Pathfinder took a drink she had not ordered from a man standing at the bar, drank it, and handed his cup back to him.

She came back to where Oliver, Windrunner, and Yokel were waiting, took her cape, and wiped off the meager amount of sweat she had accumulated.

"What?" Pathfinder asked, looking around at them all.

Oliver, Windrunner, and Yokel all in sync stated, "Nothing, nothing, nothing."

"That's what I thought."

"How did you—" Oliver began.

"I just pretended he was you," she said emphatically.

"What is your problem!" Oliver asked. Did she know his choice? Was she talking with Iris? Was there a big conspiracy against him? Did they have some secret network of girls who told each other everything instantly at all times?

Pathfinder snapped, "Nothing!"

Oliver took that as a sign the argument was over, and they all watched as more contenders fought. A mess of bloody mud was forming in the makeshift ring as fighters of all sizes and shapes battled one another, drunkenly encouraged by their sponsors. Pathfinder found herself in two more matches, coming out of each unscathed. She couldn't be touched, or so everyone started to assume, and soon enough, more wages were bet on her than her opponents.

The bell rang and a final match was set between her and a large young man about Roc's size and build who hadn't spoken a word all night. His sponsor was waiting behind him, with a young woman standing next to them. The young woman was in discussion with the fighter, using a hand language that was similar to the one Yokel and Oliver knew.

Pathfinder was all bravado as she entered the circle and the large silent young man readied himself. By this point in the night, Pathfinder's tactics were known to everyone: She went for the legs and tried to quickly finish her opponents off. A bell rang and they engaged in combat, but instead of going low, Pathfinder went high and climbed up the young man, trying to grapple his torso with her legs and arms. He became agitated and fell, landing on top of her, wiggling to avoid any type of arm bar or chokehold.

The young man managed to turn over and pin Pathfinder under his chest and they simultaneously began to go for a chokehold, the young man with his forearm and Pathfinder with her legs. The crowd was in a frenzy, yelling and screaming as both contenders started to drift to sleep.

Pathfinder was the first to release, passing out entirely, while the young man rolled off her, clearly in a daze but managing to stagger to his feet in victory. Half the crowd rejoiced in their winning wager while the other half threw their tickets onto a sleeping Pathfinder in disgust. Oliver, Windrunner, and Yokel ran to their fallen comrade, trying to wake her.

Pathfinder blinked her eyes rapidly, her senses starting to come back. "Did I win?" she asked hazily.

"You did great," Oliver consoled.

"But, no, you did not," Yokel added as Pathfinder jostled her body in a tantrum of defeat. Oliver was holding her and although she didn't push away, he didn't press for more of an embrace. Even now, in the middle of their mission, with his choice so clearly Iris, he couldn't help but wonder if he had made the correct choice. Pathfinder lay against him, her chest compressed and pushed up by the battle brassiere, and Oliver thoughts faltered for a moment, lusting after what could have been. Pathfinder's body reminded him so much of Iris's, and when Oliver thought of Iris, he recoiled at his wandering heart and silently cursed himself for his internal betrayal.

Windrunner scuffled Pathfinder's head lovingly and walked away, searching the crowd as the herald announced a new prize for the next round. Pathfinder's tears streamed down her face as she cradled into Oliver's arms. "I'm sorry, I just couldn't last. I buggered out and now we've lost the chance to help Po." Oliver tried to dismiss her failure, but a small part of him agreed with her, knowing he might have won if only he had fought instead.

Her choker vibrated slightly against her windpipe and she sprang up, searching the room for Windrunner. Oliver and Yokel followed her, confused, until they met Windrunner at the corner of a long hallway, crouching down and eavesdropping on a conversation.

"You promised us the elixir if we fought!" a young woman yelled.

"Tck-tck-tck, no, no, no, I said I would sponsor you in the fight, but the prize is mine. I have my own plans for this." Ridhan was clearly underneath the hood of the sponsor, and the young woman hastily relayed the message with her hands to her large fighter who had defeated Pathfinder. He became agitated and moved aggressively toward Ridhan but was stopped by four Spider's Web guards, encircling their small group.

"Tck-tck-tck, but I'm feeling generous, how unlike me. On the east docks tonight on the big island, you will find an unlimited source of this potion, or so I've heard."

The young woman stepped toward Ridhan but was met with the tip of a blade from a guard.

"Why don't you give us that elixir and you can find this unlimited source yourself," she said.

Ridhan put the vial into his inside pocket and smiled. "Tck-tck-tck, you better mind your manners." He leaned in. "I know what you are." Ridhan turned and left, with his guards flanking him. The young woman and young man spoke with their hands and then vanished in the opposite direction.

"What do we do?" Yokel asked.

"We split up. Pathfinder and Yokel, you follow Ridhan, see where he's taking the vial. Do not engage!"

"Where are we going?" Windrunner asked.

"We follow the other two and see exactly what Ridhan was talking about." They tapped fists together and set off on their respective assignments.

Oliver and Windrunner made their way to the East Bay piers on Goldflower, searching for any hint of what Ridhan mentioned. A group of dock workers was waiting for a ship that was just arriving into port. The East Bay piers sat out far along the water, allowing larger ships to dock without fear of running aground.

"This looks interesting," Oliver said as they found a hiding spot behind some large crates.

"Ugh, it smells like rotting fish," Windrunner protested, tugging at her mask.

"Not any worse than, no, I'm lying, it's pretty bad." They looked at the crate they were hiding behind and found the source of the smell.

"Nothing is ever easy with you, is it?" Windrunner sighed.

"If it was, it wouldn't be me." While they waited for the ship to dock, Oliver's mind raced with thoughts of Pathfinder and Iris. "Hey, do you know what's wrong with Pathfinder tonight? She seems unusually mad at me."

"Unusually mad?"

"I'm used to a certain level, but tonight seemed excessive."

A shimmer of sound and a wave of emotions came upon Oliver once more, and for the briefest of moments, his perspective changed once more to Windrunner's.

Windrunner looked at Oliver and tried to figure out how to break the news to him. She felt for Oliver, knowing his heart pulled and pushed in all sorts of directions. He was much like every other teenager in the world his age, or at least the ones she'd met. They felt their feelings so strongly, sometimes overwhelmingly so, but didn't always know how to handle them. She could feel their confusion and struggle, but she hadn't quite understood how to manage all those foreign emotions.

The shimmer released and Oliver felt once more within his own perspective.

Windrunner finally answered. "Ollie, sometimes people just need some time."

"Time for what! I didn't do anything to her!"

"But didn't you?" Windrunner posed, and Oliver decided that she too was just as confusing as every other girl he'd ever met. He thought if he could only ask Reagan, she would know the answers to his problems. Then again, she didn't know everything that was going on.

Or did she? Reagan always did have a knack for knowing things she shouldn't.

Oliver's thoughts were interrupted by four Black Hawks approaching the docking ship, flanking the Black Prince, who was talking with one of the workers. After a moment, the worker ushered over his coworkers who were carrying a large wooden box.

"There's something wrong with that crate," Windrunner said, trying to discern the situation.

"What's in the box," Oliver said in an annoying voice. The workers used metal bars to undo the nails and out of the box fell a girl, no younger than Reagan. The prisoner looked up, scared and shackled while the Black Prince examined her intently. The Black Hawks didn't look away from their post, except for one who was looking directly at the girl as well.

The Black Prince stood up once more, handed over a bag and some papers to the dock worker, and began to retreat, when suddenly a company of soldiers with black suns on their capes strode toward the exchange.

"Oi, what have we here? The High Prince, conspiring with these traitors?" The Black Prince argued vehemently with the Black Sun Battalion while Oliver and Windrunner's attention was drawn to two other figures emerging from the darkness. The young woman and her fighter were approaching but unseen by the Black Sun and Black Hawk.

Oliver and Windrunner exchanged glances, both instantly understanding the situation. No matter what happened in the next few seconds, the young man and young woman were no match for the fight ahead of them. It would be a slaughter.

"Ollie," Windrunner whispered, but he was already standing up.

"I know, let's go!"

The two of them rushed into the scene, not stopping for a moment as they tackled the young man and young woman into the dark ocean below the dock, leaving no evidence of the four's existence.

"What the hell are you—" the young woman said as Oliver elbowed her companion in the head, knocking him unconscious briefly to make it easier to move him through the water.

Windrunner had put the young woman into a sleeper hold and was backstroking away from the shore as quickly as she could. They made their way around the cove, and after an exhausting few minutes of swimming with extra weight, landed on an empty beach. They allowed the waves and tide to carry them for most of the journey but were too exhausted to stand, let alone muster up any strength to restrain their temporary prisoners.

The young woman and young man awoke as Windrunner and Oliver lay on the beach, gasping.

"Why did you do that!" the young woman yelled as she sat up, rubbing her neck. The young man rose too, one hand on his forehead where he had been hit and the other signing incoherently.

"You... you were going… ah, I can't breathe right now," Oliver tried to say, losing energy and breath with every word.

Windrunner recovered quicker than he did and propped herself up on her elbows. "I think what you meant to say was 'thank you for saving our lives.'"

The young woman stood, brushing wet sand from her pants. "No, I did not mean to say that. We now have a problem."

Windrunner looked at the weaponless young woman and young man and decided to submit rather than fight, lying back down on her back in the process. After a few minutes of silence, the young man stood and signed his question. The young woman translated.

"Do you know what you just did? We needed what they had, and you ruined it."

"What do you mean? You needed that girl? Who was that anyway?" Oliver asked.

"It was a girl?" The young woman looked at the young man, her eyes wide.

"Yes, that was what they were trading. Why did you want her?"

Windrunner answered.

The young woman signed with the young man furiously and turned back to glare at Oliver and Windrunner. "I am very angry with both of you. We understand now we were betrayed by Lord Shipwight. We shall consider other options."

Oliver stood, wobbling to his feet and supporting himself with his hands on his knees. "Wait, tell us who you are and what you want, maybe we can help!"

The young man growled deep and took a step toward Oliver, but the young woman raised her hand to stop him.

"No, we do not require your help. Goodbye." They turned and escaped into the darkness, leaving Oliver and Windrunner alone under the planet-light.

Windrunner slapped Oliver in the stomach. "Why can't anything with you ever just be easy?"

Oliver groaned and smiled. "It's like I told you, if it was easy, it wouldn't be me."

# THE SON OF THE CHIEF
## AND THE DRAGON PRINCESS

"What odds we got on the Dragon Girl?" Roc asked as he hopped onto the seat between Yokel and Roc. Oliver and Yokel sidled slowly away as Reagan visibly choked on her lunch. "You look like…"

"You mean smells like…" Oliver added.

"Hey! You try spending every waking moment in a forge!" Roc yelled as he punched Yokel, who had not said a word but took the punishment anyway.

"Oh, well, thank you for regaling us with your presence, Your Highness," Oliver joked.

"It's for research," Roc said, grabbing a platter of food away from Yokel.

Oliver was intrigued. "Research for what?"

"You'll see," he said with a mysterious smile.

Reagan plopped onto a pillow in front of the boys. "The odds are ten to one against Kiara."

"That seems a bit high, don't you think? You've seen her fight, she can hold her own," Oliver felt the need to defend her.

Yokel chimed in. "It doesn't have anything to do with her. Aasar is just that good. He's as tall as Roc, as fast as Kit, as strong as an ox, and probably your technical equal. If you had to build a fighter out of clay, you'd build Aasar. I don't know what they feed them up in the North, but whatever it is, you should order two." Yokel's assessment was predictable but accurate. They'd all seen the first round, and they'd all come to the same conclusion.

Aasar lived up to the hype.

"Everyone has a weakness, Yok, even me. We just have to find Aasar's, here and now."

Yokel looked at Oliver. "What do you think your weakness is?"

"Myself."

Yokel looked over his notes and then looked up. "Yes, that is correct." Yokel laid out two blank pieces of parchment on which to take notes and adjusted his spectacles along his nose. Roc looked at him, then down to the arena, then back at him, shook his head, and then slapped Yokel on the back of the head. "Let's get closer, you nearsighted nerd. We wouldn't want you to strain yourself."

When they got up, Reagan took the seat next to Oliver, silently judging her brother.

"Can I help you?" Oliver asked without turning his head.

"How was your night?"

"Oh, you know, went to a party, went for a swim, the usual."

"How was the water?"

"Freezing."

"Of course. Where's Iris?"

"Still mad at me, I suppose."

Reagan sat up. "And our other friends?"

"Following up on a lead."

Oliver felt crummy. A fight with Iris, a weird not-fight-fight with Pathfinder. Losing out on the elixir for Po. Everything in his life seemed to be teetering on a knife's edge. The arena below was the only thing keeping his spirits up. He could watch Kiara do battle and sit back and relax.

"Your Highness."

"Your Royal Highness."

"Your Grace?"

"Prince Kit?"

Roc and Yokel were arguing back and forth when an answer came from the entrance.

"Please. Kit."

Reagan and Oliver jumped up in surprise as Roc and Yokel bowed and bowed, slowly retreating out of the suite.

"Kit!" Reagan yelled as she ran over and hugged the high royal. Two Black Hawks lowered their spears, but the Black Prince turned them away. He walked into the suite and extended a hand to Oliver.

"Your Highness," Oliver said, shaking his hand.

"Dragon Champion."

"Nah uh uh, there's still one match left," Oliver said with a big grin.

"I suppose that is true," the Black Prince said, rubbing his shoulder.

"Oliver didn't tag you too hard, did he?" Reagan asked, grabbing a lotion and applying it to the prince's shoulder. She smiled and he smiled, and Oliver would have been happy if someone had come in and spooned his eyes out of his head.

"No, no, he didn't tag me too har—ah, ah, oh that feels wonderful."

"Family secret," Reagan flirted.

"Aren't all secrets family?" the Black Prince posed. "It was quite an exquisite match, if I am to be honest. I had always pegged you as a swordsman such as myself, Lord Quartermaine, but the weapon you used, collapsible kali sticks? That was a wonderful surprise." The Black Prince's effortless joy at his loss was discomforting to Oliver. Did he not care about winning or losing?

"You're taking this a lot better than I would have expected," Oliver said.

The Black Prince stood and leaned on the railing. "I suppose it is rather odd to understand my motivations. I do not compete to win or lose, that has never been particularly useful to me. No, I'm in search of something far more elusive and much more valuable." The Black Prince turned his head to Oliver, who stood next to him. "Perfection. The perfect move, the perfect match, the perfect moment. Are we not imperfect creatures in this vast world? Yes, but I think we can be more."

Reagan chimed in with her own opinion. "No one is perfect, Kit."

"That may be so. But there is something more than what we are, and I intend to find it."

Oliver looked out onto the arena field, watching Kiara and Aasar warm up as the herald announced their names. Every great fighter yearned for that perfect move or perfect match. They all knew it was folly, but it was the search, the journey, the struggle to find it that continually pushed them to become better. What the Black Prince seemed to search for was something beyond that, Oliver thought.

"Sometimes it's better to be lucky than perfect. That's how I beat you today. Luck."

"Ahh, luck, the great equalizer. No, I don't think it was luck. You were much better than you were when we sparred a few months ago. I underestimated you, and for that, I apologize."

"Your Highness, you have nothing to apologize for."

The Black Prince looked into Oliver's eyes, squinting ever so slightly. "Please, I think after out match, you can call me Kit."

Knowing a fighter and understanding how they fought was deeply intimate and very telling of who they were as a person. Once a fighter was in the ring, they were as vulnerable as they would ever be, and that intimacy between fighters often turned into lifelong friendships.

"Of course, Your Highness," Oliver responded, with a wry smile.

"I do have one question that I haven't been quite able to understand," the Black Prince said. "How did you know your plan would work? It would have been the smart play to just double down on your sword work. You are by far the best swordsman in Soraya, and I say that as the second best. But you didn't stick to what you are best at. Instead you went with a completely untested and unorthodox method. Few people would be foolish enough to try that in a tournament like this. Fewer would be brave enough to try it at all."

Oliver took the complex compliment to heart, knowing that the Black Prince was a true competitor and a chivalrous fighter. To admit defeat but also the superiority of your opponent took a measure of humility that no one Oliver had ever met possessed.

"You know, I wanted to think of something elegant and poetic to say, something bards and stewards would repeat for ages to come when they recounted tales of our fight and friendship, but a thought has just struck me that I think is more in line with who I am. You ask me how I could have put so much faith in an unsure plan. How I could try something so cavalier and downright crazy."

"Not my words, but the sentiment, yes."

"Well, my family has a saying." Oliver took a breath and a long pause, giving weight to what he was about to say. "Put your faith in people, not steel. It wasn't just my plan, but my team's plan." He looked past the Black Prince to his sister. "I put my faith in them, and they have yet to let me down."

Even as Oliver stared at Reagan, a shimmer of sound arrived once again, and this time it was the Black Prince whose thoughts and emotions he could feel.

Kit pondered the phrase, enjoying its simplicity and meaning. He had not yet had the privilege that the Quartermaines seemed to have in regard to family or friends. His various bastard brothers and sisters would much rather see him at the bottom of the ocean than help him in any capacity. Even his tutors were only as good as their ambition to please his mother. What friends he may have had were nothing more than pretenders and schemers. No one in this world truly knew him and he could count on no one but himself. It weighed on him, and his mind often wandered to a question he had never had a sufficient answer for. Why, out of all his siblings, did his mother take an interest in him?

From all that Kit had known, his father was nobody; one among many of his mother's lovers. Why then claim him outright, over any of her other bastards? This one kindness his mother showed him was the reason for his loneliness and ostracization. But being with these Quartermaines always felt like home. Not the palace in Land's End but the country cottage where he grew up in the hills between the Romirian and Northern Tribes borders. Oliver was a fine opponent in the ring, but it was his familial respect that Kit adored about the boy. He now counted Oliver as a brother, always at odds with one another when it came to the ring, but nevertheless, always with a foundation of respect.

The shimmer of sound released once more and a smile grew on Oliver's face as he understood just that bit more of the Black Prince's true character.

The Black Prince took a breath. "Wise words to live by." He laughed. "It's too bad you defeated me today, I was very much looking forward to meeting the Dragonbender."

Oliver and Reagan looked at each other in amazement. Humans and dragons had been at uneasy odds with each other for centuries, neither courting the company of the other. The Northern Tribes actively patrolled the border of Soraya to repel any dragons who might wander into their lands. The Dragonbender never, ever, ever met with any human, not even the High Queen herself, or so they thought.

Taking notice of their surprise, the Black Prince explained. "It's a secret few know, but the Dragonbender presents each Dragon Champion with a gift from the Dragonlands, as a token of our uneasy alliance."

"How do you know that?" Oliver asked excitedly.

"There are former Dragon Champions in the Black Hawks, and they like to impress when they've had a bit of wine." Oliver's mind raced. The poem about the champion and magic that so fascinated Ridhan must be what he was interpreting.

They heard a loud cheer from the stands, signaling the match was about to begin. The Black Prince smiled and put a hand on Oliver's shoulder. "Well, I believe that is my cue to return to my seat." Oliver bowed courteously and the Black Prince left but not before turning at the door. "Oliver, do make sure to say hello to my mother for me, will you?"

Oliver looked at Reagan, confused. "But only the Dragon Champion meets with the High Queen."

The Black Prince merely smiled and nodded before leaving.

"He's a lot," Oliver said, anxious to watch the match.

"You have no idea," Reagan answered.

The two Quartermaine siblings watched the match from their box, as they had all tournament and at the tournament five years prior. As expected, Kiara was using her twin dragon-hook blades whereas Aasar used his long handle warhammer, leaving behind his customary shield. The two fighters readied on either side of the inner ring floor, a gulf of space between them. Unlike the Starfall City Tournament, the Dragon Championship was fought on the dirt ground within the large inner arena, with no floor seats available to the crowds. There were no rounds, and scoring was the same as it was everywhere else in the world: first to thirty won.

"She's got to use her speed against him or she stands no chance," Oliver said.

"It's not going to matter much, he's faster than everyone else." Noticing Oliver's look of annoyance, she grimaced. "Sorry, Ollie."

"It's fine. You're right, he's fast. It's as if all that muscle doesn't slow him down but rather adds to his speed. Let's see how she'll react to it."

The match started and Kiara ran forward in a blinding display of attacks, aimed at not allowing Aasar any room to retaliate. It was a smart idea, for if Aasar wasn't allowed to get his hammer swinging, he wouldn't be able to get a hit in on her.

They both wore light armor plates, sacrificing protection for that added speed they so desperately needed. Kiara's strikes to Aasar's armor didn't do the amount of damage she would have wanted, but they achieved their goal of scoring points, and she took an early six to zero lead.

Kiara kept up the attack, but her right foot slipped and she hesitated for less than a second. That hesitation, however, was all the time Aasar needed to push the attack back to her, wielding his hammer with a grace and fluidity that was rarely seen even with a normal staff. He secured three quick points until Kiara was able to find a way to defend against the butt of his hammer.

"Here's the thing," Reagan said. "It's that he doesn't just use his hammer but the entire handle and pommel. It's as if he's fighting with three weapons, not just one. There's the heavy head of the hammer itself."

"The handle that should really be described as a staff," Oliver added.

"Right, and the butt of the staff, which he uses almost like a boxer would use a jab."

"So he basically stole our strategy, except…"

"… except he doesn't need to use a gimmick to connect them," Reagan finished.

The match continued, Kiara using all the available area to her advantage, trying to stay out of range of the hammer's head. Although this saved her on defense, it didn't allow for easy counterattacks, or attacks of any variety.

"She's starting to wear down," Reagan remarked.

Oliver nodded. "Aasar doesn't even look like he's broken a sweat yet. This is unbelievable."

As time moved on, it was apparent that Kiara was losing stamina, putting a lot of her energy into defending, while Aasar was unrelenting in his attack. Every time it looked as though the match would offer either fighter a reprieve, Aasar took the opportunity to push another attack, often coming away with a point.

As the score neared twenty-five to eighteen, Kiara saw what Oliver and Reagan recognized. If she kept up the way the match was heading, she would lose. Kiara took the opportunity of an overhead swing from Aasar to once again put her effort into an all-out attack. She flowed into and out of different forms so elegantly that Oliver forgot he was even watching a fight. To him it was more like watching an expert painter mix colors to create the perfect tapestry of art.

A particular move she enlisted was to use the notch of her swords to slide along the staff when Aasar jabbed for a strike. He briefly let go to save his hands, and Kiara's attack allowed her to pick up three points, pushing her to twenty-one. But her energy failed her and in an instant, Aasar was able to grab hold of his hammer once more and countered with a quick succession of moves that pushed him to thirty. Upon the final point, a horn blasted signaling the end of the match, and the crowd, who had until then been content with ooohs and ahhs, burst out into cheers and screams.

Aasar dropped his hammer and fell to a knee, having been thoroughly tested as he had not been the previous round. Kiara sheathed her swords behind her back and sat down in the dirt, breathing heavily and on the brink of exhaustion. Aasar got up from his knee reluctantly, his body not appreciating what it was being forced to do, and walked over to Kiara, extending a hand down. She took it and he lifted her up, embracing her in a hug. They talked while still entangled, patting each other on the back.

Oliver stared out at the field with his fists clasped under his chin, watching his opponent shaking hands with people in the crowd. Aasar was an almost perfect fighter in every imaginable way.

Almost.

"So, Ollie," Reagan began, looking wholly dejected, "how do you expect to beat that?"

Oliver smiled and tossed a grape from their box down to the stands, hitting Yokel in the head. "The prince wanted a perfect match, and that's what I'm going to give him."

She joined in on the aerial bombardment, nailing Roc in the ear with her grape. "Yeah, but if he's a perfect fighter, how will a perfect match from you result in a win?"

"Because, baby sister, he's not perfect. I found his mistake."

# THE DANCE OF THE WATER DRAGONS

"You clean up nice," Kiara said as she walked over to Oliver, who had just arrived at the banquet hall. As was customary, the High Queen held a private dinner for the contenders in the Dragon Championship and the High Court, which consisted of the High Queen herself and various lords trying to curry favor with her.

"I've been known to wear a suit well enough from time to time," Oliver responded with a wink as he signed the guest book. Names of every Dragon Champion contender for centuries were scribbled in the book that now included two Quartermaines.

"Looks like we're just one shy of a full boat," she said as she walked away to her seat to set her glass down. Her hair was a soft lavender color now, and she wore a fire-red long dress, with a single strap over her left shoulder and a slit along her right leg. Oliver was mesmerized by her beauty once more but determined to keep as far away as possible. The last thing he needed was another infatuation. He was blowing things with Iris and somehow also upsetting Pathfinder, and although Kiara's exuberant energy was enough to lift his spirits on even a bad day, he'd learned his lesson.

Girls were complicated and boys were dumb.

A herald walked in and immediately began talking with the Black Prince. Kiara started to make her way back to Oliver who, noticing her destination, turned and walked away.

The Black Prince clapped his hands once. "Honored guests, it seems my mother will be unable to dine with us this evening, as she apparently has not attended one of these dinners in"—he whispered to the herald and then turned back to the guests—"never." Upon hearing those words, the various lords left the banquet hall, grumbling, leaving only the eight contenders.

"Well, this should be a bit more interesting," Oliver said to the others.

The Black Prince chuckled. "Interesting is one way to describe it. Come, let us all enjoy the evening."

They sat down, spreading out along the table that was meant for many more guests. The Black Prince then commanded they all join him on one end, sitting next to each other. The kitchen slaves brought out the first course, which was eaten in silence, not one of the contenders wanting to be the first to speak. As they were served the second course, Oliver, agitated by the lack of conversation, finally spoke up.

"So, a Tribesman, a Southerner, and a Floater walk into a tavern. The Tribesman says…" He looked to Aasar to help him out, but Aasar hesitated, not quite understanding what was expected of him.

Oliver lowered his head and prodded him with his eyes until Aasar said, "I'll have a beer."

Oliver jumped in and repeated, "I'll have a beer, said the Tribesmen to the barkeep. The Southerner said, 'I'll have a wine,' and the Floater said…" Oliver was now looking at Tyvis, who sat unmoving and didn't respond for nearly a minute. After the silence was too much to bear, he finally answered with a loud grunt. Oliver's mouth was hanging wide at the response when suddenly the Black Prince started to laugh, followed by everyone else at the table.

"That has got to be the worst joke I have ever heard," the Black Prince said, unable to control his laughter. "And what's more, your punchline was a grunt!"

Oliver had tears falling down his face as he bellowed alongside his fellow contenders, finding common ground at the ridiculousness of the conversation. Tyvis was the only one who stayed silent, though a smile had started to creep along his cheeks, which Oliver took as a small victory.

"Ahem," coughed Aasar, speaking up between mouthfuls of food, "what I want to understand is how you Southerners consider this grape piss to be worth drinking. If you want a real drink, you need to try an aged whiskey. Now that will put some hair on your chest. Or scales on yours, Dragon Mistress."

Samaje shook his head. "No, that's not the question you should be asking. Now I say this on behalf of everyone here, possibly everyone in the known world, but how in the Nine Hells did you end up with the name HaHa?"

Everyone laughed an uneasy laugh until they saw HaHa joining in.

"You see, the day I was born," he said, "I came out of my mother's womb with a big ol' smile on my face. My grandmama had to describe what I looked like to my mother, because she was in such pain her eyes were closed. Grandmama described me as the happiest baby in the world, having come into it laughing. So, for my name day she christened me HaHa."

"That is actually a really sweet story, Haha," Kiara said.

Everyone around the table agreed, Tyvis giving his now customary grunt in approval. The fighters spent the rest of the evening sharing stories from their homelands and laughing more than any of them had expected. After the fifth course and many bottles of wine, beer, and other drinks, their lips had loosened and none of them held back about any of their thoughts. A few times, Oliver or Kiara had to settle arguments between two or more fighters, acting as the mother and father of the group. But tempers never lasted longer than the moment when either Oliver or Kiara would make a joke to defuse the situation.

Then, the conversation took a turn Oliver had hoped it wouldn't. Aasar had finally had enough beers to kill a small cow, but not enough to withhold his thoughts about Kiara.

"Aye, Dragon Girl, how is it you don't have any scales? Only dragons I've seen have scales. But then again, their heads are mounted on the wall of our great hall."

Kiara's face had turned redder than her dress, and she began to pass a knife between her fingers. "You Southerners have no respect for any creature, not even your own!"

"I'm not a stinking Southerner, no offense, Little Quartermaine."

"None taken." Oliver wore the badge of his region proudly.

Kiara was now pointing her knife at Aasar. "Are you South of the Dragonlands?"

"Aye."

"Then you're a Southerner. And we don't have any of you Southerners' heads in our halls. By the time we're through with you, there's nothing left, not even bones." She bit the air, and the echo of her chattering teeth may as well have hit Aasar in the face.

"You filthy, scaley… You know how many of my kin your kind has slaughtered?" Aasar was becoming more and more belligerent with every word.

"Filthy!" Kiara yelled, now standing. "I'll have you know I took a bath just tonight! When's the last time you could say that?"

Aasar, shocked, smelled his shoulder and answered. "Last week."

"No," a small voice said between the two bickering fighters. It was Tyvis, who now had every eye on him. "A month. I can smell you from here."

Aasar smelled his shoulder once more. "Aye, more likely a month."

"At least you fight better than you smell," Kiara said, a cold expression on her face masking her humor.

Aasar smiled. "You don't fight so bad yourself, for a Scale."

Oliver raised his cup for a toast and even with the tension still in the room, the other seven fighters did the same. "I think it's only appropriate Tyvis give the toast," he said.

Tyvis grunted and the contenders laughed and drank and drank and ate and drank.

Oliver, who had been too preoccupied as peacemaker to think about Kiara in her stunning dress, was now outwardly staring at her with uncomfortable thoughts and even more uncomfortable pants.

"Don't forget to blink, Lord Quartermaine," HaHa said as Oliver fumbled his goblet of wine into his shirt.

"I, uh." Oliver not only was fumbling his wine but now his words as Kiara winked at him. He was feeling the buzz from all the merriment of the evening and was just about to say something he'd regret when HaHa interrupted him.

"It's okay, my lord, even slaves like me from Hampstead know, the Dragon Princess is hot!"

Kiara raised her cup to him, acknowledging the compliment, while Oliver's face turned redder than Kiara's dress.

"Even I am not mean enough to insult Scales as such," Aasar said.

HaHa looked at the semifinalist. "Uh, I think you're confused, bub. That was a compliment."

Aasar put his cup down on the table a little harder than he most likely had intended. "No, a compliment would be if you called her cold, like the beautiful first snows of winter."

Oliver wanted to add to the conversation, but now he was imagining Kiara in a blue and white dress, a snow queen of beauty. The Black Prince inserted himself into the conversation instead.

"No, cold is when someone is withholding and lacking affection. Did you mean 'cool,' Aasar?"

"No, cool is… how do I describe it for you people." Aasar searched the ceiling for answers but couldn't quite find them.

"Cool is a state of being, indescribable and awe-inspiring at the same time," Oliver answered, still staring at Kiara. "But down in the South, 'hot' means beautiful beyond measure."

Aasar stood up from his chair and wobbled a bit before announcing his intentions. "You Southern folk and your words. I will take my leave now. I have a match to prepare for, oh master of words."

Aasar nodded his head toward Oliver and left. He was followed soon afterwards by the rest of the contenders until only Oliver, Kiara, and the Black Prince remained. Before Oliver could make a move to leave, the Black Prince stood, pushing his chair back and rubbing his belly lightly.

"I haven't had that much fun, well, ever. It was good to be amongst like-minded people. But it's time for me to take my leave. You two will be able to see yourselves out?"

Kiara and Oliver stood quickly, bowing their heads and saying, "Your Highness."

When the Black Prince left, Kiara made her way over to the chair next to Oliver and sat down, bringing her cup of wine with her.

"So," she said, putting her feet up on his lap. Oliver was about as uncomfortable as he had ever felt in his life, but for some reason made no attempt to remove her from the position she had taken.

He so loved to play with fire, no matter how often he was burned.

"So," he replied, unable to see how this conversation would go. To him, Kiara was a great void and no future or path could be ascertained by any of his tricks. Or maybe he just didn't want to know the future with her and live only in the present.

"You've been avoiding me all night. Don't think I haven't noticed." She sipped her wine, never breaking eye contact with him.

"I have not," he lied.

"Oh, so that wasn't you when I walked over before and you hightailed it in the opposite direction?"

"I wouldn't describe it as a high tailing per se."

"Then how would you describe it 'oh master of words'?"

"Evading, with style," he said with a smile, taking a sip from his cup. She shook her head at the joke but allowed it, nonetheless.

"So," she started again.

"So," he replied, enjoying this game they were playing.

"Is it my breath?"

"No, it's not your breath."

"Because I am part fire dragon, which sometimes leaves hints of…"

"It's… wait, you're part fire dragon?"

Kiara ignored him. "It's what?"

Oliver searched for a way to explain how he was in utter turmoil over two women already and that adding her to the mix was a recipe for disaster. That having her in his life was impossible, because just the thought of her would consume him. He knew it. He knew himself. She was exciting and new and exhilarating and wonderful and amazing and beautiful and funny, and he felt such joy with her.

He had a lot of feelings.

But he knew that if he allowed her into his life, even for a moment, the briefest of moments, that she would occupy a place in his heart he was scared of letting her occupy. He could tell. Just like he could predict a fighter's move in the ring, he could predict how she would affect him.

"It's me. You can say it. I know how I can be," Kiara lamented.

Oliver let his heart take over. "What do you mean by that? You're amazing!"

"I know, I was just making sure you knew too!"

"Wait a moment, you…"

"Look, little hooman, I'm a dragon. Dragons know what they want."

"And what is it that you want?" Oliver asked, excited and terrified in equal measure.

She stood up quickly. "I want to show you something. Follow me," she said, grabbing his hand and pulling him behind her.

"This is my favorite place in the entire world," Kiara said as they made their way through the thick bushes that lined the cliff of the island. She had taken them both on a boat across the southwest channel to Emerald Island. The small island was complete wilderness and the only island where humans weren't allowed. She had known exactly how to avoid the reefs that lined the coasts of the islands, guided by nothing but the waxing planet light.

"My father showed me this place when I was younger. He said it was where he first met my mother." Tears glistened in her eyes. They came out of the thickness of the forest and looked upon the open sea. Stars blanketed the sky, and a small patch of grass created a soft bed for the two of them to sit on as they dangled their feet over the edge of the cliff, the rolling waves singing a song as they broke upon the rocks.

"Tell me about her," Oliver asked, trying not to think about his own lost mother.

"My mother? Oh, she was, she was my hero. Once, I was caught trying to see a dragon egg hatching, and instead of getting into trouble, she let me watch, with her by my side. She had such a way with hoomans, and dragons, and Da. Everyone who ever met her loved her instantly, as if they were just drawn to her."

"I know the feeling," Oliver interrupted, stealing a quick glance at the Dragon Princess.

Kiara smiled, embarrassed, and continued her story. "I had never seen Da happier than when Mother was singing and dancing around a fire. He doesn't dance anymore." Her voice softened and she became silent once more, letting the ocean speak instead.

"What happened?" Oliver asked, shifting his body closer as he turned to her.

"Before I was born, she and Da had spent a long life together, and as is with my kind, eventually you lose yourself and revert back to who you were meant to be."

She looked off into the ocean, and Oliver searched his mind temple for anything he knew about dragons or their culture. He was sad to find out that it was little to nothing at all. Dragons rarely interacted with humans, and those that did, did not survive to tell any tales. Dragon culture was totally lost to him, and he was fascinated by this girl who had knowledge he didn't have.

"What about your mother?" Kiara asked, placing her hand next to Oliver's.

"Oh, she's gone now. Died about—" The memory of his mother's passing hit his chest like a warhammer. "Almost five years now."

Kiara didn't speak but let the silence linger. Oliver wanted to tell her stories, but he still hadn't moved to that point in his grief yet. The Dragon Championship held many dark memories for him, that one chief among them.

"So, your father is the Dragonbender?" he eventually asked.

"Yes. King of the Dragons. Leader of the Drakes. He has many names."

"And that makes you a princess?"

Kiara looked at Oliver, raised an eyebrow, and smirked. "You hoomans and your royal fantasies. Is that why you like me, because I might be a princess like in your stories?"

"Who said I like you?"

"You mean you don't like me?"

Oliver was flummoxed but kept, for some dumb reason, speaking. "I didn't say that."

Kiara leaned in closer, actually too close, making things very uncomfortable for Oliver. "So you do like me. Well, I like you too."

He was confused, utterly confused, but also not confused. He did like Kiara. Maybe? What would Reagan do in a situation like this? Poke logical holes, obviously.

"You barely know me!"

"I know you well enough. I know you fight with heart, but you hold back."

Does everyone know my weakness? Nine Gods!

"I know you keep the peace, even when a dumb hooman and a dumb dragon say some dumb things." She moved even closer, avoiding Oliver's lips and whispering in his ear as she rested her chin on his shoulder. "I know your friends would do anything for you. I know you are honorable and kind. But most of all, you have a cute butt." Her giggle burst into Oliver's eardrum and she recoiled as her own laugh caused her to double over in pain from laughter.

"You're crazy," Oliver said, rubbing his ear.

"But..."

"But I like crazy."

A sound from the ocean caught Kiara's attention and she grabbed Oliver's hand and pulled him closer, using her other arm to point straight out into the night. "Look!"

Oliver intertwined his fingers with hers and followed her hand out, peering into the darkness. Suddenly out of the water jumped a massive animal with a sound like a combination of a honk and roar reverberating through the air. Then another one of the animals jumped in the opposite direction, singing back to the first. A symphony of sounds were then sung as more and more of the animals leaped and splashed over and around each other, the music from their voices soothing and entrancing.

Kiara picked up on Oliver's confused excitement and leaned in close to whisper. "Those are water dragons. They never walk on land but roam the seas in search of lost sailors and souls. It's said that to see a water dragon is a signal of safety and relief, but to witness a water dragon dance is something much different."

Oliver turned his head, now mere inches from hers, and stared into her eyes. "And what would that be?" His blood was moving so fast, he thought he might explode from the heat while his stomach had dropped about three feet.

Kiara let go of his hand and turned her body, grabbing his face with her hands. "Close your eyes," she commanded.

"Why am I…" Oliver said as he grabbed her wrists.

"Just do it," she implored, and he relented, closing his eyes.

"Listen to their song," she said as she let go of his face.

"I'm listening but I don't—"

"Shhh," she said, shushing him with a finger over his mouth. "Listen with this." She put her hand on his heart. Oliver took a breath and relaxed, letting the sounds of the water dragons fill his every thought. He felt Kiara's hand release from his chest and suddenly all went silent.

He was thrust into a dark room once more, images flashing before him faster and faster. A sword in a glass stone, a castle in the sky, the blue darkness of the ocean, the heat of brimstone, Starfall City on fire, a castle by the sea crumbling into the ocean. Then he was falling, with images of people rushing by. Of Roc bloodied and Iris crying. Of Reagan hanging by her hands on a pillar, and Yokel bound to a prisoner's row. Of his father forging unyielding metal and of Pathfinder and Windrunner revealing their identities to that of faceless people. Finally, of Po lying on the ground, motionless.

He finally landed and saw a person beckoning him to come. Oliver stood and walked to the person, each step creating a ripple as he moved.

"Haralabos?"

"Water dragon dance?" Haralabos responded.

"How am I... Wait, how did you know that?"

"There's no time for that. Why haven't you answered me?"

"Well, because you're kind of a jerk and I've been a little busy."

"Do not tarry! The Spider's Web has the Codex!"

"It's okay, Ridhan doesn't have the key—"

"Yes, he does, he hasn't realized it yet, however," Haralabos said, exasperated.

"What? How many are there?"

"Three. Recover the Codex! The High Queen is gaining confidence."

"Who has the other key?"

"I've already told you. Po is the key. Open my damn book!"

Oliver was whisked back into the present. He opened his eyes and found Kiara staring at him awkwardly. Oliver tilted his head, and she spoke up.

"Your eyes... they were glowing. Is that something hoomans can do?"

Oliver felt a rush of concern fill him and he stood up quickly. Kiara followed him.

"What did you see?"

"I honestly don't know," Oliver said, trying to organize his thoughts. Kiara took his head with her hands and bent it down, touching his forehead to hers. He instantly felt calm and not the loneliness he felt in his vision. "What was that?" he asked as he pulled away from her, holding both of her hands in his.

"It's a trick we dragons use," she said, pushing their hands up with their fingers interlocking. They pushed and pulled in and away from each other flirtatiously.

"Did you have a vision?" Oliver asked.

"Yes," she responded, a smile appearing on her face.

"Care to tell?"

"Nope," she said as they swung in and out from each other.

"So, then, what do you want?" Oliver asked and they stopped swinging and entered into each other's arms.

"I told you, dragons know what they want."

She leaned in for a kiss and Oliver closed his eyes, letting the moment take him. But he didn't go through with the kiss and instead pulled away quickly.

Kiara stood there, rejection clouding her eyes. He wasn't sure he knew what to say, so he said the only thing he could think of.

"I'm sorry, Kiara."

"So, you don't actually like me?"

"No, I do like you. I really do."

"Hoomans are confusing."

"It's not you. It's me. I'm… I have someone in my life like that already. I shouldn't have led you on like that. It's just you were so…"

"Amazing?"

"Yes."

She smiled. "I know, and I know you."

"So, no hard feelings?"

"Don't think twice about it, Ollie." Her voice was hard, as though she was choking down emotion. "I think you should go now. I'm sure that someone else in your life is waiting."

The shield she had put up to cover the rejection had fallen. There may not have been hard feelings, but Oliver knew there would be hurt ones.

He took a step toward her, but then began to retreat to the forest trail from where they had come. But even as he made his way to the trail, he stopped and leaned against a tree. Lightning magic wrapped around the crown of his head and yanked it into the tree.

"Ow! What was that for!" He looked down the path, the one that would lead back to Goldenflower and back to his friends and to Iris. Then he turned and looked at the path leading back to Kiara. He needed to make a choice, and once more, he didn't know which to make.

Kiara stood where Oliver had left her, her face in her hands, vigorously trying to wipe away the embarrassment of what had just happened, muttering to herself.

"What was I thinking? He's a hooman and he already has a mate. That was stupid, Kiara, you know better than that. Oh, 'dragons know what they want.' What kind of line is that?"

She let go of her face and turned around, only to find Oliver standing behind her stony-faced. He rushed to her, grabbed her hip and head, and pulled her in for a kiss. After a few moments, they pulled away from each other. Kiara was looking utterly confused.

"Yeah, okay. I'm going to go now," Oliver said, and he raced back into the darkness of the forest.

# THE PERFECT STONE

Oliver was more confused that he had ever been. Was this how every boy in the world felt? But he was also kind of happy. He couldn't describe why, or even why he had kissed Kiara; it just happened. Now, the night before the biggest match of his life, he was wandering a rocky beach on Goldenflower. He hadn't had the courage to head home with the potential of facing his friends, Iris, or even Pathfinder. He wanted to keep this night to himself as long as he could. So, he stood at the edge of the water, skipping stones into the dark ocean.

"Shouldn't you be asleep?" Aasar asked as he approached.

"Same could be said for you, uh, Prince Aasar?" Oliver responded as he continued his obsessive stone skips.

"I am not a prince," Aasar replied, picking up a stone and joining in. "Each of the twelve tribes has a chief, but unlike your southern kingdoms, it is the greatest warrior that is crowned chief, not the blood of our ancestors."

"So, your Chieftainson? Is that a title?" Oliver wanted to know the motivations of his opponent, for maybe that would give him some insight into their match.

"Aye, my father is chief, and his father was chief before then. Our family has led our tribe for over ten generations, so I am expected to take my father's place one day."

"You're expected to be the greatest warrior, you mean."

"Aye."

Oliver absentmindedly counted his skips; he'd gotten it up to five and now was aiming for six on every subsequent throw. He thought about his opponent, so much being expected of Aasar, but it didn't seem as though Aasar shied away from it. His acceptance for who he was supposed to be was intriguing, and a smile of admiration crossed Oliver's face as he noticed Aasar toss.

"You'll want to move your arm a bit out to the side," he suggested.

Aasar looked at him and followed the advice, getting his stone to skip up to four bounces off the water. "What is it that you fight for, Southerner?" he asked.

Oliver couldn't explain his true motivations, but he divulged his old ones. "My brother competed in this championship five years ago and won, and everyone just assumed I would follow him. It probably didn't help that I had a talent for fighting."

"Aye, I was most impressed with your fight against the High Prince."

"I know."

"Oh?"

"I noticed a few of my moves during your match against Kiara." Oliver gave Aasar a sideways glance and smile.

"Aye, Scales was some type of fighter, I will give her that. It was the first time in a very long time I was truly worried about the outcome of a match."

"Yes, she's something else. So, what is it that you fight for, Aasar?"

"It is as you said. It is expected of me. But there is more, I suppose. To be crowned the Dragon Champion would signal to everyone I am the greatest fighter in Soraya, but it would also signal to the other tribes that when I invoke the Ascension Ritual, I will not be opposed. Without it, I will most assuredly not be crowned warchief."

"Warchief?" Oliver asked, watching his stone sink after the third skip.

"Each tribe in our lands has a chieftain but no one ruler over all the tribes. There is a ritual between the tribes for the chief among chiefs, the warchief, and that one warrior rules over all tribes. It is the greatest honor one can achieve. It is what I was raised to be."

Oliver stopped skipping stones and looked out into the darkness. "Would it be so bad, Aasar? To not do what is expected of us? To not have to follow what everyone else wants from us?"

"Aye, for me, it would," Aasar admitted, putting down his stone and sitting on a large boulder. Oliver sat on a similar boulder next to him. "You Southerners know very little of our ways in the North, but all is not as well as it seems. The relationship we have with the High Queen is constantly strained, and the peace between us and the dragons is tenuous. There are forces within our tribes that would incite war were it not for my father, the warchief. If I do not ascend and take his place, then I am fearful that the Northern tribes will be thrown into chaos, and the peace my family has worked so hard to maintain will be lost."

"I know what it's like to feel the weight of the world on your shoulders," Oliver admitted.

"What weight do you carry, Southerner?"

Oliver contemplated how much he could actually tell Aasar. At the end of the day, he was his opponent and enemy. But that's not all they were. They were part of a small club of sorts: contenders in the greatest tournament in the land. That bonded them like nothing else could.

"I'm not just fighting because of expectations, I'm fighting for my friend. I'm fighting for my city, and in some way, probably all of Soraya."

"Aye," Aasar reflected.

"The entire Northern Tribes way of life hinges on you winning tomorrow, doesn't it?" Oliver asked.

"I have trained my entire life for this moment. There is no other plan. I consider you a great opponent and, if I can, a friend." Oliver nodded in agreement as Aasar continued. "But know this, tomorrow when we are in that ring, I will not hold back. I must win."

"I'd expect nothing less." A long silence followed while the two opponents enjoyed the sounds of the ocean and each other's quiet company.

"So, what would you do if you were warchief? Like, the first thing you would do?" Oliver asked, trying to lighten the heavy conversation.

"I do not know. I have spent my entire life so focused on becoming the warchief that I have never stopped to think about what it would be like."

"You know what I would do?" Oliver said. "I'd throw the biggest party the North had ever seen!"

Aasar laughed. "I'd have delicacies from every corner of the world."

"Venison from Kandahar."

"Lemon cakes from Starfall."

"Spiced rum from the Southern Isles!" they both said as they laughed at the idea of pirates at a Northern Tribes feast.

Oliver settled down and then spoke again. "But really, what would you do first?"

Aasar looked at Oliver, then his face darkened. "The North has many secrets. Things that one should never speak about. I would wish to eradicate those secrets."

"You won't have to wish," Oliver suggested.

"A wish is all I could hope for. It's a secret and a stain upon our souls, or mine at least." Aasar grew quiet again, and Oliver let the conversation breathe for a moment.

"Once you become warchief, you can change that. You can do whatever you want, however you see best. Just because our parents or our grandparents or people hundreds of years ago were upset about something, that doesn't mean we have to listen to them."

Aasar stood up, fists clenched tightly. "Aye, you are right. Once I am warchief, I can do what is right. I can save her." He took a stone and skipped it into the ocean. After another successful fifth skip, it sank, and he was pleased with himself.

Oliver stood and skipped his own stone. After the sixth skip, he offered a bit of advice. "It's all in the wrist."

Aasar clasped Oliver's shoulder with his big hand. "I shall see you in the arena tomorrow, Southerner."

Oliver continued to skip stones after Aasar left, watching them descend into the darkness. Although their talk hadn't done much to relieve the problems his heart suffered, it did give him much to think about for his match. He looked at the smooth stone in his hand and skipped it. It died after only a few touches of the ocean. Dismayed, he opted for a smaller stone, but the weight didn't provide enough force to make it very far. Unlike Aasar, who was able to quickly and consistently flick his stone five skips, Oliver was more variable.

He picked up a stone that seemed heavier than any he had used before, and then it hit him. Not a stone but an idea. The smallest kernel of an idea, but an idea, nonetheless. He and his team would make it grow though, and he raced back to his practice room.

"You can't fight with no armor!" Reagan pleaded as Oliver finished stretching.

"Rea, too loud," Oliver said, rubbing his head.

Yokel walked over. "What's wrong with you?"

"I think I'm still drunk." Oliver did a quick run in place, jumping his knees to his chest and spinning around. "I'm okay, I'm okay," he said before wobbling and finally finding his balance.

Reagan grabbed Oliver's sword from the cabinet and threw it to her brother. "So, we're agreed then, armor."

"No," Oliver answered, swinging at an imaginary opponent. Testing out his theory in his head.

"Chainmail at least, Ollie!"

"No. We got here with no armor, that's the horse we're riding on."

"No, that's the horse you're dying on," Reagan snapped back.

The door to the practice area opened and Roc walked in with an exact replica of the modified warhammer Aasar used. "Am I late?"

"You're right on time," Reagan snapped as she took the warhammer and shoved it into Oliver's chest. She took his sword and handed it to Roc.

"So, this is what you've been working on all this time?" Oliver asked, admiring the craftsmanship. "It looks exactly like the real thing."

Roc used the sword as an extension of his arm and pointed out a few of the intricacies. "It could have been better, but I wanted to replicate it as best I could. Aasar doesn't know the weight distribution is off, and he'd get more power in his swing if he just—"

"How about we don't tell him until after tomorrow?" Oliver suggested.

"You boys done with your love fest?" Reagan asked.

Oliver marveled at the weapon some more before holding it out for Roc, but Reagan disagreed.

"Nope, nope, you get the fancy hammer, Ollie. Now you have to get past the three of us."

Yokel's head jerked up. "Three?"

"Yes, grab a staff. I have the tonfas. Roc, you get the sword."

Reagan, Yokel, and Roc circled around Oliver.

"Reagan," Oliver said, "shouldn't I be using my own weapon?"

"No, you need to know what Aasar knows. You need to know how that thing moves, how it handles, and how to beat it."

Without hesitation, Reagan pounced and Oliver used the warhammer to block, finding it easier to wield than he had expected. Oliver tried to mimic Aasar's movements and strikes from what he had seen and found there were very few, if any, weaknesses when facing a single weapon. But it was strangely hard to transition against differing weapons. Yokel would attack with a staff and although defending was relatively easy, the following attack from Reagan and her tonfas would send Oliver to the ground. Even Roc's sword sent his mind spiraling in every direction. Aasar may have been a master of this warhammer, but surely he would be thrown off by the use of a variety of weapons.

After a while, Oliver was able to understand the minor idiosyncrasies of the warhammer and used the advantages to make quick work of Yokel and Reagan. Only Roc was left, and he seemed up for the challenge.

"Let's go, rich boy," Roc taunted.

"Dude, you're rich now too," Oliver said, pointing out that their differences in wealth were no longer as great, given Roc's victory at the World Championship. True, he may not have had as much wealth as Oliver, but then, no one did.

Roc came in with a flurry of haymakers, but Oliver and the warhammer defended them well until finally Oliver used the hammerhead to hit the broadside of the sword. It cracked and broke into pieces.

"Rea, this just might work," Oliver huffed out.

Roc crawled over to a bucket of water. "What might work?"

"Our strategy for how to beat Aasar," Reagan answered.

"What strategy? We demolished Oliver," Roc said after dunking his entire head into the bucket.

Oliver smiled and threw him a towel. "Exactly. I'm not going to defeat Aasar with one weapon, I'm going to defeat him with all of them."

# THE DRAGON CHAMPIONSHIP

Oliver tightened his gloves up to his forearms. He had never felt this nervous. Nervous, yes, whether it was during the Starfall Tournament, or the first time he kissed Iris, or the first time he rode a horse. Those were nerves of anticipation and excitement. He knew what the outcome of each of those events might entail, or at the very least he knew what to expect.

The Dragon Championship was something he couldn't predict, nor did he know what to expect. He had a plan, but even the best laid plans were hard to execute. He didn't even know quite what he wanted. Winning meant another step toward magic, toward helping Po, toward what Haralabos wanted. But was that what Oliver wanted?

Yokel walked up to him with a hooded cape, a deep blue lined with an ivory white. It matched Oliver's new blue suit that was accented with silver seams, a suit made just for this championship match.

"What are you thinking about?" Yokel asked.

"Just realizing how happy I am to have a friend like you, Yok." Yokel was at a loss for words as he finished putting the cape in place. "I've never properly said thank you. You... you've always been there for me. You always believed in me, even when I didn't believe in myself. You were, you are, a true friend, Yok."

Yokel stared at him. Rarely, if ever, could Oliver remember anyone giving Yokel a compliment, let alone talking to him in such a genuine way. Yokel suddenly embraced Oliver in a tight hug. Oliver was feeling weirdly emotional, and luckily for him this was Yokel and not Roc, so the emotions wouldn't be followed with a punch.

"You know I'd do anything for you, Oliver," Yokel said.

Oliver hugged his friend back. "I know, Yok, and I need you to do one last thing for me."

"Anything you need."

"Go up to the box and enjoy the fight."

Yokel went over to grab his notes, but Oliver protested. "No, no notes. Just, just enjoy yourself, Yok, you deserve it."

Yokel looked at him and then at the notes apprehensively. "Oliver," he said as he headed to the door, "just, be yourself."

Oliver nodded. "Wouldn't be anyone else."

After Yokel left, Reagan came over, handing Oliver a sword. It wasn't the best sword he could have used, but his normal sword had broken during the sparring session. He gave it a few test swings, thinking through what he would see when he emerged from his room into the arena.

Unlike any of the previous fights in this Championship, or in any tournament for that matter, this final bout offered an added complexity. Instead of the weapons being brought in by the fighters themselves, the arena was filled with crates that each hid a weapon inside. After each minute of the fight, a small fuse would blow the seal holding the box together, revealing a new weapon. This was the advantage Oliver was hoping to exploit.

"I know it's not the best sword, but it'll do until the first crate opens," Reagan said as she sat next to Oliver, fidgeting. She had become increasingly nervous in the hours leading up to the match.

Oliver put an arm around her shoulder. "I'll be okay, Rea, I promise."

Tears started to trickle down her cheek. "I know, Ollie, it's just, last time we were here, in this same room..."

"It won't end up the same way, I promise." He gave his sister a kiss on her head and stood up, cracking his neck and trying to shake the nerves from his body.

Roc sat on the other side of Oliver, silently staring at the wall.

"What about you, any words of encouragement?" Oliver asked.

"Uh, don't break a leg?" Roc offered up, but even as he joked, it seemed like his mind was wandering. "Oliver, I..." Roc began, standing up uncomfortably. Oliver stood also, and before Roc could finish, Oliver punched him in the crotch.

Roc doubled over and groaned. "Yep."

Oliver bent over to meet his pained face. "Pathfinder and Windrunner here too?"

"They promised to watch the whole match." Roc gave Oliver their customary handshake and waddled out of the room but not before turning his body to move past Iris, who was blocking the doorway.

"You came," Oliver said, walking up to her slowly, as if he didn't want to startle her into disappearing.

"I came."

"Think I have a chance of winning?"

"What do you think?"

"I think, yeah, maybe I do."

"Then that's what I think too." Iris's eyes were glassy and her lips quivered. "I'm sorry."

"Me too."

"Don't die?"

"Once was enough for me." Oliver pulled her in tightly and kissed her on the forehead. She took his head and kissed him back, this time a long passionate kiss as if they loved each other. Oliver smiled, happy to be back in her good graces.

"I love you," he whispered, trying to speak the truth and make it so.

"I love you, too," she answered. Then she left, leaving only Quartermaines in the room.

Reagan snuck under her brother's arms and hugged him for luck. "Nothing is ever easy with you is it, big brother?"

Oliver smiled, "If it was easy, it wouldn't be me."

"Well, I'm going to head up to the box, Ollie. Good luck, and… I'm sorry."

Oliver stood there, confused, then shook his head and tried to mentally prepare for his fight. Three bangs on the gong sounded along the hall signaling three minutes until the start of the match.

Oliver paced around the room, trying to control his breathing as he drowned in his thoughts. He was contemplating not only the match but also the consequences of winning. "I know what I'm supposed to do, but I don't know if that's the correct choice. What should I do? What would Wiggin have done?" he asked aloud in the empty room.

"Well, first off, he would have worn armor instead of whatever Johanous had sewn together. But dang, Ollie, those are some nice threads," a muffled voice at the door said.

Oliver didn't turn, recognizing the voice immediately though he hadn't heard it in years. Anger started to churn inside him. This was the last thing he wanted at this moment. He should have been preparing for the fight of his life, not this uninvited guest.

"Shouldn't you be pillaging a village or ransacking a small keep?" Oliver said, trying his hardest to stymie his hatred.

"I have a new posting. I thought you might be happy to see me, Ollie."

"Don't. Don't say my name. You don't get to do that anymore."

"Ollie, I'm still—"

"I said don't."

"Okay, okay, relax." The Black Hawk walked in, taking stock of the room. He touched the wet stone grinder with familiar fingers, a smile hidden by his Black Hawk helmet.

"Why are you here?"

"Why so hostile? Can't I wish you good luck? Or am I not allowed that either?" His black armor barely made a sound under the weighted red cape that swayed slightly while he moved around the room.

"No, you are not. Now please leave." Oliver was doing his best to remain civil when all he wanted to do was punch this Black Hawk in the face.

"Oliver, I came here to say—"

"I asked you to leave," Oliver repeated, brandishing his replacement sword.

The Black Hawk looked at it, and his shoulders slumped slightly. "I heard your sword broke. You loved that sword so much, it's a shame. Here, I have something for you."

Suddenly Oliver became aware that the Black Hawk was actually holding a long package wrapped in a cloth. Oliver took the package begrudgingly and unwrapped it, revealing an oddly gray sword.

"The Shadow Sword?" Oliver said in amazement. The weapon was the pride of the Quartermaine family; the first weapon made at the Forge in Starfall. The weapon, he now knew, forged by Satine.

"You know the stories. Never dulls, never breaks, never rusts. Trust me, I've tried my hardest to test all three of those things."

Oliver shoved it back. "No, I can't take this."

"Yes, you can, I've even added the blade guard for you."

Oliver didn't want to agree, but he also had coveted this weapon since he knew what weapons were. It was the sword above all swords, and the only one of its kind. Now it came with an added layer of emotional complexity he wasn't sure he was ready for.

"Thanks," Oliver eventually said, relenting to his desire. Two bangs of the gong sounded in the hall, signaling thirty seconds until the beginning of the match.

The Black Hawk made his way to the door. "I'll take that as my cue to leave. Good luck, baby brother, see you on the other side."

Oliver stood holding his family's sword, so many thoughts and questions in his head. He desperately wanted more time to talk, to ask questions of Wiggin, but the fire of pain he felt burned his thoughts to ash. In the end, he could only muster a bitter question.

"You weren't even there. You didn't come back. We needed you and you didn't come back. Why didn't you come back?" He felt like he was eight years old again, crying at the latest injustice his little mind thought he suffered.

"I'm sorry, Ollie. I really am. I miss her too." The Black Hawk lowered his head but kept walking, leaving familiar footsteps trailing in the dirt and letting the door close behind him.

Oliver was alone once more, and he knew now what it meant to be a Dragon Champion. It was the most famous title in the world, and the loneliest. For a moment, Oliver looked at the sword in his hand and thought about throwing it to the ground, not wanting to accept the help. But suddenly, the stone ceiling above the platform opened, and he jumped on the rising platform, new sword in hand. He sheathed it, threw on his hood, and crested into the open arena as the crowd began to cheer.

He raised his right hand above his head, wiggling his fingers and standing straight up with his head bowed. A small group of people in the crowd joined him, raising their hand above their heads and letting out a low guttural sound, steady and unbreaking. Not wanting to be left out, the rest of the stadium joined in, creating a noise as if a hundred thousand bees had begun humming at once.

As Oliver's platform settled into place, he lifted his head and looked around, spinning and staring at everyone, imploring them to keep their hands raised. As the crowd began to crescendo in energy, Oliver threw his left hand up to join his right. He turned his palms outward and spread the air away, pushing quickly down with enormous force as if his arms were wings. Jumping up with excitement and letting out a holler of excitement, as did the crowd, he began to jog around.

A large horn sounded and the crowd quieted as Aasar ascended on his platform to the arena. Oliver looked around, not quite understanding why the crowd wasn't cheering, but it soon became apparent when Aasar dropped his warhammer and raised both his hands. He yelled a loud grunt and clapped his hands once over his head and the crowd clapped and grunted with him and kept their hands raised as he had. He clapped twice, and so did the crowd. After the third round of clapping he picked up his warhammer, yelled incoherently, and spun the weapon in a dazzling display of showmanship.

"Damn, that was pretty good," Oliver admitted to himself. He looked around the stadium, the sheer size starting to make him feel small. He let the feeling wash over him and then focused. Looking up at his family's box, he saw Reagan trying to hide her apprehension with a forced cheer. Yokel stood next to Iris and Roc, and all were at the edge of their box, as close as they could be to the field.

Oliver looked around at the other boxes filled with lords and ladies of various noble houses. Below them, filling out the stands, were people from all around Soraya. He saw the High Queen's box, three Black Hawks surrounding the High Queen herself, with a fourth joining late. The Black Prince wasn't in the box but rather sitting with Kiara and the other contenders in the front row of the crowd. He panned around the stadium, hoping to glimpse the Knight Angels, but a final blow of the horn sounded, and he was startled back to the task in front of him.

"Okay, Oliver," he said to himself, "it's time." He closed his eyes and focused, letting himself become one with his surroundings. Oliver knew he couldn't use Form Zero to find his balance, lest he accidentally summon his lightning magic in front of the High Queen. So he tried the old-fashioned way.

His mind and his heart were racing, and the earth trembled slightly beneath his feet with the dirt shifting. He felt his heart beating and with every pump, he felt out of control. He thought of his family but quickly dismissed it. He thought of his friends, of Yokel and Roc, even of Po, and pushed it aside. Thoughts of the mysterious Knight Angels fluttered away and then he thought of Iris and lost track of his heartbeat. None of these thoughts were strong enough to anchor him, not even Iris, and he let her go too.

Time stood still, waiting for Oliver to respond, and he let it stay that way until he was ready. As a child, the thought of his family had steadied him, and over time that had transitioned to his friends. Iris had been his focus recently, but now she only caused more turmoil. Oliver thought that maybe he had never truly been balanced before. That maybe his abilities and skill had overcome that fact, and that failing had finally caught up with him.

Today, of all days, was the worst to have this epiphany. Oliver tried once more in his mind, starting with the dark emptiness of nothing. His mind was cast into the ocean, stretching and pleading for the surface. Then breath and life washed over him and he saw a face, and as he looked upon it, a peace and understanding that he had never felt before overwhelmed him. He felt ready for any obstacle, and the ocean disappeared, as did the face he saw, and he was once again in darkness.

"I can't do this alone," he said.

A crackled voice spoke to him. "You were never alone."

Around Oliver appeared nine mirages of beings of various colors, made of odd energies. In front of him was the yellow-white lightning being he'd seen before.

The lightning being crackled. "Are you ready?"

"Yes." Oliver opened his eyes and time snapped back into sync with his own reality. Aasar began to move forward but stopped suddenly as the sky darkened above them and the shadows of the Coliseum coalesced into one blackness. The sister moon that also orbited the planet above had moved in front of the sun, eclipsing its light. Oliver felt odd, as if he wanted to vomit and explode at the same time. His head started to throb, and his mind grew hazy, and he looked at his family's box, where candles and lanterns had been quickly lit. They were attending to someone inside and not paying attention to the field.

As complete darkness fell, Oliver peered, trying to see what was happening, but his eyes burned with fire. He thought he saw a small commotion in the High Queen's box, but he couldn't be sure. All around the stadium people murmured and screamed.

He fell to one knee, wanting to crawl out of his skin and plunge into a volcano. He tried to focus on his breathing, but each breath became heavier and heavier. The dark halo lasted for minutes, and when he felt he could not contain the agony any longer, light began to slowly pour over the land. The pain receded until it was mercifully gone, although Oliver felt as though pieces of himself had been ripped away. He rose back to his feet, and the memory of the pain melted into nothing. He looked around at the stadium, where it seemed everyone was in a similar position, feeling as though nothing was different.

The crackled voice spoke in his head once more. "Now we are ready."

The horn sounded again, signaling the beginning of the match, and Aasar began to move forward once again, twirling his warhammer. "Best of luck, Southerner."

Oliver took his sword out and spun it in his hand. "See you on the other side, Warchief."

They met in the middle of the arena, the crowd bursting into excited noise as they clashed weapons and exchanged attacks. Oliver's new sword was even better than his original, and it moved with a grace and power as if it had a mind of its own. They fought back and forth, neither one able to penetrate the other's defenses. The crowd was hot with anticipation as every near hit induced them to a premature cheer.

For all of Oliver's preparation, he hadn't expected Aasar to be as offensive as he was. Oliver pressed the attack at the beginning, moving in and out of various forms with ease, but Aasar sacrificed a parry for an offensive session that should have cost him a point if his warhammer handle had been an inch shorter.

Oliver could feel the muscles in his shoulders and thighs starting to reject the continued assault, but he pushed through, listening for a sign. He had guessed which crate would open first by stealing glances at the Field Archer. Oliver had been subtly moving their bout closer and closer to the crate, and just as his shoulders required a break that would not come, Oliver tumbled around the crate as the fuse exploded and the crate opened, revealing two tonfas.

Aasar hadn't expected Oliver to retreat in such a manner, nor to time it with the opening of the crate, and he stumbled to the side as his overhead attack missed its intended target and took his body with him. Oliver sheathed his sword quickly and took the two weapons, ready to initiate his plan.

He pushed the attack, the tonfas spinning awkwardly and unexpectedly as they were designed to. Aasar was taken aback, letting through five points in less than a minute, but regained his composure to land two hits of his own, although luckily for Oliver those points came from Aasar's staff and not the hammerhead.

As they moved toward another crate, Oliver had to defend against an expected strike with the hammer after leaving himself vulnerable while scoring another point. The hit with the hammer would have taken his head clean off if he had not put both his arms up together, the tonfas acting as shields for his forearms. Just as his weapons shattered from the impact of the hammer and Oliver fell, another box opened. It was on the other side of the arena, and it was a pair of sais.

Aasar had taken a splinter near his eye and was furiously trying to clear it. Oliver rolled and then ran for the open crate, hearing Aasar's footsteps behind him. As Oliver reached for the set of new weapons, Aasar leapt in the air for a thunderous overhand strike. Oliver turned at the last possible moment and parried the strike, rolling out of the way.

He spun the sais in his hands, getting used to the weight and feel of the weapons. The sais were fairly straightforward. A metal baton sprang from the center of the handle, flanked by two curved prongs. It was a perfect defensive weapon against a sword, as the shape of the weapon allowed for an easy capture of a blade, but against the warhammer it needed a bit of improvisation.

Improvisation put a smile on Oliver's face. It harkened him back to the summer and his match with Sir Declan. It wasn't the only thing that reminded him of that match.

Aasar didn't appear to care much for Oliver's reminiscing and pursued his opponent. If Oliver could get inside Aasar's long reach, he might have a chance. However, Aasar seemed prepared and compensated by keeping Oliver at arm's length. Oliver was able to spin into an area where the hammerhead couldn't impact the fight, but Aasar was ready and used the butt of his staff to gain two quick points against Oliver.

Then Aasar did something Oliver had never seen. He pulled the warhammer down so that he was holding it at its base. He then began boxing Oliver, using the hammerhead as an extension of his fist. Oliver did all he could to defend, but his weapons were no match for this type of action, and the short range of the sais offered little help for a retreat. In a flash, Aasar had scored six points and Oliver had suffered six hits to his torso. He stumbled back at the last hit, the distance offering a reprieve from Aasar's attack, but his body hurt.

Hurt, but not broken, thanks to Johanous's suit, and as Aasar let his hammer slide in his hand, a new crate revealing a staff opened directly behind Oliver. Oliver tossed the sais, upset about the lack of help they offered, and picked up the staff, windmilling it around with a smile. It would be a fight of length against length, and Oliver had been studying Reagan for years to know exactly the best way to use it.

He pushed into the attack, using the staff like a warhammer, but the lack of a hammerhead allowed him to adjust his form to that of a sword. Aasar seemed unfamiliar with the unconventional technique, and Oliver regained the lead with nine points while Aasar gained three.

Aasar scowled and caught Oliver's staff with his hammerhead, snapping it in two, thereby giving Oliver a set of kali sticks. Oliver moved swiftly into kali attacks, matching five more points to Aasar's five points. Oliver was now only ten points from victory, and he considered how he could survive for the remaining amount of time. His muscles were burning, and the pain and stress was starting to creep into his thoughts, distracting his mind from Aasar.

He looked into Aasar's eyes and saw that he too was fighting the urge to surrender. His swings with the warhammer were less precise and often left him vulnerable to a quick counterattack. The only problem Oliver faced was that he was so exhausted from defending with the rapidly degrading kali sticks that he took those opportunities to regain his strength instead of pressing an attack.

The match had stalled at the current score for over three minutes. Oliver's kali sticks had become useless when suddenly a flaming arrow was loosed over their heads and into the remaining crate, blowing the fuse and revealing the contents. In the middle of where the crate once stood was a spiked mace, a weapon that would most assuredly injure Aasar and absolutely kill Oliver if either of them were hit with it.

A memory instantly came to the forefront of Oliver's mind. Five years prior, and a crate revealing a spear. That fight had ended in tragedy and also resulted in a schism in Oliver's family that had never healed. Oliver pushed the memory away and looked at Aasar, shaking his head no. Aasar nodded in agreement and they both walked to the center of the ring, regrouping and catching their breath for the final attack.

Oliver threw his broken sticks to the side and dropped to a knee, grabbing some sand and sifting it through his hands. Aasar leaned against his warhammer, the hammerhead indenting the hard dirt. If the crowd was cheering, Oliver didn't hear it. It was as if the world was in silence, and as he sifted the sand, he felt clarity and assurance about what he would do. He saw the paths ahead of him, much like he had with Sir Declan. He made his choice.

Aasar initiated the attack and Oliver waited until the last available moment to look up, unsheathing his sword and parrying. He could now hear the crowd in full force. The brief recess had reenergized both fighters, and they moved with an elegant speed.

Oliver invented new combinations as he fought, using every form he had ever learned, whether for the sword or not. Aasar's talent with the warhammer was on full display, switching between long circular swings and quick hammerhead jabs. After both fighters transitioned from attack to defense, Oliver had come away with nine points and Aasar had scored eleven. The score was tied, with the championship point in the balance.

Now was the moment Oliver had hoped for throughout the match. The weakness he had uncovered would be Aasar's undoing. He knew precisely what to do and how to win, and he moved in for a strike, feinted, then slid the blade down to the hammerhead, causing Aasar to let go in an effort to save his fingers. The warhammer dropped to the ground. Oliver spun, sheathing his sword in one motion while kicking up the handle of the warhammer and catching it as he came back around, holding it across his body as his opponent stumbled to a kneel, unarmed.

Oliver knew this was not the way he wanted to win. It felt cheapened or somehow less honorable to win against a defenseless opponent. He'd done so in the Southern Tournament but only because he was forced to. Only because that opponent didn't respect him. Aasar was different, and Oliver flipped the hammer around and held out the handle. Aasar grabbed it and stood back up as Oliver retreated a few steps, spun back around, and took his sword out once last time.

Oliver smirked. "Your move, chief."

The two opponents moved into an attack again, each simultaneously attacking and defending, when Oliver used a flurry of moves and attacks to create an opening to strike. He saw the opening, as did Aasar, who braced for the loss of the championship, but Oliver didn't strike, instead parrying a weak jab by Aasar and moving in for an overhead slash, exposing his entire torso. Aasar saw the move and spun around, dropping to a knee quickly and jabbing into Oliver's chest as Oliver attempted to bring down his sword. Both fighters held their pose for what seemed like minutes before Oliver finally backed away, sheathing his sword and bowing to his opponent, the new Dragon Champion.

The crowd erupted as Aasar used his warhammer to stand and look around. The entire stadium was in rapture, the final match having lived up to their wildest expectations. Oliver finished his bow and looked at his friend, who was barely able to stand on his own. Oliver then looked at his family's box, seeing the various expressions on the faces of his family and friends. Yokel looked utterly disappointed and confused, unable to review his notes to see what the mistake was. Roc and Iris were cheering and clapping reluctantly.

Regan was not cheering, but rather smirking and shaking her head. She nodded her head to Oliver in approval and he nodded back, knowing she had seen it too.

Oliver walked over to Aasar to congratulate him but couldn't hear anything Aasar was trying to say over the crowds cheering. Suddenly three horns sounded and the large gate at one end of the arena opened, revealing a dozen black-armored soldiers. Oliver and Aasar saw a tall, finely armored man with sharp features and long black hair pulled back with a small circlet on his head. The man had such disdain on his face, Oliver thought the man might keel over from disgust right there and then.

Oliver looked to Aasar. "Who in the Nine Hells is this guy?"

# ENTER THE DRAGONBENDER

The coliseum fell silent except for the mocking clap coming from the disgusted man.

"Well, well, this is a joyous occasion. I see here we have the Dragon Champion!" He beckoned his soldiers to surround Oliver and Aasar. Oliver felt like a deer being surrounded by wolves, and it was not a feeling he very much enjoyed. He looked up to the stands and saw that Reagan was no longer in the box. One of the Black Hawks leaned in to speak with the High Queen but was waved away after a few moments. It looked to Oliver as though the High Queen was enjoying whatever this strange man was doing.

Oliver took stock. All the soldiers as well as the tall figure had dragon insignia on their breastplates, similar to Kiara's but with a small variation to the dragon itself. The man stalked arrogantly around Oliver and Aasar.

"This is what passes for a Dragon Champion these days? Tsk, tsk, and here I had come all the way from the Dragonlands to see you. You disappoint me, hooman."

Aasar stood up straight, not allowing his fatigued body to betray him. "Your kind will not disrespect me."

"I will do as I wish, filthy hooman, and you will not talk to me unless instructed to," the man hissed. He took out his sword and pointed it at Aasar and his warhammer, gesturing up with his head. "Pick it up... pick it up, pick it up, pick it up."

The man seemed almost deranged. Was this another Ridhan? Nine Gods, Oliver couldn't be that unlucky.

Aasar didn't move. The tall man's eyes burned with manic rage as he began to scream.

"I said pick it up, hooman! You want to be the Dragon Champion, then you will fight a true dragon!"

Oliver was confused, but it seemed as though they would not get out of this situation without a fight.

And Oliver was in no mood for another fight.

Aasar glanced at Oliver. "Stand back, my friend, I will handle this," he said, but he didn't mask his haggard expression well enough. Aasar was truly an amazing fighter, and the current Dragon Champion, but even the best fighters in the world were useless when that exhausted.

The man attacked Aasar with a speed and ferocity Oliver was not expecting. He seemed stronger than even Aasar, stronger than a human should be, and he moved with such speed that Oliver thought there must be magic at work. Aasar on his best day would barely be a match for this man, but he was absolutely outclassed in his current state.

After a few strikes that pushed Aasar to a knee, the tall man started to gloat to the hushed crowd. "This, this is your champion. He is a sorry..." and he struck Aasar again, who was unable to defend himself "...excuse..." and another attack followed "...for your champion." The tall man kicked Aasar to his back. "Oh, come on," he said, "I didn't even try. If this is the best you hoomans can muster, I must say, I will have an easier time than I thought." He sneered at Aasar. "Rise, you maggot. Rise so I may strike you down like the disease to this world that you are. A dragon gets what he wants, so rise!"

The man's voice pitched erratically, and he stalked toward Aasar as the Dragon Champion held himself up on one knee by his warhammer, not wanting to die in disgrace. The deranged man raised his sword and slashed down for a fatal hit along Aasar's exposed neck but was stopped mid-swing by a smoky sword.

Oliver parried the slash away and spun into a back kick, sending the tall man flying to his back. Oliver stood in front of Aasar, looking around as quickly as he could, expecting to be attacked by one or more of the soldiers at any moment.

The man sprawled on the ground and threw his feet and arms around in a tantrum. He then got to his feet and started screaming. "How dare you attack a dragon! How dare you attack Sekou!"

Sekou moved in for an attack on Oliver, but Oliver felt a rush of excitement and smiled, thinking only one thought: "Time to stop holding back."

Then, the crackled voice spoke to Oliver. "My turn."

Oliver defended against Sekou's attacks and pushed forward with his own combination. As strong and fast as Sekou was, Oliver matched him. He knew what it was; the lightning magic was flowing through him, giving him the power he needed. Sekou once again found himself on his back after being kicked in the head with a roundhouse from Oliver.

Sekou was incredulous, wiping his hand across his mouth and looking at the blood. His anger erupted into a berserk rage. He ran at Oliver, screaming and using a series of moves and combinations that few if any in the world could have stopped. Oliver, however, calmly saw the path ahead and within fifteen seconds had sent Sekou back to the ground, a front kick to Sekou's chest denting his breastplate.

"How dare you—" Sekou began.

"First of all, don't talk in the third person, it's lame. Second, don't get back up." Oliver stood there defiantly guarding Aasar, who was now on both of his feet.

"You dare!"

"Believe it, dumbass. You want him, you have to get through me!"

Sekou retreated outside the circle of soldiers. "Kill them!" he screeched, and the soldiers unsheathed their swords in unison, starting to descend as a single unit on the two fighters. "Kill them both!"

Oliver looked at Aasar, who was shifting his weight back and forth in anticipation of the ensuing battle. "Guess I should have just let him have you," Oliver joked. Aasar laughed and readied his warhammer.

As the soldiers came within a few feet of Oliver and Aasar, the crowd started to cheer and yell, causing the soldiers to hesitate for a moment. Suddenly, two soldiers were thrown into the others as Reagan, the Black Prince, Tyvis, Haha, and Kiara moved into the middle of the circle to stand back to back with Oliver and Aasar.

"Thought we'd join the fun, big brother," Reagan said as she readied her weapon.

"Did anyone bring anything to eat? I am starving," Haha said, and the entire group turned their heads to look at him. "What?" he asked as they all laughed and returned to their defensive positions.

"So, what's the plan?" Kiara asked as the soldiers regrouped and began to advance once more. "Please tell me you have a plan."

They all looked to Oliver, who took the command without hesitation. "First to thirty wins?" he asked with a smile, and each of the fighters in the small circle yelled and banged their chests.

Oliver took two fighters, pressing the attack before they could cross the final few feet to him. "That's five!"

Kiara spun around and crossed behind Reagan, taking the soldier flanking her left by surprise as Reagan pressed straight against her enemy. Kiara yelled out, "I have seven!" as she moved on to the next soldier.

HaHa and Tyvis teamed up and traded blows against each other's enemies, the soldiers unable to determine where the next attack would come from. HaHa's laughter could be heard over the yelling of the crowd and the cries of the soldiers as they slowly learned that they were outmatched even though they were not outmanned.

The Black Prince had taken on three soldiers, pitting their attacks against one another in a way that only he was capable of. After two had accidently taken each other out of the fight with injuries, the Black Prince put the remaining soldier down with ease. "Regarding the rules, does it count if they hit each other?" he yelled.

"No!" Reagan replied as she dispatched her soldier and moved on to help Oliver. "Double twelve with a twenty-three?" she yelled as she parried a slash from behind him.

"Nineteen with a triple eight?" Oliver countered. Reagan agreed and they moved as one single unit, dispatching the soldiers with a combination of forms.

"You were a bit slow coming out of the double parry," Reagan teased.

"Really?" Oliver asked annoyingly as they turned their attention to their friends.

Kiara had finished with her soldier, as had Tyvis and Haha with theirs. Aasar was just moving into a finishing smash with his Warhammer, then he turned back to the circle. The soldiers crawled to their master's feet as Sekou stood in shock.

He screamed in frustration and anger. "Enough! I am a dragon and you will show me the respect I deserve, you hooman pieces of filth!"

"Oh no," Kiara said.

Sekou looked like he was struggling to crawl out of his skin. The fighters gathered as one and backed up until the wall and the intruders were well in front of them on the opposite side.

"Unlike our father, I'm not afraid to be who I truly am!" Sekou screamed as his body twisted and transformed and grew, his armor melting into scales. Smoke appeared around him, filling the area where he once stood. His soldiers followed suit, though the smoke around them was smaller in size and scope. After a few moments, the silent crowd in the stadium was startled by a growl and hiss followed by a deafening roar. Out of the smoke where Sekou once stood came a powerful black dragon, spikes along its back and tail and an arrowhead-shaped head staring with lizard-like eyes. Sekou spread his wings out from his back, revealing four massive legs, and roared again, louder and with more malice.

Twelve smaller wyvern stepped out of the smoke where the soldiers once stood. They yelped and flew up to land on pillars around the crown of the Coliseum. They perched, hissing and spitting out small streams of flames, guarding the exits so the crowd might not escape.

"Do you know this guy?" Oliver asked as the group formed into a phalanx.

Kiara dropped her gaze to the ground. "He's my brother."

"That's your brother?" Reagan asked incredulously.

"Well, half-brother, but wholly bad for us. He hates me but he hates hoomans more."

"Well, that's just great," Oliver answered. "What do we do?"

Kiara looked frightened. "I, I don't know. All my life, I've done my best to avoid him. He embodies everything I've fought against in dragon culture, but that's not all. He's as dangerous as he looks, and I've never been a match for him."

HaHa chimed in from the back of their phalanx. "If he's your brother and he's a dragon, why don't you turn into one too and even the odds a bit?"

Kiara turned around with a terrified look. "I've never undergone a transmogrification."

"A what?" HaHa asked.

Aasar answered. "It means Scales can't turn into a dragon."

"Can he spit flame?" Reagan asked.

Kiara nodded solemnly. "The last time I fought Sekou, it cost me everything."

Oliver looked around at the fighters, who were staring in awe at the beast in front of them. "Everyone behind me, as close as you can!"

"Ollie, what are you doing!" Reagan yelled as she grabbed Kiara and put her directly behind Oliver.

"I don't know, but all I know is that thing looks like it's about to smoke us like a pig on a spit."

Sekou grumbled and rattled in his throat as he stared down at the puny humans. He was easily six to eight meters tall, Oliver reckoned, and even longer from snout to tail. His wings curved in and his body looked as though it could withstand a castle falling on it.

Oliver looked at his friends as Sekou reared back, inhaling. He needed a miracle and fast, but what? He could use the lightning magic, but there was no way he would be able to summon it in time, and even if he could, he wasn't certain he could control it.

The group could try and run, but given the oblong shape of the inner arena, they would soon find themselves without an escape. Sekou started to jut his head forward, opening his mouth, and a bright light within his throat seared alive with flames.

The crackled voice spoke again. "Look down."

Out of the corner of his eye, Oliver noticed movement, and just to his left, not half a meter away, the false door to his preparation room was ajar, and Yokel was standing there looking as awkward as he always did. Yokel tossed him a triangular object and in one motion, Oliver sheathed his sword and snatched the object out of the air, strapping it to his left forearm tightly. Directly behind him was Kiara, with Reagan next to her, and Tyvis, Haha, the Black Prince, and Aasar compacted closer than they thought possible behind, as the Shield of Kandaheart opened to reveal ring upon ring of expanding protection.

Oliver felt the push of flames on his arm and he fell slightly back into Kiara and Reagan, who held him steady as Sekou's fire pushed him with such force he thought he was being hit by a train. Somehow, the shield created enough protection that not one of the fighters felt the flames kiss their skin. In fact, the shield had seemingly thrown the flames up and away.

"We can't hold on like this forever!" Reagan yelled.

"We won't have to, he can only keep it up for so long!" Kiara responded, holding her arm past Oliver's head and pressing her hand on the shield.

"What's the plan, Southerner!" Aasar yelled from the back. Although the flames may not have been hitting them, they were all sweating profusely from the heat, and the shield itself was starting to singe the hairs on Oliver's arm.

Oliver looked back at Reagan and gave a smirk. "One, twelve, and twenty-four?"

"That never works!"

"Bound to work sometime," Oliver answered, feeling the flame start to diminish in strength.

"What the Hells are you two going on about!" the Black Prince yelled.

"Listen to Reagan! We have five seconds!" Oliver replied. He found his center and balance again. The plan was simple, but whenever he and Roc had tried it, they could never generate the force needed. He would just have to hope Reagan could figure out a way to make it work.

Sekou's flames receded and he pulled his head back to gaze upon the carnage. But as the smoke dissipated, the hoomans he had tried so hard to burn were still alive and spreading out around him. Reagan, Haha, and Tyvis had moved to Sekou's left, trying to distract him with attacks to his legs and tail. Kiara and the Black Prince had moved to his right, looking to attack his other legs and torso.

None of their attacks were fruitful; the dragon's hide was too hard and they had to worry about being smashed by his legs or whipped with his tail. Sekou looked amused at the antics of such insignificant creatures, but amusement soon became annoyance as they distracted him from his true prize. Sekou stared at Oliver with his reptilian eyes.

Oliver had used the distraction to ready himself. He had made a ramp with the Shield of Kandaheart by placing it on Aasar, who was crouched and loading up the strength in his legs. Oliver picked up the warhammer and nodded to Aasar. He looked to the stands as the crowds screamed in terror, unable to leave for fear of the twelve wyvern atop the stadium, waiting to pick them off.

Everything in Oliver's mind told him the plan would not work, that the physics and the arithmetic did not match up. But something within his heart and soul said that it was the right thing to do, that it would work, against all the odds.

"It will work," the crackled voice said.

"This is some way to die, I suppose," he said aloud as he began an all-out sprint toward the ramp. He hit it with his right foot and Aasar unloaded his legs as Oliver stomped on the top of the ramp with his left foot, vaulting himself up and forward. Oliver flew, aiming directly for the dragon's head, warhammer in hand, but it was not enough and Oliver knew that. He would miss his mark by two meters and fall to the ground, directly at Sekou's forelegs.

However, when Oliver should have been falling, he kept rising, still moving toward his target. Not letting the moment slip by, he cocked back the warhammer and whipped it forward, smashing it against the side of the dragon's head near his eye socket.

The force of the hit sent him falling immediately, and he would have hit the ground directly on his back, certainly breaking it, if he had not been bumped by a flailing Sekou onto his friends below. Everyone scrambled to their feet and back to the edge of the arena while Sekou screeched and moaned in pain.

The cries of his wyvern echoed through the stadium, and they descended into the arena, looking to help their master, but Sekou grabbed one of them by the neck and flung him into the wall, killing him instantly.

"Uh, I think we may have just made him angrier," HaHa said.

The injured dragon turned his bloody dead eye upon them, releasing a roar that reverberated within his throat and sent a shudder down each fighter's spine.

"Anyone else have any bright ideas?" Oliver asked.

Suddenly, a deafening roar came from overhead and a giant shadow blocked the sun. As the figure landed, blinding everyone with the sudden release of sunlight, no one said a single word. Before them stood a huge golden dragon, bigger than Sekou and immensely more ferocious. The Golden Dragon hissed and snarled at Sekou, who replied in like manner, chomping the air in front of his snout as a warning.

The Golden Dragon let out a roar louder than any noise Oliver had ever heard. Everyone clamped their hands over their ears for fear they would never hear again. The smaller wyvern fled, leaving their dead compatriot behind. Sekou snarled and snapped at the Golden Dragon, then flapped his wings and ascended into the sky, moans and roars of despair and anger fading away.

The Golden Dragon moved to where Sekou had been standing and sniffed around as if searching for something. He turned back to the group, and his eyes grew thin. He snarled.

"Throw down your weapons!" Kiara yelled.

"How about no?" Oliver kept his sword up in a defensive pose.

The Golden Dragon snarled again and bit the air toward the group and Oliver reconsidered.

"Okay, okay," he said as he and the rest of the group threw their weapons down.

"Da," Kiara said, extending a hand toward the dragon. "It's me, Kiara." Oliver did a double take. "Da?"

Tears started to fall down Kiara's face. "Da, please, you can fight this, I know you can. You're so strong. Just come back to me."

The Golden Dragon lowered his snout and pressed it against her hand, sniffing cautiously. A sudden noise from the crowd pushed the dragon's head back and he shook, hearing the sounds of his kind in the far distance. He roared and reared to his hind legs and flapped his wings into the air, leaving the Coliseum.

"That was the Dragonbender," Aasar said in disbelief.

After a moment had passed and the danger had seemingly subsided, the crowd exploded into a frenzy of cheering and clapping. Oliver and the other fighters found themselves in the middle of the arena, the adulation of a hundred thousand people putting smiles on their faces.

A horn blasted and the crowd quieted as the Championship Chairman walked out into the arena carrying a large gold trophy, trying his best not to let his robes get dirtied. The dead wyvern shuddered and the man jumped with a high-pitched squeal.

"You don't have to worry about that one," HaHa said as the herald looked at it in disgust.

"Lords and ladies, may I present to you Aasar of the Northern Tribes, your Dragon Champion!"

Everyone in the Coliseum cheered as Aasar stepped forward, getting a few pats on his back from Tyvis and the Black Prince who were standing near him.

Aasar stood next to the Chairman, towering over him, and looked to the crowd. He raised his hand and within seconds everyone hushed to hear what their Dragon Champion would say.

"Today, I am not the Dragon Champion." The people gasped but kept quiet once more as he raised his hand. "I may have won the match, but there is only one amongst us who is truly a Dragon Champion, for we are all witnesses!" Aasar beckoned Oliver over and embraced his friend in a strong hug.

"I know what you did. I saw it too. You proved yourself then, and you proved yourself when you saved me from the scaled one. You are the true Dragon Champion, my friend," Aasar whispered in Oliver's ear.

Oliver choked up at the thought of what this meant.

The herald raised his hand in the same manner that Aasar had to quiet the crowd, although it did not work. He huffed with irritation then looked to Aasar who once more quieted the people.

The herald continued. "Ahem, lords and ladies, it is my honor to present to you, for the first time in this Championship's history, your two Dragon Champions!"

At this, Aasar grabbed Oliver's wrist and flung it into the air with his own as the stands started to cheer and chant the Quartermaine name. Oliver looked around and saw Roc and Iris jumping with excitement. He looked to his friends in the arena, who were clapping and cheering along with him. Kiara gave him a wink and a smile, and the Black Prince gave him a courteous nod.

Oliver looked up toward the High Queen to see her gaze fixed on him. He felt a tingle in his mind and the crackled voice whispered, "Murderer."

# THE HIGH QUEEN OF SORAYA

On the westernmost peninsula of Goldflower sat the High Queen's monstrous castle. The rumor was that it once belonged to the Dragonbender as his southern home, but when the islands were gifted to Soraya, the High Queen insisted the castle be hers. Maybe that's why dragons and humans never found harmony together, or maybe it was just spite. Either way, the castle was said to hold many secrets about the beastly culture that now only the High Queen knew.

Oliver had never been inside the castle before, but its reputation for being creepier than the Sixth Hell was not unmerited. Spires rose high into the sky, overlooking the ocean, and Oliver could only imagine how deep its dungeons may have gone. As he entered through the outer gate, a familiar figure approached him.

"How did it go?" Oliver asked Aasar as they passed each other.

"As I had expected. She offered me positions within her armies, and I declined, as she knew I would. The Warchief and the High Queen conduct much business together, so there was not much left to talk about." Aasar seemed more reserved than usual, as if he was withholding some truth that was too hard to divulge.

"Interesting," Oliver said. "And that was all?"

Aasar hesitated. "Yes."

Oliver put a hand on his friend's shoulder. "Well, if you're ever in Starfall, my home is the big one on top of the hill."

"Aye, and if you are ever in need of assistance within the North, you need not but ask." Aasar clasped Oliver's shoulder and then left, while Oliver was ushered into the castle by the High Queen's attendants.

He made his way up the stairs to a long hallway, littered with Black Hawks every few paces on either side of the walls. He walked, not making eye contact with the motionless guards. As he approached the door at the end of the hallway, he saw two Black Hawks standing on either side, and just as he was to enter through the door, both of their spears moved down quickly, crossing each other to form an x, impeding his progress.

Oliver looked at the Black Hawk to the right, staring into familiar eyes that filled him with instant anger. "I was invited," he said curtly.

The Black Hawk on the left answered him. "Your weapons, my lord."

Oliver unbuckled his sword belt and leaned it against the wall. The left Black Hawk removed his spear and stood back into his normal position, while the right Black Hawk kept his spear slanted. "And the knife," he said.

Oliver looked at him with disgust and removed the knife from his boot and threw it into the wall. The right Black Hawk removed his spear, and Oliver thought he saw a smile beneath the helmet, but it was probably only his eyes playing a trick on him.

Oliver followed the Hawks into the room, and they forcefully seated him in a chair, then flanked him on either side as he sat and looked out a colorful window behind a large oak desk. The High Queen was nowhere to be seen and Oliver anxiously fidgeted as he waited. He rolled his shoulders, the bruises from the match earlier in the day still fresh on his body.

"So, what happens if one of you has to pee?" Oliver asked. The two Black Hawks didn't react, not even to look at him. "Is this what it was like for you? Is she really as intimidating as they all say?" Oliver asked. "So, what did she promise you? Money? Fame? Power? Women? Men?"

The Hawks subtly shifted.

"How does it feel to protect someone so—"

He was unable to finish his sentence due to the tip of a spear pointing directly at him, being blocked by a second spear. It appeared that the left Black Hawk didn't take kindly to the forthcoming insult but was rebuffed by the block from the right Black Hawk.

"We do not allow disrespect to our queen," the left Black Hawk said.

"Her Majesty requested his presence and he will not be touched," the right Black Hawk countered, and they both returned to their positions.

"Still trying to protect me?" Oliver said. "It won't make up for what you did."

"And what did I do, Oliver? What did I do to deserve so much hate from you?" the right Black Hawk asked unexpectedly.

"You left."

"Yes, I left. But don't you dare sit there and pretend to judge me and understand. You don't know what it was like."

"I think I'm about to," Oliver said as he heard the doors open behind him. He stood and bowed immediately, waiting for a command to allow him to rise once more.

"Well don't just stand there like that," the High Queen said as she motioned for him to stand.

"Your Majesty, it is truly an honor to be in your presence. May the Nine bless—"

"Cease the pleasantries," the High Queen said without looking up from the book she had fingered through as she walked behind her desk. She dismissed the Black Hawks with a wave of her hand and Oliver stood awkwardly waiting.

She was tall for a woman and didn't look a day over thirty years of age. Oliver couldn't get past her beauty. She had features that would shame even the prettiest woman in the South. Her dress hugged her curves but kept her breasts hidden to the imagination. A crown adorned the top of her head and sparkled in the light when she moved. Songs and ballads had been written over the years about her beauty, but in that moment, Oliver thought they had never done her justice. The High Queen had ruled this land for hundreds of years but seemingly never aged. The Nine Gods had blessed her centuries ago, stating she was the chosen vessel of their will and thus was granted immortality. Warrior, leader, and religious symbol, she was everything a person could achieve in a hundred lifetimes—because she had lived a hundred lifetimes.

Standing now in front of this seeming goddess sent Oliver into a tailspin of thoughts. Was he attracted to her right now? Was he awed by her power?

The High Queen slammed her book closed and rubbed the bridge of her nose. "So, you are the other Dragon Champion. It seems as though your family has a penchant for doing things... how would I say, unorthodoxly."

"I apologize for any grievance I may have caused you, your Majesty," Oliver said, eating the words as he said them.

The High Queen ignored him and moved to a table adorned with different sizes of bottles filled with various liquids. She poured two glasses and brought them over to Oliver, handing him one and leaning against the desk.

Haralabos had tried to warn him against her, but warn him against what? This woman was wonderful, beautiful, sexy, intelligent... Oliver's brow furled. Why was he thinking this way? She smelled incredible and—

"Tell me, Lord Quartermaine, are you happy?"

'Of course, your Majesty."

"And, are the people in your little Southern city happy?"

"We live by the mercy and strength of your grace."

"Ah, but that is not the question, is it. Answer your queen, are the people happy?" She took a sip of her drink. Oliver drank from his cup and the liquid felt as though a thousand shards of glass had torn down his throat and into his stomach. Oliver suppressed a cough and began to try and answer the question.

Suddenly he felt lightheaded and his mind open to any suggestion. A burning sensation started in his hands and moved throughout his body until he heard the crackled voice once again. "Not this time."

Regaining his composure, he answered her. "I believe the people are happy, your Majesty, because they know your guidance and leadership protect the—"

"Enough! I expected more from a Southerner, but it seems you are the same as all the others." She started to shuffle through papers. "As you know, the Dragon Champion is afforded any number of opportunities. Assuredly by now many kings and queens have offered you positions of high rank within their courts and so forth."

Oliver stood there barely listening, devastated by what the High Queen had accused him of.

"Too many kings," Oliver blurted out, immediately recognizing that he had just spoken out of turn and without permission in front of the most powerful person in the world.

The High Queen looked quickly to Oliver, her eyes squinting slightly. "What did you say?"

"I'm sorry, Your Majesty," Oliver said, lowering into a bow. "I spoke out of turn."

"I asked you a question."

"Too many kings, your Majesty. I had attendants waiting in my preparation room before I even returned underneath the stadium. As you said, they came armed with positions within their courts. I simply was saying there were—"

"Too many kings," the High Queen repeated, scratching her left breast as if it would never stop itching. Maybe it was an old injury from her time of conquest.

Oliver thought about all he had learned this past year, and all that Haralabos had told him. How the High Queen had defeated his Knights of Nine, and how Haralabos wanted Oliver to destroy her. Haralabos had made her out to be a monster, but she didn't seem so bad, and from everything he could tell, Soraya had never been more prosperous. Haralabos must have been mistaken, or maybe Oliver was caught in the middle of some ancient grudge he knew nothing about.

He pondered whether it was the High Queen he should be helping and not some half-dead has-been from a time long ago. Did she know of the threat of the Spider's Web? The thought of mentioning magic in her presence sent a chill down his back and he dismissed the idea. If there was anything he shouldn't discuss with the High Queen, it was magic.

The High Queen stared silently at Oliver as he daydreamed. Then he noticed the silence. Then she noticed the silence. Then Oliver panicked and said the first thing that came to mind.

That was his mistake.

"So, your Majesty, what did you think of the match?"

A single eyebrow raised, and she answered his question with one of her own. "Informative. Do tell me where you procured that Relic."

Oliver looked away. Relic? Where had he heard that word before?

Oh no.

"I'm sorry, my queen, what do you mean?" Oliver lied.

She walked over to Oliver and bent down, and he could smell her perfume and see the large necklace hiding the treasures beneath her dress. Was the High Queen flirting with him? Was this a sign? Was he supposed to refuse an advance from the most powerful, influential, and seductive woman in all the world?

Would Oliver be the Black Prince's new stepfather?

Oliver laughed, but only on the inside as High Queen Amukamora whispered into his ear. "I think you know exactly what I mean." She caressed his cheek with the back of her hand and he nearly melted in his seat.

The crackled voice spoke up once more. "Murderer."

Unthinking, Oliver relayed the message. "Murderer."

Fire raged in the High Queen's eyes. "What did you say?"

"Nothing, Your Majesty."

She pushed away from Oliver and straightened her dress, rubbing her left breast once again. She spun around quickly, a stern expression on her face. "I will give you the same offer I give every Dragon Champion. You may be a Captain in the Imperial Army, commanding your own squadron of soldiers."

"That is entirely too generous, Your Majesty."

"My attendant will draw up the papers," she said, moving back behind her desk.

Oliver spoke up quickly. "I apologize, but you misunderstand." She looked up quickly and bore down at him, waiting for him to finish his response. "I cannot accept. I believe my fate lies elsewhere."

"You will take the position of Captain, and you will be stationed at the Gate of Kandaheart, as your brother was. Prove yourself useful to me, I will consider something more suited to your station."

Oliver looked at the High Queen, wondering if this was the same pitch she had given his brother all those years ago. What had she said to make him turn his back on his family? To turn his back on Oliver.

Growing impatient, the High Queen continued. "I only make this offer once. Do not think to test me. Tell me what it is that you want." Her famous temper was starting to simmer, and the conversation seemed to cause her itch to return.

He didn't know if it was the drink, the stress of being in her presence, or the lightning magic now reverberating through his body, but Oliver felt oddly combative. Dangerous, even.

"I've been told a dragon knows what he wants, and being the Dragon Champion, I must decline your offer."

"I've always hated you Quartermaines. Every last one of you." Her voice was steady, but she may as well have been screaming at Oliver. She took her glass and smashed it against a wall, and the doors opened behind Oliver and there were spears at his throat in an instant.

The High Queen fixed her hair and flicked her hand. "He may leave now."

Oliver left and pulled his knife out of the wall of the hallway as the Black Hawks closed the doors behind him. Beginning to walk down the hall, he heard a grunt from behind him and turned to see the right Black Hawk motioning toward the sword Oliver had left behind.

Oliver looked at it then turned to keep walking. "Keep it, it's yours anyway."

# AROUND THE WORLD IN ONE NIGHT

"**Y**ou have to go to the banquet!" Reagan yelled.

"I don't want to." Oliver was lying in bed, emotionally drained, physically exhausted, and mentally racing. All he wanted was to curl up and fall asleep.

"You're the Dragon Champion, you're expected to go!" Reagan said, whacking him with a pillow.

Oliver caught the pillow and pulled it tightly over his head. "No. You can't make me."

Reagan jumped up and frog-splashed on top of her brother, who groaned and yelped at the assault on his many bruised ribs. She took another pillow and continued to hit him. "You have to go to the banquet, you have to dance, and you have to—"

"Blah, blah, blah, blah, blah, blah… blah." Oliver teased.

Reagan found the soft spot near her brother's armpit and started to torture him in the most inexcusable way possible. Oliver shrilled as the tickling onslaught continued and at one point made many threats of punching his sister in the face if she did not retreat. She did not retreat but instead tickled him even more until he had fallen on the floor and was literally crying from laughter and pain.

"This is a blatant disrespect of my personal space!" Oliver yelled as he tumbled around on the floor, tangled in a mess of blankets.

Reagan stood on top of the bed, hip jutted out to one side and her arms crossed. "So, you gonna get dressed or do I have to call in reinforcements? We all know Roc doesn't play nice when it comes to a tickle attack." She unfolded her arms and moved her fingers like the legs of a spider, and Oliver forfeited any notion he would be able to sleep early.

He stood, threw his blanket at her in protest, and walked into his closet, rummaging around for something to wear. The banquet was the dinner that immediately followed any tournament, and just as Roc had been expected to go to the Homecoming Banquet, Oliver as one of the Dragon Champions was expected to attend this one. If this was a smaller tournament in some no-nothing keep, he might have gotten away with skipping out. But this wasn't some no-nothing keep, and his sister was correct, as usual.

Nine Gods, he hated when she was right.

After dressing in a silver suit with blue inlays, he spun around in front of the vanity mirror, admiring himself. Reagan sat at the edge of the bed, giggling.

"Oh no, if I have to go, you do too. I'll see you in the carriage." Oliver threw a pillow at her head and exited the room before she could reciprocate. He turned in a circle, undecided where to go, until his feet took him to Iris's room.

"Knock, knock," Oliver said.

"People typically knock and not just say it."

"Big day today, huh?" Oliver asked, leaning against the doorframe.

"Yes." She carried on reading her book.

"So, there's this party that I'm invited to, and I was wondering if you might want to possibly maybe attend with me?"

"No, thank you."

"Why not? We're supposed to be together. How would it look if I show up without you?"

Iris snapped her book closed and just stared at Oliver, shaking her head.

"What?" Oliver asked.

"You don't get it, do you?"

Oliver slouched to the ground. "Obviously I don't."

Iris sat on the ground in front of him. "I come to this island and we fight. I watch you today and it's the most nerve-wracking and dangerous thing I've ever seen. YOU WERE ALMOST BROILED BY A DRAGON. But when do I see you? Now. I've spent all day waiting for you and you come to me now, because you need something." Her voice cracked.

Oliver sat in stunned silence.

She continued. "We're supposed to be partners. We're supposed to love each other, and it seems like I just don't matter to you. Not like I used to."

Oliver grabbed her hand, and she let him. He didn't have the words to express his feelings nor his confusion. "I do love you," he said.

"I love you too but is that enough?"

Oliver couldn't contain himself any longer and tried to pull her in for a hug. "Of course it's enough. It's more than enough." He hugged her tight and never wanted to let go. He wanted to rededicate himself fully to her, right here and right now. He would forget every confusing feeling he ever had and love this person he was with. Oliver and Iris would go to the banquet, dance and kiss and everything would be as it should be.

"You should get dressed," Oliver said, kissing her on the top of her head.

"Why?"

"So we won't be late for the banquet."

"I'm not going."

"What do you mean? You have to go! I love you and you love me, remember all that?"

"I'm still upset with you and I don't want to go to a fancy party in front of all those fancy lords from all over Soraya who will be judging me the moment we walk in."

"Are you kidding me!"

"You don't understand, I can't, I just can't."

"Fine."

"No, now you're mad at me," she cried.

"I'm not mad at you."

"Yes, you are."

"No, I'm not, I said it's fine. I'll just go by myself."

Oliver felt betrayed. He had just fought in the most epic battle of his life and was crowned the Dragon Champion in the most dramatic way possible. He'd just gone toe-to-toe with the High Queen herself and rejected her offer. He was so tired but also so excited. He wanted to celebrate, to dance, to drink, and to do all of that with the person he loved. What was Iris's problem? Why she was being this way?

He stormed off, leaving her to her books. He wanted to do the right thing, he wanted to love her fully, but he was angry and once again confused. Confused about what he should be doing, who he should be with, how he should feel.

"No Iris?" Reagan asked at the carriage.

"No."

"Do you want to—"

"No."

"Okay, okay. Don't bite my head off," she said as they got into the carriage.

"I'm sorry, it's just frustrating. I'll be okay."

"It's probably for the better anyway," Reagan began. "You never know who might be at a party like this one."

Oliver just stared out the carriage window. Anger and sadness clouded his mind, but at her words a single ray of light burst through.

"What do you mean?" He turned to see his sister wearing a silver mask that covered the top half of her face.

"It's a masquerade banquet. Anyone can be anyone there." She handed Oliver a mask of his own, simple and elegant. They sat in silence the rest of the ride, letting the dimming light of the oncoming night produce the quiet sounds of the island.

Oliver wondered if Pathfinder would be there, wearing an entirely different mask, or whether she would still be scouting Ridhan's fortress for a weakness. He missed her so much, and this trip had not produced the kind of time he had planned to spend with her. He missed his friend, at the very least, and the way she made him feel special.

Although if it was a special feeling he was after, there was only one person on this island who caused a raging fire within his body. The Dragon Princess most assuredly would be at the banquet, and that friendship was new and exciting and something entirely different. There was a connection between them that ran deep, be it from their brief time together overlooking the ocean or their time battling her brother.

What a strange family, but I'm one to talk.

His pain about his hot and cold relationship with Iris caused his heart to physically ache, but the prospect of merriment and, dare he think it, fun at the banquet lifted his spirits, even if only slightly. Reagan was right, as she always was. He needed to go to the banquet.

The Coliseum had been transformed into a riot of tents, each one its own unique setting with its own unique people. Each tent represented a kingdom of Soraya, and in the middle stood a much larger tent, which obviously represented Romir, the only kingdom without a Dragon

Champion contender.

Oliver put on his mask and hopped out of the carriage before it made its way up the line to the entrance, unwilling to wait any longer. He scooted past the heralds and into the first tent he could hide in, followed by Reagan. They looked around in awe at the Mercyhold tent.

The tent was filled with decorations from the small mountainous kingdom. Oliver had never spent much time in the region, beyond a quick stop for the occasional tournament, but the natural beauty it was known for radiated everywhere. Oliver gazed in amazement and turned to his sister.

"So, Rea, where should we start?"

"Sorry, Ollie, but I already have a date," she said with a wink.

"You know I hate you, right?"

Reagan stood on her tip toes and kissed Oliver on his metal mask cheek. "Love you too, big brother. Try and have some fun tonight." She disappeared through an exit, off to another showcased kingdom, and Oliver was stuck, alone, swaying awkwardly to the Mercyhelfian music.

He wandered over to a table, unable to recognize anyone with their masks on. No one seemed to recognize him either, which felt somewhat peaceful. The food being served in this tent were all the delicacies one would expect from Mercyhold—berries and nuts, fish and venison, hearty vegetables and birds of every type, save any birds of prey. And of course, there was the staple of the marshland coast, rice. Every delicacy was complemented with rice in various forms. Oliver tried to mingle but often found himself on the outside looking in as he never could quite get the hang of their particular dialect of Sorayian.

"Interesting place. Almost reminds me of home," a voice said next to him. Oliver smiled, recognizing the voice. It was Kiara, dressed in a silver strapless gown that hugged her body at every curve and feature. Oliver eyed her down to the ground, stunned by her beauty.

"My eyes are up here, Ollie. Do you mind if I call you that? I really like it, but you said only your sister calls you it, and I definitely don't want to be confused with her. She sure is something else. Mostly people call me Kiara, though from time to time someone will try Kiki, to which I say, 'I am not a delivery service,' but they never understand."

Oliver put a finger over her lips to shush her. "You look incredible," he said. He marveled at her raven dark hair streaked with white strands.

Kiara blushed and smiled. "You don't look half bad yourself, though your tie is a bit…" And as she talked, she adjusted his tie for him, looking up into his eyes and never at the tie itself.

"How did you know it was me?"

Kiara wrinkled her nose and sniffed. "You hoomans have your own scents." She laughed and downed an entire cup of wine before looking around for more. Oliver was transfixed. This curious girl radiated joy and had a bounce to her life he envied.

Glover Danson walked over to Kiara and Oliver, removing his mask quickly to let them know it was him. "Oliver, congratulations! Kiara! It's so nice to see you in my tent. I'm sorry about earlier today. Samaje and I were, uh, occupied. When we finally made it into the stands, Oliver and Aasar were being cheered as Dragon Champions."

Oliver shook Glover's outstretched arm and smiled. "Don't worry about it. So, you and Samaje?" Glover's face quickly shied away as Kiara giggled and Oliver gave the contender a hearty punch to the shoulder.

A commotion at the entrance of the tent heralded Sekou's arrival. He was a human again, wearing a patch over his smashed eye.

Kiara spit out her drink and almost laughed at the sight of him. "Uh oh, I think we're in trouble."

"Why do you say that?" Oliver asked.

"Because he knows your scent too."

"Who's the pirate?" Glover asked.

Oliver put his cup down. "You know all that craziness you missed today? Well that's the guy who started it all. Would you be so kind as to buy us a little time to escape?"

Glover clapped Oliver's shoulder and kissed Kiara's hand lightly before heading to intercept Sekou. Kiara giggled and took Oliver's hand as they rushed through the back exit and into another tent themed after Kandaheart. If Romir was a beacon of the future and what was to come, Kandaheart was an ode to the past. Kiara was visibly impressed as she looked around. Kandaheart was the oldest kingdom in Soraya and it loved its traditions and its palette of neutral and earth tone colors.

"This place is magnificent," Kiara said as she twirled around, taking in the walled labyrinth kingdom.

"You've never been to Kandaheart before?" Oliver asked as they moved through the crowd.

"No, I've never been anywhere south except for Dragon's Treasure."

"Oh, well then."

Oliver pondered as the dragon girl took him from statue to statue and painting to painting, admiring everything and everyone. The native Kandaharim were dressed in their traditional robes, and Kiara took it upon herself to ask each one about the intricacies of their jewelry and patterns. Her curiosity was infectious and there wasn't a person they met who didn't go into long-winded stories as she attentively listened. Oliver felt a quiet peacefulness as he observed his odd friend. For all his gregariousness, she may have been more "Oliver" than Oliver was.

"We have to go now," Oliver interrupted.

"No, you've got to listen to this," she said as she tugged Oliver closer to her. Oliver smelled her perfume and wondered if he could tell the difference between a human and, well, whatever she technically was.

The Kandaharim sipped his drink and continued his story. "... and you must understand, my Dragon Princess, I wouldn't tell anyone this except you." Kiara giggled flirtatiously and the man was giddy to divulge his secret information. "There are rumors coming from the mountain pass. An army gathering within those mountains, an army of those foul creatures."

Oliver had one eye at the entrance but couldn't help but listen to Old Man Deptok's story. Oliver had recognized the plump man's deep, rattling voice but let the anonymity stay with the storyteller. He did have one minor plot hole to poke into Deptok's tale, though.

"Isn't that why the Imperial Army is stationed there?"

Deptok motioned them with a finger. "The goblin army isn't amassing on our side of the mountains, but on the other."

Kiara looked concerned, but Oliver's concern was more immediate, and he took hold of Kiara's head and pointed her toward the raging "dragon in the pottery shop."

"Sorry, my lord, you've been lovely, but we must be going." Kira kissed him on the mask and pulled Oliver as they laughed all the way into the next tent.

"Hold up, hold up, hold up," Oliver huffed. "I have an idea."

"Ooooohhhh, I like ideas. Tonight, is a night full of ideas!" Kiara sang. She was utterly crazy, possibly on some type of drift, but Oliver didn't care.

"You've never been anywhere in Soraya, so how about we visit. I'll show you the world, or at least the world in these tents…"

Kiara's brow raised. "Intriguing, little hooman."

"… and you use that super nose of yours to let me know when your brother comes by. I'd like to survive the night."

Kiara's tapped her nose. "Fair trade. So where are we now?"

"Hamstead," Oliver said, following the circular route around Soraya. Hamstead was a minor kingdom, technically part of Kandaheart, and only represented here because Romir had failed to send a championship contender. Because Hamstead had sent HaHa Dix, they were afforded a tent of their own, albeit smaller and less glamorous than the others.

Kiara's nose had identified HaHa, who joined them on their quest to travel the world. Because the Hamstead tent offered less to do, they soon made their way into the Northern Tribes tent. That tent was the most eclectic by far, with each of the twelve tribes represented in their own unique way.

"Reagan? What are you doing here?" Oliver asked, surprised.

"Told you I had a date, Ollie," she said as Aasar spun her around, letting her make him look better at dancing than he was.

"I see you have found yourself a date… or two," Reagan said as she finished her spin. "What are you all up to?"

HaHa was the first to respond. "We're running from Sekou."

"And going for a tour of Soraya," Kiara explained, pulling Oliver close. Reagan shot Oliver a look, who tried to avoid eye contact with his sister as much as he possibly could. He was saved by the sound of manic Sekou screaming as he tripped into the tent.

"That's our cue! Where to next, Ollie?" Kiara asked and he felt an elbow to his kidney as he mentally traveled through the country in his mind.

"Ow! Next is Land's End. Let's go!"

HaHa took out a small pellet and tossed it into the air. "This might help." He threw it over at Sekou, and smoke as well as an odd odor filled the room while the friends escaped into Land's End. Oliver, Kiara, HaHa, Aasar, and Reagan stood stunned at the dreary dullness of it all. Land's End had no character, no ambiance, and no fun. There wasn't even any music playing. Oliver was pretty sure someone was dying from boredom, but it was just Haha audibly whining about being in this place.

"So, this is the capital?" Kiara asked. "How…"

"Lame?" Oliver offered up.

"Boring," Haha said.

"Quaint. I was going to say quaint," Kiara corrected.

Aasar looked at Reagan, who interpreted. "It's a nice way of saying it sucks."

"Sucks?" Aasar looked confused.

"What she means is, it lacks culture," a voice from behind them said. "Welcome, contenders, and Reagan." It was the Black Prince, and they all bowed accordingly. "What brings you all to our humble tent?" With the lack of music, they could hear Sekou causing destruction in the Northern Tribes tent and the Black Prince shook his head. "Ah, yes, I heard he was here."

Oliver began. "Yep, her brother is—"

"Half-brother," Reagan corrected.

"I knew I liked you," Kiara said.

"And he's been tracking us because—" Oliver started to explain.

"He can smell you. I know a thing or two about dragons." The Black Prince winked at Kiara, who blushed into Reagan's shoulder. Oliver felt a pang of jealousy, and quickly put it in a box and buried the feeling deep within his mind temple, hoping to lock it away forever.

HaHa slapped the Black Prince on the back, and two Black Hawks stepped forward in an instant, but the Black Prince put up a hand to wave them off. Haha was undeterred by the Hawks. "We're on an adventure, Your Royal Royalness. You coming with?"

They all looked at the Black Prince and he stared around at the dreadful room. He turned to the two Black Hawks.

"There's a man venturing after my friends and me."

The Black Hawks looked at each other and bumped fists before wheeling around and heading toward the Northern Tribes tent.

"That will occupy him for a while. Shall we? I hear the Floating Isles have some exquisite ales." The Black Prince led the way and the rest of the group looked at each other gleefully and hollered as they followed him.

The Floating Isles were as strange as their people. Large stones floated in the air, as their islands did, and no one's feet touched the ground below. The group jumped and stepped from stone to stone as they pushed and pulled each other, floating and flying around the tent.

"Tyvis! We're on an adventure, will you come join us?" Kiara called as she floated around him. Tyvis was sitting with crossed legs, sipping a cup with both hands.

"Everyone is doing it!" Reagan giggled as she bumped into Kiara.

"These are so much fun!" Oliver and HaHa were swinging around in circles on their floating stones. Aasar looked out of his element as he spun around uncontrollably, whereas the Black Prince mastered his stone and stood watch, waiting for a sign from their hunter. He signaled to the group and they floated to the next exit, Tyvis roping the larger Aasar like he had caught a deer in the forest.

"You're in?" HaHa asked excitedly.

Tyvis grunted and everyone yelled, "HE'S IN!"

They made their way into the Southern tent, a riot of colors. Its culture was as if every tent in all Soraya had merged into one perfect tapestry. Even the dryness of Land's End seemed to come through.

"Home sweet home," Oliver said as he took a cup of wine and toasted. "Cheers!"

A rush of people from every entrance to the tent plowed through them and the group of friends was split apart. Oliver tried to find Kiara in the crowd, but the different masks and people confused his eyes. He searched and searched but found no sign of any of his friends. But he did see a familiar sight, with a familiar mask.

"Fancy seeing you here," he said, tapping Pathfinder on the shoulder.

"Excuse me, do I know you?"

"I'm just a Southern lord, looking for a dance."

Pathfinder turned away. "You know I hate that."

Oliver was feeling the effects of all the different drinks he had consumed throughout the evening. "Oh come on, remember our dance in Romir?"

Pathfinder grabbed him by the collar, anger in her eyes. "Yes, I remember. Do you?"

The sight of Po lying in the alleyway flashed into his mind, and his enthusiasm fell, but before he could answer her, Kiara came from behind and pulled him away.

"There you are! We've been looking all over for you!"

"And who are you?" Pathfinder asked coldly.

Kiara put her finger on Pathfinder's mouth, shushing her. "It's a secret."

Oliver thought Pathfinder might remove her mask and bite Kiara's finger off but was relieved when the Dragon Princess pulled him away and into a sea of people. He could hear HaHa laughing above the music and crowd, but not above Sekou's tirade as the one-eyed man stormed into their tent.

"We've run out of tents!" HaHa said as the group met up once more.

"No, there's still one more," Reagan said, pulling the train of people into the middle tent of Romir. Oliver dropped his cup and no one in the group made a sound or took a breath. Bigger than all the other tents, this one spanned most of the arena and was adorned in iron and steel and machinery of all kinds. Yokel would have loved it.

And he did. Oliver spotted his gangly friend trying to talk to a much older woman in a peacock mask.

"YOKEL!"

Yokel turned around, shaking. "Uh, do I kn-know you?"

Oliver picked him up in a big hug. "It's me, you dumb goof."

"Oh." Yokel laughed nervously. "Oliver, what are you doing here?"

HaHa tumbled over, put his hands around Yokel's shoulders, and pointed to the vast tent in front of him. "We're on a mission from a god."

Oliver and HaHa burst out laughing and Yokel tried to join them but could only muster a half measure, since he didn't understand the joke.

The orchestra in the tent had just finished a song and began transitioning into the next when Kiara ran over and excitedly pulled on Oliver's arms. "Oh this is one of my favorites. Come dance with meeeeeee!"

"Duty calls," Oliver said to Yokel as he was whisked away.

Yokel tried to grab Oliver. "Oliver, wait, wait, don't," but it was too late.

Kiara and Oliver walked briskly to the center of the quickly emptying dance floor. She spun around, letting Oliver walk her into the beginning of a classic waltz as the music started. She followed him for a few steps then pulled herself in, moving up to his ear.

"So, Ollie, who are we trying to make jealous tonight?"

Oliver caught a memory and put it aside as he smiled. "Everybody."

She spun out and as the tempo and the beat of the music increased, they increased the pace of their waltz. Then Kiara started to improvise, sometimes alone and sometimes with Oliver. It took Oliver a few tries to find her rhythm, but once he did, they put on a display of dancing like none in the room had seen that night.

Oliver spun Kiara into his arms and lifted her up, holding her by one arm and his other hand intertwined with hers. He turned on his heel and she never lost eye contact with him, even when it seemed he would undoubtedly lose his balance. But he never did, and when he put her back down, everyone clapped. They moved in such perfect sync it was as if they had rehearsed the routine hundreds of times. He spun her one last time and ended in a low dip where he held her leg up and their faces were mere inches apart.

The song ended and they held the pose, breathing heavily into each other, not wanting to let go of the moment. The spectators finished clapping and a new song began, and more people joined them on the dance floor. Oliver slowly brought Kiara out of the dip and held her closely. He wanted this moment to last as long as it possibly could; he was mesmerized by this incredible dragon girl. Oliver felt three hearts beat as one as their chests pressed together, and Oliver didn't know what to do next. He couldn't let go of her, fearing it was a mirage and she would disappear the moment he let go, but he also couldn't kiss her, not here, not like this. They had shared a kiss once, and the memory of it was perfect and untouchable. Kiara turned her head to lay it on his shoulder, then abruptly pulled away.

Oliver looked around, confused. "Pathfinder?"

But the mask was wrong, and her true identity was confirmed when the mask was taken off to reveal Iris, a mix of anger and tears covering her face. She turned and ran and when Oliver tried to pursue her, he was stopped by a masked Roc.

"Let her be," he advised.

"No, it's not what it looks like. I have to explain," Oliver offered as his mind fought against his drunken euphoria.

"It's not going to do either of you any good if you fight right now."

"It was just a dance," Oliver explained, losing confidence.

"Tonight is not the night, trust me. I'll talk to her." Roc patted Oliver on the back and left.

Oliver's mind was reeling, and he put his head in his hands to try and make sense of it all. Why was Iris here? She had made such a big issue about not coming and now she was here. He was so confused.

"It is a strange thing," the Black Prince said as he offered Oliver a cup. "You can spend your entire life looking for perfection, and when you find it, you resist."

They both looked out at the dance floor where they saw Kiara, standing alone where Oliver had left her. His heart ached but he didn't know what for; all he knew is that he felt horrible. Kiara disappeared into a group of dancers, and Oliver stood there panicked.

"Ollie, go get her," Reagan said, a drink in one hand and Aasar on the other.

"Go get who?" Was he supposed to run after Iris or run after Kiara? Reagan didn't give him an answer, but his heart did, and his feet moved to the chase.

"Can't a girl step away for some fresh air alone?" Kiara said as she took a sip of her drink on the empty concourse of the Coliseum. Oliver joined her where she stood on a balcony overlooking the arena full of tents. It had taken Oliver three separate bribes with the slaves to find her, and by then his cup was as dry as his throat.

Oliver grabbed her drink and gulped it down entirely as Kiara protested. "Hey! That was mine!"

Oliver shook the liquid in his mouth. "I'll get you a new one back in the tent."

"Oliver, what are we doing?"

"Showing you a tour of the world and trying to avoid your—"

"No, I mean, what are WE doing. I have never met a more confusing hooman, I swear." She began pacing around, and Oliver tried to gather his thoughts. He knew what she was asking but he didn't have an answer; at least not a good one.

"I don't know," he finally said.

"Then why are you in such a tizzy?"

"What's a tizzy?"

"You know, a tizzy. Like, 'oh she's all in a tizzy because she couldn't get her own drake,' things like that."

Oliver looked at her. "First off, you can't use the word in the definition of the word. Second off, that's not a real example."

"Yes, it is. That actually happened with a girl I knew when I was younger."

"Oh yea? What was her name then?"

After a longer than normal hesitation, Kiara replied. "Tizzy."

They both laughed at the ridiculousness of the conversation and then sat quietly for a moment.

Oliver was the first to speak. "I don't know what to do. I don't know what I want. I'm not a very good dragon, it would seem."

Kiara grabbed his hand and interlaced her fingers with his. "No, you are not. That's one of the things I like about you."

"You like me?"

"Like about you," she answered, booping him on the nose.

Oliver smiled. "I haven't had this much fun in a very long time."

Kiara pulled his hand playfully. "Dragons are fun."

"You're telling me. My heart is in such a weird place at the moment."

Kiara put his hand on her chest, and he felt a single beat under his fingertips. "Dragons have two hearts for two kinds of love. One for the clan and one for the mate."

"What's it mean when they beat together?" Oliver asked.

Kiara noticed her own heart beats and pushed his hand away, scooching back and looking anxiously for her cup.

Oliver didn't know what to make of his comment and cast around for a change of subject. "So, what did you think of Soraya?"

"It was quite peculiar."

Oliver thought about each tent they had traveled through and wondered how well they actually represented the world he knew. Then he wondered how well he thought he knew the world. Then he spiraled into contemplating if he knew anything at all.

"You're such a curious little hooman," Kiara said, cocking her head.

"I know," Oliver said. "But why this time?"

"You spend all this time in your mind, when the world in front of you is alive and wondrous."

"The world isn't like it is in those tents, dragon girl. It's nothing like that at all. It's full of people, and for the most part, the people are good. But a few are bad, and their voices are loud and destructive."

Kiara cupped his face in her hands. "Tell me about these bad people."

"They're very bad people," Oliver said through smushed lips. He grabbed her wrists and pulled them down. "I don't know who they all are, but I have to stop them." The weight of his burdens sat heavy on his shoulders, and he felt like he might collapse. He always felt this way, but still he trudged on. "Because I'm not just Oliver Quartermaine."

"You're a Dragon Champion."

"No." Oliver knew he shouldn't do what he was about to, but he felt like he needed to. For some reason, he needed Kiara to be tethered to his life, even if it meant that tether was through a secret. He stood up and moved into Form Zero, dancing with himself until the lightning magic sparked to life around his hands.

Kiara's eyes widened but she didn't run, which Oliver was relieved to see. She came close to touch the lightning, but just as she was about to be shocked, the lightning magic dissipated. She cupped his hands tightly and looked around for any spies.

"You shouldn't have done that," she said.

"I'm tired of hiding."

"Hoomans don't have magic."

"I do."

"Your queen will have you killed if she finds out." She hugged Oliver tightly. "Why you?"

That was a question Oliver didn't want to think about. He was never supposed to have the lightning magic; it was always meant for Po. But the thought of letting go of it was one Oliver hadn't come to terms with.

"It was an accident," he finally responded.

Kiara pulled away slightly and looked deep into his soul with her violet eyes. "What will you do then? Play pretend in fancy tournaments for the rest of your life?"

"No, I think those days are over for me." Oliver thought about Po and Haralabos, and Ridhan and the Spider's Web, and knew that once he returned to Starfall, nothing would be the same. "I think I'm meant for more."

"Like what?" Kiara asked mischievously.

Oliver smiled. "Like saving the world and saving magic."

"That's a lot for one hooman to do. If you were a dragon, maybe you could pull it off, but you, Oliver, can't do it alone."

She was right, Oliver thought, he couldn't do it all himself; Satine had told him as much. He would need help, and he could find it. He had his friends, Po and Yokel and Roc. He had Pathfinder and Windrunner, and even Reagan. But that was not all. He'd spent this championship, and more specifically tonight, sparking new friendships, and together, he thought, they could do anything. The time for pretending was over for Oliver, and he wanted to go out on his own terms.

Oliver took Kiara's hand and raced back down to the Romirian tent. Kiara jerked Oliver to a stop, sniffing and pointing to the center of the tent. "He's here." In the center of the dance floor stood Sekou, who was awkwardly sniffing the air where Oliver and Kiara had danced.

Oliver walked up to him. "Hey, worm!"

Sekou's eye widened as he saw his prey approaching him. "You dare disrespect me?" he yelled, but before he could finish his insult Oliver punched him between his eyes, knocking him out. Oliver jumped and shook his hand as it was definitely some kind of broken.

"You idiot!" Kiara yelled, spitting into her hands and placing Oliver's broken one between them. "Dragon heads are notoriously thick!"

"Yep, I know that now!" Oliver yelped as he struggled against the pressure of Kiara's grip. She let go and he looked at his hand, which was now less broken but still bruised. The Black Prince, Aasar, Reagan, HaHa, and Tyvis encircled Oliver as he bent down and unlaced his boots, setting them on the ground. He was standing on the spot of his final match with Aasar, the final match of his career. Tournaments were no longer in his future, for he knew now what he needed to dedicate his life toward.

The Black Prince was the first to follow him, his boots coming off quickly and placed next to Oliver's. HaHa, Aasar, Tyvis and Kiara all did the same while Sekou lay unconscious on the ground next to them. The tent was silent, until HaHa yelled, "Your Dragon Champion, everybody!" The music started back up, and the friends whooped and yelled, starting a raucous and energetic dance that spread to everyone else in the tent.

In the middle of the dancing, Oliver pulled Kiara close. "I'm not alone," he whispered, and they all danced the night away, even Tyvis, who had absolutely no rhythm.

# QUEST: IMPOSSIBLE

"It's impossible." Pathfinder slugged back a goblet of ale underneath her mask.

"Speaking purely academically, I'd have t-to agree," Yokel said, poring over the improvised blueprints of the Shipwight Fortress.

Oliver looked them over and sighed. "What if we—"

"Nope," Windrunner answered.

"But here we could—"

"Can't be done," Pathfinder interrupted.

"What can't be done?"

At the entrance of the practice room, which was now their makeshift staging area, stood Roc. All this time on the island and they hadn't told him of their schemes, but it seemed as though Oliver couldn't avoid it any longer.

Oliver prepared for the fight that would ensue. He prepared for the berating, for the anger, and the argument. He was scared that this would be the moment when he lost his best friend forever.

"Roc, let me explain," he began.

"What can't be done?" Roc asked again.

"It's not what it looks like."

"Oliver, just tell me."

"We're breaking into the Shipwight Fortress on Silverfox. We're doing it for Po. Ridhan has something that can help him walk again. We're going to break in and take it."

"I'm in."

"Roc, it's a magic elixir, like in Romir. I know how you feel and I—"

Roc put his hand up. "It's for Po. I'm in. Whatever it takes."

Oliver shook hands with his friend and brought him over to the table, where they still had no plan. Roc looked over the drawing and mused aloud at the different options while simultaneously discarding them.

"We need more people. That's the problem," he finally surmised.

Oliver looked over the map again, muttering in a call and response with Roc and Yokel.

"This will be just like when we—"

"Yep," Roc answered.

"But we did that with Wiggin and—" Yokel added.

"Yep," Roc answered again, this time with a big grin.

Oliver counted on his fingers. "We'll need like, what, three more people?"

"Four," Yokel corrected.

Oliver thought of the other Dragon Champion contenders but didn't know how well they'd take to the idea. Breaking into the fortress was one thing, but the magical element of the mission was another. Kiara might have been up for it, but he had no idea where to find her. Reagan had not come back after the banquet the previous night, so Nine Gods only knew what trouble she was up to. What he needed was people he could trust but also people who wouldn't mind a little magic.

He walked away while the others discussed guard shifts and other minutia. He pulled out Haralabos's book and opened it with his ring, hoping that the man in the in-between could provide some answers.

You summoned me?

"I take it you know what's going on?" Oliver whispered.

Yes.

"So, any bright ideas?"

Now you come to me?
You cast me aside for days, with all that has happened, and now you ask for my help?
No.

"You want the Codex back? Then we need your help."

Haralabos did not respond. Oliver pleaded. "You know I'm right."

The blotch of ink appeared in the book as Haralabos gave in.

You need more people.

"Yes, that much we've figured out. But who can we trust to help us?"

You need a drink.

"I'm not thirsty."

Ask for a Blue Cactus.

"Are you kidding me right now?"

Stop arguing with me, you petulant child.

"I hate you."

I hate Quartermaines.

Oliver closed the book and hid it as he tried to come up with an excuse to leave. He thought maybe an elven goodbye was in order, or he could say he was going into town for supplies. He inched casually toward the door.

"Going somewhere, Ollie?" It was Windrunner's metallic voice.

"Uh…"

"Haralabos give you an idea?"

"How did you know… Never mind. Yes. You four work on the plan. Ridhan leaves in the morning, so we have to be ready by nightfall. I'll be back with a team, so let's meet on Blue Ivy Island. At last light, look to the east."

Oliver took a horse into town and to the same nondescript tavern. The horse had again taken to the hay trough happily, and Oliver opened up the book to talk with Haralabos again.

"Here I am, now what?"

Did I say stand around or did I say get a drink?

"You're kind of the worst, you know that?"

The tavern was packed, almost every seat taken by any number of travelers. He spied a notice on the wall claiming this was the favorite establishment of one Oliver Quartermaine, the Dragon Champion. Oliver chuckled and noticed most of the patrons drinking Dragon's Fire.

"My friend! Another Dragon's Fire?" the barkeep asked Oliver, who was scanning the room.

"I was thinking of something a bit different this time. Have you heard of a Blue Cactus?" Oliver was excited by the idea of a new drink.

"Oh, yes, of course! The Elven drink!" The man pulled out an assortment of bottles and spices. After a few minutes, Oliver was handed a cup of blue liquid, which he held up to the light.

Oliver took a sip of the sweet drink and shuddered a bit but nodded in appreciation. "This is oddly satisfying."

"Yes, the elves knew how to make them."

Oliver turned to take stock of the room. "Everyone else enjoying Dragon's Fire? I hear it's the favorite drink of... me." The barkeeper anxiously began to apologize, but Oliver stopped him. "It's fine. Tell me, is everyone drinking Dragon's Fire?"

"Yes, yes, except that one over there."

Oliver flipped the man a coin and went to sit in the same booth he had sat in only nights before.

"Lovely evening isn't it, Loranne?"

The Stranger glared at him. "What are you doing here, hooman?"

"I came for a drink, and company."

"Too much company was your problem, if I recall correctly."

"Not like that."

"Oh, you've solved your problems of the heart?"

"Actually, no, they've gotten worse."

"Worse?"

"They're both angry with me."

"As they should be."

"And there might be someone else." Oliver's face was suddenly wet with the lukewarm liquid thrown from the Stranger's cup. "I deserved that."

"Are all hoomans like you?"

"No one is like me."

"So first it was Tulip, and then the Pathfinder." The Stranger's voice curdled with contempt at the second name.

"It's Iris, and yes, Pathfinder, but now there's—"

"Two hearts not enough for you, hooman? You're worse than a dragon."

"Well, it's funny that you should mention dragons because—"

The Stranger straightened up quickly. "You're not talking about that she-dragon princess, are you?"

Oliver looked away awkwardly.

"Are you jesting? I wouldn't trust her as far as I could—"

"You don't even know her. Or do you know her? Wait, you know her? Can you tell me—"

"Yes, I know her, and no, I will not talk to her."

Oliver's excitement was swiftly dashed, and he looked at the Blue Cactus in his cup and swirled it around, remembering why he was here.

"So, Nymara."

"It's funny that you think you are getting closer when it's the exact opposite."

"Have you had any success in retrieving the, uh, package?"

The Stranger became agitated and her lips barely opened in response. "No."

"Like I predicted. Lucky for you, I'm here to help."

"I don't need your help."

"I think you do, and we need yours."

"We?"

"I'm putting together a team. We already have five, and you make six."

"You think you can enter that fortress with only six people?"

"No, Shirley, but I think we can with nine."

"You hoomans and your affinity for that number." The Stranger shook her head. "Who will be the other three?"

Oliver finished his drink and looked around, noticing a familiar couple in the back corner. "Follow me," he said, pulling the Stranger's hand.

She followed but not without initial resistance. "Fine, but don't call me Shirley."

"You!" the young woman from the night at the docks said.

"Me," Oliver answered.

The larger silent young man pointed aggressively at Oliver.

"Me again," Oliver once more answered.

"And who is she?" the young woman asked, looking at the Stranger.

Oliver looked at the Stranger and back to the young woman. "I honestly have no idea."

"What are you doing here?" the young woman asked while the large young man fidgeted in his seat.

"What's his problem?" the Stranger asked.

"He cannot speak."

"Are you two, uh, together?" Oliver asked.

"We're twins."

"Ah, twins. You know I knew a pair of twins from Mercyhold. Swore they could read each other's minds but were always reluctant to show me, regardless of how much money I offered."

"What are you doing here, Dragon Champion?" The Sister sounded more serious, more annoyed.

"My friend here, Carroll?"

"No," the Stranger answered.

"Right, so my friend here needs this, uh, book, and it's kind of in a tough place."

(*What kind of place?*) the Brother asked with his hands as his sister interpreted.

"Oh, just Silverfox Island."

The Brother looked at his sister with a glint in his eyes, but she frowned.

"The near-impenetrable fortress? Impossible."

"But doable," Oliver suggested.

"Why should we help?"

Oliver only had one thing he could bargain with that would mean anything to these two. It was the same thing he needed for Po's legs. He would have to choose whether the Codex was worth Po walking again, or if Po walking again was worth betraying these two strangers. In the end, Oliver silently promised himself he would find another way to help Po and he leaned in.

"Because that's where the elixir you want so badly is. You help us, and we help you."

The Sister discussed the issue with her brother before finally turning back to Oliver.

"We will help you."

Oliver clapped his hands together. "Perfect, now all we need is—"

A scream from outside had the four of them out of their seats and rushing outside and down the street until they came to a crowd looking up at a figure standing at the edge of the roof of a building. With an unknown compulsion, Oliver climbed up to the roof, followed by the Stranger and the Twins.

"Hey, what are you—" Oliver stepped back, recognizing the Fool from Romir. A rush of emotions and thoughts flooded Oliver's already fuzzy mind and he turned and paced around, trying to breathe.

"Who is he?" the Stranger asked Oliver.

The Fool answered. "I'm nobody, love, I'm nobody."

"What are you doing?" Oliver asked.

"I'm ending it all, mate. I can't do it anymore. I thought I could, but I can't. He dies, every time. It's a nightmare I never wake up from, and now I'm here on this island, and I still can't forget. I'm the reason your little mate is dead." The Fool inched backward, his heels now over the edge of the roof.

"He's not dead."

"What did you say?"

"He's crippled, but he's alive, I swear to you."

"A fate maybe worse than death then." The Fool turned to look over the edge, letting one of his feet slip down.

"Stop!" Oliver yelled, frantically taking a step closer to the Fool. Oliver felt compelled to help him, because for some odd reason, he felt the same. He recognized this Fool's agony; he knew the dark spiral it led to. He too felt responsible for Po's situation, but he had his friends to help him through the depression. This Fool had no one, and Oliver thought that, had circumstances been different, he might be standing where the Fool was now.

The Fool continued his lament. "I've failed enough. I've hurt enough people."

"Then stop failing and help us," Oliver said.

"Help? I can't help anyone, mate."

"You can help the kid. You can help Po."

"Is that the kid's name? All those times and I never learned it. Couldn't bring myself to. But I can't help him now. He'll be dead because of me."

"He's alive because of you," Oliver stated. "And we can get his legs back, if you help us."

"You don't get it, mate! You don't understand." The Fool was crying. "It hurts… so much."

"I do understand."

Tears streamed down the Fool's face. "How could you possibly understand?"

"Because I've been there before, and I know the way out."

The Fool sniffled. "What's the way out?"

Oliver put out his hand. "Together."

The Fool looked into Oliver's eyes, then at the strange girl behind him and the silent duo behind her. He sighed. Oliver felt that if he could just save this Fool's life, he might be saving his own in a way.

"Alright, mate, together." The Fool reached out his hand to meet Oliver's, but his boot slipped, and he stumbled over the edge of the roof.

Both his hands were grasped tightly by Oliver and the Stranger, who were both pulled up by the Twins. The Fool laughed uncontrollably, while Oliver just shook his head.

"I suppose this makes nine?" the Stranger asked Oliver.

Oliver looked at the planet's place in the sky and jumped to his feet. "Yes, it does, but we've got to hurry. I'll explain on the way."

Oliver and his four new team members met up with his friends at the edge of Blue Ivy Island, staring across the small channel at rocky Silverfox island.

Roc frowned. "Who are these people?"

"Some new friends," Oliver answered, taking a drink of water from Yokel.

"Wait, I know you," Yokel said.

"Look, mate, I know I done ya wrong, but I'm here to help," the Fool said. Roc looked at Oliver, who shrugged. "So," the Fool went on, "what's the plan, eh? We just supposed to sashay up to the gate and knock nicely?"

Pathfinder looked around at the additional support Oliver had managed to wrangle up and shook her head disapprovingly. "We enter at these two points."

"One of those is a sewer," the Stranger said.

"Yes," Pathfinder said, annoyed. "And the other is through a secondary entrance by the dungeon. Both will be heavily guarded."

"You missed one," Oliver said.

"No, I didn't," Pathfinder replied.

"How do you do that thing with your voice?" the Fool wanted to know.

"The front gate," Oliver pointed out.

"We can't use the front gate, you moron," Pathfinder said.

"He's not a moron," the Stranger defended.

"Oh, and who exactly are you?"

The Stranger stepped up to Pathfinder. "Listen, little hooman—"

"It's Pathfinder." The Stranger's eyes lit up with fury and she looked at Oliver, who was shaking his head emphatically. Windrunner stepped between them.

"Let's just listen to what Oliver is thinking?"

Oliver looked across the channel. "The sewers and dungeon will both have teams of guards."

"So will the front gate," Roc said.

"But what if the front gate had *most* of the guards?"

"A diversion. That could work." Windrunner started working through the calculations with Yokel.

"We still have one problem," Pathfinder pointed out. "We have no exit plan."

(*No exit plan?*) the Brother asked.

"It's the one flaw," Yokel answered, somehow understanding the silent young man.

Oliver thought about the options and then saw something curious break through the water before going back down. "That could work," the crackled voice inside his head told him.

"I think I have an idea for that. Maybe."

"Maybe? We can't go on a maybe," Pathfinder argued.

"Who's itching for a fight?" Windrunner asked.

The Twins both stepped forward along with Roc, who leaned on his fancy warhammer.

Oliver gave the orders. "Remember, your job is to delay them as long as possible, then meet us on the east rampart."

"Please not the sewer, please not the sewer," Yokel prayed.

"Yokel, Pathfinder, and I will take the sewer," Windrunner announced.

Pathfinder snarked at the Stranger. "I hope the dungeons are reasonable enough for you, princess."

"That's fine," Oliver said as he pulled the Stranger away.

"Looks like it's us, love," the Fool said, flicking the Stranger's hair with a knife.

"Ollie, you sure we can escape?" Windrunner asked.

"Nope."

"You never make things easy, do you?"

"Where would the fun be in that?" Oliver joked. "Okay everyone, masks up, hoods on. See you on the other side." He held his hands wide and clapped as his old friends followed suit and his new friends looking to each other in confusion.

The darkness of Black Sunday gave them cover as they crossed the channel in small rowboats. Oliver felt the cool ocean water filter through his fingers as the Fool and Stranger rowed.

"How exactly did we get stuck with this job?" the Fool complained.

"Shh!" Oliver said. "I'm looking for something." At the halfway point, he signaled them to stop. As they drifted on the gentle waves, he peered into the darkness for a sign of the other boats but saw nothing. He looked into the deep beneath them, and still saw nothing.

Oliver stood, rocking the small boat back and forth. "Head to the dungeon door, I'll meet you there."

"What do you mean you'll meet us there?" the Stranger asked.

Oliver simply smiled and dove into the water, the complaints of his shipmates fading as he swam deeper and deeper. He searched and searched but the cold water stung his eyes and his lungs burned fiercely. Maybe this was a mistake, or at the very least a horrible idea. But the lightning magic had encouraged him, so if he died again, it would be her fault.

Moving into the motions of Form Zero, he summoned the lightning magic to his body, illuminating the ocean around him, and when his glowing blue eyes opened, they were met by the unmistakable eyes of a water dragon. Oliver was in a cocoon of air, into which the water dragon stuck its head.

"I don't know if you understand me," Oliver began, "but I need you to send a message to someone we both know. Tell her, tell her I need her help. I need a dragon's help."

The water dragon blew a mist into the air cocoon, which evaporated upon touching sparks of lightning magic.

"Tell her we need an escape from the eastern rampart of the fortress above. Tell her to look for my signal. Can you do that for me, please?"

The water dragon crinkled its nose, which reminded Oliver of Kiara, then withdrew its head and disappeared into the depths. Oliver looked around and said a quick prayer to the Nine Gods he didn't believe in. He pushed his hands behind him, shooting out lightning that propelled him to the small dock by the rocky dungeon door. He emerged from the water like a dolphin leaping through the air and landed with a thud amongst six guards who had all fallen victim to his friends' aggressions.

"That's four to a deuce, love," the Fool said before noticing Oliver. "Oi, nice of you to join us after we did all the hard bits."

The Stranger helped Oliver up. "I hope your little swim was useful," she said.

Oliver had never used that amount of lightning magic before, and his energy was spent.

"I can't go on," he said. "I'm dead. I'm so tired. It's sleepy time now."

The Fool took a vial from a necklace and popped it open. "Just a drop, mate."

The liquid hit Oliver's lips and he jumped out of their hands and started racing around the small dock. He felt incredible, like he could reach the top of the fortress in a single bound.

"What was that!" Oliver asked but horns blew, signaling that their friends had reached the front gate. "Never mind, let's go."

In the dungeons, they stayed in the shadows. Oliver had never been in this fortress before, but he'd seen enough schematics of castles and fortresses that he had a general idea of what the layout might look like. He was sure Yokel would guide the other party similarly, and if the distraction at the main gate held, they actually might make it out alive.

"This stinks," the Stranger said softly as they made their way past festering wounded prisoners and the occasional dead one.

"I know. The Shipwights are horrible," Oliver said, thinking of how Lord Shipwight used this fortress as his real seat of power, controlling the ocean south of the Floaters with an iron hand.

"No, I mean this literally stinks."

"Oi, you've got quite the nose on you, love," the Fool responded.

"She's a bounty hunter," Oliver offered, as if it answered the unasked question.

"Still, I've not seen a sense like that except for—"

The threat of an arrow between his eyes from the Stranger's bow stopped him short. They found a stairwell but paused at the top for fear of alerting more guards. As if on cue, a horn sounded and the guards hurriedly left their posts.

"That's a lot of guards," Oliver pointed out. If this was just a fraction of the manpower of the fortress, Roc and the Twins wouldn't last for very long.

"Then we don't have much time. Where to now, hooman?"

Oliver leapt from the doorway and ran down the hall, looking for any sign or marking he could recognize. If Ridhan had the elixir and the Codex, it would most assuredly be in some hidden room. But they didn't have time to search every nook and cranny.

"Tck-tck-tck, Your Highness, you misunderstand."

Oliver, the Stranger, and the Fool ducked behind some curtains just before Ridhan and the Black Prince walked by, followed by two Black Hawks.

"No, it is you who misunderstands, Lord Shipwight. My mother has given me a task and I fully intend to succeed. You wouldn't want the Black Sun Battalion to pay you a visit instead of me."

"Ever the bold one, Prince Kitanchulee, to threaten me in my own home, a fortress that hasn't been taken since before the dragons bequeathed these islands to your mother."

The Black Prince stopped and pointed a finger at Ridhan. "You would do well to mind your manners, my lord. You are not the only one here who possesses power." Both Black Hawks pointed their spears over the shoulder of the Black Prince, but Ridhan was unfazed.

"My power doesn't come from my mother, my prince."

"Nor mine from my father," the Black Prince spit back.

"Tck-tck-tck, I like you. You remind me of my love. But that is another story for another time. Come with me and I shall give you what you seek."

They turned the corner, toward the dungeons Oliver had just come from.

"Should we follow?" the Stranger whispered.

"Maybe." Oliver fumbled around, the pressure of their task wasting precious time. He pulled out Haralabos's book instinctively and opened it.

"What's that?" the Fool asked, but Oliver ignored him.

"How do we find the Codex?" Oliver asked.

Follow the lightning.

"Why is a magic book talking to you?"

"What does that mean?"

Oliver ran through every scenario of letting his companions know his secret, but he had no time and no choice but to trust them.

"It means this," he said as he put the book away and summoned the lightning magic. It danced around him and then flew off ahead of them.

The Stranger stared at him. "You have magic?"

"It's a long story. You two follow Ridhan. I'll follow the lightning." Before Oliver could let them argue, he was off. He followed the lightning magic around corners and through hallways until it took him to an inconspicuous door that had a nine-pointed star etched into the top corner of the doorframe. Oliver inspected the door for any traps or how to pick the lock. Failing to open it, he took a few steps back, then charged it with his shoulder. A frantic search began for the elixir, the Codex, and anything that might be of use, but as Oliver tore through the room, defeat washed over him.

"It's not here," he muttered.

Oliver went to pull out the book to ask Haralabos but instead noticed a painting on the wall. It was a portrait of Ridhan, majestically holding the Staff of the Seas. But the last time Oliver had seen the staff, it had been turned into a trident, unlike what the painting portrayed. He walked over to the painting, noticing a raised section of the staff, and pressed it. An audible click sounded, and the staff's two prongs jutted out into the painting, followed by the movement of the wall itself.

Behind the wall was a treasure trove. All manner of alchemical and magical items were in the room. In the middle, on a pedestal, lay a simple book covered with a cloth, and next to it, a vial that looked exactly like the elixir Oliver needed. He inspected the room for any boobytraps but found none. It was almost like Ridhan wanted this to be found.

Oliver took the elixir in one hand and with the other he opened the book to verify its contents. This was the Codex, the book of magic that would help Po save the world, and the elixir that would restore his legs. Oliver had everything he needed, but also everything that would betray his new friends. The Stranger needed this book so she could return home, and the Twins were fighting who knows how many guards so that Oliver could retrieve the elixir for them.

Haralabos's book seemed to agitate on its own and he pulled it out.

What are you doing?
You have what you need, leave this place!

"I can't betray them like this."

This is a war. Sacrifices must be made.

"Not my war."

You insolent child!
They will never stop looking for the Codex.
They will never stop searching for magic.

Oliver thought quickly. Ridhan would never stop looking for magic. It was everything to him. Even if he gave the Stranger this book, she would never be safe. Nor would her family. Ridhan was resourceful and would probably get his hands on it again. The Codex needed to be destroyed before anyone else took it, but all the knowledge it contained would be destroyed as well.

Before he could talk himself out of it, he summoned the lightning magic and whispered, "Find Yokel." It flew off, and Oliver felt a moment of pride that his lightning magic worked as he hoped it would. He opened the Codex and began to read every other page. One single look and the first page was imprinted into his mind temple. Another look and the third page was there.

"Oliver?" Yokel yelled as he stumbled into the outer room. Oliver ran out and grabbed him and rushed him to the pedestal. "Yok, I need you to do something and you can't ask questions. We don't have time. I need you to read every other page in the Codex, starting with this one, and commit it to memory."

Before Oliver could explain any further, Yokel began.

"Oi!" the Fool gasped as he fell into the room. "You have to come quick, it's…"

Oliver rushed to his side and propped him up, taking a quick look at the bleeding gash along his temple.

"To the dungeon, he's got some Relic. All your mates are there, but he's insane."

"Yokel, you done?" Oliver yelled.

Yokel popped out of the secret chamber with a proud smile and the Codex in hand. "It's complete."

"Yok, you're the best." Oliver took the Codex from Yokel's hand and turned to the Fool. "Burn this place to the ground, make sure the window is open, then meet us on the eastern rampart."

Oliver raced out of the room with Yokel and back down toward the dungeons. The few guards he met never stood a chance. He bounded down the steps, unconsciously readying his lightning magic, should it come to that.

At the bottom of the steps, Windrunner lay crumpled in a ball, fighting against ropes that slithered and squirmed like snakes. Her mask was off, revealing Reagan's face as she rolled in and out of the shadows. Oliver would have been in shock if it all didn't make complete sense. He bent down to help her, but she urged him to continue even while the magical rope wrapped around her mouth.

Against his instincts, he obeyed and turned the corner of the room. The Black Prince was down the darkened prison hall, fighting off a horde of released pirate prisoners with his two Black Hawks. They would surely have been overwhelmed in a matter of moments if not for the Stranger who had come to their aid.

Directly in front of him, amongst broken tables and miscellaneous implements of torture, Pathfinder and Ridhan were dueling. Pathfinder's mask had been ripped off as well, evidenced by the cut she bore across her cheek, and her hood had fallen away from her shoulders.

"Tck-tck-tck, who would have thought my beautiful little flower was the Knight Angel giving us so many problems. But even a flower cannot withstand the strength of the Spider's Web." He parried her slash and kicked her in the sternum, sending her flying back into Oliver's arms.

Iris looked up at Oliver, gasping for air as she touched his cheek. He held her hand, for fear it would accidentally unmask his own face, and laid her down gently. "I always knew it was you."

"No, you didn't," she said, coughing up blood.

"No, I didn't," he said with a smile. It was the quickest of quiet moments, but he treasured it beyond any other. The two people his heart yearned for most were one and the same, which explained so much and left him with just as many questions. All his confusion and all his worry melted away, and he finally had clarity. His heart was full, and his mind was clear.

He kissed her on the forehead. "My turn." He stole her choker and put it on his throat, then unsheathed his sword to dance in the lamplight while Ridhan spun his spear around.

"You seem familiar. Do I know you?" Ridhan asked.

In a metallic voice, Oliver answered. "I'm the Lightning Knight."

"Tck-tck-tck, I doubt that." Ridhan lunged.

Oliver's skill and knowledge quickly outclassed Ridhan, but when Oliver should have dealt a final blow, he was instead sent backward by a gust of air emanating from the Staff of the Seas.

Ridhan laughed and kissed his magical weapon. "You never stood a chance, you Wanting Knight. None of you did. Soon I will have more magic than just this staff, and you all will—"

A flying knife hit the wall just above his head.

"Now, now, who said you could have all the fun?" the Fool yelled. He bent down next to Yokel, who was trying desperately to help Reagan with her wild ropes.

"How many of you are there?" Ridhan asked incredulously.

Oliver picked up the Codex and held it up to the light for Ridhan to see. "This look familiar?"

"You dare!" Ridhan stabbed his staff into the ground, sending a blast of wind in all directions and throwing everyone from the Black Prince and the pirates to the Fool and the Stranger to the ground. Everyone except Oliver, whose lightning magic clung his boots to the ground.

"Give me that or all your friends die!" Ridhan yelled.

Over the howling air Oliver yelled, "You want it? You can have it!" He threw the Codex up between them and Ridhan dropped his staff to reach for it. The rush of wind subsided and while the Stranger yelled at Oliver, the lightning magic from his boots coursed up around his body and away from his outstretched hand. The bolt of lightning hit the Codex as Ridhan caught it, and the magical book exploded, sending Ridhan and his staff through the wall into an antechamber and collapsing the roof and walls around him. All that could be heard was Ridhan's maniacal laugh as the dust settled.

The room was crumbling around them. Oliver scooped up Iris and raced toward the steps. He looked down the tunnel where the Black Prince and prisoner pirates had been, but massive rocks and bricks now blocked the way.

"Easy, love, we best be off now," the Fool said as he pulled the Stranger from under a pile of bricks.

"This whole place is coming down!" Reagan yelled as they ran through the halls.

"Yes, who would have thought the dungeon was the keystone to the whole structure," Yokel commented.

"Shut up and move, Yokel!" Oliver yelled.

On the eastern rampart they met Roc and the Twins battling what was left of the guards. Iris squirmed out of Oliver's arms and steadied herself. All nine friends fought the guards, even while the walls of the rampart groaned and shook beneath them.

"Now would be a good time for that escape plan you promised!" Roc gasped. Blood was dripping from various cuts and he looked like he might collapse at any moment.

"Wait for it!" Oliver yelled as he swept the legs of a guard, the Fool finishing the guard off with a kick.

"We're running out of time!" Iris yelled as she tripped over the crumbling rocks. A guard attacked with a clean overhead strike but was sent over the side of the rampart by the Stranger, who extended a hand to help Iris to her feet.

"Wait for it!" Oliver said once more as he was kicked in the side. He would have been cut down if not for Reagan at the last moment. She offered him a hand up after she had disposed of the guard. "So, baby sister, are we not going to talk about your alter ego?" Oliver asked as they each took out guards.

"I think we might have bigger problems," Reagan responded. At least fifty more guards had appeared and were now surrounding the group of nine. Yokel and the Brother were both on the ground, barely moving, while the rest of the fighters could hardly stand, let alone take on the oncoming horde.

Oliver looked up into the sky, noticing the stars twinkling in and out of focus. But they weren't twinkling, they were disappearing and reappearing.

"Okay, now!" he yelled. He turned and leaped over the side of the rampart toward a certain rocky death below. With no other choice and too tired to think clearly, everyone followed him over the edge, Roc carrying Yokel and the Stranger carrying the Brother.

The jagged rocks below hurtled toward them faster and faster until suddenly the nine were instead lifted into the air. Not lifted but carried into the night sky by winged dragons.

"About time you showed up!" Oliver yelled as he sat on the saddled back of the dragon, holding on to Kiara tightly as the dragon banked. He looked around and saw his other friends clutched in the taloned feet of Kiara's dragon friends. Everyone was accounted for, including the unconscious Yokel. Oliver shook his head. Yokel would surely regret missing out on this flight.

"Water dragons are notorious for their miscommunication." Kiara laughed as her dragon spit fire along the rampart toward the guards below.

"Can you take us all to the Quartermaine estate?"

"A dragon CAN do anything."

"MAY you please take us to my house on the island?"

"Yes, yes, we may." Kiara whooped and whistled to the other dragons.

They flew high in the night sky, hidden by clouds and darkness. Oliver motioned to fly by Reagan, who was dangling from her dragon's claws as if she were a bird.

"Ollie, isn't this amazing?" Reagan yelled.

"You have no idea," he replied as he squeezed Kiara tightly. But in the moment of euphoria, he wondered if the Black Prince had made it out alive.

Oliver turned to Reagan. "Get everyone on a ship tonight. Make sure the Twins get this." He tossed her the elixir and she gave him the Whisky Danger hand signal. "I'm going back for the Prince. I'll meet you in Starfall." He tapped Kiara's shoulder and motioned for her to bank back toward Silverfox, then he watched his friends fly south toward Goldenflower.

"By the way, thanks for catching me," Oliver spoke into Kiara's ear.

She smiled and turned nuzzled Oliver with her cheek. "Whenever you need me, I'll always find you."

Oliver panicked briefly at the touch, but then relief washed over him, for they had done the impossible. He stretched out his arms wide, pretending that he too was a dragon.

# THE KEY

Oliver and Kiara banked so harshly around the edge of Silverfox that Oliver almost fell out of the saddle. Kiara giggled as he held on to her for dear life, and he suddenly felt at odds with his heart.

He had just found out the most glorious news that the two people his heart most yearned for were one and the same. Maybe it shouldn't have been such a surprise, if he thought more about it. In fact, the more he put the pieces together, the dumber he felt. All the signs were in front of him; he had just failed to catch on.

"I wonder if anyone else knew," he whispered to himself as the dragon he sat on descended toward the ocean. "Oh, Nine Gods, if Yokel knew and I didn't…"

"What did you say?"

"Nothing. The entrance should be just there." He pointed to where his small rowboat had docked, but it was missing. The entrance to the dungeon had caved in, and Oliver felt a wash of sadness. Had he condemned his friend to being buried alive? The dragon landed on the dock with silent grace. Oliver hopped out of the saddle and examined the area for a way to move the rubble. But the rocks were too heavy for him to make any progress.

He instead studied where the rowboat should have been and noticed a piece of parchment lying by the post. It read "The Shipwights have the Codex" and was signed only by a symbol of a Spider's Web.

"Curious," Oliver murmured to himself. "Sounds like there's something rotten in—"

Kiara's whistle made him turn. "We should leave now," she said, pointing out into the ocean where lights flickered from three separate ships. Whether it was pirates or Shipwight ships, Oliver and Kiara didn't want to find out.

Oliver took the parchment and jumped back into the saddle, holding Kiara tightly as the great beast leaped into the air, pushing its mighty wings down and sending them flying above the clouds.

"Where are we going?" Oliver asked, noticing their continued journey south instead of east to Goldenflower.

"You'll see," Kiara said playfully. Oliver embraced the opportunity to fly some more and began to relax his hold on his rescuer, when suddenly the dragon descended in a spiral, forcing Oliver to clutch Kiara and scream like a child.

They landed on Emerald Island, at the very same cliff where Oliver had kissed Kiara, and Oliver jumped off immediately, falling to his knees. He took in the dark scenery and a mix of emotions flooded his heart. This was the scene of his kiss with Kiara, but Oliver's heart for Iris was full and complete.

Oliver sat on the edge of the cliff and let his legs dangle while their dragon ride flew away. The rush of air from the dragon's wings almost pushed Oliver off the cliff, but Kiara caught him before he fell.

"That's two," she said.

"You mean three. One for the beach. One for the fortress. One for just now," Oliver corrected. There was an easy comfort knowing he owed her a debt. Something he could always tether himself to her, even if he couldn't call her his own.

"The fortress was for free, since you asked my mother and all."

"That was your mother?" Oliver yelled.

"Yep, yep. I'm surprised you were able to talk to her."

"Why?" Oliver asked. The more Kiara spoke, the more he learned about the mysterious dragon culture, and the more he wanted to hear.

Kiara threw a rock over the edge of the cliff. "Because she typically eats hoomans who fall into the ocean."

She snuck a look at him and burst out laughing at the expression on his face. He didn't know whether she was being truthful or not, but he didn't care either way. He liked Kiara and he was pretty certain she liked him back. But he loved Iris.

"So…" Oliver began.

"So…" Kiara replied, staring out into the night sky.

Oliver said a thousand different words in his head, but none aloud. He didn't want to lose Kiara, but he also knew that he couldn't keep her. Not like he wanted. Not in any way that would be fair to Iris or to Kiara. "So, I feel like we're in a weird place."

"We're in my favorite place," Kiara stated, still peering out into the darkness.

"No, I mean us. I feel as though I've led you on."

"You have."

"I didn't mean to. You know I have someone in my life already. Tonight, I just found out something important I didn't know before, and any confusion I might have had about our relationship has been put to rest. I love her."

Kiara looked over at him and smiled. "I'm happy for you, little hooman."

Oliver felt a rush of relief. She wasn't taking this too hard. He was being faithful to Iris. Maybe he could still be friends with Kiara. "Thanks," he finally said. There was a piece of him, the smallest of pieces, in the deepest of places in his heart, where he wanted Kiara to not be happy for him. To fight for him and run away across the world with him. But he extinguished that flame and felt at peace with the fact that he had finally chosen. For good this time. Definitely no more choices to be made. The ink was dry. All was set in stone.

Oliver kept telling himself more variations of the same turn of phrase until he finally relaxed in the silence between them, enjoying his friend's company as the ocean waves crashed below them.

"So why did you bring me here?" he asked.

Kiara took his hand and placed it over her heart, and Oliver immediately felt uncomfortable again, in every way possible. "The last time I was here, I had a vision. A vision of a boy who danced with lightning. He beckoned me and I followed. I'd always thought it was a vision of someone else, but then you showed it to me. You showed me the lightning magic, and I knew. So, now we wait."

Oliver was transfixed. "Wait for what?"

The breeze that had been blowing softly against Oliver's face stopped as if all the air had been sucked away, and a huge blur of golden motion passed in front of him. Oliver fell back in shock, away from the cliff's edge.

"For him," Kiara replied with a smile and laugh.

The golden dragon circled and then landed in the clearing near Oliver and Kiara. Kiara extended a hand and the golden dragon snarled before sniffing and touching it with his snout as she muttered a phrase Oliver was unable to make out. Smoke began to envelop the animal, and just as quickly the dragon disappeared and a man with chestnut hair and a scraggly beard took its place.

"Da," Kiara said as she moved in to hug him tightly.

"My daughter, it is wonderful to see you with these eyes once more. I feared I would not come back this time," her father said between the kisses he placed on each of her cheeks.

"I can't lose you, too," Kiara pleaded.

"You will never lose me, hatchling," he replied with a smile. "Is this him?" He looked at Oliver.

Oliver dropped to a knee. "Your Gr— Your Maje— Actually, I don't know what to call you."

"This is Oliver Quartermaine, the Dragon Champion," Kiara stated.

"One of them at least." The Dragonbender chuckled. "Please, please rise, little hooman." The Dragonbender raised his hand and Oliver felt the ground beneath him contort into a seat that hit the back of his knees, causing them to buckle and him to sit. Oliver couldn't take his eyes off the man's hand. The forefinger wore a sapphire ring that contained every shade of the ocean all at once. His middle finger wore a ring that contrasted between orange, yellow, and red. His heart finger held a grey and white pearl, and his pinky finger was adorned with an emerald. The black diamond on his thumb was faded and cracked, and while Oliver stared blankly at the hand, the jolly-faced man spoke.

"You look very familiar to these eyes. Have we met before?"

"My brother was the last Dragon Champion, Your Royal Dragon-ness."

"Ah, that is right. But he does not share your eyes. No, you have the look of someone I knew a very long time ago, but that is neither here nor there. Tell me, how fares your brother?"

Oliver stifled the urge to burst out in a rage of explanation and instead decided to keep it short and to the point. "I've heard he is doing well, Your Grace."

"You've heard? Hmm, if you would hear a bit of advice from an old dragon: Family is the most important part of your life." He pulled a smiling

Kiara in tightly.

"I thank Your Royalness for his wisdom."

The Dragonbender looked at his daughter. "Does he always speak like this?"

"No, sometimes he stutters," she joked, and Oliver gave her an annoyed glance.

Oliver rose out of his seat, having decided he very much didn't like speaking this way to this dragon. "If you'll excuse me, dragon-sir, you aren't exactly what I expected."

The old dragon raised a bushy eyebrow. "Oh, and what did you expect?"

"More, uh, regal?"

The dragon waved his hand around in the air. "Live the hundreds of years that I have, and you'll find that being regal is a young dragon's game. At our heart, dragons are a jovial species. I tried being solemn between one hundred and thirty and two hundred and seven and you know what I learned?"

"I haven't the faintest idea," Oliver said, completely mesmerized by the conversation.

"Nothing. I learned nothing. Dragons are the top of the mountain, hooman, so no matter how we act, no matter what we do, we'll always be at the top. So, I figured, why not have a little fun with it?"

Oliver was one part terrified and one part astounded by the dragon king, and he realized where Kiara got her exuberance.

"I see you've shown him our spot," the Dragonbender said, giving Kiara a sideways glance. She shied away and he continued without missing a beat. "So, Dragon Champion, what will you do with your newfound glory? Women, parties, maybe a castle all to your own?"

"I'm a Quartermaine, so I believe the castle and parties won't be an issue," Oliver responded, starting to get a bit of his bravado back. Sure, he was talking to probably the most powerful creature in the entire world, but Oliver had gone toe-to-toe with the High Queen, so he was feeling confident.

The Dragonbender looked at him. "I remember your family. How is the Inventor?"

"My father is at the Forge as we speak, working on his latest project."

"A man after my own hearts. Fire and—"

"Brimstone, yes we know, Da. Ollie has places to go, so how about you do what we discussed?"

"Of course, of course, my hatchling. Dragon Champion, come here." They walked to the edge of the cliff, just the Dragonbender and the Dragon Champion, and peering down, Oliver felt a bout of vertigo. The Dragon put his giant hand on the back of Oliver's neck and sighed a deep, old man's sigh.

"Undoubtedly, my daughter has told you of her mother."

"Not very much, Your Highness."

"She's quite taken with you, you know. I can't recall her speaking of any hooman the way she spoke of you. You'd be smart to remember that a dragon may have two hearts but only one father, and if you break either of hers I will—"

"Da!" Kiara yelled behind them.

"I think you get my meaning, hooman. But that's not why I'm here." The Dragonbender walked back to Kiara, who punched him in the side, and Oliver had never felt so jealous.

"Kiara's mother was once friends with a man who could control lightning. They ventured together in this world trying to save it, and for that, we ultimately lost her. I loved that dragon with boths heart I had, but she was resolute in her faith in the lightning knight."

"You're talking about Haralabos."

The Dragonbender's eyes narrowed. "You're a clever little hooman. Yes, Bos was the lightning knight, and our friend. Before he was defeated by your High Queen, he passed a message to my mate. That one day, there would be someone who would control the lightning magic once more, and that I should look for the Champion and tell them the key to magic."

"I'm not the Lightning Knight," Oliver confessed.

The Dragonbender looked at his daughter, who ran to Oliver and grabbed his hands. "Yes, you are, I've seen it."

"No, this isn't my magic. It wasn't meant for me. It was meant for my friend, Po."

The Dragonbender walked over to Oliver and sniffed him. "It is not your magic, but it does listen to you."

"I'm not the one you're looking for."

"Maybe, but my Kiara says you are the man I seek, and therefore I am to tell you the key to our lost magic."

"I already know what the key is."

The Dragonbender took Oliver's hand, which had on it the ring from Po's grandfather. "Yes, I can see you wear it already."

"What? No, this isn't the key, Po is."

The Dragonbender cocked his head. "No, this ring is the key."

"No, Po is."

The old Dragon scowled and his orange ring glowed and a ring of fire encircled them both. "Listen little hooman," the Dragonbender said, trying to take the ring off Oliver but failing to do so. "This is the key. Bos's ring. This will restore magic!"

"Da!"

The flames dissipated and the Dragonbender relaxed once more. "Apologies, hatchling, but you didn't tell me your hooman was as stubborn as Satine."

"You know Satine? My Satine?"

The Dragonbender sighed and shook his head. "Quartermaines."

"We get that a lot," Oliver said with a wry smile.

"Ha-ha! This one has spunk. I like him."

"Me too," Kiara answered, looking at Oliver. He looked at the nine-pointed star on the ring, trying to put the pieces of the puzzle together. Was Po meant to wear the ring when he read the Codex? Was it so simple? All this time, they had the answer with them, but Oliver had been too stupid to realize.

Oliver jumped up and did a little jig to celebrate. He finally knew what to do, and he could finish his quest. He hooted and hollered as the two dragons watched him.

"Hoomans are weird, Da."

"Yes, they are, but that's what makes them interesting, I suppose. It's a curious bit of magic they all possess."

Oliver stopped and looked around anxiously. "I need to get back to Goldflower. No, I need to get back to Starfall!"

"I can help you with that." Kiara whistled loudly with her fingers. A winged dragon thundered through the forest trail and eagerly awaited her directions. Oliver climbed onto the dragon and Kiara clucked within her throat as she slapped the shoulder of the beast. Oliver held on for his life as the dragon sprinted toward the cliff's edge.

"Wait! I didn't get to say goodbye," Oliver yelled as the dragon leaped off the cliff. It spread its wings, catching the air beneath them and rising up into the clouds before turning north. Any sadness Oliver had at the lack of a proper goodbye melted away as he spread his arms wide and glided through the air as the planet-light broke the horizon.

# THE LIGHTNING MAGIC

"I still can't believe all of that happened!" Po said.

"Honestly, neither can I," Oliver responded.

"I always knew Pathfinder was Ms. Iris."

"No, you didn't."

"Well, I kind of knew."

Oliver ruffled his young friend's long hair. "Oh really?"

"Uh, well no. But it does make a whole lot of sense now."

"Doesn't it?"

They watched as the ship they had been waiting for came to dock. Then they patiently waited for their friends to disembark. But the passengers leaving the ship were bloodied and bandaged. In the midst of the crowd, Iris and Reagan limped down the ramp, followed by Roc who was carrying Yokel, and finally the Fool.

Iris hugged Oliver so tight he thought he might never breathe again. Reagan slumped to the ground next to Po, leaning on the boy's wheeled chair.

"What happened?" Oliver squeaked out.

Roc laid Yokel down, who was finally opening his eyes. He had a large bruise on the side of his head, and dried blood caked his collar.

"Pirates, mate," the Fool responded. "Bloody pirates. They attacked three of our ships at once." The Fool became silent at the sight of Po in the wheeled chair.

Roc added to the story. "They came out of nowhere. We never stood a chance. Not after what we'd already been through. They took the brother and sister captive."

"And your other friend, she took down one of their ships and nearly another before she was thrown overboard," Reagan said.

"We only managed to escape because something in the water attacked the third pirate ship and they turned tail and fled," Roc finished.

Oliver smiled quickly at a thought before kissing Iris and bending down to Yokel, checking on his wounds. "You alright, Yok?"

"I'm alive," Yokel responded, coughing up a bit of blood. "But, Oliver, I'm sorry."

Oliver looked around at the rest of the group, eyebrows raised. "Yok, you have nothing to be sorry about. You've been brilliant."

"No, Oliver. I can't remember it. Any of it. The Codex, it's gone."

Maybe the blows he had sustained had caused his loss of the Codex memory, Oliver thought. He sat down on his butt and sighed heavily. Knowing half of the Codex wasn't enough. "Reagan, did you give the elixir to the Twins?" Oliver asked, hopeful that she hadn't been able to before they were captured. It was selfish of him, but all he cared about in this moment was his promise to Po.

"I gave it to them as soon as we got to Goldenflower. I'm sorry, Ollie."

"Then I've failed. I'm sorry, Po. Without that elixir or the full Codex, you won't be able to walk again."

The Fool bent down to a knee and took Po's hands. "Hey, kid. Do you remember me?"

Po's eyes lit up. "You're the Fool from Romir."

"I'm the reason you're in this chair."

"You're the reason I'm alive."

"You know kid, I relive those days so many times, but I can never forgive myself for what happened to you. I'd like to fix that, now." He pulled a vial from his necklace and snapped the neck off. "Bottom's up, kid." The Fool took a gulp and then passed the remaining half to Po.

Po looked at the Fool, then to Oliver. Oliver nodded, and Po drank. The Fool backed away and everyone waited, anxious for any visible sign he had been healed.

Nothing.

No sparks of magic, no fireworks overhead.

"I don't feel any different," Po said sadly. He took the blanket off his legs, revealing the atrophied limbs. Oliver took a small pebble and flung it at the young boy's legs. It bounced off and Po instinctively yelped and kicked out.

The realization hit each of them in succession as Po jumped out of his seat, falling over due to the weakness in his legs. With Oliver and Roc's help, he was able to move and walk around, tears streaming down his eyes.

"Thank you, thank you," Po said to where the Fool once stood. But the Fool was not there, nor anywhere. He had disappeared without a trace or even a goodbye.

"I can't believe this," Iris said.

"I can," Oliver said.

Roc shook his head. "We did it. We destroyed the Codex, we got Po's legs back. There's no more Haralabos, and Ridhan is probably still buried under hundreds of feet of stone. We're done with it all now. We're done with magic."

Oliver wanted to explain that it wasn't over and that he had magic of his own. He wanted to tell Roc that now that Po was healed, Po could still be the hero the world needed. They could still save magic.

Reagan sighed. "I think we're all overdue for a very long sleep."

"Roc, would you be so kind as to help me take Yokel home?" Iris asked.

"We'll take Po home to the Workshop," Reagan said, pulling Oliver over.

Roc laughed. "See you all in two weeks. That should be enough sleep for me."

"Three weeks for me, please," Yokel said, still holding his head.

After Roc, Yokel, and Iris left, Oliver sat in Po's chair, trying to figure out his next step.

"What are you doing sitting around for? We have training to do," Reagan said, smacking him in the head.

"What training?"

"Po isn't going to learn magic by himself, and you're the only one we know who has it. Without the Codex, you're the only one we've got."

Po leaned on Reagan and smiled proudly, nodding his head. His legs seemed to be filling out even as he stood, the elixir not only restoring the boy's ability to walk but all the damage his muscles had taken. Oliver knew he was going against Roc's wishes and behind his back, but maybe it was for the best. At least for now.

"Po," Oliver started, "I think you're going to love this."

The three of them walked from the docks to the Shears, going down to the secret level where they found their mentor sitting in a chair, reading a book.

"You can read?" Po asked.

"You can walk?" Azel replied sarcastically.

"Once I received the lightning magic, Azel got her sight back," Oliver explained.

"Ooooohhhhh," Po responded, smacking his head. He wandered around the room, taking it all in for the first time with wonder and amazement.

"I take it your trip to the islands was fruitful?" Azel asked.

"Very. You can add one more Dragon Champion to your ranks," Oliver answered. "Although, we did lose the Codex again."

Azel perked up. "Who has it now?" she asked.

"No one. I destroyed it."

"I see," Azel responded, touching her staff.

"So now we have no way to properly learn magic, or train Po," Reagan said.

"No? If only you knew someone who had read the Codex. Maybe even wrote it."

"That would be helpful, but we don't know anyone like that," Reagan answered with a curious smile on her face.

Azel walked over to a slate board and with a piece of chalk, wrote "The Laws of Magic."

Oliver's jaw dropped. "Wait, you're telling me *you* wrote the Codex?"

"You forget, I have been around for a very, very long time." She began to write out a list of different rules and terms on the board while Oliver, Reagan and Po sat anxiously waiting. When she was done, she turned and set aside her cane.

Oliver stood. "Does that mean you know what it says?"

Azle looked at him with a sad expression. "I'm sorry, but no. I may have written it, but that knowledge is lost to me; a final gift to me from the High Queen herself." She perked up with a smile after a moment of thought. "But there are things that I have always known, even before the Codex was written.

"There are three Laws of Magic that can never be broken. The First Law: Magic has a price. Always. Every magical action has an equal and opposite reaction."

The image of a small obelisk disintegrating into dust flashed across Oliver's mind.

"The Second Law: There are many different types of magic, and your mind and body can only process one at a time. To try and harness more is to court madness. That is why we imbue objects with magic, so they might burn up instead of our minds." Azel paused, taking her walking cane and pressing it to Oliver's chest. They both were pulled into a kaleidoscope of imagery. She released it and Oliver let out a held breath.

"This cane allows me to unlock certain "minor magic" within my students. Not enough to drive the mind to madness but enough to make a difference. I believe all three of you have experienced it in your training."

Reagan popped out of her seat. "When time stands still." Azel smiled and nodded and Reagan sat back down, shaking her head in amazement.

"The Third Law," Azel continued, "is that magic can neither be created nor destroyed, for there is a finite amount of it in the world."

Oliver's forehead crinkled. "If magic can't be destroyed, then why are we trying to save it?"

Azel sat back in her chair, spinning her cane on the stone floor. "Magic can be converted into other magics or even disappear entirely, lost to us forever. When the world was infantile, the Elven magicians were masters of time magic. They misused their power and ultimately time magic abandoned them, leaving our world." Azel looked away, tapping a rhythm with her fingers.

Oliver thought about the in-between, of the river of stars, and of a curious phrase he had heard. "But elves still use time magic, don't they?" he asked.

Azel stared at him, squinting her eyes ever so slightly. "Before the time magicians lost the magic, they tethered a small piece to this world. Elves commune through that piece of time magic so they might have everlasting life."

Reagan sat at the edge of her seat, fiddling with her fingers. "So, the High Queen banished magic hundreds of years ago, but because of the magical items still in the world, a tether still existed. Which means, unless we find real magic, once those items are gone, so too will magic."

Azel stood. "Yes." She walked to the door that led to the training chamber. "How powerful you are at using magic depends on how much you train it, like any other muscle in your body. Oliver, when you've used your lightning magic, how did you feel afterward?"

Oliver looked at his hands, imagining the swirls of bolts. "Exhausted. Like I've run for three days without rest."

"Exactly, but you can tame that exhaustion over time, with practice."

Oliver looked away and took a breath. "It's not my magic, though. It was meant for Po."

"The lightning listens to you, Oliver. There are ways to transfer it, but they require a totem and it is extremely dangerous."

Reagan frowned. "Why is it so dangerous?"

Azel looked at her cane and then to the portrait on the wall. "Magic is unique to each person, and to transfer your magic to someone else would be the same as trying to give someone your heart or your blood. Your magic may not be compatible with someone else's mind. Furthermore"—she paused before tightening her grip on her cane—"to rip out magic from a person, to take something so fundamental to them… the consequences are indescribable."

Oliver hated each and every one of these new laws and rules. Ordinarily, he would love rules and order and procedures, but something inside him rebelled against it. Magic, he thought, was more than what Azel was trying to shape it as.

"Haralabos said Po was to be the Lightning Knight, so if there's a way to give him my magic, then we have to try." He didn't want to give up the lightning magic, he really didn't, but he wasn't supposed to even have it. If Po was to be the hero and save the world, Oliver would need to make the sacrifice.

Azel composed herself and took her cane and opened the door of the practice room. "Master Pondarion, we can try and transfer the magic to you, or we can look for other ways. The choice is yours."

Po stood up and looked around the room with wide eyes and that determined look he so often wore. He smiled and nodded. "I can do it."

The practice room was littered with metal poles and stakes crisscrossing each other to create a barrier around the walls and ceiling and leading to the ground. By the door stood a large metal birdcage, big enough to hold multiple people.

Azel placed her ring on the floor and moved into Form Zero, muttering some indecipherable words that caused the ring to float above the ground and spin, before she stumbled back into the arms of the students watching her.

"Reagan, take us to the cage. You two, stand around the ring," she instructed. Oliver and Po stood on either side of the floating ring while Azel shouted instructions. "Oliver, summon your lightning magic. Po, mimic his movements."

Oliver started slowly, working his way to more intricate movements, hoping against hope that this might fail. He loved Po and knew what Po was meant to be, but still Oliver resisted the idea of losing a part of himself.

Lightning sparks appeared around his body and jumped toward the metal around the room and to the spinning ring. The crackle of the air snapped and splintered all around them, and Oliver felt the rush of power and peace that accompanied the magic. Azel and Reagan stood unaffected by the lightning as it jumped and whipped through the air, creating a storm of light thunderclaps. The lightning magic started to coalesce into a sphere around Oliver and Po.

"Hello," a crackled voice called.

"Hello,' Oliver responded aloud.

"You hear it too?" Po asked.

"You know what I am?" the crackled voice asked.

"You are my lightning magic," Oliver responded confidently.

"I am not your magic."

"I know," Oliver answered. "You're his."

"No, he is not my knight," the crackled voice countered with a tinge of sadness.

"Your knight? You mean Haralabos. He gave you to me, but it was a mistake. You were meant for Po."

"I am not some trinket that can be possessed and given away," the voice yelled.

"I'm sorry, we just—"

"Excuse me, lightning magic, sir," Po said. "We could use your help. I think I'm supposed to be the Lightning Knight, like my ancestor Haralabos. But I don't have the lightning magic. So, you see, it would be kind of hard to be the Lightning Knight without, well, you."

There was a brief silence in the void of their minds, then a sudden storm appeared and the familiar boom that followed a lightning strike sounded. Sadness and disappointment washed over Oliver at the absence of the crackled voice. He worried they had failed and that the lightning magic would be lost to both of them.

In desperation, Oliver begged. "Please, you have to help us. I can't fail again." He was looking at Po, who shook his head. Po left his position and walked over to Oliver and hugged him.

"Po, what are you doing? You need to stay over there for this to work."

"This is more important," the young boy said as he squeezed Oliver tighter.

The crackled voice spoke once more. "Torn away and now cast aside. I am a fundamental force, and they dared lie to me. I shall seek out the truth."

The cocoon of lightning surrounding them shot bolts into Oliver's body, and by extension, Po.

"Oliver, where are we?" Po asked nervously.

"In my mind temple."

Oliver looked around cautiously. They were standing at the foot of the stairs leading to the behemoth of knowledge in front of them. Lightning and thunder boomed overhead as if they were caught in a rainless storm. Suddenly, the lightning magic materialized into the form of a woman. Peace filled Oliver as he realized that she was not lost to him yet.

She touched Oliver's cheek. "Curious little being you are. I sense it, buried deep within you. It calls to me." She dematerialized and lightning streaked into his mind temple.

"I don't think he's a he at all," Po said.

"How did you…"

"It's like our minds are tangled up like two pieces of rope," Po answered, rubbing his forehead. "Gee, Oliver, how do you live like this? My head is melting!" Po's exaggeration wasn't totally unfounded, but Oliver bent down to the young boy.

"That big building in front of us is how. I keep everything I know locked in there. If I close a door, then it doesn't open until I say so. If I didn't do this, I would probably be as crazy as Crazy Old Maurice down by the Bluefish Tavern."

"Oh, Crazy Old Maurice is really crazy," Po said, nodding. "How did you learn to do this?"

"My brother," Oliver answered with a faint smile.

The slight crackle of static in the background snapped their attention toward the mind temple. Oliver wondered what the lightning magic was doing in there. It felt as though she was talking with someone, but the only people here were Oliver and Po. Then she materialized once more, bowing in front of Oliver.

"You are powerful, young magician, and you are correct, I am not your magic, but rather I now am his." She gestured toward Po who wore the same face he had when Roc and Oliver had asked him to join Whiskey Danger.

"Does this mean I'm losing you?" Oliver heard, or rather felt, a banging inside his mind temple from the locked door he had kept buried for so many months. The pounding became louder and louder until the door began to crack.

The lightning magic took Oliver to the door and pointed. "You must release her."

Oliver was in tears, his chest heaving as he failed to catch his breath. "I can't. I'm not ready. Please don't make me."

"This is the way," the lightning magic stated in her crackled voice.

Oliver shook his head furiously, wishing for anything but to open the door. He knew what was behind it, he knew what it would mean. He sobbed. "I'm sorry, I just can't."

The lightning magic bowed her head. "Then you will lose me."

Was he strong enough to do what she asked? Strong enough to face the memory, the feelings? Strong enough to keep the lightning magic he so desperately coveted?

"I used to have a door like this," Po said in a small voice.

Oliver sniffled up his dribbling mucus and wiped away his tears. "Uh?"

Po walked to the door and touched the strained wood. "I think, I think everyone has a door like this. It makes it easy to forget the pain and sadness." Po turned to Oliver and took his hand. "But it also makes it hard to remember the good and happiness."

Oliver squeezed his young friend's hand and then let go to place his hand on the doorknob. "I don't know if I can do this, bud."

Po put his hand on top of Oliver's. "Then we do it together."

The door opened and they walked in, but instead of a room of memories, they were in front of Oliver's mind temple once more. Streaks of bolts that made up the swirling body of the lightning magic moved faster and finer until they resembled skin and clothes and a body and a face. Standing in front of them was the figure of a human wearing a Southern-style white and gold suit trimmed with black.

Oliver fell to his knees. "Mother?"

"No, young magician. I am the lightning magic, and you will not lose me." She bent down and cupped Oliver's face with her hand. "I shall serve you as I have been instructed, and I shall serve him as I was meant to."

Oliver's heart was turning over on itself. He knew this wasn't really his mother, but he didn't care. It'd been so long since he'd seen her face or heard her voice. He was almost delirious with relief at finally letting go of the pain he had buried inside.

The lightning magic turned to Po and touched his forehead, sending streaks of lightning under his skin and knocking him to sleep. Oliver caught his young friend in his arms.

"Will he be okay?"

"Yes. He needs a moment of rest for me to learn his mind."

Oliver caressed Po's hair as bolts simmered under the skin of his face and his eyes twitched. "So, what now?"

"Now, I am yours to command."

"So, I am your master?"

"Yes," the lightning magic answered, although there was a note of disdain in her voice.

Oliver thought back to the night on the rooftop when they'd all pledged themselves to Po. "People aren't meant to be masters. They're meant to be in service of one another. I don't want to be your master."

The lightning magic scoffed in disbelief. "You dare reject me?"

"No. Just changing the terms."

"Humans and their schemes," the lightning magic spat.

"Not a scheme. A partnership."

The magic in the guise of Oliver's mother paced back and forth, looking at the temple again and again before finally saying, "We shall be partners, Oliver."

It dawned on him that he had a name, but she didn't. "What do I call you?" he asked.

"I do not have a name, for I am from the beginning and will be long after the end."

"Oh, well, that's uh… nice. How about I call you Isadora?"

"My name is not Isadora," the lightning magic said in protest, but Oliver being Oliver, he didn't care.

"This is a fun dynamic we have going on here, don't we, Izzy?"

"I do not care for you at this moment."

"I get that a lot," Oliver said, extending his hand. Isadora took it and Oliver and Po were thrust out of his mind and back into the slowly dissipating cocoon.

Reagan ran out of the cage and over to Po as the last of the bolts jumped between metals.

"What happened?" she asked, checking Po's body for any sign of injury.

"You're not going to believe it," Oliver said.

Azel approached him. "I've never seen magic like that before, gods-son. It was truly remarkable. Did the transfer work?"

Oliver looked over at Po. "Why don't we find out."

Reagan helped Po stand, and he mimicked the basics of Form Zero that Oliver had done earlier. Small sparks surrounded his hands and arms before quickly leaving him, but even that smallest amount of magic sent him running around the room screaming in excitement.

Azel put a hand on Oliver's shoulder. "I'm sorry, Oliver."

"For what?"

There was a strange look in her eyes. "It is not easy to give up a power such as that."

Oliver held out his arm, modifying part of Form Zero to quickly summon his lightning between his fingers in an elegant dance. Po stopped running around as he witnessed Oliver's magical dexterity. Azel fell to her knees, taking her ring off the ground and crying softly.

"Azel, what's wrong?" Oliver asked in concern.

"I thought magic was lost to us forever. I thought the High Queen had taken it away from this world. But now we have hope." She took Po's and Oliver's hands in her own. "We have both of you." She looked to Po. "We have our hero, the Lightning Knight returned." Then she turned her head to Oliver, placing her ring on his hand. "And we have his guide. Just as I trained Haralabos and all the Knights of Nine, you will train Po."

Oliver sat back on his butt, taking it all in and fidgeting with the new ring. He now had three rings on his hands, and he couldn't quite reject the idea of what that meant. He had everything he wanted. He had Iris, and he had magic, and Po could now be who he was meant to be. Excitement thrilled through him and he stood, moving back and forth, quite unable to decide on his next move.

"Now what?" he asked.

Reagan stood up with him, mocking his movements. "Now you learn how to use the lightning magic. You both do."

Po stood up and started imitating both of them. "Alright! But how do we learn?"

Azel stood up last, using her cane. "I don't know. Form Zero is just the foundation. Without the Codex, you will have to discover other forms some other way."

"Well, I guess that leaves only one thing then," Oliver stated.

"What's that?" Po asked.

Oliver stuck out his fist and uncurled it in front of Po's face. "It's time for you to learn Form Zero. Empty Hand."

But Oliver's hands were not empty, for lightning magic danced among his fingers.

# THE PRICE OF MAGIC

Po lay on the stone floor of the practice room, his narrow chest heaving. Oliver lay opposite him so that their heads nearly touched. He felt just as exhausted. Reagan sat cross-legged, gleefully watching the two magicians beg for a reprieve.

"Rea, I don't think I can even stand," Oliver protested.

"I think I'm dead," Po joked.

"What? Did you think this would be easy?" She slapped them both on their stomachs and made her way over to the practice dummy at the far side of the room. "Again!" she commanded and Oliver rolled over to push himself up.

"We better not make her angry," he said as he offered a hand to Po.

"This is her being nice?"

"Po, come stand next to me," Reagan instructed.

The three of them had spent every day for two weeks working on their forms, and although Po had progressed sufficiently to the point where he could at least summon his lightning magic, Oliver had plateaued. He couldn't control the lightning and it often resulted in a few singed hairs on Reagan's head.

Po stood on one side of the wooden practice dummy while Reagan stood on the other side. Oliver looked at her in bewilderment. "Rea, what are you doing?"

"It's not what I'm doing, it's what you're not doing. Every day we come here and every day you suck."

"Hey! I don't suck!"

Po looked at Reagan and then back to Oliver. "Uh, I'm sorry, Oliver, but you suck real bad."

They were both right, Oliver knew it. Something was off about him this week, but he couldn't quite put his finger on it. Maybe it was lying to Roc or maybe it was just a culmination of everything. Maybe he just needed a holiday with Iris. A month or two or twenty would do the trick, he thought.

"I'm sorry, I think I'm just tired," he finally said.

Reagan shook her head vehemently. "No, that's not it. You're holding yourself back again. This is what you do. Your light shines too bright and then you hide. You hold back, for what? So you don't offend? So people won't notice you? What is it, Ollie?"

Oliver balled his fists. "It's not like that, Rea."

"Yes, it is. You know it, I know it, and Po knows it. Hit the dummy."

"You're both in the way."

"Hit the dummy."

"Reagan, this is crazy! I'm going to kill you both!"

Po spoke before Reagan could counter. "Oliver, all we do is crazy. You can do it. I believe in you." The young magician planted his feet firmly on the floor and Reagan closed her open mouth, letting Po have the last word. Oliver sighed and closed his eyes, trying to reach Isadora.

"Please, help me," he begged in his mind.

The crackled voice of Isadora answered. "Find balance, young magician."

"That's all you got? Find balance? I am balanced!"

"Are you?"

"Ugh. No. But I don't see how that will help me not kill Regan and Po!"

"Tonfa Form Twelve."

"What? I don't have a—"

"Tonfa Form Twelve. Find your balance."

Oliver was kicked out of his own mind by the metaphysical being. He looked at Po's steadfast expression and Reagan's wry smile. He breathed in and out, finding the calm at his center, then moved into the tonfa Form Twelve as Isadora had instructed. Without the actual weapon in hand, Oliver found his fingers and wrist compensating for the movements, and the lightning magic formed around his arms and shot out in front of him directly at the dummy, leaving Po and Reagan untouched.

"How did you…" Reagan asked in disbelief.

"OLIVER THAT WAS INCREDIBLE!" Po yelled as he ran over to topple his mentor.

"What'sa matter, Rea? Didn't think I had it in me?" Oliver asked while trying to escape Po's tackle.

"Honestly, Ollie, I thought we were going to die." She laughed and gave her brother a swift kick to his feet before heading back into the main room of their secret hideaway. A banging on the door followed by a muffled yell startled the three friends and they all jumped up and readied themselves for a fight with swords in hand.

Iris tumbled into the room, breathless. "They have my parents!" she gasped, staring directly at Oliver with eyes full of tears.

"What are you talking about?" Oliver rushed forward and pulled her into his arms.

"The Spider's Web. They have my parents in a warehouse at the docks. They're going to kill them. Please, we have to go!"

Oliver kissed her on the forehead and without hesitation grabbed his gear and rushed out of the room, followed by the others. By the time they reached the docks, Yokel and Roc were waiting for them.

"That building there with all the guards, that's where they are," Yokel said.

Oliver gave Yokel and Roc a strange look, and Roc explained. "We were with Iris when they took her parents."

"Why would they take them?" Po asked.

Iris unsheathed her sword. "Because my family is trying to stop the Spider's Web, and someone betrayed them." She started to run toward the guards but Roc and Oliver held her back.

"What are you doing?" Oliver asked.

"I'm going to save my parents!" She struggled to break free but was restrained once more.

"You against five guards?" asked Roc.

"I like those odds."

"Just hold on a moment. There's always a better way," Oliver said, looking at Yokel.

"The roof, follow me!"

Without asking more questions, they followed the master strategist around the perimeter to the back of the warehouse building where they scaled the side with ropes. On the roof, large skylights allowed them to peer into the scene below.

Lord and Lady Kentaro sat gagged and tied together, surrounded by ten robed figures. Oliver noticed hints of steel glittering in the shadows behind the Spiders, a sign that the guards out front were not the only ones on the premises.

Yokel glanced at Oliver. "It seems we may be outnumbered. Do you happen to have any other reinforcements coming?"

"Nope, tonight it's just us. Hit them hard and hit them fast, and above all, get the Kentaros out of there. That's the mission, everyone clear?"

They all nodded, and Oliver and Roc quietly cut the window seal open and dropped silently onto the rafters, fanning out across the ceiling.

In the torchlight, one of the Spiders took off his hood, revealing himself to be Ridhan. "Council, thank you for joining me here tonight. I trust the trip was not too inconvenient."

Oliver looked back at Iris, who silently slapped her forehead. The Kentaros hadn't been betrayed; rather, Ridhan had come back from the dead with the knowledge of Iris's other identity.

A voice from one of the tall robes spoke up. "We do not appreciate being summoned so. What is the meaning of this?" The tall man looked around. "Where is Goldentooth? And Moonclerk?"

Ridhan gestured toward the Kentaros, who were desperately trying to escape. "I give you Goldentooth and Moonclerk, traitors to our cause. They are spies for the enemy."

The tall Spider took half a step forward. "You dare to accuse members of this council of treason? What proof do you have?"

"A Spider has no need of proof when prey has been caught in their web."

"You have become more unstable and unpredictable since we brought you into our fold. We warned your father, but he did not see fit to heed our warnings," said a shorter council member with a higher-pitched voice. The council member snapped a finger and nine armored guards stepped out of the darkness.

"I'm sorry to inform you, but this council has taken a vote, and we will not be requiring your services any longer, young Shipwight."

The nine guards stepped in front of each of the council members, save for Ridhan, and brandished their knives. Ridhan, for his part, seemed unfazed by the threat, his voice sounding erratic as he asked a simple question. "What is magic?"

"Your final words are fitting," the tall Spider said.

"Tck-tck-tck, wrong answer," Ridhan said, and with the snap of his fingers the armored knights spun around and stabbed each of the council members, their screams and pleas a prelude to the silence that would follow.

Ridhan walked between the guards and dead Spiders and stood in front of the Kentaros. He waved a hand airily at the bodies on the ground. "They never deserved magic. None of them."

Through the door came Ridhan's father, Lord Shipwight, flanked by guards. He surveyed the death in front of them and clapped his hands. "Well done, my son. Well done, indeed. Now I will take command of this wretched Web once and for all. My name will be the most powerful in the entire South."

Ridhan's face was crazed as he turned to face his father. "What is magic, Lord Shipwight?" he asked with emphasis on the title.

"Shut your mouth, you insolent child. Magic is a fool's dream. It doesn't exist. Real power is what you can exert on your enemy."

"You're just like them. You don't see my vision."

"Enough of this! I will not hear any more of magic from your lips," Lord Shipwright yelled.

Ridhan snapped his fingers again, and every guard in the warehouse took their knife and slit their own throats, falling where they stood into a pool of blood.

Lord Shipwight looked around, aghast. "What is the meaning of this!"

Ridhan muttered words in a strange language and Lord Shipwight fell to his knees, holding his head and screaming in pain.

Oliver dropped down out of the rafters and summoned the lightning magic, moving forward quickly to save Lord Shipwright. "Ridhan! You need to stop this!" But Ridhan turned his head and muttered another phrase that sent Oliver flying backward into some crates.

"Nine Hells, this is going to be one of those nights," Oliver muttered to himself as he stood back up. Reagan, Roc, and Yokel joined him and began to flank Ridhan even as Lord Shipwright's guttural cough signaled the end of his life.

"I remember you. You're the one who stole my lightning magic. Who are you?" Ridhan asked as he stood behind the Kentaros, using them as a human shield.

"Don't you know? I'm the Lightning Knight," Oliver said in his masked metallic voice. Oliver never truly felt like the Lightning Knight, but he enjoyed the idea of helping to build the name's reputation, especially since it seemed to irk Ridhan so much.

"So you are, but who am I then? Tck-tck-tck, a Shark?" He muttered some more words and blew to his right, sending a powerful stream of water at Yokel, Po, and Reagan that knocked them back into some crates. "No, no, no!" Ridhan yelled. "Maybe a dragon?" He muttered more words and blew to his left, sending fire from his mouth at Roc and Iris as they tumbled behind cover. "No, that isn't it, is it, my sweet Iris? I like your friends, but do they know? Do they know who you truly are?"

Oliver summoned his lightning magic, even in his exhausted state, and sent warning sparks into the air. "Last warning, Ridhan. Let them go."

"Tck-tck-tck, you don't understand. You're just like the rest of them." He put his hands on the prisoners' shoulders and Iris yelped in anguish, knowing her parent's lives were literally in the mad boy's hands.

"Ridhan, you can't do this. Don't you see what you've done? You've killed your own father!"

"He didn't see my vision. None of them did. Only one person does. He would join me, you know. He has never failed me." Another spell and everyone was knocked to the ground once more, except Oliver.

"I'm sorry, Ridhan, but he wouldn't join you." Oliver took off his choker and removed his mask. "Please, just let them go," he asked with an outstretched lightning-enveloped arm.

"Tck-tck-tck, my love? Oh this is a surprise. Or is it?" Ridhan looked down over the top of his nose at Oliver. "You know the truth, don't you? What is magic?"

Oliver moved into tonfa Form Twelve and threw a lightning bolt between Lord and Lady Kentaro's heads toward Ridhan. As much as Oliver wanted to save Ridhan, he knew it was a lost cause. The stakes were too high, and the death toll was too much. Oliver had to end this tonight.

But before the bolt could reach Ridhan, the Staff of the Seas appeared in his hand and redirected the lightning to the roof, sending debris falling around them. In the commotion, Oliver ran forward and jumped over the prisoners, tackling Ridhan. They tumbled to the ground, the Staff of the

Seas falling away as Oliver tried to throw another bolt, but he was fatigued and this bolt was weaker and more erratic. Ridhan spoke another incantation and broken pieces of roofing combined in the air in front of him to form a shield. As the shield disintegrated from the bolt, Ridhan, unharmed, shot a plume of fire from his hands toward Oliver. Instinctively, Oliver threw lightning to meet it, and the two elements met in a concussive blast that sent them both to the ground.

Iris and Roc scrambled to untie the Kentaros while Yokel and Reagan attempted to engage with Ridhan. Ridhan spread his hands wide, sending fire and setting Yokel ablaze. While Reagan attended Yokel's burning clothes, Po summoned his own lightning magic, sending sparks in the general direction of Ridhan.

As the three of them engaged with their magic, Oliver felt his body waver. Between all the training and this fight, he didn't know how much longer he could last.

"Destroy the Staff," Isadora said in Oliver's mind. He looked at Ridhan who was laughing maniacally as he began to overwhelm both Po and Oliver. Then he noticed it, the Staff of the Seas, on the floor not a yard away.

"Can you hold him?" Oliver asked Po, who nodded and redoubled his effort.

For the briefest of moments, Oliver stopped his stream of lightning and somersaulted away, giving him a clear shot at the staff. He tried to summon the lightning magic once more, but it sputtered and failed. He was spent, and Ridhan knew it. Oliver looked at Po, who was about to be overwhelmed by Ridhan's fire, and from the deepest parts of his mind and soul, Oliver summoned the lightning magic once more. This time, it was wild and unruly, uncontrolled, bolts sparking in every direction. Before Oliver could stop it, an explosion erupted within the warehouse.

Oliver was barely conscious as he was dragged from the crumbling building. He couldn't quite tell what was happening, but he knew his head was throbbing and his left arm felt limp.

Roc sat Oliver up against a crate on the dock and they watched the building burn. To his right, Oliver saw Yokel, scarred and still smoking, and Reagan coughing and dazed. Iris was supporting her father under his arm while her mother limped behind them. Oliver tried to grab Roc to ask what was happening, but he was already gone, heading back into the inferno that engulfed the warehouse. Oliver's thoughts mixed together, and his left eye became blinded by blood dribbling from his forehead.

A window and wall exploded. From the smoke emerged Roc's large figure, carrying Po on his shoulder and dragging Ridhan. Roc laid Po at Oliver's feet, but the young boy did not move and his eyes did not open.

Oliver bent over Po, praying to Nine Gods he didn't believe in that his friend would be okay. He put his hand on Po's chest but didn't feel the thump of a heart or the breath of his lungs. Instead he felt the fractal pattern scars of burned skin and immediately recoiled in fear of acknowledging the truth. In agony, Oliver fled into his mind temple.

"ISADORA!" he screamed as thunder and lightning encompassed the sky of his mind.

The lightning magic appeared, but her bright glow was dulled and faint. She looked at Oliver, held his cheek, and then dissipated into the netherworld of Oliver's soul.

"Fix him," Roc said coldly as Oliver returned to reality.

Oliver coughed. "I can't."

"You lied to me," Roc stated, grabbing Po's small hand and holding it to his cheek. "I will never, ever forgive you."

Oliver lay on his back, sobbing dry tears and choking on his own air as the crackle of the burning building continued. Oliver reached out for Roc's hand, for Iris's hand, for anyone's hand, but none were there to comfort him. Oliver was alone.

Po was dead, and it was all his fault.

# CONSEQUENCES

Oliver sat, waiting for Professor Lortho to return to his office. He could hear excited murmuring from his fellow students in the halls; the last day of the term had arrived. None of them knew about Po's death, and Oliver wondered if any would even care. To them, Po was just a poor boy from the Narrows. They would never know who he truly was nor the kind of hero he was to become.

"Mr. Quartermaine, I did not expect to see you here," the stout professor said as he entered.

"I'm sorry, Professor, but I've come with news of my final assignment."

The professor pulled a chair next to Oliver and sat, looking him in the eye. "Oliver, I've heard what's happened and I think—"

"What is it that you think, Professor?" Oliver interrupted.

"I think it is a tragedy that someone so young and full of promise is lost to us."

Oliver let out a breath, trying to control the anger he felt at himself that he was directing at the professor.

"I found magic, but it's lost now." Oliver's voice broke. "Po was to be the hero. He was the one to save magic. Now he's gone, and..." He couldn't continue.

"From what I hear, he wasn't our only hope. You have it too, is that not correct?"

Oliver shook his head, a coldness washing over his emotions. "Not for long. I want to get rid of it, I want it gone." It was the lie he told himself over and over. He didn't want to lose Isadora, but he also felt he had to punish himself. This was the price he had convinced himself he needed to pay. The price of the magic he so foolishly played with.

Professor Lortho put a hand on Oliver's shoulder and took a deep breath. "You know, destiny is a funny thing. I knew a woman once who talked of the future all the time. More often than not, the future was not exactly how she had predicted it. The future is malleable, and it is up to us to write it. Maybe you were meant to carry on for Po."

"I was never meant for this. I was selfish and now... now my friend is dead because of me. Because of my magic."

The professor searched the room. "Maybe there is still a way for you to—"

"I don't want it anymore. I can't have it. Don't you understand? I need to get rid of it. It's my fault, Professor. It's all my fault. How can I go on living with his magic when I was never supposed to have it? Please, help me. Help me get rid of it."

"You mean to pay a penance then."

Oliver turned his head away. "Yes. I need to pay for what I've done."

The professor stood and stretched his back. "Before humans were gifted magic, it belonged to the elves, in the lands beyond the Sunset Mountains. They will help you pay your penance."

"Elves are extinct."

Professor Lortho smiled. "So too was magic, but we both know better. It is a perilous journey, and you would be wise not to take it alone."

Oliver thought about Roc and Yokel, who had followed him on an odyssey across Soraya. Maybe they would now follow him across the unknown world. Iris would join him, obviously, and possibly Reagan too. "Thank you for understanding, Professor. I'm sorry I couldn't complete your assignment."

"As am I, Mr. Quartermaine. But the future has a way of surprising you. Safe travels."

As Oliver made his way through Starfall and into the Narrows, he basked in his knowledge of the city: On this corner lived a baker who was in love with the seamstress who had moved in across from him, who happened to be dating a banker who didn't love her back. In that apartment lived a ten-year-old boy who might grow up to be a Starfall City Jousting Champion, if only given a chance. And over in those gardens lived Madam Lysel, who would tell your fortune if you brought her flowers. He thought of all the parts of the city he loved and how he might not see them again for many years, if ever.

The Narrow Gate felt smaller, but maybe it was Oliver's mind that felt constricted. So many questions raced through his head about the journey that lay before him. He was sure, that no matter how perilous things got, his friends would be there to help him. Once he told them of his plan, any hard feelings would surely disappear. They would obviously understand what he was giving up, and how he was doing it for Po.

His questions melted away as he approached the Whalebone Tavern, deep in the Narrows. As they had every year, the Quartermaines held a party to celebrate the end of term at the Institute. His friends were compelled to go to the party with the promise of drowning their sorrows in drinks all night. Roc had spent an inordinate amount of time at the Whalebone since Po's death, party or not.

Oliver heard the sounds of clouds bumping into each other above, and the leaves on the few trees that dotted the street turned over. A couple of students were kissing passionately just outside the tavern door, and Oliver patted the boy on the back as he passed him, throwing him a wink of approval. Oliver entered, bombarded instantly by the sounds of music and voices.

"Oliver! Great party, man," a recently graduated and not so recently drunk student yelled as he spilled his beer onto Oliver's hand. Oliver knew the student's name, as he knew everyone at the Institute, and smiled, looking around the tavern to gauge the atmosphere. The place was packed to the walls with boys and girls, all celebrating their recent milestone.

"Thanks, Todd," Oliver replied, turning Todd back around and gently pushing him in the opposite direction.

A few girls crowded Oliver.

"Oh my Nine, Oliver Quartermaine! You are as dreamy as they say you are."

"Chloe, shush! You know he's taken."

"I know that, Jules, I was just commenting on the Prince of Starfall's outfit here."

Oliver was in a daze. "Prince of what?"

"Oh, aren't you silly, pretending not to know your own nickname." Mishe came in close and whispered, "If you ever want to know what it's like to be with a Princess of Starfall, you know where to find me."

Alarmed, Oliver tried to back away quickly, but bumped into Todd again. He grabbed him and hurriedly thrust him between himself and the three girls. "Oh, ladies, please meet my very, very good friend Todd. He's basically me, except a bit more, uh, well, here you go." Lucky for Oliver, the ladies were all so out of their minds from the night of celebrating that they moved on to Todd without a moment's notice, pulling him in every direction, trying their best to steal his affection and a kiss.

If this was to be his last night in Starfall, Oliver would try to muster an ounce of celebration. He took a cup of wine from a server and held it in the air, toasting his lost friend. "To Po!" The tavern answered him back, though they probably didn't care who they were toasting.

Todd came by again, the girls firmly attached, and pulled Oliver in closely. "Seriously, man, thank you!"

Oliver rustled his hair and moved away, trying his best to make it through the crowd and over to the bar. He was stopped by every student along the way, offering their thanks for the party while Oliver toasted to Po in response.

He took a bottle of wine from the bar and scanned the room once more. He could feel a goofy smile on his face as he searched the crowd. He found Yokel, who was trying his best to dance with two girls at once while holding two drinks in his hands. Although Yokel had taken Po's death as hard as the rest of them, there was nothing a bit of alcohol couldn't solve with the skinny boy.

He found Todd once more, who was tongue deep with Mishe. Oliver thought about how weird it was to be celebrating when Po was gone, but it was what they all needed, and what Po would have wanted. He would have wanted them to get obliterated rather than mourning for so long. Oliver could only hold on to despair for so long, and this party felt like a welcomed release after the weeks of grief.

He found Roc and Iris, standing in a dark corner. They did not look to be celebrating. Roc had shown no emotion since Po's death, and Oliver was sure he would explode soon. Iris had wept for three days straight and was still heartbroken.

Oliver grabbed another bottle of wine and hopped off the bar in the direction of his best friend and the love of his life. He would offer them a drink, tell them of their upcoming journey, and all would be well.

As he made his way toward them, he was waylaid by groups of students creating an artificial wall with their dancing. Iris seemed to be arguing with Roc, but Oliver couldn't hear what they were saying. As stoic as Roc was, Iris was just as animated, and amongst the shadows and dancing light, Oliver felt at peace. He loved her so much, her beautiful face accented by those brown eyes that could stare directly into his soul. She was everything he wanted in the world, and together there wasn't anything they couldn't do. His heart was warm—maybe from love, maybe from the wine, he really didn't care. He had a purpose now, one last quest: to rid himself of magic.

He swam amongst the students but made little headway. Finally, after observing their argument for longer than he wanted, he came within a few feet of his friends. Roc looked down at Iris, who had stopped talking and was waiting patiently for an answer. Roc took Iris's face within his large hands and kissed her.

Oliver's heart shattered. He stopped breathing. It was a ruse, a vision. His mind had been poisoned, or he had had too much to drink. Yes, that must be it. This was simply a nightmare.

"Iris?" Oliver asked. "Roc?" He dropped the bottle of wine and closed his eyes, shaking his head and backing up. "No, no, no, no, no."

Iris and Roc gaped at him. Roc's cup slipped to the ground to meet the shattered bottle. Oliver backed into two guests, bumping them as they danced. Embarrassment washed over him and he turned and fled from the tavern into pouring rain.

"Oliver, wait!" Roc yelled. He pulled Oliver's shoulder around and Oliver shoved him back with both hands, tears mixing with the rain pouring down his face.

"Don't touch me!" Oliver yelled, pointing a finger at his friend. "You don't get to touch me." Pure rage was rising in his body, and he did nothing to quell it. "I can't believe... you... you're my best friend..."

Roc held his hands out in front of him, trying to keep Oliver at a distance. "It's not what it looks like. Oliver, I'm sorry, we were both... I don't know, it's just all confusing."

Oliver's expression washed over with cold, unfiltered anger at the person in front of him. He filled with pure, disciplined hatred. The dark mind temple was back, as was the emotion he had first felt in Romir.

Unlove.

"I was going to ask you to go with me…" Oliver started, trying to manipulate the situation even more to his favor.

"Go where, Oliver?" Roc asked.

Yokel had made it out to the thunderstorm and was standing next to Iris as Oliver and Roc squared off.

"We were going to head west. I wanted to—" Oliver began, but he had miscalculated.

"Are you joking? After all we went through. Po is dead. DEAD! Because of you! And you want to just up and leave? That's what you do, isn't it? Things get tough, things go wrong, and you leave. Well I'm not leaving, and neither is anybody else. We're done following you."

Oliver's stomach dropped.

"You don't understand, I have to leave!"

"I do understand. WE do understand. You've done this all year, and we're sick of it," Roc countered.

"It's what Po would have wanted," Oliver said, but he knew it was a lie. Deep down, Oliver knew Po would have wanted him to carry on his legacy. But Oliver's mind was made up. He would journey over the Sunset Mountains to rid himself of his magic.

Roc shoved Oliver. "He would have wanted to be alive! I told you, I told you from day one that we shouldn't mess with magic. Then I told you again, after Romir, when Po almost died. I thought we were through with it, but I was a fool. You lied to me. You've lied to me ever since I met you. We were never friends. I was just some boy you could use, and I let you. Well no more."

"Po—"

Roc shoved him again. "Don't you say his name! Not anymore. You used him for your own adventures because you were a bored little lord. Well I have news for you, we are not expendable. Po was not expendable. And now you want to leave?"

Oliver was reeling. He felt anger and pain and suffering and grief and drunkenness and rage and sorrow and too many more emotions to feel or think clearly.

Yokel ran between them and spread his arms wide. "Why are you two fighting?"

"Go ahead, tell him. Tell Yokel what you want to do."

"Oliver?" Yokel asked, rainwater dripping off his scarred cheek.

Oliver looked at them both, just as he had when his mother died, imploring them to leave their home, for him. "I want us to go—"

Roc interrupted. "He wants us to leave. AGAIN. Like we'll do anything the Lord Quartermaine commands. This is our home too. We're angry too! But we're not leaving."

Yokel put his hands down, shaking his head no at Oliver.

"Yokel, please," Oliver begged, but his friend was speechless.

Iris moved to stand behind Roc, making her choice clear as well. Then Oliver remembered the kiss, and the unlove surfaced again.

"Oliver, I love you but… Roc is right," Iris confessed.

"You stand with him?" Oliver asked coldly.

"Oliver, it's—"

"You stand with him and not me. You too, Yokel?"

Yokel didn't respond, but neither did he move from Roc's side. Iris grabbed Roc's hand, planting her boots in the mud.

Oliver's voice quivered and cracked. "I loved you."

"Did you?" Iris started in a rage. "Or did you love Pathfinder, or did you love some random girl from some random land. Who did you love? Do you even know?"

"I loved you," Oliver repeated. All his emotions swirled and mixed, and one rose above the others: betrayal. Betrayed by Yokel, betrayed by Iris, and betrayed by Roc.

"We're not going with you. Stay here, where you belong," Roc commanded, but Oliver's gaze fixed on Roc's fingers intertwined with Iris's.

"You choose him?" Oliver asked.

Iris opened her mouth to respond, but nothing came out. Light flashed in the clouded sky, followed by the booming of thunder, and rain poured on them even harder.

"She stands with me, Oliver." Roc answered. "I, I love her." Iris turned quickly to look at him, a look of surprise on her face.

Quicker than Roc was anticipating, Oliver moved and punched him on the right cheek, sending him reeling backward. Oliver turned around and walked in a circle, shaking out the pain from his knuckles.

"Oliver!" Iris yelled as she went to Roc's aid.

"No, that's it. I'm sick of this. No more!" Roc yelled as he pushed Iris aside. "You think this world revolves around you? You think you're the center of it all? The hero of this story? Well you're not. Po was the hero, you're just the villain." Roc wiped the cut on his cheek. "I love her, and I have for a while. While you were off playing gods with magic and lives, while you were gone and treating her like she didn't matter, I was there for her. I fell in love with her." He put his fists up in a boxer's stance, readying himself. "I'm willing to do what you never were. I'm willing to fight for her. Come on!"

Oliver felt sadness, anger, hate, betrayal, but now most of all, loss. The loss of his best friend and the loss of the love of his life, all at once. The loss of Yokel, who was always there for him, and the loss of Po, who was his hope. But then the cold hatred took over, and he stopped thinking. The only thing he wanted at this moment was to hit something.

"I've been waiting for this for a long time," Roc yelled as he protectively moved in front of Iris. Oliver flew into a blur of motion, deflecting the one punch Roc was able to get off, and quickly hit him with a succession of punches under Roc's right arm and chest, sending him stumbling back.

"You don't belong here, Lord Quartermaine." Roc coughed as he held up an arm for Iris not to interfere. "She chose me, Oliver. How's it feel? How's it feel to be the one who wasn't chosen?" Roc pushed forward with two haymaker punches. Oliver deftly avoided his attacks but didn't return any, toying with his prey.

Roc continued to berate Oliver even as his attacks failed to make contact. "You're the reason he's dead. You're the reason she's heartbroken. You're the reason Yokel is scarred. You're the reason for everything wrong with us!" Roc was in a rage, but his attacks were slow and uncoordinated. Instead of using his strength to his advantage, he tried to match Oliver's speed. Oliver returned with a left hook to Roc's ribs and an uppercut to his chin, and Roc went sprawling to the ground on his back.

Roc rolled onto his feet instantly and pushed away offers of assistance. He yelled a guttural, primal scream and charged, aiming to tackle Oliver to the ground and use his size and strength to win the fight.

But Oliver's world was now as broken as his heart. He was losing control again, just as he had in the warehouse. He was so tired of holding it in, of holding back, of not letting his true power come forth. His chest pounded and his body trembled, and it was all so agonizing and tiring. He was so tired of everything and everyone. His emotions were too much to bear, and he held out his hand, flicked his wrists, and moved his fingers subconsciously, and the lightning magic sprang forth, encircling his fist as he punched Roc directly in the chest. The lightning magic dissipated, but even as Roc twitched from the lightning punch, Oliver jumped on top of him, pinning his arms down with his knees and continuing his assault by alternating between Roc's face and chest. With every punch, Oliver felt relief at letting his emotions free.

A punch to Roc's left cheek. The anger for holding back all the time. A punch to Roc's sternum. The sorrow for failing his friends in every meaningful way. An elbow to Roc's right temple. The loss of the future that Oliver had planned, now turned into ashes.

Punches landed in quick and powerful succession, Oliver yelling while Roc's body bounced and reacted to each hit. Oliver could hear a crowd around him cheering for the fight, but soon the cheers started to turn to groans at the sight of Roc, who was quickly approaching a point from which no one would return. A scream sounded in Oliver's ear and two small hands tried to pull him away. The two hands were joined by two more, larger, and Oliver snapped out of his rage to see Iris and Yokel separating him from his prey.

Yokel held Oliver back, and Oliver pushed away with his hands and body, signaling he didn't need to be restrained anymore. Iris knelt by Roc, who was having trouble breathing, blood pouring from the cuts on his face. She was crying and trying to wipe away the blood that was mixing with the rain, muttering something to Roc that Oliver couldn't discern. Seeing that he was not needed as a buffer anymore, Yokel went to offer what help he could to his broken and bloodied friend.

Oliver looked around, shame and guilt washing over him at the sight of the faces looking back at him. They were faces of horror and fright, and their gazes dropped repeatedly to Oliver's bloodied and bruised knuckles. He looked down at his hands, the instrument of such easy destruction, and turned to leave.

"Oliver! How could you?" Iris cried out, running after him and stopping a few feet away when he turned to face her. The love he had once felt was overcome by the sense of betrayal, and as he looked at her, the only thing in his mind was the most spiteful of thoughts.

"I never realized it until now," he said.

"Realized what?" she replied, walking into his trap. There was still time; he could just walk away. But he didn't. Instead, with dead eyes, he looked at his former love, and with all the malice and vitriol he could conjure, he hurt her in the most poisonous way he knew.

"You weren't worth it," he said, and he turned and walked away, leaving Iris crying as she fell to her knees.

Oliver ran through Starfall, desperately trying to escape the rain and his regret. He had lashed out against the people he was closest with. He stepped into an alleyway, leaning against the wet wall as he slumped down, trying to breathe and finding it difficult between the tears and emotions. His mind was moving faster than he could keep up, and he sobbed, feeling more alone than he had ever felt. In an instant, he had thrown away his life, his future, and everything that was good.

He sat in the rain, letting it pour over his body. He didn't know what to do next. A part of him wanted to run back and apologize. To try and win back Iris's heart and give up his quest to rid himself of magic. But he couldn't do it. He didn't have any friends anymore; he had just made sure of that. The only thing he had left was the final quest.

Oliver stood and entered his mind temple, hoping to put an end to his emotional suffering.

"Your magic is angry," Isadora said as she walked alongside Oliver.

"Why are you angry?" Oliver asked as he closed doors on the memories of his friends.

"I am not your magic, young magician. Your actions tonight, they have angered it." Oliver dismissed Isadora's comment and continued to close doors. The memory of his first tournament with Roc and Yokel, shut. The night of the Homecoming banquet, locked. A party with a small bespectacled young boy holding on to his mother's dress, closed.

"You should not do this," Isadora suggested.

"Why not!" Oliver snapped back. "I can't take it anymore, so I'm shutting them out."

Isadora put her hand on Oliver's as he held a doorknob. "This isn't the way."

"What is the way?"

"I am not that kind of magic."

Oliver let go of the handle and took a step back. "What do I do?" he asked desperately.

"You listen to your sister, because she knows everything," Reagan said behind them.

"Rea? How are you... I don't care." Oliver ran over and picked her up in a hug. He didn't care if she was real or just a figment of his mind, he was happy to see her.

"Ollie, you have to leave. People are talking about tonight, about what happened." Oliver looked at his sister, confused. "They're saying someone used magic to attack students. The Black Sun Battalion will be here within a fortnight. You have to leave. I've already sent your things to the station, but you must leave tonight."

This couldn't be just his imagination. Oliver jumped out of his mind temple and found that Reagan was holding his head while the rain poured down. "Rea? I'm so sorry," Oliver cried as he fell into her shoulder.

"I love you, Ollie. But you can't be in Starfall any longer. You have to go be a hero."

"It was supposed to be Po," Oliver protested.

"Yes, but now it's you. Time to be the hero we need."

He hadn't the will to tell her what his true intentions were for his journey. He just wanted his sister with him. "Will you come with me?"

Reagan held him tightly. "I have to stay here, big brother. I have to protect our city, and our friends." Oliver understood but silently rejected it, nonetheless. He didn't think he could do this quest alone, but he had no choice. After everything he had done, he had to vanish without even a goodbye. A small idea grew in his mind, and Reagan let him go, cocking her head as if she already had heard it.

"Say it," she commanded.

"Tell them it WAS magic," Oliver said. "Tell them everything. Magic is real and that the Lightning Knight is back. Tell them Po is the Lightning Knight and that he will save us all."

"They'll be searching for a dead boy."

With the Black Sun Battalion searching for Po, Oliver would have a chance of making it to Kandaheart and then into the Sunset Mountains.

Oliver smiled. "It'll give people hope."

Reagan kissed his forehead. "And it will make Po a legend."

# MAGIC WAS REAL

Oliver let his head bump slightly against the window as fields and forests passed him by. He looked down at the small wooden box in his hands. Along with his belongings that his sister had sent, his father had left for him a box and a note.

My Son,
This was always meant for you.
W.Q.II

For the entirety of the ride through the Floating Isles, the Starfire Bay Coast, and even Mercyhold, Oliver had been unwilling to open the box. He felt as though if he opened it, he might solidify his choice to leave. Weeks had passed on his journey and he had barely moved from his seat or even inventoried his belongings. A single bag with what he assumed was his gear and weapons, along with this box, were his only possessions on this quest. He hoped to stay with his uncle in Kandaheart, gather supplies and make a plan, and then head into the Sunset Mountains.

It was all very overwhelming, and he had done his best to control his emotions, but the images of the night at the tavern, of the night at the warehouse, and so many other regrettable nights caused his heart to palpitate.

In a single moment, in a single night, his heart had been overcome with a poisonous darkness so deep and strong he thought he would never feel love again. He let that feeling once more fill his chest, then he breathed slowly to expel the emotion from his body. It didn't leave him, however, so he repeated the process over and over, getting lightheaded as he began to hyperventilate.

He had seen panic attacks before, in other people. Oliver had prided himself on the fact that he could control his emotions. He had never felt as he did now. He tried to think calming thoughts, of the ocean, of the night sky, of anything that would steady his breathing, but everything failed. His chest pounded with the thought that he might be dying, and the only image in his mind's eye was that of Roc and Iris kissing.

"Here," a small voice said. A small, scruffy-haired boy, no older than six maybe, was looking up at him with wide green eyes. He held a small empty animal skin pouch, not large enough to hold anything of significance. Oliver looked at the boy, confused.

The small boy held the pouch to his mouth and breathed into it, the pouch inflating and deflating with each breath. Oliver held out his shaking hand, urging the boy to hand him the pouch. He snatched it from the boy's hands and immediately put it to his mouth, and his breathing slowly came under control.

The boy smiled and held out his hand, requesting his pouch back. Oliver granted his request and nodded in thanks. The boy took the pouch and attached it to his belt, but remained there, staring at Oliver.

"Can I help you with anything?" Oliver asked, to no answer. The small boy stayed motionless. It felt as though he was peering into Oliver's very soul. It made him very uneasy, vulnerable.

"Do you have a name?" Oliver asked, and once again received no response. If he didn't know better, he would have sworn this was a statue instead of a person. Oliver became increasingly frustrated, his fuse quicker than it used to be. "Little boy, I asked you a—"

"I'm not a little boy, I'm seven."

"So, he does speak. Okay, Seven, I'm Oli—" He stopped abruptly. He didn't feel like Oliver anymore, or anyone he recognized. He had once again fallen into the dark hole of not knowing who he was. He hated the feeling and had thought his confusion of identity was over. But here he was, unable to even tell this boy his name.

"My name isn't Seven, that's how old I am. My name is Simon."

"Well, it's a pleasure to meet you, Simon, I'm—"

"Simon! Why are you bothering that man? I'm so sorry, my son has a tendency to wander off." A woman was tugging her son away, apologizing for the intrusion. Oliver had never ridden on a train before that wasn't in a private car, and the cramped-ness of the seats was surprising.

"It's not a problem. In fact, Simon was just telling me how old he is. Quite the young man you have here."

Simon's mother smiled and pulled her son in close for a prideful hug. She looked around at the almost full train car, searching for a seat.

"Please, sit," Oliver offered, moving his pack from the seat next to him and onto the ground. She sat, uneasily looking around the car.

"So, what brings you on your journey?" Oliver asked, trying to start a conversation. She didn't respond, continuing to scan the faces of the other passengers. He thought she was maybe twenty-two or twenty-three years old. "Are you waiting for your husband?"

"Huh? What?" she said, finally turning her attention to Oliver.

"Your husband, is that who you are looking for?"

"No, I don't have... I'm not looking for anyone. It's just Simon and me. His father isn't in our lives, and that suits us just fine. We don't need a man or anyone else to help us."

"Easy there, I was just asking. Seems you're a bit jumpy."

"I'm not jumpy. It's... It's nothing. I don't need to explain myself to you."

Oliver sighed, not quite understanding what this woman's issue was but deciding he didn't have the energy or passion to follow up. He turned his head and looked back out the window in silence, watching as a station approached. The train's loud whistle sounded, and the train rumbled to a stop. Simon and his mother jumped much too quickly out of their seats and exited the train.

"Uh, bye," Oliver said sarcastically to their backs as they passed by his window, walking briskly and looking around in every direction. Oliver tracked them as they scurried into the station and down the steps.

He felt an odd sensation of rejection, and it left a poor taste in his mouth. His meager attempt at politeness had been rebuffed, which reminded him of his friends' rejection, and suddenly the poison in his heart returned, and all sense of caring for anything in the world left him. Oliver let his head lean against the glass of the window once more, the smooth surface sending a refreshing cooling sensation along his skin.

Odd movements caught his eye just as he was about to be lost within his thoughts. Four suspicious-looking men, dressed in black and wearing cloaks that disguised their identities, seemed to be following Simon and his mother down the stairs.

Oliver watched them, recognizing their body language as sinister. He tried to forget about it, but when he closed his eyes, all he saw were Simon's huge deer-like eyes staring back at him.

"They're fine, they're fine. I'm sure lots of people go down those steps. It's a train station after all," Oliver said aloud. But the sight of the men nagged at him. "They're not my responsibility, I'm not a hero," Oliver said aloud once more, banging his head against the window lightly. After many weeks of being alone and lost in his own thoughts, the idea of being any type of hero left a sour taste in his mouth.

"You could be," Isadora's voice said, and he turned, finding no one near him. He looked frantically for a voice, but he was alone. Small sparks danced between Oliver's fingers, and he quickly tightened his fist.

"Leave me alone!" he said aloud. The two people passing him gave him a strange look. Ever since leaving Starfall, he had worked hard at keeping Isadora at bay. He was scared of what the lightning magic was doing to him, or rather what it was turning him into. He felt like one of the monsters rumored to be on the other side of the Sunset Mountains, although he was pretty sure those were only tall tales to scare children.

Isadora yelled back in Oliver's mind. "Lightning does not wait and watch. Lightning is meant to strike!"

But Oliver was hesitant. What if he lost control again and the lightning magic killed someone else? "I can't—" But before he could finish his thought, lightning enveloped his head and smashed it against the window. Oliver rubbed his head and sighed, understanding there was no refusal to this request. "I thought you were supposed to serve me?" Oliver asked as he picked up his pack and made his way toward the exit.

Isadora's crackled voice answered in reply. "No, young magician, we're supposed to be partners."

"Simon, we have to keep moving."

Oliver could hear Simon's mother urging the boy down some stairs into the alleyways between the buildings of this small town. Simon moved as quickly as he could manage, but it was not fast enough for his mother, and as she dragged him, he tripped and fell.

"Well, well, well, you finally showed up. You know, you were quite hard to find, but we have the best tracker money can buy, and you aren't as slick as you seem to think," a low and scratchy voice said as the four black-clad men surrounded Simon and his mother.

"I told you," Isadora's voice seethed.

"Shut up," Oliver whispered from his position on a catwalk high above the group.

"I don't have any money," his mother pleaded. "We're nobody, we don't have anything you would want."

One of the men bent down to stare into her face as she kneeled next to Simon, shaking. "We don't want your money. You know what we want." And he looked to Simon, who had a defiant expression on his face. The man reached his hand out to ruffle Simon's hair but was met with a slap across his face. The sinister man caught the woman's wrist when she went for a second slap.

"Now is the time to act," Isadora urged.

"Not yet," Oliver protested. He had convinced himself that his hesitation was in order to better understand the situation below, but he and Isadora both knew it to be a lie. He was still too scared to make a move. Still too scared of his own power.

"That'll be enough out of you!" the man yelled, throwing Simon's mother to the side as he scooped up her son. Simon began to flail, trying to escape. "We don't need you, ma'am. Just the boy-o," the kidnapper said. He looked to his comrades and hissed an order. "Make sure she's not breathing when you're done with her."

Simon managed to grab the kidnapper's arm and bite down, falling to the ground with a yelp as his kidnapper yelled in pain and wound up for a kick.

"You little piece of—"

He was thrown off balance by a blow to his head and fell down and stayed down, groaning.

"Now, what exactly are you trying to do with my little friend over here?" Oliver said in a metallic voice as he swung his sword in front of him. All the pain and guilt he had felt for weeks had vanished. All the suffering and self-doubt disintegrated faster than a used-up magical item. He wasn't thinking about Starfall, or his friends, or Po. He wasn't thinking of his failings or depression. The only thing on his mind was protecting Simon and his mother. For weeks he had spent every moment sulking and spiraling deeper and deeper into the darkest parts of his mind and soul. The darkness within him subsided, but Oliver didn't know how long this feeling would last, nor if the darkness would come back stronger than before. All he knew was that he needed to protect Simon and his mother.

"Get him!" All three rushed at Oliver.

"I've got, like, a really good feeling about this," Oliver smirked as Simon's mother scrambled over to her son and clutched him tightly against her chest. As quickly as Oliver had entered the fray, the three men had fallen.

As the last of the attackers fell, groaning in pain, Oliver bent down and grabbed him by the collar. "Who are you?"

The man spit blood, missing Oliver's face by inches and smiling with red teeth. "You can't stop the Nine Hands from getting them. You're just—"

Oliver punched him with the hilt of his sword.

Oliver sheathed his sword, contemplating the new information. The Nine Hands were one of various syndicates throughout Soraya, and if Oliver's memory served him correctly, which it always had, this particular group was known for one thing: never breaking a contract. He bent down, searching the fallen Hand for clues. The man wore dark leathers, with a monstrous red hand as an emblem on his chest. Oliver checked his pockets but found nothing but a few knives and a folded piece of parchment. He read the orders and turned around, looking at Simon and his mother. The woman had picked up a sword and was holding it out defensively.

"If you want to live, you'll come with me," Oliver said, straightening up. He extended a hand but was met with the tip of the sword. He bent down, easily pushing the sword to the side with his finger. When he pulled down his mask, her eyes widened in recognition, but she still didn't move. "This note says your name is Kate Winters, is that correct?"

Kate nodded slowly, her eyes now wider than Simon's. Oliver extended his hand slowly. "We need to go, right now."

Kate and Simon followed Oliver through the small town to the other side, where they came upon a carriage hall. Oliver handed her the orders and she read them, tearing them up after she was done.

"Care to explain why the High Queen wants your son?" Oliver asked.

"It's... It's his father. We've been running for years, but we have nowhere left to go. I thought we could escape Starfall without notice, but it seems my help was no help at all. She said we would be fine."

"Who said? Never mind, there's no time for that. Who is his father?"

"I... No, I can't tell you. You'd be in too much danger. We've already put you through enough as it is. The bounty on our heads... You better leave us alone."

Oliver pulled her away from Simon and spoke softly. "Look, Kate, can I call you Kate? Listen, those orders didn't say anything about you, they only mentioned Simon. As far as the bounty is concerned, you're just collateral damage to get to him. Which means you both need to disappear. Somewhere where they won't find you..." Oliver looked north and snapped his fingers. "I know just the place."

He walked into the carriage hall and talked to an older man, who was accompanied by his wife. Oliver handed a bag of coins to the old carriage driver and they shook hands.

"Okay, so this gentleman and his wife have agreed to take you to Kandaheart. When you get there, head directly to the Fifth Ring and to the library, and ask for Steward Aleventi. Mention his nephew sent you. Tell him 'All stories were meant to be told.' He'll understand what it means."

"What?"

"Just repeat it. We don't have a lot of time. Five of the Nine Hands are still out there, and once they find the four at the station, they'll undoubtedly try to block all the escape routes. It's now or never. Do you remember what to do?"

"Uh," Kate fumbled, "go to Kandaheart, to, to the library, and, um..."

"The Fifth Ring Library. Ask for Steward Aleventi."

"Ask for Steward Aleventi," Kate repeated.

"And say?"

"I'm a friend of his nephew's. All stories were..."

"Meant to be told," Simon piped up.

"Steel trap, this one," Oliver said as he ushered Kate and Simon into the carriage.

"Th-thank you... Wait, we don't know your name," Kate said as she turned in her seat.

Oliver closed the door and stepped back, wondering what he should tell her. He still didn't feel like Oliver, not the real Oliver anyway. He was suddenly ripped into his mind temple, where he saw a boy sitting at the foot of the stairs, waving for him to come over.

"Po?" Oliver fell to the step below the boy.

"Hi, Oliver," Po replied in his usual upbeat manner.

"You're not alive," Oliver whispered.

"No, but I'll never be truly gone. We're connected, Oliver, more than anyone else. We shared something no one else has."

"Magic," Oliver said, and a thunderous boom sounded above them.

"Yes, and because of that, I will always be a part of you, tethered throughout time."

Oliver tried to take the boy's hand but found he was clasping his own hand instead. Confused, he looked at Po, who smiled his wide smile.

"As long as we share magic, I'll always be here for you, Oliver."

"Po, I—"

"I know what you are doing, and it's okay. Really, I promise. I know you're scared, but you don't have to be brave all the time…"

"I only have to be brave once," Oliver finished.

"The world needs a Lightning Knight," Po said. "Not just a story of one." Oliver backed away from the steps and turned, finding Isadora in the form of his mother. He hugged her, despite knowing it wasn't the woman who raised him.

"I miss you, so much," he cried.

Isadora rubbed his back. "You will find, young magician, that the dead never truly die, when there are still those who remember them. Those that you've lost, they live on, within you."

Oliver lifted his head from her shoulder and looked back at Po, who was wearing his Carpenter outfit and wobbling back and forth to a beat Oliver could not hear.

"I feel so lost. Like I can't control myself, or my thoughts, or my emotions, or anything," Oliver confessed to them both. Po stood up and nodded, disappearing into the mind temple. Isadora stood next to Oliver, looking at the magnificent building.

"Your magic, I can feel it. There is something not right with it. I will do my best to help you, but I fear this is a task I will not be able to complete alone."

"What if it's never fixed? You know where I'm going, you know how this ends for us."

"You must do what you feel you need to."

"You know that means I'll lose you, and him."

Isadora took a long breath. "Yes, young magician, I understand. But until then, I will do my best. I would only ask for one favor."

Oliver was thrust back into the real world, as Kate repeated herself. "We don't know your name."

"I'm the Lightning Knight."

The carriage jerked forward and they were carried off while Oliver stood, embracing the moniker. He looked at his hand, letting the light glean off the ring with the nine-pointed star emblem. The ring that Po had given him. He would try to be the hero Po was meant to be, and in doing so, hopefully honor the boy. At least until he finished his final quest.

Magic was real, and Oliver meant to forsake it.

# EPILOGUE:
## THE STRANGER AGAIN

Oliver vanished west into the forest. He had paid some children from the village to spread rumors that he had taken Kate and Simon with him, hoping to lead the Nine Hands in the opposite direction from where the mother and son were actually headed. His time spent exploring the Forest of Kel with Roc and Yokel turned out to be fortuitous, because he was able to leave visible trails and clues to his whereabouts, leading the Nine Hands on a wild chase. After a few nights, he doubled back, checking to make sure the Nine Hands were still following him, and after a full week he was confident that not only had he managed to get them sufficiently lost within the forest, but also that he had given them the slip.

The only problem was, he too was lost. Not only that, he had survived on little more than small game and berries for the entirety of the chase, and he was starving. So, when he caught the scent of roasted venison and followed it to a smoldering fire and a deer hide tanning in the sunbeams, he was cautiously optimistic. It seemed as though this site was abandoned at the moment, but even if it wasn't, he wasn't planning to tarry for long. He just wanted a bit of food for his rumbling stomach.

Just as he parted the bush, the sound of a bow being pulled near his ear and the press of an arrow on the back of his neck stopped him. He put his hands up, saying in his real voice given his choker was in his pack, "I give up."

"Oliver?" The arrow was removed from his neck.

He turned with a goofy and confused look on his face. "Cindy?"

"No." The Stranger un-nocked her arrow and put it back in her quiver. "You know I could have killed you."

"What are you doing here?" Oliver asked, his hands still in the air.

"I could ask you the same question. Where is your flower and all your other friends?" She started gathering her belongings and putting them in her bag.

"I heard you were attacked by pirates!" Oliver yelled as he jumped at her and clasped her in a hug. The Stranger stood there frozen.

"Why do hoomans always insist on hugging?"

"I am so glad to see you," Oliver said as he let her go. His stomach grumbled and he stole a glance at the venison. Rolling her eyes, the Stranger nodded, and Oliver quickly ran over to eat while she recounted her journey thus far.

"I was captive on the ship and we managed to stage a mutiny. When we docked, we all went our separate ways and I took on a bounty." She handed him the bounty message for Simon and Oliver threw it into the fire.

The Stranger punched him in the chest and then took a stick to try and rescue the piece of parchment. "Why are you the most insufferable hooman I have ever met?"

"You can't collect that bounty," Oliver said from his position on the ground.

"Why is it you tell a bounty hunter she cannot collect on her bounty?"

"Because it's wrong."

"There is no right and wrong, there is only the bounty."

"This time it is wrong," Oliver argued, propping himself up on his elbows. "Besides, I already sent Simon away where no one will get to him."

The Stranger looked at him, the fire reflecting off her eyes. She took out an arrow and nocked it once more. "Why would you interfere?"

"Because it was the right thing to do."

The Stranger grunted in frustration, letting her arrow loose to land between Oliver's legs and much too close to his manhood. "You don't understand. First you destroyed my only means of returning home and now this. I should have never trusted hoomans." She loosed another arrow that landed between Oliver's arm and side.

He somersaulted backward and onto his feet, taking out his sword to defend against another attack. "I can help you get home!" He had destroyed the Codex, but in his head, there was still half of the book. Maybe that would be enough.

She loosed another arrow that grazed the top of his hair. "I should have never trusted you. I should have never trusted anyone."

"But we're friends!" Oliver pleaded.

"I have no friends. You let people into your life, you trust them, and they disappoint you. They let you down. They betray you. If you don't look out for yourself, then no one will."

"You're not listening to me!" Oliver said as he dove behind a tree trunk.

"I'm finished listening to you, hooman."

Oliver stepped out from behind the tree with his arms spread, dropping his sword. "You're right. I failed you. I've failed a lot of people. Friendship is a myth, like elves are. People will only disappoint you if you give them the chance. Go ahead, take the shot. I deserve it."

The words felt all too real as they left his mouth. The betrayal by his so-called friends, the revelation that the Stranger didn't count him as a friend, regardless of their brief adventures together. There was an emptiness in his chest, and all he could do was fill it with sad acknowledgment. All his life Oliver had been eager to allow people into his heart, willing to give them a second, third, tenth chance. He welcomed anyone into his circle of friends, knowing full well that it left him vulnerable to disappointment. He thought he had been lucky enough to not see those repercussions, that everyone loved him and truly wanted to be his friend. Truly cared for him. As he thought of it, of each and every person he had met, he noticed the pattern he had been so blind to before. The only people who cared about him were obligated to, because of his last name. He was alone now, as he always had been, and the Stranger's words made that ever so clear.

"Oliver, you are not supposed to be like that."

"Why? You are."

"Because ever since you sat in my booth, you've always believed in everyone, even strangers and fools. You're supposed to be the one someone like me counts on. I lost my hope in friendship a long time ago, but that doesn't mean you have to."

"Why do I have to be the beacon of friendship for everyone? You don't even know what I've done. I don't deserve friendship." Even before he finished speaking, the revelation of his words struck him in his chest. All his feelings could be summed up so simply that he choked up.

He didn't deserve friends.

He deserved to be alone.

The Stranger put down her bow and looked at him thoughtfully. Eventually, she responded. "Trust me, you deserve friendship."

"I can't even trust myself," Oliver admitted.

The Stranger's eyes softened. Oliver stared at her, vulnerable and defeated. He was wary of letting her close, letting anyone close again. He didn't feel as though his heart could take another person in his life, another disappointment.

"You used me just like everyone else," he said.

"Excuse me?"

"You heard me. You're just like everyone else. You used me, and I let you. Just leave," he responded, dejected.

"First off, jerk-hooman, I didn't use you. You're the one who sat in my booth and you're the one who offered to help. Don't try and turn this around on me. Second, this is my camp, so you can leave."

Oliver looked at her and sighed, sheathing his sword and turning to walk away.

"Oliver, wait. I didn't mean it."

He kept walking. He didn't want to turn, didn't want to stop. The darkness inside him felt like it was taking over and he decided to give in. Giving in would be easier than trying.

An arrow buzzed by his head and stuck into a tree trunk inches from his face.

"I said, wait!" the Stranger yelled, her bow nocked with another arrow.

Oliver turned and took his sword out. "You don't want to do this, girl," he said in a patronizing manner. She loosed another arrow and he deflected. She repeated the motion, moving faster and closer with every arrow. After the sixth arrow she was close enough to the oblivious Oliver, who was busy defending himself from the onslaught, and she hooked the bow around his head, pulled it harshly, and let go, letting it smack into his face.

He dropped the sword and yelled. "What in the Nine Hells!"

"You don't get to walk away from me," she said as she held the tip of his own sword to his chest. "What is wrong with you? This isn't the hooman I knew. One moment you're full of hope and the next despair. Why can you not trust who you are?"

"You want to know why I can't trust myself? This is why." He summoned the lightning magic. It enveloped his entire body, and he threw a small bolt at the sword, hitting it and sending it ten feet behind her.

She looked at him, but not in fear. The defiance on her face made him angry. Why wasn't she afraid? Everyone should be afraid. He was afraid. He let the anger take over and began to throw out lightning bolts, moving his arms and body without thought, sending explosions all along the forest floor.

The Stranger followed his form, or was it a different form? Suddenly her eyes were blazing yellow, and as Oliver threw his arms forward to release lightning at her, she did the same, sending a concussive blast of air.

The two forces met and combined, enveloping both fighters in each other's magic. Suddenly, Oliver was in the darkness of his mind again, looking around anxiously. As he turned, he saw the Stranger, standing with her hands folded across her chest and a pensive look on her face.

"What happened?"

"You tell me, dumbass-hooman."

"You've got a sailor's mouth, you know that?"

"And you've got a funny way of treating your friends, you know that?"

A crackle and a loud boom sounded simultaneously and suddenly, Isadora and another figure were standing on either side of Oliver and the Stranger.

"It is good to see you again, my friend," Isadora said to the figure made of glowing dust.

"If only it was under different circumstances," the dustman said, looking at Oliver.

"What did I do?" Oliver glanced at Isadora, who looked angry.

Isadora ignored him. "Have you spoken with it yet?" she asked the dustman.

"Wait, who are you two?" the Stranger asked.

"I have not," the dustman responded.

"Let me bring you. I could use your help," Isadora said, and with that, both magical entities disappeared.

"Oliver, what is happening?" the Stranger asked, turning about, looking for danger.

"What did you do out there?"

"Out where?"

"Out there? Outside of this place. You threw something at me."

"You were throwing lightning at me first. I just reacted."

"Interesting." Oliver put his hands to his head to think.

"Interesting? Interesting how? Where are we? Do you know those two things?"

"Sort of," Oliver said, trying to think and answer at the same time.

"I thought I was going crazy," the Stranger said softly. "For as long as I remember, he's always been with me, urging me in different ways, but it was only ever a feeling. Then he became a voice."

"You're not GOING crazy. You are crazy," Oliver said with a smile. "But it's okay. I'm crazy too. Those things, they were magic." The Stranger's eyes widened. Oliver continued, hoping more information would set her at ease. "The lightning lady was my magic. Her name is Isadora."

"My name is not Isadora," Isadora said as she reappeared with the dustman.

"He does that with you too?" the Stranger asked.

The dustman walked over to Oliver and the Stranger. "We have spoken. I will help you and the lightning, young magician, but I am not your magic." He looked at the Stranger and tilted his head. "I am hers."

Oliver and the Stranger landed on their backs, breathless from the force of the blast of their magics.

The Stranger struggled to move. Oliver rolled over and then dropped his face into the dirt, his arms too weak to push himself up.

"What was that?" the Stranger asked as she turned her head to Oliver.

"That was Isadora. She's a jerk sometimes," Oliver responded as lightning lifted his head up and dropped it to the ground once more. "I mean, she's really quite lovely. You should name yours."

"Name my what?"

"Name your magic." Oliver forced himself up, brushing dirt from his shirt.

"My magic? I can't have… That's impossible," the Stranger said as she joined him. He brushed some dirt from her shoulder and looked at her.

"Well, it's possible and you have it. I think you should call him Teigen." Oliver was swept off his feet by an unseen force and thrown to his back again. "I think Tei-guy likes the name."

The Stranger helped him up and looked around. "You don't understand,

I CANNOT have this magic," the Stranger implored. "What does this mean?"

"It means you're not alone."

She looked at him. "I suppose not. But this cannot be correct."

"Why not?"

"Because it's impossible for me to have this magic. Unless…"

"Wait, what was that?"

They whipped their heads around to see nine armed men, all adorned with the red hand insignia on their chest, surrounding them.

"They're here for me!"

"They're here for you?"

Oliver's sword was on the ground, too far away, but the Stranger's bow was close. He rolled quickly, picked up the bow, and threw it to the Stranger, landing in a fighting stance. The Hands descended upon them and the Stranger loosed four arrows before they had made it three steps. Oliver settled into a ready stance and played out the paths in his head.

With all the members of the Hand surrounding them and working together, there were few options available. To complicate things, Oliver didn't fully understand how the Stranger fought, or if she could use her magic on command, and therefore many paths were hidden to him.

He stepped forward and took on three Hands, trying not to get turned into a position where he would be surrounded. The Stranger traded her bow for Oliver's sword and was fending off two opponents of her own as more moved in around them both. The only way they could survive was to work together, so he backed into the Stranger, getting a few moments reprieve as he tripped one of the Hands into another, stealing a sword.

"We need to work together!" he yelled.

"I'm fine alone. I can handle this, get out of here!" she yelled back as she took an arrow from her quiver and jammed it into the shoulder of one of her opponents.

"The only way we both make it out of here is if we work together!"

"I don't need your help!" She backed away from an oncoming slash, bumping into Oliver who had his strike parried from the man in front of him. The parry and unforeseen bump caused him to lose his weapon, and he looked at it and then at his opponents, and everyone realized at the same time that he was defenseless.

"Summon me!" Isadora's voice crackled, but Oliver still feared the power within him and his lack of control. He'd almost lost it on the Stranger just moments ago, and if it hadn't been for her own magic, he was afraid of what might have happened to her.

"I can't," Oliver said, doing his best to dodge the attacks and stumbling backward over his pack. The wooden box his father had given him had broken, revealing the black rectangular handle of a sword but no blade to accompany it. He turned his head to see a Hand rushing at him with an overhead strike. At the last moment before a fatal hit, Oliver grabbed the black handle and instinctively held it up. A bit of lightning magic coursed along his arm and into the handle and a long sword blade emerged, shining brightly.

Clink.

Oliver was saved from a mortal strike, and he looked at the sword in wonder and disbelief. But in that moment of hesitation, the Hand member recovered and hit Oliver in the head with the butt of a sword. As Oliver fell, unconscious, another bit of magic emanated from his head and traveled down his neck, along his arm, and into the sword handle, returning the magical blade to the place from which it had emerged.

Oliver shook his throbbing head. His arms were bound tightly behind him and around the trunk of a tree. Night was upon them, and the Nine Hands members were sitting around a fire, eating the Stranger's venison. The Stranger herself was sitting directly in front of him, tied similarly, a deathly look of annoyance on her face.

"What, what happened?" Oliver asked groggily as he continued to shake the buzzing noise out of his head.

"We've been captured."

"Well… That's not great, is it. So, what's our plan?"

"Our plan? Our plan? No, there is no OUR, there's just me. I'm getting out of this by myself. You're the reason we're even in this mess."

"What did I do?"

The Stranger struggled against her ropes as she leaned forward to answer. "Everything. Nothing. Ugh!"

Oliver tried to crack his neck but scratched it against the bark of the tree instead. "Look, the only way we make it out of this is if we're in it together.

Do you trust me?"

"No."

"That's actually fine, but you should listen to me. I know you don't want to believe it, but you have magic, and I do too. For some reason, that means we're bound together." He laughed briefly and nodded at the ropes binding them.

The Stranger didn't acknowledge the pun but yielded to Oliver's offer. "Fine."

"Good," Oliver said, fidgeting with the ropes, trying to gauge their tightness. "Now, if we're going to work together, we should try to communicate better. That means you listen to me.'"

The Stranger looked away, rolling her eyes. Suddenly she shook her head back and forth, muttering to herself. After a few seconds, she looked back at Oliver.

"No, that means you listen to me," she corrected. "We only have until the next Dark Day to escape before they realize I lied, and they kill us."

"Dark Day? Lied? Where are they taking us?"

"Into the Sunrise Mountains."

"Sunset Mountains, you mean. Why would they do that?"

"Because they think they will receive a bigger reward from the—"

"Goblins."

"Yes," the Stranger said, looking at her legs. "If there is one thing goblins hate most in this world, it is—"

"Hoomans," Oliver answered again, this time using the foreign dialect. The Stranger shot him a sharp look, but before she could answer, he continued. "So, what's the plan, Cynthia?"

She closed her mouth and stared at him, reading him within the darkness. After a few moments of reflection, she spoke once more. "The plan? I'm working on the plan, and my name isn't Cynthia."

"I know," Oliver responded playfully.

The Stranger looked at him, letting another long moment pass. "It's Piper."

## ABOUT THE AUTHOR

Born in NYC and raised in Maine, Sean Valiente grew up reading fantasy stories and watching way too many movies. Living outside Boston with his wife, he now writes his own stories, hoping to inspire others as he was.

www.ingramcontent.com/pod-product-compliance
Lightning Source LLC
Chambersburg PA
CBHW020001120726
47903CB00004B/1084